The Ruins

T.H. Hernandez

Cover Art © 2015 by Mark Sgarbossa (www.popgroovy.com)
Interior Graphics © 2015 by Suzanne C. Walker (http://pajamapress.com)
Edited by Barbara Trageser and E.J. Hernandez

Ordering Information:
Quantity sales. Special discounts are available on quantity purchases by corporations, schools, associations, and others. For details, send an email to the above account with the subject line of "Bulk Discount."

The Ruins / T.H. Hernandez. -- 1st ed.

Library of Congress Cataloging-in-Publication Data is available

ISBN 978-0-9908688-4-2

*To Mattea, Noah, and Grayson for inspiring me every
single day.*

Book 1 – The Union

100 Years After the Second U.S. Civil War

"Sadness flies away on the wings of time."
—JEAN DE LA FONTAINE

Destiny

The scents of honeysuckle and fresh-cut grass float on a late summer night breeze. I stare up at clouds from the chaise lounge on the balcony. A thick marine layer inched its way in from the coast hours ago, blanketing the sky and obscuring the stars I was hoping to see. With the moon hidden and the Union lights off for the night, darkness envelopes me.

Grief, guilt, heartbreak, fear, loss, and abandonment swirl in my head, creating a vortex of pain and confusion keeping me awake. Three days ago I was planning a future with the boy I love. Cyrus was going to come back with me. We were going to figure out a way to warn the Union or stop an attack on it. Together. Now his brother is dead, and Cyrus stayed behind, unable to ignore his sense of duty, unwilling to abandon those who needed him most.

Over the soft murmuring of desalinated ocean water burbling through the aqueduct on its way to homes throughout the Province,

I hear the door slide open behind me. I sit up as my bio-dad, Eddie, walks out and sits next to me. "Can't sleep?"

I shift to my right, giving him more room. "No. You?"

He shakes his head, his wavy, cinnamon-colored hair sweeping his shoulders. "My grandmother used to say if you can't sleep, it means you're awake in someone else's dreams."

That's a comforting sentiment. Is Cyrus dreaming about me now? Or is he like me, too afraid of the nightmares to close his eyes?

Eddie presses his lips together and studies me for several long seconds. "Are you ready to tell me where you really were all summer?"

His question catches me off guard. I thought he bought my story, the one I told him when I came back. The one Lisa fed him while I was in the Ruins. Posing as me, she texted my mom and Eddie from my tablet with regular updates on our fake adventures sailing off the southeastern coast. When I first showed up here yesterday afternoon, he didn't seem to care where I'd been or what I'd been up to, only that I was here at all. I'm definitely not ready to have this conversation with him.

"I don't know, are you ready to tell me where you were for the first twelve years of my life?"

He shifts his weight on the chaise next to me and sighs. "I'm not sure how many times I can apologize."

"You think another 'I'm sorry' is going to fix everything?"

"Look, I know I was a lousy father to you, but—"

"You weren't a lousy father, you weren't any kind of father at all. You were non-existent."

He rubs his palms on his thighs and stands. "You're welcome to stay here as long as you'd like, but you might want to ratchet the anger down a few notches." He moves toward the door before turning back. "You're going to have to forgive me some day."

I raise my head and turn toward his dark silhouette. "Why? You think sending me a ticket and letting me hang out with your new kids makes up for everything?"

"No," he says quietly, "because hanging on to all that resentment isn't healthy." He walks back into the house, sliding the door closed behind him.

With a heavy sigh, I fall on my back and stare back up into the blackness. Seriously? After being nothing to me for three-quarters of my life, where does he get off being all parental right now?

My breaths come short and raspy, my arms pumping as my feet pound the earth. Lungs burning, I glance over my shoulder to make sure I'm out of arm's reach and trip over a tree root, falling to the ground. Lucien stares up at me with unseeing eyes, a bright red stain spreading across his midsection. I push myself up, spinning into Dantel's chest. He lurches back, blood pouring from his mouth as I shoot him over and over.

A scream tears from my throat, my heart racing as fast awake as it was in my dream. A thin layer of moisture coats the lounge chair, as if it's broken out into a cold sweat, too. The chill is enough to send me back inside to burrow under the blankets. It still feels wrong to sleep in a bed while my friends in the Ruins are roughing it on hard ground. But sleeping on the floor out of guilt isn't something I'm prepared to explain to Eddie yet.

The remnants of my nightmare continue to haunt my waking thoughts. It might've only been a dream, but it's wrapped in truth, tied with a bow of reality. Whoever said time heals all wounds must be talking about a lot more time, because I feel just as shattered as I did in the moments after Lucien's death. I haven't been able to cry since that day, though. Maybe we're born with a finite number of tears, and once they've been shed, they're gone forever.

Rolling to my side, I force my thoughts to something else, to a way to stop a group of unknown rebels in the Ruins from attacking the Union. Without any information on who's behind the plot, what their plans are, or when it'll happen, I'm second-guessing my decision to come home. Why did I think I could do this? I am no one. A spoiled Union princess who's had everything she's ever needed handed to her.

When we were packing to come back here together, Cyrus said doing nothing wasn't a valid alternative, but I have no idea what I can possibly do. He said he believed in me, but he doesn't know me. Not the real me. He knew the Ruins version of me. The girl who escaped from kidnappers, barely surviving long enough to be rescued. I was just playing a part, pretending to be someone else. That's the girl Cyrus fell in love with. I want to be that girl. Not the Union girl who doesn't even know what she wants to do with her life. The one who got Lucien killed.

Turning onto my back, I stare at the ceiling, willing my mind to shut up. I crawl out of bed and pad over to slide the window open before snuggling back under the blankets. Through the opening, I can hear the water gurgling past and finally drift off, lulled by the sweet sound of fake nature.

A steady knocking pulls me from sleep, but I refuse to go without a fight. I burrow deeper under the comforter, trying to escape the relentless assault. When it's clear I can't win, I sit up and rub my eyes. "Come in," I croak, my voice adjusting to being used for the first time today.

Eddie pokes his head in. "You have a call." His voice is flat, as if he's talking to a stranger.

With a sigh, I get up, shuffling down the stairs to the great room and pick up the phone. "Hello?"

"Morning, Evansville."

"Hey, Bryce. What's up?" Now it's my turn to show no emotion.

"We're meeting at Lisa's this morning. Want me to come get you?"

"No, that's okay. I need to shower and eat breakfast." I'm still pissed at him for lying to me about everything from his name to his career. The fact that the smugglers he was investigating kidnapped me isn't something easily forgiven. "What time's everyone getting there?"

"They're only waiting on us. Do you know where she lives?"

"No." I feel like an idiot for telling him I'd meet him someplace I don't even know how to get to.

"I'll be by to get you in an hour," he says, the smile evident in his voice.

After taking a quick shower, I dress and brush my teeth. When I spit out my toothpaste, I startle at the stranger staring back at me from the mirror. My features are the same — wide-spaced hazel eyes that appear brown or green, depending on my mood, small nose, full lips — but the short blond hair is still foreign after seventeen years as a redhead. So are the muscles and tanned skin from spending my days working outside in the Ruins all summer.

I apply some product to my hair, trying to get my curls to behave and slip my feet into flip flops before bounding downstairs. It's too quiet in here, Eddie and the kids must have gone out. A plate of muffins sits next to a fresh pot of coffee. I pour myself a cup and grab a muffin. When I slide my finger along the edge of the counter, it lights up, displaying the central controls. I swipe a few times, selecting a music channel.

The front door opens, and two giggling children spill into the apartment, followed by Eddie.

"Eban!" Quinn, my two-year-old half-sister yells, running into the kitchen and shoving a fist full of crushed flowers into my hand. A smile splits her face, her pale blue eyes wide.

"Thank you," I say, scooping her up for a kiss.

Eddie walks past me without a word and reaches into the cabinet above the refrigerator, handing me a small glass vase. The tension hanging between us is heavy and ugly, but I don't know what to say or do to diffuse it. Our problems are not going to be fixed with a word or simple gesture. I put the flowers in the vase and add water, setting it on the counter for Quinn to see.

"Pwetty." She nods her head with enthusiasm, her red curls bouncing, which makes her nod harder until she giggles.

A knock at the door indicates my escort is here. I kiss the top of her head and high-five my half-brother, Liam, before heading to the door. "Be back later," I call over my shoulder, slipping out the door before Eddie can ask any questions.

2 Playing a Part

Bryce and I walk down the path from Eddie's apartment to the commuter station, and it's hard not to notice the differences between here and where I grew up back east. Even something as simple as a sunrise or sunset is turned upside down, with the sun setting into the ocean instead of rising out of it. The Western Province is pristine, new, white, clean, the only color coming from the flowers and plants. By contrast, the Eastern Province is dark and rich, like an old city with a storied past.

We hop a train heading north and grab seats in one of the enclosed areas, giving us some privacy. I glance at Bryce, trying to decide how I feel about him this morning. Not in a particularly forgiving mood at the moment, I settle on pissed but no longer homicidal.

"How'd things go last night?" he asks with a lift of his brow after he catches me staring at him.

"Not well." I shift and twirl a piece of stitching that's pulled loose from the seat. "Eddie asked me where I'd been the past couple of months, and I accused him of being a deadbeat dad, basically telling him he didn't even have the right to ask the question."

"Ouch."

"Hey, he can't just show up when I'm nearly grown and decide it's time to be a father." A grin breaks out on Bryce's face, and I realize he was teasing me. "Lying doesn't come naturally to me, so I lapsed into doing what I do best, antagonizing him. Seriously, how do you do it? How do you lie to people so easily about... *everything?*"

The grin slides off his face, and he becomes suddenly fascinated by his knuckles. "It's like playing a role. Were you ever in a school play?"

"Yeah, once. I played a toothbrush in an oral hygiene production in Grade Two."

He laughs. "Really? I'll bet you were cute." I glare at him, and the laughter dies in his throat. "Well, it's sort of like that. You become this other person and play a part."

"I guess."

"It's not easy, but you find ways to be as truthful as possible. Like embellishing or half-truths. Instead of telling your dad, I mean Eddie, you were kidnapped and taken into the Ruins, say you were exploring. It's both plausible and mostly true."

"It's okay to call him my dad, you know. I call him Eddie, but technically, he is my father."

The train slows, pulling into the station, and I stand to follow Bryce through the crowd as he guides us to the stairs. He leads me down a couple levels and out onto the main sidewalk. The structures here are concrete and glass, providing more of an urban grunge feel in stark contrast to the spotless white stucco where Eddie lives.

Bryce navigates an alley between rows of buildings, stopping at Lisa's place, which resembles a box with windows. She's in a bustling area of the Borough with everything she could possibly want located within a few short blocks of her apartment.

Bryce knocks, and Lisa flings the door open seconds later, her blond hair tumbling past her shoulders. She squeals when she sees us and wraps her arm around my neck in a hug, her other hand gripping an oversized magenta coffee mug.

Still in pink flowered pajama pants and a gray tank, she kicks the door open wider with her foot so we can enter. Her apartment is a cube of space with wood floors and narrow windows set up high in bare concrete walls. A Japanese shoji screen blocks off one corner I assume hides her bed. A red fuzzy couch sits in the center of the space flanked by a pair of saffron colored armchairs with a cobalt acrylic coffee table in the middle. Along the side wall is a galley-style kitchen, and four teal padded barstools are pressed up against a narrow island, forming an eating area.

"This place is great, Lis," I say, looking around. "Like a box of crayons threw up in here."

"I know." Her dark eyes shine with obvious delight. "It's small, but it's mine."

Part of me is envious. I'd love to have a place of my own like this. And I guess I could've, if I'd figured out what to do with my life and applied for an internship somewhere. Instead, I'm stuck living with a man I barely know who just happens to have spawned me.

Colin saunters into the room from what must be the bathroom — the only door in the entire apartment other than the front door. He plops onto the couch and stretches out his lanky legs, propping his feet up on the coffee table. His dark messy hair is even wilder this morning, spilling into chocolate-colored eyes, tangling with bushy eyebrows.

I sit next to Colin, resting my head on his shoulder. He kisses the top of my head. "Morning, EvTay."

Bryce sits in one of the armchairs, which have bizarrely long seats, meaning either his legs will stick out straight in front of him, like Quinn when she sits on the couch, or he needs to slouch back so his feet can reach the floor. He chooses the latter.

"Hey," Lisa calls from the kitchen area. "How'd it go with Eddie last night?"

"I got into a fight with him," I mumble. She lifts an eyebrow, and I blow out a steady breath. "Yeah. He asked where I'd been over the summer and I asked where he'd been for most of my life. Not one of our better father-daughter bonding moments."

She studies me for a long moment before smoothly changing the subject. "Do you want some coffee?"

"Always," I say, taking the plum-colored ceramic mug.

The front door opens, and Jack sweeps in, carrying a bag of what I assume are baked goods based on their heavenly yeasty aroma. He gives Lisa a light kiss, but it's enough that Colin's jaw clenches in response. We swarm the island to find fresh bagels and cream cheese, Colin, Bryce, and I taking ours back to the living area to eat.

"So, what's the plan?" Lisa asks, mouth full of bagel.

"I've been thinking a lot about this," Jack says. "We need more information. There are still too many unknowns to come up with any kind of a plan yet."

I set my mug down and glance around the room at my friends. "So then what *do* we do?"

"Investigate," Jack says, running a hand across his jaw. "Find out everything we can."

"I have an idea—" I start, thinking about the plan I came up with out in the Ruins.

"Give us a chance to sort through what we've already learned before you go off and do anything, okay?" Jack cuts me off. "These are dangerous people."

I narrow my eyes, pissed he didn't even let me finish. "How much time are we talking about?" I ask, working hard to keep my voice even.

"Only a few days," Bryce says. "Just long enough to see what we can dig up. Then we'll regroup. The more information we have, the better plan we'll be able to develop."

Jack glances at Bryce. "We should get going. They'll send someone out to look for us if we don't show up for our debrief." He leans over to kiss Lisa before walking to the door.

Bryce pushes his plate across the coffee table and sets down his cup. He starts to follow Jack to the door but turns back to me, as if he's going to say something. Instead, he gives his head a slight shake and follows Jack outside without a word.

Once the door closes behind them, Lisa eyes me. "So what's going on with you two anyway?"

I let out a long sigh. "I have no idea."

After Lisa and Colin take turns in the shower and get dressed, we decide to kill time by exploring the neighborhood. Shopping isn't going to stop an attack on the Union, but it beats sitting around doing nothing while Jack and Bryce do their thing.

Outside, the early September morning is warm, promising to be hot by afternoon, but nowhere near as hot as it was out in the Ruins. Back-to-school shoppers swarm the sidewalks along with others who are trying to eke out the most of the last few days of summer. Unfortunately, the fresh air and mild exercise don't ease my edginess at not doing anything productive.

"Why the scowl?" Lisa asks me.

I didn't even realize I was and work to relax my facial muscles. But rather than blow her off and give her some lame excuse for my mood, I go with the truth. "The reason I came back was to make something happen. Hell, if I knew we'd just be sitting around, I'd have stayed with Cyrus."

Her jaw clenches and I realize how snarky that sounded. "Jack and Bryce are cops, Evan. These guys...they're *really* dangerous."

"No shit. I know that better than anyone. They kidnapped *me*," I slap my chest with my hand. "They killed Lucien. You think I don't know what they're capable of?"

I've never yelled at Lisa before, and her stunned expression tells me maybe I've gone too far. She did come out to the Ruins to rescue me, even though I didn't actually need to be rescued.

"I'm not saying that," she says. "But, well, it's...don't hate me for saying this, but you have a habit of acting first and thinking second. Jack deals with information, and he makes plans based on that information."

Colin shifts his feet, hands stuffed into the pockets of his cargo shorts, looking like he'd rather be anywhere but here.

"He didn't even listen to my idea," I mumble, but I let it drop because arguing with her isn't going to accomplish anything. She won't really get it anyway. That this is personal to me, my mission, or fate, or whatever, and I feel like it's being hijacked from me.

We walk in silence, a cloud of tension hanging over us until Lisa drags us into a clothing store. Holding a shirt against my chest in front of a mirror, I get an idea. "Let's find a salon. I want to color my hair."

"Your roots aren't showing yet," Lisa says.

"I'm gonna go back to red."

"I've never seen anyone with your hair color," she says. "Good luck finding it in a bottle."

"I know, but I want to at least try. For Quinn's sake." She lifts an eyebrow. "Quinn said I can't be her sister because her sister has red hair."

She nods as if she understands, and with two younger siblings who look like carbon copies of her, she probably does.

We stumble upon a salon a few blocks down with a sign saying they take walk-ins. I meet the colorist and explain what I want. Her eyebrows disappear into her bangs, but I pull up a picture on my tablet of me, Lisa, and Colin from last year to show her. She glances at the screen and excuses herself, returning with a stash of supplies. After checking the picture a couple more times as she mixes, she sits me down and applies the color to my hair. When she's done, even though it's still wet, I can tell it's close. As long as I'm here, I see a stylist who fixes the hatchet job Cyrus did on my hair.

Glancing at my reflection with fresh eyes, the way I think Quinn will look at me, I'm pleased with the results.

"I'm starving," Colin announces before we've taken more than a few steps outside the salon.

"Wow, it's been two whole hours since you ate something. I'm surprised you're still conscious," Lisa says.

Colin shoots her a look, then shrugs and leads the way to a bistro. We sit on the patio and people-watch while Colin inhales three sandwiches, Lisa picks at a salad, and I eat the first burger I've had in months. A boy about Quinn's age squats nearby and carries on an animated conversation with the pigeons camped out next to our table.

"So, do you want to talk more about what happened out there?" Lisa asks.

I glance up and meet Lisa's anxious gaze. I shake my head, and her shoulders drop. I know she's hurt, we used to talk about everything. "I'm sorry Lis, I'm not ready yet."

She reaches out her hand, resting it on my arm and gives me a nod of understanding. Or at least I think that's what it is. I finish my burger and wad up the paper, tossing it onto my tray. Lisa abandons her salad, and we clear our table before heading out to do a little more shopping.

Lisa gets a few things for her apartment, and I pick out a pair of purple sparkly barrettes for Quinn and a T-shirt for Liam that says, "Don't blame me, I'm the middle child."

Our last stop is the music store. An enormous screen is suspended from the ceiling in the middle of the store, rotating through images of various performers. Epic Vinyl pops up with none other than Eddie McIntyre front and center. He looks so young, it's gotta be from at least ten years ago. Definitely before I knew him.

I was such a huge fan of the band before I knew Eddie was my father. Their music was all about growing up, fitting in, finding your place in the world, and I could relate to the lyrics. But now it just pisses me off. All the time he was making his fortune off of songs about finding himself, he walked away from his most important responsibility.

Lisa tugs on my arm. "Come on, we can go."

"No, it's okay. I mean I live in the guy's house, an image on a display is no big deal, just…*really* surreal."

Colin is in a listening booth, shaking his head to the beat of some rock song while a couple of girls check him out. Lisa's listening to some sappy ballad with a dreamy smile on her face. Colin glances over at her, a flash of pain crossing his features.

I let out a small sigh. A broken heart is just another thing he and I have in common at the moment.

3   Broken Hearts

Quinn and Liam snuggle on the couch next to me while we watch a movie. Their mom will be here any minute to pick them up for the weekend, leaving me alone with Eddie. I'm trying not to stress about that, but I can't help thinking how awful the next two days are going to be.

A knock on the door only amps up my anxiety as I brace for a confrontation. Ashlynn, Eddie's soon to be ex-wife, blames me for the end of her marriage, and she'll be less than thrilled to see me bonding with her offspring. I'm not sure how a grown woman can blame a twelve-year-old girl for the fact that her husband kept a big secret from her, but that's my step-mommy. She's an even bigger piece of work than Eddie.

When I open the door, instead of Ashlynn, I find Jack and Bryce. Jack puts a finger to his lips and shoves a scrap of paper into my hand. *We're going to tell you we're going camping. Don't ask too many questions. Try to sound excited.*

I tear my eyes away from the note and glance at Jack. His eyes are pleading with me to go along with the instructions, and Bryce is nodding like a deranged bobble-head in encouragement. I swallow hard and nod.

"Hey, Evansville," Bryce says. "We're going camping this weekend. Want to come?"

"Sure…I mean yeah, sounds like fun."

Bryce gives me a small smile. "Good. Why don't you pack a bag? We have a few things to do, but we'll be back to pick you up in an hour."

"Okay."

Bryce reaches out and squeezes my hand before following Jack down the sidewalk. My gaze drops back to the note, searching it for a clue to what the hell that was all about. The click-clacking of Ashlynn's stilettos draws my attention. She pauses, tilting her head to the side and studies me with icy blue eyes.

"Evan. Nice to see you." Her voice is as cool as an arctic blast. She pushes into the house, waving a manicured hand in dismissal. Her willowy form sashays into the living room, her blond bob swinging across her shoulders. There's no denying the woman is beautiful, but so is a poison dart frog.

Eddie makes his way down the stairs with the kids' bags and hands them to Ashlynn without a word. Quinn and Liam finally notice their mother and fly off the couch.

"Mommy!" Liam yells, launching himself at her.

Ashlynn bends down and pulls both children into her arms, a serene smile crossing her painted lips. Okay, so she loves them. I guess it's good to know she's capable of loving someone other than herself. She rises with stiff movements and turns to Eddie. "I'll have them back by bedtime on Sunday." She spins, breezing past me on her way out. "Evan," she says with a curt nod, not bothering to close the door behind her.

"What on earth possessed you to marry that woman?"

Eddie sighs and retreats to the kitchen. What is it with rock stars and vapid, narcissistic models? Suddenly I remember I need to pack, and better yet, I don't have to spend the weekend with Eddie.

I follow him into the kitchen. "Eddie?"

He glances up from the counter he's been staring at, and I almost feel sorry for him. Lines crease his forehead, and his face is drawn. For the first time I can recall, he appears older than his thirty-eight years.

"I, uh…I'm going camping with my friends this weekend."

"Have fun," he says, his voice flat, emotionless. "When will you be back?"

"Sunday." At least I think so.

"Do you need anything? There's some camping gear up in the closet. You're welcome to borrow whatever you need."

"Thanks." I feel like I should say something else, although I don't know what. What do you say to the man who abandoned you and is now being abandoned by his wife? "Hey, I know how it feels"? "Join the club"? But the weird thing is, I do feel kind of bad for him. Before I can come up with anything more to say though, he heads back upstairs.

I slide the zipper of my duffel bag closed just as a knock comes on the front door. Eddie answers it, and I see my friends on the porch over his shoulder. Eddie greets them with a nod and pulls the door open to let them in. He met Lisa and Colin years ago in the Eastern Province when he was attempting to connect with his long lost daughter. Recognition replaces the indifference on Eddie's face, and he smiles, shaking their hands.

"Eddie, you remember Bryce. This is Jack. Jack, this is my…my Eddie. Eddie McIntyre."

Jack shakes Eddie's hand with genuine enthusiasm. "It's nice to meet you, sir. I'm a big fan."

Eddie's smile grows wide. This is his world, the one he knows how to live in — the one with adoring fans. "Good to meet you, Jack."

Great, he can turn it on for a complete stranger, a fan, but his own daughter? I get stony silence.

Bryce reaches out and takes my bag, slinging it over his shoulder. I stand next to Eddie, not sure if I should hug him goodbye. He makes the decision for me, reaching an arm around and giving me an awkward pat on the back.

"Have fun," he says, closing the door behind us.

We make our way to the express elevators in silence, no one finding it necessary to clue me in. Gliding down one hundred levels without a word spoken only increases the already building tension spiraling inside me, but asking questions when everyone else is quietly clenching their jaw, won't get me anywhere.

Once on the ground, we take a commuter train the twenty-five miles out to the coast, emerging from the dark station into bright late morning sun. It's a perfect Western Province day, all blue cloudless skies and yellow sunshine. We walk out to the boardwalk, a cool ocean breeze skating across my skin, fluttering strands of hair. The crashing surf is interspersed with screeching seagulls and children's laughter. This is the most I've felt at home since getting back to the Union. Cleanliness aside, this is as close to being in the Ruins as I'll get here.

A four-wheel-drive sand cruiser shuttles us to the check-in tent. We step out onto a path of groomed sand lined with solar luminaries that will light up at dusk, creating a glowing walkway. A campground employee leads us to a grouping of three white canvas tents adorned with strands of solar lights. Each tent has two cots, a small table with a vase of fresh honeysuckle and gardenias, and two folding chairs. Lisa and Jack dump their bags in one tent, and I follow Colin into another, setting my bag down. I suppose I could have let Colin and Bryce bunk together, but I don't want to be alone.

The flap from the tent falls into place, and I spin around. "Colin, what the *hell*—"

He cuts me off, putting a finger to his lips. I'm trying hard not to freak out, but he's making it difficult. His eyes roam over my face, his mouth pressed in a tight line. "I've got my ticket for the Northwest. I leave in a week."

"Oh." I drop into one of the chairs. Over the past couple of days, I haven't thought much about him leaving. We both lapse back into silence. After a few minutes, I get up and go peek outside, looking for the others. Jack, Bryce, and Lisa head toward us with grave expressions. Turning back to Colin, I realize it's the same expression he's had the whole time we've been in here. Something really bad is going on.

They file into our tent, and Jack pulls a palm-sized electronic device from his pocket, moving it over the seams of the tent, the cots, the table. After glancing at a display on the front of the device, he motions for me to approach and sweeps it over me from head to toe. His shoulders relax and his jaw loosens for the first time since he arrived at my door this morning.

I raise both eyebrows, waiting for someone to clue me in, not sure if I'm allowed to speak yet.

Jack glances at Bryce before turning to me. "Someone bugged Lisa's apartment."

"What do you mean 'bugged'?"

"I was helping her put up some speakers when I found a tiny Union-issue listening device. I swept her place with this and discovered twelve in total."

"That's insane."

"We checked our place, too, and found another dozen there," Jack says. "We need to check your dad's place."

"Why would anyone do that?

"You were gone a long time and so were we," Bryce says, hands stuffed in the front pockets of his jeans. "Apparently someone noticed. We checked everyone's clothing because we don't know who planted the bugs, what all they had access to, or how long ago. We figured we'd be safest out here."

A sliver of fear pierces me. "What did we say in Lisa's apartment?"

Bryce shifts, pulling his hands from his pockets. "I don't think it was anything specific. What about you at your dad's?"

I shake my head. "Nothing. What about you guys at Lisa's place before I got there?"

"Nothing much I can remember," Jack says, dropping the device into his shirt pocket.

"What's going on?" I ask, sinking onto my cot, my voice barely above a whisper.

"I don't know," Jack says. "But we've stumbled onto something even bigger than we realized."

Even though our tent is bug free, I feel dirty, like I need a shower. I wander down to the water and stare out at the waves. They crash ashore, spraying me, inching forward, reaching up to tease my toes. The surf rushes back out, pulling some of the sand with it, my feet sinking deep.

"Are you okay?"

I startle at Lisa's voice. She moves to stand beside me.

"I don't know," I say. "Sometimes I think maybe I am, but a few minutes later, I'm not sure."

She puts her arm around me, and I lay my head on her shoulder, feeling fortunate to have friends who care. We watch the raw power of nature in silence, and a sense of calm begins to edge out some of the unease. Not a lot, but enough for me to at least get through the rest of this day, and maybe that's all I can ask for right now.

"Hey, there you are," Colin says, making his way like a sloppy drunk through the loose, dry sand. "I'm hungry."

"Of course you are," I say under my breath, but Lisa and I follow him to the mess tent.

Bryce and Jack find us while we're still in line and sneak in between us. Dinner conversation is reserved, stilted, and afterward, we make our way back down to the water for the sunset. There's something lonely about the sun disappearing behind the horizon, leaving us abandoned in the dark.

We return to our tents, and I grab a sweatshirt before joining the others at the fire ring outside our tents. The guys gather wood, while Lisa and I make a coffee run. We drag our chairs out and sit around the fire, sipping coffee, and finally talking.

"What are we going to do?" Lisa asks, a slight quiver in her voice.

"First we need to find out who bugged our places," Jack says.

"And then what?" I ask.

"After that…I don't know." Jack blows out a breath. "We'll have to figure it out then."

Great, more waiting. We're spinning our wheels. Every day we don't do something is one day closer to an impending attack.

"So, should I show up at work Monday morning like nothing's wrong?" Lisa asks.

"For now," Jack says. "I think we all need to go about life as if everything is normal for as long as possible."

"What should I do?" Colin asks.

"You need to stick with your plans," Jack says, taking a sip of his coffee. "Any deviation will raise a red flag."

"And what about me?" I still haven't declared a vocation even though I was supposed to have done so by now.

"I've been thinking about that," Bryce says. "I want to keep you close, and I have an idea." He gives me a small smile. "What if you went into journalism?"

"Journalism? What do I know about journalism?"

"Probably a lot more than you think. And I can help."

Jack glances from me to Bryce. "What are you thinking?"

"I have some samples I wrote a couple of years ago. She can take them down to Western Provincial and offer them up as her own. They should be good enough to get her an internship at the crime desk. We'll give her a few weeks to get settled, then we can send a request over for an embedded reporter for an investigation we're working."

It's not uncommon for reporters and detectives to work together. It helps create the kind of sensational journalism Unionites crave. Because the Union has a low crime rate compared to other countries, journalists have resorted to a tabloid style of reporting that looks nothing at all like overseas news sources or the pre-war stuff we studied in school. It wouldn't be horrible to be a writer. Plus, working with Bryce and Jack beats sitting around and waiting for them to do their thing.

"What makes you think they'll let me do it?" I ask. "I don't have any experience."

"No one does when they start an internship," Lisa says, settling back in her chair. "That's the whole purpose of your first year. On-the-job training."

"No, I mean why would they let a brand new intern, with no experience, work as an embedded reporter?"

"We can request a young female because we're undercover and need her to be able to pose as the girlfriend of one of us," Bryce says, rubbing his jaw. "If it works like it does for other teams in our precinct, they'll send us over four or five candidates, and we'll choose you."

"But what if they don't give you my name?"

"We'll say none of the ones they offered are what we're looking for and ask if they have anyone else. A friend of mine works over there, if I have to, I'll call in a favor."

I stuff my hands into my sweatshirt pockets as the chilly air starts to burrow deeper beneath my skin. "Okay, so let's say by some small miracle this does work, aren't they going to expect me to submit stories from time to time? I can't just go off and not report, can I?"

"I'll help you, but I know you can write. I was in your class, remember? We'll say we need to hold off on some stuff because of the sensitive nature of our investigation with the promise of a big story when it's over. Trust me, they'd rather send a green intern than give up one of their seasoned reporters. That way if something happens to you, they won't be out one of their valued writers. Or worse, if a decent story doesn't materialize, they won't have wasted a prized talent on a bad lead."

"It's brilliant," Jack says, smiling broadly.

"Yeah," Bryce says with a smug grin. "It solves two of our immediate problems. Evan will have a vocation, and we'll be able to keep her safe. Plus she'll have access to the investigative resources of the news site, which could come in handy."

I try not to get too confident about it working, but I have to admit, if it does, it's a pretty damn good plan.

Damn Good Plan

Colin and I arrange our cots so the ends meet at a right angle in the corner of the tent. Lying on our backs with our heads together, we talk.

"What's going on with you and Bryce?" Colin asks.

"Nothing. That was over before it even began."

"He cares about you."

I twist around, but it's too dark to make out Colin's expression. "I never thought you were a fan."

"I wasn't before, but he was really broken up when you were missing. After Jack was ready to throw in the towel, Bryce refused to give up. Even after Lisa and I began to wonder if we'd ever see you again."

"Wait, I thought Lisa said she always knew you'd find me."

"That's what she said, but I know her, and there were times she wasn't sure about any of it. Not Bryce, though. He just kept going. You don't do that for someone you only sort of like."

I push up on my elbow and study him for a few moments before dropping to my back, trying to process this new information along with the events of the past week. At first, we only needed to find a way to stop an attack on the Union, but now we have to figure out who's monitoring us and why. Because as long as someone is listening to everything we say, doing anything meaningful to stop the attack is impossible. So trying to make sense of what Colin said about Bryce isn't even on the to-do list. Although I'll admit it was easier for me to be around Bryce when I thought he was the bad guy.

"All I'm saying," Colin continues, "is hear him out. I saw the look on his face when you were with that guy from the Ruins. I know that look."

Of course he does. It's the same one he gets whenever he sees Lisa and Jack together. I reach out to take his hand, squeezing it. He squeezes back and I don't let go until his hand falls from mine. Sleep doesn't come for me though, and I give up trying after tossing and turning for an hour. Grabbing my sweatshirt, I step outside into the chilly air. My feet take me down to the water without any prodding from my brain. The tide is low, providing a large swath of hard-packed sand that's easier to walk on than the loose stuff.

I stroll along the shore, eyes down, deep in my own thoughts. Colin's words from earlier and Sonia's that day out in the Ruins about life being too short for regrets mix together in my head like thought soup.

"Whoa," a voice startles me and I glance up seconds before crashing into Bryce.

"Sorry, I didn't see you."

"Trouble sleeping?"

"Yeah." I pause. "But I'm glad I ran into you — literally."

He turns and falls in step beside me. "Why's that?"

With a deep breath, I launch into an unrehearsed apology before I chicken out. "I never meant to hurt you. Well, maybe I did…or not."

He laughs. "What are you talking about?"

"Cyrus. The guy in the Ruins."

"Oh." All humor is gone from his voice now.

"I guess there was a part of me that wanted to hurt the guy I thought you were — the smuggler more interested in business than my safety. That guy doesn't exist, so I'm sorry I hurt you, but the guy I fell for on the train doesn't exist either. Not really."

A slow breath of air escapes his lips. "Let's start over." He stops and reaches out his hand to mine. "Hi, I'm Michael Bryce Cooper…but you can call me Bryce. I like the way it sounds when you say it."

I shake his hand, smiling. "Nice to meet you. I'm Evan Delilah Taylor. But you can call me Evansville because it makes me laugh."

He gives me a full-dimpled smile, white teeth gleaming against dark skin in the moonlight. We turn and start back toward camp, walking in silence for several minutes, the gentle sound of the waves pushing ashore the only thing I can hear beyond my own thoughts.

"I like your hair better red."

I glance at him out of the corner of my eye. "It took me nearly eighteen years, but I think I do, too."

"What made you change your mind?"

"Quinn." I shrug. "What she said about how I'm supposed to have red hair. It also made me think about other stuff, about how things are supposed to be. Everything that happened led me to where I am now. Maybe this is what I'm supposed to be doing."

"That's a huge burden, Evan. You don't have to do it alone. We're all in this together, all set in motion by the same chain of events."

I turn toward him, searching his face. Maybe he's right. Just because this is my destiny, doesn't mean it's mine alone.

"I don't even want you involved in this," he continues. "Jack and I are trained detectives. This is what we do. I could lose my job, or worse, by involving you."

"I'm already involved, Bryce."

"I know." He glances down at the sand for a moment. "But you wouldn't be if it hadn't been for me."

This is where I should tell him I forgive him, but I don't. We've reached where we need to turn to head back into our camp, but I'm still too keyed up to sleep. "I'm going to walk a little longer."

He hesitates for a couple of beats. "I can walk with you, unless you'd rather be alone."

"No, I'd like the company."

While we stroll, we talk about things long left unsaid. He tells me more about his childhood and growing up, this time not skirting around topics to protect his cover. His words flow freely as he talks about how hard it was in the days after his father disappeared. Pain laces his voice, but I also detect a tinge of hope, as if he believes his father might still be alive.

I share more about what happened in the Ruins, not glossing over my feelings for Cyrus. I don't want to hurt Bryce, but I need him to understand what I was feeling when I was out there, why his deception and dishonesty hurt me so much.

When I'm done, he's quiet for a long time before stopping and turning to face me. He reaches out and take my hands in his. I want to pull them back, but Colin asked me to hear Bryce out, so I leave my hands in his for now.

"I won't lie to you again," he says. "About anything. Even if the truth is difficult."

"Thank you," I say, meaning it. This feels like a moment, the beginning of a genuine friendship based on shared goals if nothing else.

Scuffling sounds drag me out of a dreamless sleep. I lift my head to see Colin moving around. "What time is it?"

"Seven-thirty, I think. I'm hungry."

I roll my eyes. "Okay, hang on. I'll go with you."

Throwing on a sweatshirt, I stumble after him, heading over to the mess tent. We grab food and coffee and join Lisa and Jack at their table.

"Why do they call it a mess tent? There's nothing messy about this," I say, taking a bite of crepes Suzette, nestled between fresh asparagus with hollandaise sauce and a biscuit.

"Hey, Lis," Colin says. "If your gig at the restaurant doesn't work out, you can always come and do your chef thing here."

She smiles between bites. "I know, right?"

Bryce wanders over as I shove the last of my biscuit into my mouth, looking as bleary-eyed as I feel. He gets breakfast and joins us, taking the spot next to me. The campground has close to a hundred tents, and there's a decent crowd here for the final weekend before school starts. A group of teenage girls sits a few tables over, checking out Colin. I nudge him and he smiles at them, which sends them into fits of giggles. His smile dissolves into a frown when he glances at Jack and Lisa. I know what it's like not being able to be with the person you love, but when I peek at Bryce, I know a small part of me still has feelings for him, I'm just not sure exactly what those feelings are.

We convene in Bryce's tent after breakfast, dragging our folding chairs with us. Bryce pushes both cots over to the side so we can arrange the chairs in a circle. Jack closes and ties the tent flaps, giving us privacy. "We need a plan for the next week," he says, turning to face us. "Then we'll schedule a time and place to get back together."

"Colin's leaving before then," I say.

"That's an issue," Jack says. "And we have to be careful what we say over the phone or by text. But, I think we can use it to our advantage."

"What do you mean?" Lisa asks.

"If we remove any of the bugs, they'll know we're on to them. By leaving them in place, they'll think they have the upper hand. We'll feed them the information we want them to have, use that to help us figure out who they are."

I trace my finger along the arm of the chair, studying the wood grain while Jack talks. "So, we have to go about our lives being careful of what we say?" I ask.

"We have to act as if the bugs aren't there or it'll become obvious to whoever's listening. But we can't talk about the Ruins or the invasion when we're in any of our apartments. And Colin," Jack turns to him, "you have to assume your place up in the Northwest Province is also bugged."

"Jack, you said we don't know who planted the bugs," I say. "But, it has to be someone who knows where we were, otherwise, why would they have bothered?"

"Not necessarily," Bryce says. "It doesn't mean they know *where* we were. Only that we were off the grid for a long time, and that raised suspicions somewhere."

"Who would have been paying that much attention to a group of teens?" I ask. Then it hits me this might not be about me, Lisa, and Colin. "Or, a couple of undercover detectives… What did you tell them at your debriefing?"

Jack lets out an exaggerated sigh. "We told them about the weapons smuggling and even went so far as to say we believe the weapons might be going into the Ruins. We had to tell them something."

"But if they go out into the Ruins, if they send people out there—"

"Hold on," Jack says. "They're not going to do that. Not yet, anyway. This is still our investigation. We have to report back to our lieutenant on a regular basis, but they aren't going to send anyone out there to investigate until we do a lot more work on our end."

"How do you know someone in the police department didn't plant the bugs?"

"It's a possibility," Jack says, "and one we'll explore. It could also be someone close to you who was concerned about your delay in getting to your destination — someone with enough clout to get into several residences in the Western Province."

"No way." I push out of my chair and whirl around to face him. "I know what you're insinuating, but my uncle wouldn't do that. What about your dad? Maybe he noticed his son and partner weren't checking in as required, figured out who were the last people he was seen with and bugged everyone's apartments."

"I'm not ruling that out either, Evan, but we have to consider everything. For now, let's assume no one except the five of us can be completely trusted."

With an exaggerated sigh, I stop pacing and plop down in my chair, staring glumly at the ground. "Okay, so what's the plan?"

After spending a day walking up and down the shore, throwing out ideas, the plan we've come up with is that we don't have a plan. We return to our tents after dinner to continue our discussions. I grab some blankets while the boys make another fire. Most of the day was spent arguing, so the mood of our little group is as dark as the night sky.

"Look," Jack says, leaning back in his chair. "I get it. You hate not doing anything."

"It's not only that," I say. "But the reason I came home was to do something, and now you're telling me I have to just sit around."

"What do you want to do?" he asks.

"Finally. I've been trying to tell you, but you keep cutting me off." He presses his mouth in a tight line, as if he's forcing himself to remain quiet. "I came up with an idea out in the Ruins, a way to warn the Union citizens without threatening the Ruins. I was thinking about the Peace Patrols from the late 2000s that brokered the cease-fire to end the war. What if we went down to the lower levels and blended in, started spreading the word of what we saw out there?"

"How does that protect the Ruins?" Colin asks.

"Well, most of the people who live down below are the ones who like their privacy. They're not big on government to begin, barely use any services, and only contribute as much as they have to. So the chance they'd talk to the government is pretty low. If we tell them what we saw, that people live out there, people without anything, word would spread. You know how it'll go. Demonstrations, people demanding change. If the people in the Ruins get what they need from us, there won't be any reason for them to attack."

Everyone is quiet for a few minutes. Jack shifts in his chair and glances at Bryce before turning to me. "It's not a bad idea, but, Evan, you know serious changes like you're talking about will take years. What if the attack happens before then?"

"Yeah, I don't have it all figured out yet."

"If what we suspect is true, about the smuggling and arming the rebels, what if they planted the bugs to make sure we don't do exactly what you're suggesting?" Jack asks.

"I don't know, but all you've said is we need to find out who bugged us, and that's going to take time, too. Especially if your plan is to feed them information and wait to see what happens."

"That's not exactly what I said, it's more complicated than that."

I lift an eyebrow.

He sighs, "Okay, so that's basically it. But knowing who's behind it is key to finding out more about their operation."

"Assuming the two are connected."

"I think for now we need to assume they are," Bryce says, finally deciding to join the conversation. "At least until we find out they're not. There are too many coincidences, and I don't believe in coincidence. There's a decent chance government officials are involved, and I wouldn't be surprised if Peter Benton's one of them."

"Do you think our own government is funding an attack against us?" Lisa asks.

"I don't think the entire government is," Bryce says. "But I'd bet money certain members are involved."

"Well then we're screwed," Colin says.

"If you think there's some cooperation between the two, figuring out who bugged us may point to the connection," Jack says to Bryce. "Think about it. If anyone knew we were out in the Ruins, they have a vested interest in discovering how much we know."

"I'm not saying the bugging isn't connected," Bryce says. "But Benton could be useful in finding out who's moving freely between both worlds. When I was in his place, there was a steady stream of people coming and going. People who didn't come across as legitimate visitors to the Mayor."

"Bryce is right," I say. "If Benton's connected to the rebels in the Ruins, we could infiltrate them, learn more about their plans." That was Lucien and Draya's plan before Lucien died. I almost feel like I owe it to him to see it through.

Bryce turns to me, his eyes dark and intense. "That's by far the most dangerous option."

"Which means it's also the most promising. It could be our best chance to learn what they're up to. How else can we get that information?" I ask, fighting to keep the frustration out of my voice.

"By doing good detective work," Bryce says. His voice is calm but there's an edge to it not usually present. "I think Benton is the key to all of this."

If Alivia's dad is involved, he might know more about the rebels' plans. It might be easier to get information through him than to join up out in the Ruins. Based on what I saw and heard out there, they seemed like a bunch of drunk idealists, anyway.

Silence settles over our group, the tension building. Jack and Bryce stare each other down until Lisa breaks the stalemate. "Why do we need to be limited to only one plan?"

"We've been over this, Lis," I say. "There aren't enough of us to do everything."

"Everyone keeps saying that, but I think you're trying to make this more complicated than it needs to be. You and Bryce can go back east and check out Benton as part of your embedded reporter undercover thing. Jack and I can use the bugs to see if we can flush out the buggers, or whatever it is you call people who plant bugs."

"That could work," Jack says, smiling at Lisa.

I roll my eyes. If I'd suggested it, he'd have immediately shot me down. Colin crosses his arms over his chest, staring into the fire, a frown pulling at his lips. "What about Colin? How are we going to keep him in the loop?" I ask.

Bryce, Jack, and Lisa exchange glances, but no one offers up any ideas.

"I don't see why I can't stay here," Colin says. "Maybe I can talk Eddie into letting me shadow him or something. I mean what aspiring musician would turn down a chance to hang with a member of Epic Vinyl?"

"That's not a bad idea—" I start.

"There's no way to do that without tipping Eddie off," Jack says. "You and Lisa both need to go ahead with your plans. The Northwestern Province is only a few hours by A-Train. We'll plan on getting together every couple of weeks."

If I thought Jack was oblivious to how Colin felt about Lisa, he pretty much just shot that theory to hell. He knows, and he wants Colin and his feelings as far away as possible. Colin glares at Jack but doesn't argue. I'm not sure what Colin will be able to contribute once he's up there. This feels like the beginning of the end of his involvement.

Colin is quiet as we lie on our cots. I know he's frustrated. "As much as I hate to admit it, Jack's right. You can't stay here, at least not right now," I say. "Besides, it'll be good for you to get a little distance from Lisa for a while. You've been together in one way or another almost every day since we were in Grade 5."

"Jack's trying to get rid of me."

I stack my fists on top of each other, propping my chin up. "He's a detective, Col, if he didn't know how you feel about Lisa he wouldn't be a very good one."

He sighs, but doesn't take his eyes off the ceiling. "So, is being away from Cyrus making it any easier for you?"

"No. But I did think about what you said the other night. About Bryce, I mean. I heard him out, and I think I'm starting to forgive him." I pause, chewing on my bottom lip. "Maybe it's time for you to forgive Lisa. She didn't hurt you on purpose. You never told her how you felt."

He doesn't say anything and before long, I can hear his deep, even breathing, but thoughts of Cyrus keep me awake for a long time.

5 Forgiveness

Shaking the sand out of my sweatpants, I roll them up and stuff them in my duffel bag. Colin is quiet as he packs behind me. He's been subdued since he got up, hardly saying two words at breakfast.

"So Lisa was a bundle of energy this morning. More bouncy than usual," I say. "I guess she's pretty excited about her internship starting tomorrow."

"I think I'm gonna head up to the northwest early," Colin says, his voice flat, emotionless.

I grab his arm, spinning him around to face me. His eyes are downcast so I can't tell if he's serious. "Why?"

He shrugs, but we both know why. "Can you at least wait until after my birthday on Wednesday?"

He runs a hand through his hair and lifts his head to look at me. My eyes plead with him. "I don't know, EvTay."

"Please? Pretty please? I want to go out and do something fun for a change, but it won't be fun if you're not there."

"I'll think about it," he says, but his tone is less than convincing.

I zip up my duffel and drop it by the opening, turning to face Colin. "You're going to brood up there all alone. Why not brood here among friends? Stay at our place if that would be easier."

He lifts his eyebrows. "You're inviting me to stay at Eddie's when you two are barely speaking? Sounds like fun, but I'll pass."

I drop the subject for now and pick up my bag, slinging it over my shoulder. Colin reaches out and takes it from me. "I'll wait until after your birthday, but I'm leaving on Thursday." He pushes past me, leading the way to the sand cruiser for the ride back to the train station.

Jack falls in step beside us carrying his and Lisa's bags. "When you get home today, try to get your dad out of the apartment so I can sweep it for bugs. It would be nice to know."

"I'll try."

"If you manage to get him out, send me a text. If I don't get a text from you, I'll assume it's a no-go."

"Okay."

After saying goodbye to the others at the commuter station, Bryce walks me to Eddie's. He sets my bag down next to the front door and stuffs his hands into his pockets. Several seconds pass with him staring mutely at the ground. Uncomfortable silence settles between us. Even though we sort of cleared the air the other night on the beach, our relationship is in an awkward place.

"Thanks, Bryce. I'll talk to you later," I say, more to break the stalemate than anything else.

He glances up, his gray eyes locking onto mine, and nods before turning and striding down the sidewalk. I stare at his retreating form and wonder what we're doing. I'm pretty sure he wants more than friendship from me, but I'm in love with someone else. Someone I'm never going to see again. With a heavy sigh, I push open the door and head inside.

Eddie's on the couch watching a football game on his huge display wall. He turns and mutes the sound when he sees me. "How was it?"

"Fun." I pause, trying to think of how to get him out of the house with the game on. "Hey, Eddie, can we talk?"

He blinks a couple of times then stares at me for a few seconds. "Uh, sure." He slides his finger across the control panel on the arm of the couch and turns off the screen.

"I was thinking we could go for a walk...to the park, or something."

"Sure, but we can't be gone long. I want to be back before Ashlynn shows up with the kids."

"What time is she due?" I cross to the door, eager to get him out before he changes his mind.

"Not for a couple of hours, but sometimes she brings them home early if she doesn't want to deal with baths."

"Nice." I loathe that woman.

He follows me outside, and I remember I need to text Jack. "Um, I have to use the bathroom first, I'll be right back." I grab my tablet and text Jack from the bathroom before rushing back out to join Eddie. We walk in strained silence, the sharp thwacking of our flip-flops on the pavement only fueling my anxiety.

Eddie stares at me, waiting for me to tell him why we're out here. I have no idea what to say and end up vomiting a lame apology. "I wanted to say I'm sorry. For the other night, for what I said. I didn't mean it. I just didn't want to be interrogated about my summer."

"Okay." The word comes out slowly, as if he's testing it out. "But for future reference, you can tell me you don't want to talk about something. I am capable of understanding."

I make my way over to a park bench and take a seat. Eddie sits next to me, close but not touching.

We're quiet for a few minutes before he asks, "Is that all you wanted to discuss? We could have had this conversation at home."

"I know, but it's a nice day. I'm learning to appreciate the Western Province weather."

"Ah, okay." After a few more minutes of awkward silence, Eddie stands.

We haven't been gone long enough. "That's not all," I say before mentally grasping for something else to talk about. I pick up a yellowing leaf from the seat next to me and twirl the stem between my thumb and forefinger, racking my brain for a new topic. Eddie glances at me expectantly, and I blurt out the most insane thing ever. "Do you think it's possible to be in love with one person and interested in another at the same time?" Where the hell did that come from? I've decided to forgive Bryce, but that doesn't mean I'm interested in him.

His eyes widen for a second. I've never asked him for advice. About anything. Ever. He stammers for a few seconds then starts talking without really saying anything, as if he thinks I'll take the question back if he doesn't respond. "I...I, well, I don't know. I suppose it's possible. I'm no expert, but I guess, maybe… Is this about Bryce and Colin?"

A laugh that sounds more like a snort escapes. "Not Colin. He's like a brother. We don't have that kind of relationship, and anyway, he likes someone else. I met this guy over the summer…" My voice trails off as thoughts of Cyrus take over. I bite down on my lip to keep it from trembling and take a deep breath. "And fell in love with him. But…I don't think I'll see him again. Some things…happened and I don't know if he wants to see me. He didn't leave me any way to reach him."

Eddie stares at me as if I've explained myself in a language he can't even understand. "I'm the wrong person to give romantic advice, but it seems to me if the other guy's out of the picture, and you like Bryce…it is Bryce, right?" I nod. "Then why not see where that goes?"

I wasn't actually looking for advice, just something to fill the time, but there must be some sort of subliminal reason I chose this question to ask. And his answer is logical. Can logic ever be applied to matters of the heart?

"You're only seventeen," he continues.

"I'll be eighteen on Wednesday."

"Still too young to be thinking about settling down. Learn from the mistakes your mother and I made. Trust me, what you want now, at seventeen or eighteen, isn't the same as what you'll want at thirty-eight."

"You didn't settle down when you were eighteen," I remind him with a hint of bitterness. "And are you saying I was a mistake?"

"No, of course not." He turns to me, his eyes intense, all traces of unease from earlier gone. "I am so proud of you, and Liam, and

Quinn. I know I can't take credit for how you turned out, but I'm still proud to be your father. Just because I don't want you to become a parent at nineteen doesn't mean I'm sorry you were born."

I nod, although I'm not sure I understand. If he doesn't want me to make the same mistakes, then I must be a mistake.

He sighs, running a hand through his hair. "If I had to live my life over, I wouldn't change anything if even *one* of those changes meant I wouldn't have you three kids."

"Oh." I turn and glance out across the park, not wanting to get into some sort of sappy father-daughter thing, so I stand and continue walking along the path to pad the time.

"Have you chosen a vocation yet?" Eddie asks. "I'm not trying to pressure you, but it's September. You can work for me doing something. I'd hate for you to end up stuck in a community service position that makes you miserable."

"Thanks, Eddie, but I think I want to be a reporter. I'm going to go apply for an internship tomorrow."

He stops and stares at me, eyebrows raised. "I didn't realize you were interested in writing. That's…that's awesome, Evan, and a good choice for you. I'm impressed." He definitely seems pleased, which makes me almost feel bad for lying to him.

"So, um, how early do you think Ashlynn will be back with the kids?"

He checks his watch. "Any time now. We should head home." We turn and start back toward the apartment, following the serpentine path through shaggy grass.

While we walk, he tells me about the journalists he's met over the years. "Hey, you could specialize in fashion or even cover music or do restaurant reviews."

I nod in response, wondering what he'll say when he finds out I've been assigned as an embedded reporter with undercover detectives.

When we get back to the house, I check my tablet and see a text from Jack. One simple number that sends an icy chill careening through my veins.

12

6 Making Mistakes

With one last glance at my reflection, I decide I'm satisfied with the results. Lisa dragged me out to do some birthday shopping this morning, and I splurged on something to wear tonight. The dress is black with large, pale pink roses. It's form-fitting to my waist before flaring out over layers of pink tulle ruffles that hits mid-calf. Even though I'm no slave to fashion, I can't deny it feels pretty damn awesome to wear something fabulous for a change.

"Evan," Eddie calls from downstairs.

"Be right there." I arrange a few curls away from my face and spritz them then apply a thin layer of lip gloss. Slipping on a pair of blush patent-leather heels, I fling the door open.

"Oooo," Quinn says as she goes bouncing past my room in a persimmon-colored dress and brown cowboy boots.

My friends are waiting in the living room, and Colin lets out a wolf whistle as I descend the stairs, making my cheeks redden. But it's the way Bryce's gray eyes lock onto mine, as if there's no one else here, that heats my blood. Yeah, getting dressed up was totally worth it.

"Reservations are at six, so we'd better get going," Eddie says, herding us out the door.

After an early dinner with Eddie and the kids, the rest of us head to the Rocco Blue nightclub to continue the celebration. Bryce takes my hand and threads a path through the maze of sweaty bodies, as the loud bass pounds in my chest and frenzied music pulses through my veins.

I let Bryce lead me, unsure of our destination until we stop at the bar. Leaning in close to my ear, he asks, "What do you want to drink?"

In addition to officially being an adult, I'm now of legal drinking age, although I'm not much of a drinker. "I'm not sure, something sweet, I guess."

He leans across the counter to talk to the bartender and is soon handing me a crimson drink in a martini glass with a sugared rim. A shish-kebob of tropical fruits are stacked on a silver toothpick, topped with a white-chocolate-dipped raspberry. "What's this?" I ask.

"It's called a Daring Escape," he says with a smile, flashing his dimples.

I take a sip to keep it from spilling over the edge, the sugar crystals tickling my tongue. The drink has a strong fruity flavor that might be cherry, and the pungent odor of alcohol and molasses from the rum. Bryce pulls me behind him, and I twist and dodge to avoid elbows and sloshing drinks, arriving at one of the few available tables.

We grab seats and sit, sipping our cocktails and taking in the craziness around us. Bodies bump and grind against one another on the dance floor, fists pumping to the beat. Two tables over, a group of girls eye Colin. Words are exchanged as they smile, before a blonde in an impossibly tight black dress slinks her way over to our table. She places her shiny lacquered nails on Colin's arm and leans in to say something to him. He blushes and smiles then pushes up from our table and leads her to the dance floor where they're immediately swallowed by the crowd.

"Wanna dance?" Bryce asks.

I nod and follow him to the dance floor. It's been ages since I last danced, and for several songs, I close my eyes and let the music move through me, wrap around me, consume me. At least until the air surrounding us becomes saturated with body heat and sweat. On the way back to our table, we stop at the bar and grab some waters. Colin's at the girls' table, his tie loosened, top button undone, stealing glances at Lisa and Jack whenever he can.

"I'll be right back," I say to the others and head over to Colin. "Can I talk to you for a minute?" The blonde looks me up and down, a scowl marring her otherwise perfect face. I give her a toothy smile. "Don't worry I'll bring him back in a few minutes."

Hooking my arm through his, I steer him around the perimeter of the club and outside. While it's quieter out here, the din seeps through porous walls and the beat thrums across my skin. We step to the side as a group enters, the music blaring when the door opens.

"What's up?" Colin asks when the door swings shut, muffling the noise.

"You're at a table full of adoring girls, but you aren't enjoying yourself. At least try to have fun. Out in the Ruins, they live each day like it could be their last, because it could be. They don't waste time worrying about what-ifs."

A breeze ruffles his dark hair, a pained expression filling his eyes. "So, what? I'm supposed to pretend I'm thrilled she's dating him when I really want to beat his cocky ass?"

I inhale and let it out slowly, "No. I'm saying we don't have to let the weight of the world crush us. We grew up always worrying about the future, never living in the moment. Maybe there's a place between the two extremes. Those girls can't take their eyes off you, but you can't take your eyes off Lisa long enough to notice."

"So you're taking your own advice and are back together with Bryce?" I glance away and chew my bottom lip. "Yeah, didn't think so." He turns and stalks back inside.

With a heavy sigh I follow him, rejoining Jack, Bryce, and Lisa, while Colin returns to the girls. Bryce takes my hand and leads me back out to the dance floor, but I can't get in the zone again.

"How about some fresh air?" Bryce asks.

I nod, realizing that's exactly what I need. We gather Jack and Lisa, and I make eye contact with Colin as we pass him, inclining my head toward the door. He gives me a brief shake of his head and returns his attention to the blonde.

While we walk, I step out of my shoes and hook the straps over my fingers, letting the warmth of the pavement settle into my feet, easing some of the pain from wearing ridiculously high heels tonight. We reach the park, illuminated by soft lighting, and stroll the lazy path. For the first time in a week, we can talk without fear of someone listening to us. Being able to speak freely is like throwing open the door and filling my lungs with fresh air after being confined in a windowless box.

"So, I got the job." I tell them. "It was like Bryce said. I showed up with the writing samples, filled out an application, and they called this morning to offer me an internship."

"That's awesome!" Lisa says.

"See. I told you it would work," Bryce says, picking up my right hand and kissing my knuckles. It's a bold move and catches me off guard. Maybe it's the alcohol, but it doesn't bother me like I would've expected. But it also doesn't make my belly flutter the way it used to.

Lisa lets out a long sigh. "I envy all those people in there." She nods toward the restaurants and clubs beyond the park. "Having fun, totally oblivious to what's going on around them. That was us a few months ago."

"I don't know, Lis. Sure, they're happier, but being blissfully unaware doesn't mean horror isn't about to rain down on them."

"Well that's a complete mood buster," she says with a rough laugh.

It is, not that it was all rainbows and glitter before, but it brings the darkness back from the edge where I'd managed to shove it for a few hours. "I think I'm ready to call it a night," I say to the others.

We stop back in the nightclub to check on Colin before heading home. I find him dancing with the three girls and pull him aside to say good-bye. Angry possessive glares are aimed my way and this time I glare right back. He can dance with them all he wants, but he's still *my* best friend.

"We're leaving," I tell him. "I'll see you tomorrow?"

He nods and turns to rejoin the trio of possessive bitches. My chest tightens, I hate that things are like this between us. I'll find a way to fix it in the morning before he leaves.

Bryce and I say goodnight to Jack and Lisa at the train station, and he walks me to Eddie's. When we reach the front door, I turn toward him, not sure what comes next, but he just smiles and says, "Happy birthday, Evansville," before turning and walking away.

I watch him go, grateful he didn't try to kiss me. Cyrus is still too much a part of my heart to even think about kissing anyone else right now. It's weird how my relationship with Bryce has evolved from that night in the park last spring. We had this crazy whirlwind romance that had him declaring his love for me in a few short days, but we never really knew each other. This feels like we're developing the friendship we didn't have before, and I like it.

My feet pound the pavement from the train station to Lisa's apartment, my lungs pulling in air, filling my chest like sharp blades. I knock on the door with harsh raps before bending at the waist, hands on my knees, catching my breath. What if Colin left before I have a chance to make things right between us?

Lisa opens the door still in her pajama pants and a tank top. Jack's behind her in nothing but a pair of sweatpants. I raise an eyebrow in silent judgment. How could she have Jack spend the night with Colin here?

"Where's Colin?" she asks, looking past me.

"What do you mean, where's Colin? Isn't he here?"

"No. He never came home last night. I thought he was with you."

"*You* were with me."

"No, I mean after we separated. I figured he showed up at your place." Her cheeks turn bright red.

"You've got to be kidding me." My hands ball into fists of anger at my sides. "You can't really be that…" I bite off the words. It's not my place to share how Colin feels about her.

"He probably left with one of those girls we saw him with," she says.

I push into her apartment and find Colin's duffel bag on the floor where it's been since he began camping out on her couch last week. "So, he just blew off his train?"

"Maybe," she shrugs.

"Not likely," I say, stalking back outside, unease gnawing through my stomach. If all this other shit wasn't going on, I could chalk it up to Colin getting laid, but I can't shake the feeling something isn't right. I'm halfway to Bryce's before I realize that's where I'm headed. Hopefully *he* takes me seriously.

My fast walk turns into a jog as I cover the remaining three blocks and two flights of stairs down to the apartment he shares with Jack. I've only been here once before, but I think I remember which one it is. I lift my hand and knock on the pale blue door then pace the small empty concrete porch. Thirty seconds pass before I knock again, louder and longer this time. Still no answer. I'm beginning to think he's not here when the lock clicks and the door cracks open.

Bryce swings the door wider, and my eyes zero in on a bare chest. My gaze drifts from his firm abs and pecs up to meet a pair of gray eyes squinted against the morning light. Confusion fills his features as he stares at me.

"Colin didn't come home last night," I blurt out, my voice breaking.

His gaze rests on my face for a moment before circling the room, reminding me we're being monitored. "I'm sure he's fine, but let me get dressed, and we'll look for him."

Stepping inside, I close the door and bounce on the balls of my feet while I wait for him. The place is decorated in neo-classic guy. A fireplace and hearth runs the length of the front of the apartment, and opposite that is a solid glass wall overlooking a weedy, overgrown garden. The limited furniture is a jumble of chairs, a couch, and a couple of mismatched tables littered with empty beer bottles.

Bryce dresses in record time and takes my hand, pulling me outside. He leads the way to the depot to catch a train back to the nightclub. "I want to retrace his steps after we left," he says. "He might've just found some company for the evening."

"That's what Lisa said, but I think there's more to it."

"It's no secret how he feels about Lisa. He might've just wanted to get away for the night."

"But his bag is still at her place. He would've had to come get it before catching his train."

The nightclub is deserted with the exception of a handful of staff still cleaning up. Bryce walks up to a lanky guy pushing a broom. "Can I talk to the manager?"

A woman in her mid-thirties approaches us a few minutes later, wiping her hands on an apron. She sweeps a chunk of blond hair out of her face with the back of her wrist. "Can I help you?"

"Yeah, I'm Detective Cooper," Bryce says, flashing his credentials. "We're looking for a friend. He was here with us last night, but we're not sure what happened to him."

She glances between me and Bryce. "Did something happen to him?"

"That's what we're trying to find out. Can we take a look at the security feed from last night?"

"Sure," she says, inclining her head. "Come on back."

We follow her past the bar and into a small office beyond the kitchen. "Here," she says, indicating a chair in front of a display screen.

Bryce sits and she shows him how to move through the video files. Bryce locates the one time-stamped from when we were here and forwards through frame-by-frame. I see us leaving for the night and Colin dancing with the girls, getting another drink, dancing some more. Then about an hour later, Colin walks toward the exit alone. A guy in a sweatshirt, hood pulled up, hands shoved into his jeans pockets, approaches Colin. They appear to exchange words. Colin nods before following the guy out the front door.

"What the hell?" I ask. "Who was that guy?" Terror sweeps through me, turning my blood to ice. "And where the hell is Colin?"

"I don't know," Bryce says, reaching over to squeeze my hand. "But we'll find him, I promise."

Bryce downloads the image of Colin and the guy plus another one of the three girls Colin was with. He thanks the manager and we walk back outside, my anxiety rising with each step.

"Now what?" I ask.

"Now we go back to Lisa's. I need Jack to help me track down the guy and these girls."

"What can I do?"

He stops and turns to face me. "Right now, nothing. This is something Jack and I need to do. I'll get back to you as soon as I can. Stay put, either at Lisa's or at Eddie's."

I start to argue, but change my mind. He needs to focus on finding Colin, not arguing with me or worrying about what I might do. When Lisa opens her door, her eyes widen, her mouth going slack. As she shifts her gaze between me and Bryce, taking in our matching somber expressions, her dark eyes fill with tears.

Bryce drags Jack outside and they walk far enough away to have an unmonitored conversation. I watch them, trying to detect what they're saying from their body language. From the hard set of their shoulders, it's clear they're both on edge. Jack returns to kiss Lisa before he and Bryce take off down the sidewalk.

When they're out of sight, I turn to Lisa. "Get dressed."

Lisa nods, tears spilling from her eyes, and disappears into her apartment. When she's ready, I drag her over to the park. The path is beginning to fill with morning runners, dog walkers, and people like us with nothing better to do. We make our way to a bench and sit.

I pull my left leg up and tuck it under me. "Colin's missing. He was last seen leaving the nightclub with some guy."

"What guy?"

"That's what Jack and Bryce went to find out. Hopefully if they find the guy, they'll find Colin."

"I don't understand."

I sigh, some of my anger giving way to fear. None of this is Lisa's fault. Sure, it would've helped if she'd noticed Colin didn't come home last night, but she had no way of knowing this would happen. "Bryce and I went back to the nightclub and watched the security footage. A guy approached Colin as he was leaving, and it looked like they left together."

Her bottom lip quivers and tears trail down her cheeks. "What are we going to do?"

"I don't know, Lis. I'm really scared, though." With nothing better to do, we wind up hanging out in the park and talking about Colin until it's time for Lisa to go to work. I walk her to the restaurant and hug her goodbye. "It's going to be okay," I say for my benefit more than hers. "It has to be."

Once she's inside, I go back to Eddie's to wait for word from Bryce and Jack. The house is too quiet and I call out for Eddie and Quinn, but get no response. Eddie must have taken Quinn somewhere after dropping Liam off at school. I plop down on the couch and click through the wall display, looking for something to distract me from the fact that my best friend is missing.

Flipping between talking heads babbling about the weather and the upcoming election and a couple dozen music channels, I end up turning it off and staring out the window, tracing patterns in the lime green velour of the couch. The fabric goes from light to dark as I push the pile one way then the other. I'm busy making intricate swirls when my tablet chimes. Lunging over the arm of the couch, I grab my shoulder bag and pull out my tablet. Colin's name is on the screen along with a fragment of the message.

Colin: Hey, EvTay, think I found something…

My hands shake as I launch the text app to read the whole message.

Colin: Hey, EvTay, think I found something. Met a guy last night who knows something. Can you meet us?

My fingers hit all the wrong letters as I attempt to type out a response, before managing something coherent.

Me: Yes, yes! So glad u r OK!!

Time crawls as I watch those the little dots bounce while he types.

Colin: Can you come to B5 L52 221W C?

Me: K. Be there soon

Colin: Bring your tablet

Me: K

Relief mixes with a healthy amount of fear. It's not like Colin to go off with some guy he just met, but he sounded normal in his text. Bryce doesn't answer his mobile phone, and I debate leaving a message, knowing anything I say is being monitored. I decide to text him from the train instead.

As soon as we pull out of the station, I realize I left my tablet on the couch. It'll take a half hour to go back for it, though. Chewing on my bottom lip, I try to recall the address Colin sent me. *B5, L52, 221W C.* I'm pretty sure that's it.

Fifteen minutes later, my nerves are a giant twisted mess as I make my way through Borough 5. I take the elevator down to Level 52 and hop a train out to C Street, my feet tapping an agitated rhythm during the entire ten-minute ride. The address is in an enclosed portion of the Union I've never ventured into. It's dark and stuffy with no natural sunlight, and smells like feet. The Union, being what it is, attempts to recreate the atmosphere of the great outdoors with piped in fresh air, potted plants, and sidewalks that mimic the outside, but it misses the mark big time.

I walk the few blocks to C Street and start looking for address numbers. My shoes scuff across the concrete surface, and I feel like

I'm a character in a bad slasher movie. This is an industrial area, mostly warehouses and manufacturing facilities, I'm not sure what Colin's doing here. A corridor leads to the 200 block where the door to 221 is ajar. The hairs on the back of my neck stand on end and my breathing becomes shallow — this slasher movie just got real.

A hand grabs my upper arm from behind and I whip around to yell at Colin for scaring the crap out of me. Instead unfamiliar dark eyes peer at me from beneath black shaggy bangs. *Oh shit.* Yep, I'm the stupid chick in every horror movie ever made. While everyone in the theater is yelling at me to run, of course I didn't.

"Well, hello princess," says a creepy voice that turns my blood cold. *Walker.*

I suck in a breath and turn to face him, narrowing my eyes in an attempt to appear determined instead of scared shitless. The shaggy-haired man locks me in place with a firm grip on my biceps while Walker reaches out and strokes a thick finger down the side of my face.

"We were hoping you'd come."

An involuntary shudder rolls through me. "Where's Colin?" I squeak.

"He's fine."

I turn away, chewing my bottom lip to keep it from trembling until the coppery taste of blood hits my tongue. "Where is he?" I whisper.

"If I'd known what a pain in my ass you'd become, I'd have had you killed along with your friend."

My heart pounds as fear is replaced by rage at his casual mention of Lucien's death. I lean forward and spit at him. A rush of air ruffles my hair a split second before the back of his hand connects with my cheek, rocking my head to the side. Sharp white pain radiates out from my face, and a stinging heat rushes across the surface of my skin. It doesn't matter how many times I get hit in the face, I never seem to get used to it.

Walker grips my hair and yanks my face up eye-level with his. "I'll make sure your death is particularly painful, but if you cooperate, your friend will get off easier." He nods at the man holding me. "Throw her in the back room."

Shaggy drags me by my arm down a narrow hall, shoving me into an empty room at the end. "I'll take this," he says, yanking my bag off my shoulder before closing and locking the door.

Hysterical laughter bubbles up as I take in the room and realize I'm right back where I was a few months ago. Unlike the room I was held in out in the Ruins, though, there are no windows in this one. But down here in the bowels of the Union, no one can hear me scream anyway. I slump to the floor, drawing my knees to my chest.

Soon, the lock jiggles and the door opens. Colin stumbles in, and I rush over, throwing my arms around him. He winces and I pull back. Oh god, his face. It looks like someone used it as a punching bag. His left eye is swollen shut, and his lip is busted open, dried blood crusted on his chin.

"Colin, what did they do to you?"

I place my hand under his arm and help him over to the wall. He sits, leaning his head back, his long legs stretched out in front of him. My heart aches as I sit next to him, resting my head on his shoulder. His knuckles are bruised and swollen. At least he put up a fight.

"Are you okay? I mean…where does it hurt?"

"Where doesn't it hurt?" he grunts.

"Who was the guy you met in the nightclub? Is he part of this, too?"

He turns to look at me with his one good eye. "How'd you know about that?"

"Because Bryce and I saw the footage, and you texted me…" Of course he didn't text me.

He shakes his head. "They took my tablet as soon as they grabbed me. The guy said he was a fan. Used to watch us play back home. Said he recognized me as I was walking out and started talking about our band and stuff. Then a couple guys jumped me. I'm such an idiot. I let my ego get in the way of common sense. I was just so stoked that someone liked my music, you know?"

"Oh, Col, you're not an idiot. We never should've left you alone last night."

He sighs. "It doesn't matter. They know we know, EvTay."

"What do they know we know?"

"Everything. Someone saw you and your friends near the power station out in the Ruins. They want to know who else we told. Once they're sure no one else knows, they're gonna kill us."

What They Know

olin's words pierce my heart, sending rivers of fear coursing through me. The room tilts and I struggle to catch my breath. "H-how did they find out?"

"I'm sorry, Ev, they had these electric prod things. I just wanted it to stop."

"Oh, Colin, I'm so sorry. None of this is your fault."

Bile rises up the back of my throat, and I'm afraid I'm going to be sick. I cup my hand over my mouth and crawl to the corner to dry heave. Drenched in sweat, I push up, my limbs trembling. It's not the first time I've faced death, but my friends are now in danger, all because I needed to see that stupid bombed out power station in the Ruins. Pushing up on shaky legs, I pace the small room, forcing myself to think things through. We can't stay here and just let them kill us. I won't let them kill Colin.

"We have to get out of here, I don't know how, but we have to figure something out," I mumble, thinking out loud as I burn another lap.

Colin turns his swollen face toward me. "How'd you escape in the Ruins?"

"The guy was stoned and drunk, couldn't even walk a straight line. I outmaneuvered him." I glance around the room again, dredging my brain for any idea. "How many guys does Walker have here?"

"I saw three, but they all have guns."

Yeah, I figured they'd be armed, but there must be something we can do. Guilt pushes me to search for a way to at least get Colin out. Although he won't agree to leave me behind, which means either we both escape or we both die. Colin shifts his position, letting out a long groan, reminding me he's not in any shape to help me with whatever plan I come up with. When the door opens, I rush to Colin's side, determined to keep them from separating us.

Shaggy sticks his head in the door. "Where's your tablet?"

"I forgot it."

He swears loudly and slams the door. What the hell's the big deal about my tablet?

Oh…

It has this address in my text messages. That's why they told me to bring it.

The start of a plan begins to take shape. It's not much, but I think I know how we might be able to escape.

I turn to Colin. "So, this is what we need to do."

The door flies open, and even though I knew once they realized I left my tablet behind they'd move us fast, I don't feel prepared. But ready or not, it's show time. Walker pushes into the room followed by the blond guy and Shaggy, guns drawn.

Walker's jaw clenches, the only outward sign he's anything but calm. "Okay you two, up. We're going on a little trip."

I glance at Colin, hoping he's up for this. His expression is difficult to read with his face all beat up, but his non-swollen eye swivels to me for a second and closes in silent acknowledgment he's at least willing to try. I push up off the floor, but Colin moves slowly, milking his injuries to buy us time. He grunts and moans enough, I'm no longer sure this is an act and reach down to help him up.

Walker glances over his shoulder every few seconds, as if he's expecting someone. Blondie yanks Colin up and he stumbles, groaning, fueling my fear he's not going to be able to pull this off. Shaggy grabs my arm and drags me out behind Colin and Blondie.

My eyes take in everything as we make our way down the hall, waiting and watching for the right moment to make my move. We enter a large warehouse with a wide, metal rollup door. Walker strides to the door and pulls the chain to open it. I turn to Colin, who barely nods his head. Summoning all the courage I can find, I remind myself if we don't do this we're dead anyway.

With one deep breath, I stomp my heel down on Shaggy's instep. He yelps, loosening his grip on me enough for me to wrench free. I bring my elbow up, slamming it between his eyes. He doubles over, covering his face with his hand and lets out a guttural wail followed by a string of obscenities. I kick the gun from his other hand with the ball of my foot, and it flies, sliding to a stop against the wall a dozen yards away.

Walker pulls a gun from the back of his waistband and points it at me. Adrenaline flows fast and free through my veins, making me hyper-aware of everything around me. I dive for Shaggy's gun, hoping I can get to it before Walker shoots me, and that a moving target will be harder to hit.

A deafening bang echoes through the warehouse, and I press my hands against my ears. Colin yells and every cell in my body zaps with fear.

Oh no, not again. Instinct kicks in, and I grab the gun from the floor. Rolling over, I fire at Walker, missing him by more than a foot. I scramble as he returns fire, a bullet striking the concrete floor inches from my face, sending chips flying.

A scream tears from my throat as I push up and run across the warehouse, diving behind a stack of crates as a bullet pings into the rollup door next to my shoulder.

My breathing is ragged, and I struggle to keep my hands steady. Peeking around the edge of the crates, I fire off several rounds at Walker, the casings smacking me in the face. He dives under the partially open door as my last shot narrowly misses him.

I turn and process the situation. Colin is sitting, head back against the wall, gripping his left arm with is right hand, his chest heaving. Blondie spins and presses the barrel of his gun against Colin's forehead. My eyes flick from Blondie's gun to Colin's face. His eyes are screwed shut, his mouth twisted, blood seeping through the sleeve of his T-shirt.

"Drop it. Now," Blondie says.

Dread rushes in like tiny pins, poking holes in my adrenaline rush. With a sickening sense of hopelessness, I set the gun on the ground.

"Over here," Blondie orders, his gun still pointed at Colin.

I inch toward him. One step, two. At the same moment Shaggy goes for the gun I dropped, Colin sweeps a leg around, hooking his foot behind Blondie's calf and dropping him to one knee. Before Shaggy can reach the gun, I kick it as hard as I can into the corner.

Blondie pivots toward the sound of the gun hitting the wall, allowing me to catch him by surprise. Propelling myself forward, I slam my shoulder into his gut. A sharp pain rolls through my spine, but it knocks the wind out of Blondie. Not much else, though, the dude is big.

But it's enough for Colin to get his gun and aim it at Shaggy. "Not … another … *fucking* … step," Colin says through clenched teeth.

I rush to Colin's side and grab the gun, pointing it from Shaggy to Blondie. "Down on the floor. Face first. Hands behind your head."

"Damn, EvTay," Colin says.

I smile, a little proud of myself, and retrieve the other gun for Colin.

"What do we do now?" Colin asks.

My breaths are still rapid and shallow, my heart rate at a scary level. Colin's eyes start to droop and the reality of the situation sinks in. He's losing a lot of blood, and I've got two guys on the ground who outweigh me by a hundred pounds each. How am I going to get Colin out of here, and what if Walker is outside waiting for us?

First I have to stop the bleeding. Kneeling next to Colin, I try to take his shirt off. He moans, and I realize there's no easy way to do this. "This is gonna hurt like hell," I say, pulling his T-shirt off his good arm, over his head, and slide it off the injured arm while he swears under his breath. The bullet hit his shoulder, but there's so much blood, I can't tell how bad he's hurt.

Doing this with one hand is a pain in the ass, but I can't risk setting the gun down, and I'm not sure Colin has the strength to keep the other two under control. Like me, he was functioning on adrenaline, but he's got nothing left in reserves. Using my teeth, I manage to get the shirt around his shoulder and tied, but it's not doing much good.

A noise behind me makes me jump, and Blondie lifts his head. I turn and nearly cry when I see Jack and Bryce running into the warehouse, guns drawn.

"He needs a hospital," I yell.

They take in the scene for a moment before launching into action. Jack pulls out his phone and makes a call while Bryce rushes to me and Colin.

"How bad is it? Are you shot?"

"Not me. But Colin…I don't know, it looks kinda bad."

"Jack's calling for backup and an ambulance. They'll be here any minute."

I close my eyes and let it sink in I'm not alone in this anymore. Help is on the way. Help is here. I take a deep breath, but it's like I can't get any air. A full on freak-out is coming, and I'm terrified of losing it. I need to get a grip for Colin's sake. I make myself a promise — if I can hold it together a little longer, I'll let myself have a complete breakdown later. Then I focus only on my breathing until I get it under control.

When I open my eyes, Colin's pale face comes into focus. But now I think it might be more from pain than actual blood loss. At least I hope so. Jack finishes rolling up the door to let the paramedics in. They set down a stretcher and scan Colin's vital signs. One of them notices me covered in Colin's blood, and his eyes widen as he runs to my side.

"I know I look horrific," I say, "but it's not my blood."

His name tag says Pedro, and he insists on examining me anyway, running his scanner over me before draping a blanket over my shoulders. The other paramedic works on Colin, inserting a micro-IV-port then Pedro helps him transfer Colin to a stretcher.

I stand and follow them out to the ambulance waiting in the alley, ready to climb in behind them.

"You can't ride with us," Pedro says, his dark eyes sympathetic.

"I'll take her," Bryce says, coming up next to me.

Bryce places a hand on my shoulder while I watch the doors close and Colin disappear behind them. It isn't until the ambulance is gone, I notice two police officers pushing a handcuffed Shaggy and Blondie toward a police cruiser.

Where panic and fear had been running roughshod over my emotions earlier, a surreal numbness has settled in, as if all of this is a really weird, bad dream.

Bryce and Jack talk in hushed tones before Bryce returns to my side. "Meet me at the hospital when you're done," he calls over his shoulder to Jack.

In a daze, I start following the path the ambulance took when Bryce grabs my arm and turns me toward him. He takes my face in his hands and presses his lips to mine. His kiss is hard, full of raw emotion, and I'm too stunned to respond before he pulls back. I stand frozen for a few moments, staring at him. If he's upset by my lack of response, he doesn't let on, just reaches down to take my hand and leads me toward the hospital.

The young man behind the admissions desk in the emergency room stares at me with unblinking eyes, his mouth hanging open. He pushes up and starts waving his arm frantically.

"It's not my blood," I say again. He turns back, his eyes roaming over me, looking for injuries. "Umm, Colin Jennings?"

He narrows his eyes, because no one gets shot in the Union. My association with Colin and my blood-soaked clothes have this guy taking a second and third look at me.

"He's in surgery," he says, lifting an eyebrow in silent question.

Yeah, I'm not about to tell him anything more. "Uh, do you know…how is he?"

He clicks on his tablet and shakes his head. "I don't have any information. Take a seat and I'll call you when they update his record." He pauses for a second, studying me. "Are you sure you don't need attention?"

Pulling the blanket tighter around my shoulders, I nod and wander over to sit. Two uniformed police officers and a dark-haired woman in her mid-twenties are talking to Bryce. Bryce gestures toward me and the other three glance in my direction. Bryce motions me over, and I walk toward them with tiny, unsure steps. I can't tell them what happened today without telling them everything, starting with my kidnapping over the summer.

"This is Officer Jacobson, Officer Talbot, and Detective Mason," Bryce says when I reach them. "This is Evan Taylor."

"Hi," I respond.

"We need your statement," Mason, the dark-haired woman, says, "but Detective Cooper says you're waiting to hear news on your friend."

"This is my case," Bryce says. "Jackson and I are working it as part of an ongoing investigation. We'll handle it."

Detective Mason licks her lips. "That's against protocol, and you know it."

Bryce remains calm while my anxiety ratchets up several notches. "She's our embedded reporter, and it's a classified investigation. I've cleared it with the Captain."

Mason pulls out her tablet and begins clicking. I'm not sure she's buying it and watch Bryce for any sign he's worried. Mason's tablet chimes, and she locks eyes with Bryce before turning to the two officers. "Okay, I guess we're done here." She glances at me briefly before leaving.

After they're gone and I can no longer see them outside the hospital doors, I turn to Bryce. "What just happened?"

"Jack was going to talk to his dad after booking those two clowns. If you want to keep this between us for now, we have no choice but to loop in his dad. I know you don't want that, but this is too big for us to contain without help."

"So what's next?"

"We continue with our plans. The ones we discussed. Find out what's going on and come up with a way to stop it. It's obvious now it's more complex than we thought. What you overheard out in the Ruins reaches deep into the Union."

So far, all our planning has managed to accomplish is getting Colin shot, watching everything we say in our own homes, and Walker running around loose in the Union. I'm beginning to think our plans aren't worth shit.

8 Worthless Plans

Watercolor renderings of the Union hang on sterile walls, and neat rows of gray chairs perch on a white tile floor I've paced dozens of times, waiting for an update on Colin. Piped in odors of ocean and lavender mix with antiseptic in that sickening potpourri people associate with hospitals.

Bryce slumps in one of the chairs, his gaze alternating between me and his phone. The doors slide apart with a soft hum, and Lisa and Jack rush in. Lisa's eyes widen as she takes in my appearance, zeroing in on Colin's blood all over me.

"How is he? Is he okay? I can't believe this is happening." Her unblinking gaze leaves the crimson stain on my shirt and lifts to my face. "Are *you* okay?"

"Yeah."

We stare at each other for a few moments before she wraps me in a hug. I sink into her, letting her hold me together. She pulls back and hands me a bag. "Here. I brought you something clean to wear."

"Thanks." I take the bag and head into the bathroom. After peeling off my soiled clothes, I stare at myself in the mirror. My cheek is a sickening purplish color and the outside edge of my eye is puffy. Dried blood crusts in my hair, creating a clumpy mat. I wash my face and hair, the water in the sink turning a barf-inducing red. Using the clean portions of my top, I scrub my body raw before dressing in the jeans and T-shirt Lisa brought me.

I stuff my dirty clothes into the trash and return to the waiting room. Bryce pops up and approaches me with tentative steps, his expression soft, filled with concern.

Why is he looking at me like that? "Colin?" I ask, my voice shaking.

He shakes his head and moves closer, reaching out a hand to move a piece of hair from my face, his fingertips grazing my cheek up to my outer eye. I wince, and he pulls his hand back. Our eyes lock and the kiss from earlier takes center stage in my mind.

"Umm—" I start, figuring I should say something.

"I'm gonna get you some ice," he says at the same time. Bryce disappears, returning a few minutes later with some ice wrapped in a soft towel. I place it on my face and suck in a breath.

The hours tick by at an excruciating pace, and I kill time by chewing my thumbnail, pacing, or replaying the scene in the warehouse over in my mind.

"Colin Jennings?" a female voice calls out.

I turn to see a woman in scrubs by the admissions desk. Standing on shaky legs, I make my way across the waiting room to her. A piece of her short graying hair falls into her eyes and she pushes it behind her ear. "He's going to be fine."

I close my eyes and breathe out a deep sigh, locking my knees to keep from collapsing.

"The bullet missed the bone, he was lucky. He lost a lot of blood, but we were able to transfuse him with donor blood instead of synthetic. We'll keep him here for a few days, but he'll need time to heal when he's released."

"When can we see him?" I ask.

"When he's out of recovery and settled in his room. If you want to help in the meantime, you can donate blood. We always need donors."

"We will," I assure her. "Thank you."

She nods and disappears behind the doors leading to the operating rooms. Lisa sniffs behind me, and when I turn, tears are running down her apple cheeks. Jack wraps his arms around her, resting his chin on her head. With a couple of hours to kill before we can see Colin, we head down to the lab to donate blood.

My stomach lets out a thunderous growl on the way back to the waiting room.

"Have you eaten anything today?" Bryce asks.

I shake my head.

"Let's get you some dinner."

"After I see Colin."

"Your stomach begs to differ, and you just gave blood. You need food."

"Okay," I say, mostly to get him to back off. I don't have the energy to fight him.

"I'm going to take Lisa home," Jack says, muffling Lisa's cries against his chest.

Seriously? She wasn't the one shot, hit, or covered in blood, but I walk up and give her a hug anyway. "He's going to be okay."

She nods and sniffs as Jack escorts her outside.

Bryce and I head down to the hospital cafeteria where none of the food looks appetizing. I settle on a cup of roasted tomato soup and some crackers.

My spoon is halfway to my mouth when he says, "I'm sorry. About earlier. I swore I wouldn't kiss you until you asked me to. After everything I put you through, I wanted it to be on your terms. But…" He drops his gaze to the table. "I thought I lost you again."

I set my spoon in the bowl and study him. Colin told me how he was out in the Ruins, but I was too pissed at the time to care about what *he* went through. That anger has been slowly melting over the past couple of weeks, and I can appreciate his feelings even if I don't share them. "You don't need to apologize."

He glances up at me, brows drawn together.

"It's okay you kissed me. Once."

He nods his understanding and waits for me to finish eating.

"Colin," I say, picking up his hand and lacing my fingers between his.

"EvTay," he slurs. "We make a damn good team."

I laugh, wiping a tear from my eye, not wanting him to see me cry. "Yeah, we do."

"You saved me."

"*You* saved *me*."

"This's a pretty screwed up…thing…we're in." His voice is slow and syrupy thanks to the drugs he's on.

I nod, not trusting myself to speak. Relief and gratitude expand, filling a big emotional bucket to the point of overflowing. The problem is, I think it's a big emotional bucket of tears, and I'm close to bawling. I lay my head on his hand to hide my face.

When my emotions are under control, I stand. "I have to go, but I'll be back in the morning. Do you want me to bring you anything?"

"I'm good." His dopey smile tells me he's feeling just fine.

Leaning down, I kiss the top of his head. "I love you."

"Love you too, EvTay." His eyes are closed before I reach the door.

Bryce is waiting in the hall for me. "We have to file a report. Jack and I talked and we're going to keep it as vague as possible. We'll see what we can get away with. In addition to being shot, Colin was worked over pretty hard, so we can say he doesn't remember much."

"So what do you want me to say?"

He's quiet for a moment. "I don't know yet. If Walker is connected in any way with government officials, we're all in even more danger than we thought."

"Then, what's our next step?"

"We need to find out more about their operation, how deep it goes, and determine who we can trust. Until then, I don't intend to leave you alone for even a minute."

"Are you serious?"

He narrows his eyes. "Extremely. Did you forget what happened today?"

"Of course not. But you can't…just follow me around everywhere."

"I can and I will."

We arrive at the station, and the lobby is dark, abandoned, but sounds of shuffling and murmurs come from somewhere beyond, a rectangle of light stretching across the floor. Bryce guides me down a hall behind the reception desk and into an office, closing the door behind us.

"How long till Jack gets here?" I ask, staring at a display wall with all kinds of notes and pictures on it, lines drawn between some of them.

Bryce turns off the display. "He's taking Lisa to my mom's first. She's been the wife and mother of cops long enough to know to not ask questions."

"Oh." The reality of that statement hits me hard. My mom never worries about Joe when he's working, never knows not to ask questions. I wonder if Lisa's thought through what life with Jack will be like if they stay together.

Jack strides into the office a few minutes later and sits on the edge of the desk, crossing his arms. He and Bryce exchange a look before he turns to me. "We have two problems with keeping this quiet. The first is the two officers who provided backup, and the other is the two guys we have in custody. The good news is neither of the suspects is talking and don't seem to be in a hurry to change that. So we need a plausible story that fits with what the arresting officers witnessed." He rubs his jaw, his stubble scratching against his palm. "I'm just not sure what that is yet."

What went down today was so bad, I don't see how we can make up anything that will sound remotely legitimate. While trying to come up with something, my mind goes back to what Colin told me about the guy at the nightclub posing as a fan. He could've just as easily pretended to be anything else, giving me an idea.

"What kinds of crimes do other detectives deal with? The ones not looking into smuggling and stuff?" I ask.

"Domestic disputes mostly. Occasional thefts on the lower levels. Stupid shitheads getting drunk and starting brawls," Jack says.

"What if we say Colin was dancing with one of those guy's daughters and they took Colin to scare him, but things got out of hand?"

"Maybe," Jack says. "But why were you there?"

"Yeah, I don't know that part yet. But Shaggy and Blondie can't refute anything I say without implicating themselves. So it just needs to be believable to the police, right?"

"Shaggy and Blondie?" Bryce asks, with a lift of his eyebrows.

"That's the name I gave those two guys."

He grins and shakes his head.

I think best when I'm moving, so I get up and pace the small office. "What if I was trying to get a jump-start on my new job? Colin and I were out together, and I saw Shaggy and Blondie doing something suspicious. Looking for a story, I decided to follow them. I don't know who they are or what they're up to, I was just an eager intern who got in way over my head."

Jack eyes me thoughtfully then nods. "I think we can make it work. Let's start putting the specifics together."

Two hours later, the report is finished with the details worked out among the three of us. It includes enough false leads, anyone investigating will be off in the wrong direction, allowing Jack and Bryce to figure out what's really going on.

"So you found my tablet and that's how you knew where to find me?" I ask Bryce as he walks me home.

"Yeah. I came by when we couldn't locate Colin. Eddie said your bag was gone, but I saw your tablet on the table. When he turned his back to get us something to drink, Jack swiped it. We found the text from Colin. You really should put a password on there, you know."

"I know. But it's a good thing I didn't."

"We would've hacked it, but that would've taken longer."

When we get to Eddie's, I glance at the front door, not in any hurry to go inside with those bugs in there. Plus, I have no idea what I'm going to say to Eddie. It's well past midnight, and I have a wicked black eye. I reach out to open the door and pause, pulling my hand back. Instead, I grab Bryce's sleeve, and drag him over to the park.

"I need to tell Eddie everything. They took Colin to get to me. What if they take Eddie or the kids next?"

Bryce lets out a long breath through his nose.

"But before I do that, those damn bugs need to go. I can't talk to him knowing someone's listening."

He nods. "Okay."

"Okay?"

"Yeah." He takes my hand and leads me to the depot where we hop a train to Lisa's. Jack answers the door, his hair a complete disaster, pieces jutting out in a dozen directions. A five o'clock shadow has become more of a one a.m. shadow.

"Bryce inclines his head, and Jack steps outside, closing the door behind him, but he keeps one eye on the apartment as we walk out of range of the listening devices.

"Evan wants the bugs out of Eddie's tonight," Bryce says.

Jack looks over at me and narrows his eyes. "It's our only chance to flush these guys out."

"I know," I say. "But after what happened today, they already know we know everything. Colin told them as much."

He studies the sidewalk for a few moments and sighs. "Okay, let me call my dad to come stay with Lis, and I'll meet you at your place in a half-hour."

"Thanks." A weight lifts off me, as if I've been pinned beneath an elephant that suddenly decided to wander off. Getting rid of those damn bugs is a bittersweet victory.

Jack struts into the park across from Eddie's apartment, bug detector in hand. I lead the way to the apartment, and pause before pushing open the door. Eddie stops pacing and turns toward us, running a hand through his cinnamon-colored hair. His shoulders ease and his face relaxes for a moment before morphing into a scowl.

"Where the hell have you been?" He doesn't wait for me to answer before starting in on me about how worried he's been. His eyes drift toward Jack, who's searching for bugs and destroying them by dropping them into a glass of water. Eddie's mouth drops open, and he turns back to me.

I shake my head so he won't ask any questions yet. Not until Jack destroys them all. We move into the living room and take seats on the couch as Jack works. Eddie clasps his hands between his knees, his face ashen. When Jack's done, he joins us, leaning against the wall, arms crossed.

"Will someone please tell me what's going on?" Eddie demands.

With a deep, cleansing breath, I launch into my story, telling him everything that happened after I got on the train in the Eastern Province. His face contorts as I recount my kidnapping, escape, and near death before Cyrus and the others found me. I tell him the real history I learned from Lucien, and what I overheard about a possible revolution. It's such a relief to tell him this, to stop hiding the truth.

Eddie glances from me to Bryce to Jack and back to me as if he's struggling to put all the pieces together. When I'm done, Bryce and Jack pick up the story from their point of view, explaining how they tracked me down in the Ruins and about the bugs Jack discovered in all of our apartments.

I finish off by filling him in on the events of the past twenty-four hours, from Colin not coming home last night until we arrived at his front door a little over two hours ago. Eddie's quiet for a long time, studying his palms. A really long time. Too long.

"Eddie, say something," I beg.

He glances up, weariness etched into his face. His eyes close and he lets out an exaggerated breath. Placing his hands on his knees, he pushes up and turns to face Bryce and Jack. "I suppose I should thank you for saving my daughter, but I can't help thinking if she hadn't been involved with you, none of this would have happened."

"Eddie," I say, "if none of this happened, we wouldn't know what was coming. Now we can try to stop it."

"What do you mean, 'we'? You need to stay out of it. Turn it over to the authorities." His voice has an edge to it I've never heard before.

I shift on the arm of the couch. Maybe telling him was a mistake. "Jack and Bryce *are* the authorities, and Jack's dad, too. He's like a captain or something."

"Fine, let them handle it. But you're not going to be involved."

"I'm eighteen. You can't stop me."

His eyebrows shoot up, disappearing into his hairline. "No, but I can cut off access to your trust fund."

"Only part of it. And besides, I've got a job, remember."

"You're standing here telling me you're an adult while acting like a spoiled child."

"You don't understand what we're up against, what it would mean if we were to tell the government."

"Then make me understand," he says, his voice rising in frustration.

"I told you what I heard out there. What the Union did. What do you think they'll do if we tell them we overheard a plot to attack the Union?"

He's quiet for several long moments, most likely processing everything he learned tonight and going through the possible actions the Union could take. I know what he's thinking. They're all things I've thought of.

"Please, Eddie. If you love me, let us do this our way. People live out there. People I love. I can't let them be killed. We can stop this. I don't know how yet, but we have to. The lives of innocent people depend on it."

Eddie shakes his head. "I don't know, Evan. If what you heard is true, the lives of innocent people here are on the line. Possibly the lives of my kids."

So this is about Liam and Quinn. I get that. "I love them, too," I say. "And that's why I have to do this. For them and my friends in the Ruins. Can you give us some time to try? Please?"

"We've been investigating lots of pieces of this puzzle for a while." Bryce finally weighs in. I thought he was going to let me twist in the wind all on my own. "Our captain is in the loop. Based on what happened today, I don't know how safe it is to go to anyone else, anyway. Someone in the government is involved. We're pretty sure of that now."

"You're asking me to leave the fate of the Union in the hands of a bunch of teens. Do you know how crazy that sounds?"

"Jack and Bryce are detectives," I remind him. "And they're not teens."

"I don't know," Eddie says again. "But someone put listening devices in *my* apartment, and I want to know who. So I'll give you a short window to figure out what's going on. But that's it. And I want to meet this captain."

Jack reaches his hand out to Eddie. "I should get back to Lisa," he says. "But I'll arrange for you and my dad to meet. Soon." He looks at Bryce and they do some sort of silent communication thing.

I walk Jack to the door and hug him. "Take care of Lisa, okay?"

He gives me a small nod before walking out. I close the door and turn to face Eddie and Bryce.

"I'm heading back to the hospital in the morning to talk to Colin," Bryce says. "Jack and I need as many of the real details as possible. I'd like you to come with me. It'll be helpful to have you there to fill in any blanks."

"Okay. I was planning to go see him anyway. Why don't you come for breakfast and we can go after."

"Alright."

Eddie hovers behind me, awkward silence filling the apartment. I turn and lift my shoulders in a *what the hell are you doing* gesture. He seems to get the hint. "I'm going to bed. We'll talk tomorrow." The words are terse, his voice gruff.

When I hear Eddie's bedroom door close, I sink back against the front door, my limbs numb with exhaustion. I'm not even sure how I'm still standing.

"I should go," Bryce says, moving toward the door.

"Yeah." I open the door and move so he can get past me. He steps across the threshold before pausing to turn back to me, his eyes searching mine.

"It's okay to kiss me," I say and realize I mean it. I want him to kiss me again, and this time I want to participate.

Bryce doesn't look relieved or even happy about my statement, but he does move closer, our gazes locking. We stare at each other for several long moments before he reaches up and takes my face in his hands.

He bends his head and brushes his lips across mine. It's a sweet kiss, and I try not to compare it to the soul-drenching kisses I shared with Cyrus. Instead, I close my eyes and let myself fall into *this* kiss, live in *this* moment. He pulls me closer and I wrap my arms around his waist, letting my mouth conform to his. He doesn't take the kiss any further, and it's more like our first kiss than any of the ones that followed.

When he draws back, he gives me a smile big enough his dimples pierce his cheeks, warming me. I do like Bryce and I liked that kiss. It makes me feel cared for and wanted, something that's almost as essential as breathing in the midst of everything else we're facing.

I reach up and press my lips lightly to his again. "I'll see you in the morning."

He squeezes my hand before heading down the walkway.

"Be careful," I call after him. "Text me when you get home." I watch him go until he disappears around the corner.

9 Breathing

I take a deep breath and shake my hands, trying to dislodge the nerves making my breakfast sit in my stomach like a lump of lifeless goo. Pushing open the glass door, I enter the lobby of Western Provincial News. My boots click across the tile floor, echo-y and loud, as I make my way up to the same counter where I applied only a week ago.

A girl not much older than me glances up, putting a finger in the air, signaling me to wait while she finishes a phone call. She hangs up and gives me a wide smile, revealing a row of straight white teeth. "May I help you?"

"Um, yes. I mean hi, I'm Evan Taylor. Today's my first day. I'm assigned to the crime desk?"

"Of course. My name is Stevie. You'll be working with Tony. Follow me."

She stands and moves so gracefully, I'd swear she was a dancer if she wasn't working here. She's wearing a simple tailored black dress, making me question my own wardrobe choice of jeans and a sweater. I trail Stevie, mesmerized as she seems to glide rather than walk, her long platinum blond ponytail swinging back and forth.

She leads me to an office in the back with large windows overlooking a landscaped courtyard. A man I assume to be Tony is on the phone, feet up on his desk, bouncing a small blue rubber ball off the wall across from him, letting it hit the floor before catching it. His jet black hair hints at youth, but the crinkles at the corners of his blue-green eyes and the speckles of gray in the stubble dusting his jaw make me think he's closer to Eddie's age.

He glanced up when Stevie first entered his office, but he continues with his call as if we're not here. Stevie crosses her arms, her pale blue eyes narrowed, lips twisted.

"Okay, sounds good. I'll meet you for lunch tomorrow." He clicks off his phone and drops it into his shirt pocket.

Stevie gives him a tight smile. "Tony Baxter, this is Evan Taylor. She's your new intern."

Tony looks me up and down, as if he's evaluating me for a position largely different from the one I applied for.

"She'll do," he says, dismissing Stevie with a wave of his hand.

She turns and glides back toward the lobby, and my first instinct is to run after her. Instead, I turn and face Tony, reminding myself that as rude as he is, he hasn't tried to kill me yet. Considering my life over the past few months, this puts him in the friendly category. I can do this.

Tony studies me for a long silent moment. "This job is about learning to trust your instincts," he says. "Right now, your instincts are telling you I like my coffee extra hot with a splash of cream." He turns his attention to his tablet and begins reading.

What the hell?

I guess I'm getting him coffee. The nearest coffee shop is a couple of blocks away, and as I stand in line waiting to order, I remind myself this is temporary. I should be assigned to work with Jack and Bryce soon. I can get through two weeks with this jerk.

When I return to the office, I set the cup on Tony's desk and sit in the chair across from him, folding my hands in my lap. If this is what being an intern at a news site entails, then I'll suck it up and do it, but why would anyone sign up to do this on purpose?

My eyes wander around the small office. A map of the Union is displayed on an oversized wall monitor zoomed in to our Borough in the Western Province. Another monitor behind him is tuned in to Union News Today. The sound is muted but headlines scroll along the bottom. Not much is on his desk, just the untouched coffee I brought him and a lone photo monitor cycling through pictures. Most are of the ocean or parks, but every so often, a pretty woman with dark hair smiles at the camera. She's on the beach in a white sundress, smiling broadly at the camera from an A-Train station, wearing jeans and a leather jacket holding a pumpkin.

Tony clears his throat. "Are you going to sit there all day?"

Tearing my eyes away from the photos, I blink. "What?"

"Are you planning on sitting in my office all day?"

"Um…"

He opens a drawer and pulls out a tablet, pushing it across the desk to me. "Here, edit this."

I take the tablet and skim an article about a man accused of beating a guy for talking to his girlfriend. "Should I work here? Or someplace else?"

"Here's fine." He gets up and walks out of the office, taking his coffee with him.

I read through the story then go back and read it again, looking for errors. If this is a test, I want to make sure I don't miss anything obvious, but I don't see any mistakes.

"Well?" Tony's voice from behind startles me.

I turn around to face him. "Uh, I can't find anything wrong with it. Grammatically, punctuation-wise, sentence structure, it's correct."

"Yes, and it's boring as hell."

My mouth drops open.

The corners of his mouth tip up. "News is all about entertainment these days. We're in a constant battle with broadcast programming for the attention of Union citizens. In order to compete, we have to be more entertaining than they are. This article needs to be jazzed up, more scandalous." His eyes crinkle with amusement as I stare at him. "Crime isn't what it used to be. If we want anyone to pay attention to what we do, it needs to be bigger than life, another form of entertainment. I want you to take this story and turn it into something thrilling."

"Okay…" I'm not sure what he expects from me, and I'm hoping he'll elaborate.

He lets loose a deep laugh. "I don't expect you to edit this under my watchful eye. Go home or to whatever environment stimulates your creative side. Bring me back an edited story in the morning."

I contemplate asking him what he means, but remember I'm supposed to know what I'm doing. "Uh, thanks," I say before rushing from his office and back to the lobby before he changes his mind.

Stevie glances up when I pass her desk. "So, how did it go?"

"Okay. I think. He hasn't fired me yet."

She smiles and gives me a thumbs up. "There's always tomorrow."

"Ha," I say, not sure if she's kidding.

On the two-block walk to the coffee shop, my senses are heightened as I observe everyone around me. Ever since Colin was shot, I can't relax when I'm out in public. I order a cup of coffee and take it to a table in the back before texting Bryce.

Me: At Waitless Coffee. Wanna meet for lunch?

Bryce: Be there in 10

I watch the door and unease spreads through me as if tiny bugs are crawling under my skin. Whenever someone approaches the door or stops to read the menu, my pulse races. Even though the listening devices are gone, the sensation of being monitored lingers.

When Bryce arrives, I can't hide my smile, and it's not only that I'm relieved he's here, I'm happy to see him. He slides into the booth next to me and kisses my cheek.

Over sandwiches, I explain my assignment. "I'm not sure what he wants, though. He's expecting me to be able to write the way you do."

"I'll come by after dinner and help you polish it. You'll have something to submit in the morning."

"You should come for dinner."

"Yeah?"

"Yeah."

He smiles and switches gears. "Jack talked to his dad. He's going to see what he can find out through his channels, but he'd like you to come in and talk to him."

My throat goes dry, and I almost choke on my coffee. "When?"

"As soon as possible. What're you doing after lunch?"

Bryce pulls open the door to the police station and holds it for me. Bright lights illuminate the lobby, making it appear harsh as opposed to the creepy, shadowed version of the other night.

"How should I refer to Jack's dad when I meet him?"

"Everyone calls him Max."

The girl at the front desk sits up straighter, her cheeks flushing when Bryce approaches. "Hi, Mike," she says, her voice a little breathless.

Right, Mike. I forgot *his* name.

"Hey, Sophie. We're here to see Max."

She glances from Bryce to me. "He's waiting for you in his office."

Bryce leads me down the same hall from the other night, but today, the previously empty cubicles are filled with people. We stop at a door at the end with a name plaque that says *Captain M. Jackson.*

"Wait, his name is Max Jackson?"

Bryce turns to me, eyebrows raised. "Do you know him?"

"No, but um…so Jack's name is Jack Jackson?"

He laughs. "No. His name's Christopher, but everyone calls him Jack. I don't think anyone calls him Christopher except his family. Not even when we were kids."

Weird. I've known him for months and never knew his real name. I wonder if Lisa knows.

Bryce knocks and a voice on the other side says, "Come in."

The door swings open and I come face-to-face with an older version of Jack. The resemblance is uncanny. If there's any of Jack's mother in his appearance, I can't tell what it might be.

Captain Jackson reaches out to shake my hand. "Welcome, Evan. I've heard an awful lot about you." He smiles the same lopsided grin as his son.

"Nice to meet you." There's something about him that puts me at ease. Maybe it's just the way he's so much like Jack.

"Let's take a walk." He stands and leads the way out. "Sophie, we're heading out. Be back in an hour."

We end up at a nearby park, and Captain Jackson sits at a concrete picnic table, indicating the bench across from him. I sit and Bryce positions himself next to me, picking up my hand beneath the table.

"Chris's brought me up to speed."

Chris is Jack. Right. Must remember all the characters in this story without a program.

"I can't let you be involved in police business. I'm sorry."

I chew on my lip as he studies me. "So what are you saying?"

"I'm saying I understand this is important to you, but you're a civilian."

"Did he tell you about the plan? About me posing as an embedded reporter?"

"He did, and I'm not blocking that yet. But you need to follow the rules set for the program."

"I can do that. But…Captain Jackson, you're not going to tell anyone what we saw out there, are you?"

Max's gaze shifts from me to Bryce, and they communicate something silently. "Evan, I'll do whatever I can to prevent any harm to the people in the Ruins. But to be honest, I'm still having a hard time with all of this."

I nod. "It's a lot to take in."

He leans forward, resting his elbows on the table, his blue eyes piercing mine. "I think I always knew the Ruins weren't the destroyed wasteland we learned about in school. Looking at the weather patterns over the past three hundred years, it's clear the extreme heat and droughts peaked a hundred years ago. If the coasts have become more moderate in the last century, it stands to reason the climate in the Ruins has as well. But this revolution or uprising, or whatever it is, I'm not going to sit back and do nothing."

He glances at Bryce and rubs a hand across his chin. "As an investigative reporter, I can't prevent Evan from doing her job, but I expect to be kept in the loop. The fact you waited this long to tell me anything disturbs me. We'll be discussing that further, I assure you." He turns back to me. "I won't risk the lives of the innocent people I've sworn to protect and serve, but I also won't unnecessarily put the people in the Ruins at risk."

I get what he's saying and while it doesn't make me sigh with relief, it gives me a little hope. I still wish Jack hadn't told him, but since he did, I have to find a way to control the situation, to make sure Max never feels the need to make the call that'll result in the death of my friends in the Ruins. "Okay," I say.

After Jack's dad leaves, Bryce takes my hand and walks me home.

"You've been awfully quiet," I say.

"Yeah, I've been thinking over our meeting with Max. How do you feel about it?"

"Honestly? I'm not sure. But I guess no worse than before. What about you?"

We walk several blocks before he answers. "I think Jack and I are going to be on a very short leash for a while."

With an exaggerated groan, I shove the tablet with Tony's article across the counter and get up to make a cup of coffee. I place the pods into the Supresso machine, choose my options, and press the button. It's not quite as good as what I can get at a coffeehouse, but it'll do for now. After staring at the story for the past few hours and making several attempts at a rewrite, I only have a vague idea of what to do. I just don't have experience structuring interesting news stories.

Someone knocks on the door and Quinn squeals, running from the couch. "Me get it!"

Bryce's voice carries into the apartment as he talks in low tones to Quinn. She bounces up and down as she tells him about whatever godawful show she was watching before he arrived.

His eyes leave her face and lock with mine. Something flickers in them, making me wonder just how short of a leash Max has him on.

"Coffee?" I ask.

"Sure."

We sit at the counter discussing my assignment until Eddie comes down from his studio, where he's been working on some new material. "Bryce," he says, acknowledging him with indifference. I suppose that's better than outright aggression.

I get up to help Eddie make dinner while Bryce continues with the article. Colin stumbles into the kitchen and nods at Bryce before setting the table. He's been staying with us since he was released from the hospital. With six of us, eating in the kitchen is out, so we move into the dining room, which apparently is reserved for holidays, so Quinn and Liam are hyper by the time we all sit.

"Where's the tablecloth?" Liam asks. "Are we gonna have pie? I like pumpkin."

Colin looks at me, but I just shrug. I've never spent a holiday with Eddie, here or anywhere else.

Liam turns to Bryce, all interest in proper table setting replaced by something more interesting. "So, did you shoot any bad guys today?"

Bryce smiles. "Not today."

"Oh." Liam stares at his plate as if Bryce had told him all his toys had been stolen. "Do you think maybe tomorrow?"

"What do you let him watch?" I ask Eddie.

Eddie puts his hands up. "Not me."

"Bang, bang," Quinn says.

I don't think Liam and Quinn know Colin was shot. "So, does anyone want to hear about my first day on the job?" I ask, trying to change the subject.

It works and for the remainder of the meal we discuss what I did today, what I need to do tonight, and what I'll probably do tomorrow.

Bryce and I clear the table and do the dishes before we settle down and he walks me through a complete rewrite of the article. The end result is an interesting story full of intrigue and scandal. I hope Tony likes it. After dumping the tablet in my shoulder bag, we join Colin on the couch and watch a movie — at least until Colin's eyelids begin to droop, a side effect of his pain medication.

"I'm going to bed," Colin mumbles after his chin hits his chest for the third time. "See ya t'morrow, Bryce, EvTay."

The movie plays in the background while Bryce and I talk.

"Things were rough with Max this afternoon?"

"It wasn't anything we didn't deserve. If it was anyone other than Jack's dad, we'd both be out of a job. Possibly facing criminal charges."

I turn to stare at him, my jaw dropping.

"I knew the risks," he says.

"Then why—"

"Because it was important to you."

"You did not put your career on the line to make me happy."

"No. And even if I'd wanted to, Jack never would've agreed. But we figured we had time to work this on our own. What you said about some of the guns coming into the Union is what convinced Jack to hold off. He's as worried about his dad's safety as he is ours. If this plot has roots in the Union government, anyone who knows could be in danger. I think Max understands that now. He also knows you're already in danger, as are Lisa and Colin, and keeping you on the sidelines doesn't guarantee your safety. He's not thrilled, but he gets you're probably safer with us."

Music indicating the movie credits are rolling draws my attention from the intensity of Bryce's gray eyes. He pushes up and stretches. "I should probably go."

He takes my hand and I walk him to the door. But when he opens it, the same unease I had earlier is back with a vengeance. "Stay," I say.

"What?"

"Stay. Here. I don't want you to leave."

"Yeah, I don't think your dad'll like that very much."

I slap his shoulder. "I'm not inviting you to share my bed…but stay here at the apartment. Can you sleep on the couch?"

"Sure." He gives me a small smile and kisses my forehead.

"I'll let Eddie know."

I head upstairs in search of a pillow and blanket and find Eddie sitting on his bed, reading.

"Eddie?"

He glances up from his tablet. "Hey there, Evan. Is Bryce gone?"

"Not yet. I kinda wanted to talk to you about that. I, um, asked him to stay tonight."

His mouth falls open and his face takes on the color of a ripe beet.

"Oh my god! Jeez, Eddie, don't freak out." My face is turning as red as his but for other reasons. "He's sleeping on the couch. But…I…I have this feeling. I can't explain it, but I don't want him going home alone right now."

His complexion normalizes and his face relaxes. A little, anyway. I chew on my lip, waiting for him to respond. "I guess I can understand that, in light of everything…but if he's going to be moving in here, too, he and Colin will need to share a room."

Ha. Eddie the comedian. At least he's not about to stroke out any more. "Thanks."

I locate bedding for Bryce and give him a quick kiss goodnight before heading up to my room.

10 Bad Feelings

A crash from downstairs jolts me out of a deep sleep. Adrenaline pumping, I throw off the covers and rush from my room. Eddie is standing on the top step in his pajama pants and a T-shirt, hair wild, holding a baseball bat. He puts up a hand to signal me to stay back.

"What's going on?" I ask him.

"Sounds like a fight."

"A fight?"

Downstairs, a loud smack is followed by a grunt and something clattering to the floor. Colin stumbles out of his room, wiping sleep from his eyes. He opens his mouth to say something, but stops when he spots the bat, his eyes widening.

"Bryce is down there," I plead with Eddie in a loud whisper.

Eddie scratches his head and nods. With his back against the wall, he inches down the stairs. I follow close behind, with Colin trailing me. When we reach the landing, we scrunch down to peer over the half wall. Lots of scuffling is followed by a grunt and glass shattering.

"Eddie," I whisper louder this time, "we have to do something."

With a deep breath, he rushes down, the bat high over his head. A dark figure in a hooded sweatshirt turns toward Eddie before bolting out the front door. The dull thud of a fist connecting with flesh and another grunt tightens my stomach.

I run the rest of the way downstairs toward the sounds of fighting. Two figures struggle on the floor. Bryce is on the bottom, fending off repeated blows from a second hooded-sweatshirt guy, landing a few of his own. Without bothering to think, I leap at hoodie guy, wrapping my arm around his neck.

He whips his head back and with one good shrug dislodges me. I roll away seconds before Eddie swings the bat, connecting it with Hoodie's back. He rolls to the side, yelling obscenities.

Bryce struggles to sit up. "You okay?" he asks me.

"Yeah, I'm fine. You?"

Before he can answer, Hoodie pushes up and runs to the door. Eddie's faster, though, and pins him against the wall with the bat.

I crawl over to Bryce to check on him. He tries to sit up again, but groans and drops back to the floor, squeezing his eye shut.

"We need to get him to a hospital," I call to Eddie.

"Call Jack," Bryce croaks.

Eddie turns toward us, and in that split second, Hoodie bolts out the front door, Eddie rushing after him.

Turning to Colin, I say, "Stay with Bryce," and tear outside after Eddie, my bare feet slapping against the cool pavement. Eddie's silhouetted form races down the sidewalk, the bat held securely in his left hand. He pulls to a sudden stop in front of me, his head swiveling.

"Where'd he go?" I ask when I catch up.

He's breathing hard as he recovers from his sprint, but I gotta give him credit, he's fast for an old guy. "I don't know. I...lost him."

There's no movement down either alley, and I start toward the one on my right. Eddie grabs my arm and pulls me back.

"Wait. Let's go home and regroup. They could be anywhere by now."

He's right. Alleys have doors leading to stairs that go down into the maze that is the innards of the Union. And Bryce is lying on our floor, the snot beat out of him.

We reach the apartment at the same time as Jack. "What happened?" he asks.

"Someone broke in and attacked Bryce," I say.

When we get back inside, Bryce is sitting up, holding his ribs, his head leaned back against the couch. I drop down beside him and pick up his hand. His knuckles are swollen and beginning to bruise.

Jack squats next to us. "Dude, you look like shit."

Bryce laughs and winces.

A knock has all of us turning toward the door where Captain Jackson can clearly been seen through the busted window.

Seconds after Colin opens the door for Jack's dad, the paramedics file in. Jack and I back up, giving them room to work. After scanning Bryce's vitals, they transfer him to the stretcher.

Jack follows them out to the ambulance and flashes his credentials. "I'm his partner. I'm coming." He turns to me. "I'll stay with him, I promise."

I nod and watch as Jack, Bryce, and the paramedic disappear behind closed doors, a sense of deja vu washing over me. The other paramedic heads to the cab and climbs in, driving off, red lights casting a pulsating glow against the snow white buildings.

Jack's dad approaches Eddie and thrusts out his hand. "Hi, I'm Max Jackson."

Eddie blinks a few times and reaches out to shake hands. I'd completely forgotten they don't know each other, and I'm not sure Colin has met him either. But there's no doubt who he is; one look and you know he's Jack's dad.

"I'll take you to the hospital," Max says to me.

Eddie tenses and opens his mouth to say something, but when his eyes rest on mine, whatever he was going to say dies on his tongue. I run upstairs to dress, throwing on a pair of jeans and a T-shirt.

As we head out, Max turns to Eddie. "I'll make sure she gets back home safely. Don't worry."

When we reach the hospital, I rush to the information desk. The woman sitting behind it lifts her blond head and smiles. "How can I help you?"

"Yes. I'm here to see Bryce…er, Michael…Michael Cooper."

She taps buttons on her illuminated desktop, her pointed fingernails clicking against the glass. "Are you family?"

I hesitate for a second. "Yes?"

She lowers her head and peers at me from the tops of her eyes. Yeah, no one is going to buy a white girl with crazy red hair is related in any way to the dark boy I'm here for.

Max walks up behind me and flashes his credentials. "She's with me."

The woman eyes Max and studies his credentials before looking at her desktop again. "Room 704, seventh floor, on the right."

Max turns on the same megawatt smile Jack's used countless times to get what he wants. "Thank you."

She blushes and turns away, fussing with her hair.

"What is it with you Jackson men?" I ask him.

He laughs and directs me into the elevator. "It's a gift, what can I say?"

Jack stands across the dark room from Bryce, watching the door. He pushes off the wall when we enter, and I rush up, giving him an awkward hug. He releases me and hugs his dad while I go over to Bryce. I reach out and take his hand. It's warm and soft, but doesn't respond to my touch.

"How is he?" I ask Jack.

"He's got a broken rib and three cracked ones, plus lots of bruising and swelling. They gave him some pretty good pain meds, and the nurse said he'd probably be out of it for a while. They're keeping him overnight for observation."

I want him to be okay, I *need* him to be okay. My gaze travels over Bryce's face and body, stopping at his right hand, wrapped in a bandage.

"He has some bruised knuckles. He knows how to throw a punch," Jack says with a grin.

I flex my right hand and curl it into a ball, remembering the bones I broke when I punched Montreal in the girls' bathroom the day Alivia and her friends attacked me.

"What can you tell me about what happened tonight?" Max asks.

"Not much. I asked Bryce to spend the night…on the couch at Eddie's, I mean. I woke when I heard a loud noise. When we came downstairs, one guy bolted out the front door and another guy was attacking Bryce. Eddie hit him with a baseball bat, but he still escaped."

"What did they looked like?"

I shake my head. "I didn't see either of their faces. It was dark and they were both wearing hoodies."

Max rubs his chin with his thumb and narrows his eyes a fraction. "Who knew he was spending the night at your place?"

"No one. It was spur of the moment. With everything going on, I didn't want him going home alone. Detective or not."

Max turns to Jack. "Did he text or call to say he was staying with Evan?"

Jack studies the floor with intensity. "No." I wonder if Max knows his son spends most, if not all, of his nights at Lisa's.

"We have to consider the possibility, or rather the likelihood, Bryce was never the intended target," Max says.

The air stalls in my lungs. First Lucien, then Colin, and now Bryce. People I love are getting killed or hurt because someone wants *me*.

Muffled sounds in the hall mix with the steady hum of the hospital ventilation system and Bryce's quiet rhythmic breathing. From the chair beside his bed, I can just make out the rise and fall of his chest.

Max didn't want to go without me because he promised Eddie he'd bring me home, but I convinced him to come back in a few hours and walk me to work instead. I couldn't leave Bryce, not after what happened to him because I begged him to stay. Jack offered to hang out here, but I knew I wouldn't be able to sleep anyway, so it seemed pointless to go home.

My eyes travel from Bryce's chest up to his swollen and bruised face. I move closer to the bed so I can pick up his undamaged hand. He stirs, but doesn't wake. Before I can stop myself, I crawl into his bed and curl up next to him, careful to avoid the side with the cracked ribs. I lay my head on his shoulder and kiss his jaw, my hand curling into the crook of his arm. He's warm and solid beside me, and I inhale his scent, a mixture of sweat and whatever they used to clean him up. The tears begin to fall.

Apparently I cried myself to sleep, because the next thing I'm aware of is the gentle stroking of my hair. A husky voice next to my ear murmurs, "Hey, Evansville."

I open my eyes and push up, my back aching from pressing into the side rail. Bryce's left eye is nearly swollen shut and is the color of a burnt plum dredged in something yellow. I lightly run my fingers over the bruising and he closes his eyes.

"What are you doing here?" He asks.

"I couldn't leave. Am I hurting you?"

"No. I'm glad you're here."

I rest my head on his chest while he strokes my hair with his bandaged hand, and we talk about what happened. "Max thinks you were never the target," I finish up.

"Mmm, could be. I was out cold when breaking glass woke me. I left my gun on top of the bookcase so the kids wouldn't find it, and I couldn't get to it before I was jumped. I got the feeling they were surprised to see me, so Max may be right."

The door opens and a nurse enters. She glances at me in Bryce's bed and her eyes narrow in a heated scowl. "I need to take you for some more scans," she says. I push myself up and hop down. Now that I'm no longer occupying her patient's bed, she seems less hostile. "I have to take him now, but he'll be back in about an hour."

"I'll be gone when you get back," I say to Bryce. "Max'll be here in a half-hour to escort me to work."

"Good. I don't want you going anywhere alone until we figure out what's going on."

The nurse pulls the side up on his bed.

"I'll stop by after work if you're still here," I call to him as he's wheeled from the room.

I step into his bathroom to freshen up, but there is no freshening the mess greeting me in the mirror. Dark circles sit beneath bleary eyes, and it's obvious I slept in my clothes. I'm all set to make a great impression on day two of my new job.

Means to an End

Tony clears his throat, and I glance up from the article I'm reading to find him staring at me. He studies me for a few seconds, and I force myself not to fidget under his stare.

"Your name was floated as a possible candidate for an embedded reporter."

That was fast — I've only been here a week — I don't even have to pretend to be surprised. "Um, h-how?" I stammer, trying to figure out what I *should* be saying.

"A couple of detectives are looking for an embed. Someone fresh, young, and your name was thrown out." His eyes narrow in my direction. Tony's not stupid, so I work to keep my features in the shocked and awed position. "It could be exciting, but also dangerous, so you don't have to do it if you don't want to."

I chew my lip, pretending to think it over. "What would you do if you were me?" I ask.

"The first thing I'd want to know is why someone thinks a newbie with no experience is a good candidate."

"Who should I ask?"

"I already did."

Of course he did. He's an investigative reporter. "And?"

"The assignment is with a pair of young undercovers. They're looking for someone who can pose as the girlfriend of one of them. You're the only one who can really fit that role."

"Oh. That makes sense, I guess."

He nods, steepling his fingers beneath his chin. "It does."

"Um… do you think I'm ready for something like this?" I delivered my first doctored article to Tony the morning after Bryce's beating, and he loved it. I've done a half-dozen more since then. With each one, I do more of the work, with Bryce only providing a couple of tweaks on the most recent one. Tony even took me on a few interviews, and yesterday he showed me how to get into the massive Western Provincial News databases to do research. It turns out I'm enjoying the hell out of this fake job.

"Hard to say, but I think you're on your way. You have decent instincts, but this assignment is more about gathering information. You'll be able to ask the detectives questions, but for the most part you'll just observe and report back."

I nod as he talks, wondering what, if anything, Jack and Bryce will let me report on, and it occurs to me that's probably a question I should ask. "Do you know what they're investigating?"

"Not yet." He pauses and stares hard at me again. "This is an incredible opportunity, almost unheard of at your age. Don't blow it."

"I won't," I say, unable to hide my smile. The fact he believes I might be capable of doing this job means a lot. Maybe because it's the first time in my life I'm doing something I could be interested in long term. This could be my way of making a difference, I mean after saving the world and all.

"It's yours if you want it. I'll expect you to touch base on a regular basis. I want to hear from you no less than once a week, either by text or phone. And you'll need to file articles regularly. I realize there may be things you won't be permitted to share until the end of the investigation, but you need to keep me in the loop."

"Yes, sir." I stand to leave, but pause and turn back to him. "Thanks…for this opportunity."

"Don't make me regret it."

Walking out toward the front desk, my feet are bouncy. I know this isn't real, the job has been manufactured for my benefit, but Tony's willingness to take a chance on me *is* real, and it's gratifying. Most of the time, I feel as if I'm spinning my wheels, like a non-four-wheel drive vehicle trying to move through sand or snow.

I came back to the Union to find a way to stop the attack, but instead I spend my days avoiding being captured or killed. Now, it's as if I'm no longer hovering, waiting for everyone else to do something or for some other crappy thing to happen. This is me *finally* doing something.

I grip the offending plant below its spiky leaves and pull. Although it resists being torn from its nutrient-rich environment, I'm bigger and stronger. The weed breaks free of the dirt, sending pieces of soil dancing off the roots; the clean, sweet odor of fresh earth fills my nostrils. Soft dirt and tiny rocks embed themselves under my nails, and although painful, I find it familiar, comforting.

I love the community gardens — the crisp morning air, working with my hands, being a part of something bigger than myself. When I was younger, my grungy, scraped-up hands were a trophy, a symbol of a small defiance of my parents' wishes. They wouldn't be caught dead doing community service, something only those who can't afford to pay taxes do.

A peal of laughter behind me pulls my attention. I turn in time to see Colin attempting to juggle apples with a still-healing shoulder. Lisa laughs as he misses one, and it hits the bench with a dull thud. For a moment, I almost forget we're not back in school and this isn't any other Saturday morning of community service. Although the citrus trees are a stark reminder we're in the Western Province and not back east. Well, those plus Eddie and the kids being here.

Eddie still doesn't get why I choose to work instead of paying taxes. I tried to explain it makes me feel like I'm a part of the community and not above it. He may not understand, but the fact he got up early on a weekend to drag himself and the kids out here to do manual labor means more to me than all his other bonding attempts combined.

Quinn's red curls bounce as she picks late-season blueberries, popping at least half of them into her mouth. Liam pulls a plant with long roots from the dirt, that I'm pretty sure it isn't a weed, and shows Eddie.

"Good job, buddy," Eddie says, patting his son on the head.

"Thanks again for letting Bryce stay with us," I say to Eddie when Liam runs off with his "weed."

He shrugs. "I couldn't very well let him stay by himself after he got beat up in my apartment."

Bryce doesn't think he's a target, so I'm convinced he agreed to stay with us just to humor me. But when we curl up together on the couch after everyone else goes to bed, he doesn't seem to mind. Today, he's back at work for the first time since being released from the hospital, and I'm glad he's with Jack, because he's not quite at one hundred percent yet.

"Hey, Lisa and I were talking," Colin yells at me from across the garden. "We want to do our community service at the farmers market next month. You in?"

"Sure." We have no clue where we'll be next month, but it's easiest to just agree, prolonging the fantasy that life is normal.

The bell chimes indicating our shift is over, and we wash up before heading off to a late breakfast.

"Mr. Egg, Mr. Egg," Quinn chants.

Eddie laughs, and I know the toddler has won. We'll be eating breakfast where the wait staff dress like characters from her favorite cartoon and often break out into song and dance. At times like these I wonder if this is what my life would've been like if Eddie had stuck around. I try not to be jealous of Liam and Quinn, but there are moments I can't deny that's exactly what I am.

12 Doing Something

"How do I look?" I ask Bryce.

"Beautiful, as always."

"No, I'm serious." The form-fitting jeans, knee-high boots, and long green sweater are my third outfit of the morning. "I'm not sure if I should dress like a reporter or a detective."

He kisses my cheek and takes my hand. "You look fine," he says, pulling me out the front door before I can run upstairs and change again. We navigate the crowded sidewalks from Eddie's apartment to the police station. The early October morning is crisp, although autumn in the west is not quite the same as back home. For one thing, the leaves don't turn colors here, at least not yet.

A few blocks from the precinct, Bryce tugs me into an alley and backs me up against the brick wall with a devilish grin. Placing one hand behind my head, he leans in and kisses me thoroughly.

"What was that for?" I ask, tilting my head in an attempt to figure him out, still not sure if I'm totally comfortable with this "us" thing yet.

He runs his lips up the side of my neck. "I needed one last kiss to get me through the day. Working with you all day and not being able to touch you is going to kill me."

He takes my hand again and leads me back to the sidewalk. He's not Cyrus and sometimes that's painfully obvious, but Cyrus is gone and I need to move on. Bryce is a good guy, and I do like him. It's taken me awhile to get to the point where I trust him again after all the lies. With the rest of the world crumbling beneath our feet, he's the solid earth I need right now to keep upright.

When we reach the precinct, Bryce drops my hand and pulls the door open, letting me walk in ahead of him. He smiles at the girl behind the desk. "Sophie, this is Evan. Evan, Sophie." If she remembers me from the day I came in to meet Max, she doesn't give any indication. She scans my fingerprint and hands me a visitors badge with press credentials.

I place the lanyard around my neck and follow Bryce down the corridor, past Max's office, and into a maze of cubicles filled with busy officers, support staff, and volunteers fulfilling their community service obligations. A few heads turn our way as we pass, but most people pay no attention. We arrive in a small office in the back with two desks, each with a large tablet and telephone. Dirty coffee mugs and a stack of smaller tablets, air drives, and other assorted electronic equipment are strewn about. Jack sits at one of the desks and glances up, nodding a greeting.

Bryce closes the door and I park myself in a chair across the room as they work. Bryce said we can't assume we're not being monitored here, so we go through our day keeping up our ruse. I pull out my tablet to take notes, but since they're not doing much, mostly I read. When lunchtime rolls around, we head to a cafe a couple of blocks away, giving us an opportunity to talk.

"So," I say, "Tony tells me I'm supposed to be the girlfriend of one of you. Who's the lucky guy?"

Jack's lips tip up in a half smile. "I value my life enough to know there's only one right answer to that question."

I stab my salad and twirl the fork in my hand, watching the lettuce spin. "What should I be doing back at the precinct? I hate just sitting there, but I'm not sure if I should be doing something else. What do other embedded reporters do?"

Jack takes a bite of his sandwich and shrugs. "I don't know, we've never worked with one before."

"I've seen them around," Bryce says. "They trail after the detectives, observing, asking questions."

"Great. A whole lot of nothing, then."

When we get back after lunch, I plunk down in the chair and watch them tap searches into their tablets and read through the results. I'm in real danger of lapsing into a boredom-induced coma. "What are you working on?" I ask after my eyelids close and my body jerks.

"We're tracking down leads on a guy suspected of smuggling weapons using Union trains," Jack says without looking up.

Movies always make police work look way more exciting than this. Tomorrow we're at least going out in the field. Hopefully that will be more riveting.

Field work was only slightly less boring than office work and didn't last nearly long enough. The past few days have been boring as shit. I kill time by texting with my mom, telling her how utterly dull this job is, while she badgers me to visit.

Today has been particularly long and monotonous. The afternoon drags on and I study my fingernails, picking off some of the chipped nail polish. This is just more sitting around and waiting for something to happen, but in a different venue. I thought we'd be doing *something*.

When it's time to leave, I toss my tablet in my bag and stand, ready to bolt out of here.

"In a hurry?" Jack asks, a grin splitting his face.

"What can I say, the excitement is overwhelming."

"Is this job every bit as thrilling as you expected?"

I roll my eyes. "Oh, way more."

We part ways with Jack at the train station, and Bryce picks up my hand as we walk to Eddie's.

"Bryce, we're wasting time. I know you're doing your job, but you're not getting anywhere."

"It may not seem like it, but we're making progress."

"On stopping the attack?"

"On finding out who in the government is involved. It's only the first step, but it's an important one. When we locate them, we can interrogate them, find out more. This is the best way, Evansville, trust me. If the Union has a specific target to aim for in stopping this, the rest of the Ruins will be spared."

I let that sink in. It makes sense. A surgical strike rather than a broad, sweeping attack would be better for everyone. "Okay. But how much more time are we talking?"

"I don't know. But we *are* uncovering leads."

"Is that what you were doing? It looked a lot like scratching your asses and staring at tablets to me."

He laughs and kisses the side of my head. We've reached Eddie's so our conversation is put on hold for now. When we open the door, Quinn flies across the room and jumps into Bryce's arms, ignoring her big sister. He sets her down and heads into the kitchen, poking around in the fridge for something to eat.

Leaning my head back against Bryce's chest, I settle in to watch Monday Night Football. Of all the pre-war sports that have survived in the Union, football is my favorite. Liam bombards Eddie with questions about each play and penalty until Eddie tells him to be quiet and watch the game.

Before the next play is snapped, there's a frantic knock at the door. Eddie glances at me, his brow furrowed, before getting up to answer it. Bryce hops up and grabs his gun from the top of the bookshelf, following him. Eddie peeks through the blinds covering the newly-repaired window, and his shoulders drop, tension draining out of him in waves.

He opens the door, and Jack barrels in with Lisa in tow. Lisa's face is pale, her dark eyes wide, bottom lip trembling.

Jack closes and locks the door behind him before turning to us. He opens his mouth but slams it shut when he spots the kids. "Hey, guys," he calls out to them, his tone unnaturally light.

Quinn jumps up off the couch and runs up to him, squealing, "Jack, Jack, Jack, Jack."

He scoops her up, ruffling her crazy hair before setting her down and giving Liam a high five.

Eddie announces, "Okay, bedtime," and bends down to pick up Quinn.

I take Liam by the hand and escort him to bed, tucking him in before hurrying back downstairs.

Jack inhales sharply and glances at all of us before his gaze rests on Bryce. "I found a memo." He pauses and presses his lips into a thin line. "Someone is organizing a contract killing. For us."

The room tilts, and icy slush pulses through my veins. I reach for Bryce to steady myself. Air won't enter my lungs, even though I'm gasping. Bryce rubs my back and says something to me. Blood rushes through my ears in a deafening roar, drowning out whatever Bryce is saying. Finally, his words register. "Evan, breathe. It's going to be okay."

My mind snaps back into focus and I suck in a breath. People in the Union want to kill us. "How can you say it's going to be okay? This is the least okay it could possibly be."

Another knock on the door interrupts his response. Jack and Bryce bolt back to the door, guns drawn. Jack peeks out through the blinds before opening it.

Max enters, his eyes sweeping the room, agitated tension coursing through the air. "Got your text," he says to Jack, running his hand across his jaw. "What's going on?"

Jack pulls out a small external drive, about the size of a dime, and pushes the pin into his tablet. He swipes a few times and carries the tablet over to the table. We all huddle around him, reading over his shoulder.

"This is a screen capture of something I found in an old database. It's gone now, disappeared right after I grabbed this. I'm sure it was saved there by accident. I don't even know if anyone realizes I saw it. I was doing some research on the weapons smuggling and it came up in the search."

"Is your AirNet off?" Max asks.

"Yeah. Turned it off before I left the precinct."

If I hadn't experienced the past several months, I would laugh at the absurdity of the words in front of me. It reads like a plot from a movie, except it's my life. Our lives.

RE: Project Blackbird

We have discovered a very real threat to the Project that needs to be neutralized as soon as possible. Extensive knowledge of the program has been discovered. Enough to bring down the entire operation.

Due to the sensitive nature of the Project and the high-visibility of the threat, the resolution must be complete and clean. An ongoing investigation would be detrimental to the Project.

Please submit only your best people for consideration. Once a final team has been chosen, you will be forwarded the threat details.

Eddie shakes his head. "How can you be sure this is about you?"

"It's certainly vague enough," Max says.

"What else could it be about?" Jack asks his dad.

Max scratches the back of his head. "Based on what you've told me, it's a safe assumption."

I want to believe the memo isn't about us, but everything fits. We're a threat. One reduced to a danger needing to be contained like an epidemic.

"Something we found is significant. I don't know what yet. But they're escalating, so we must be close." Bryce says, still rubbing my back.

"Do you know who created the memo, who it was sent to, or when?" Eddie asks, his face drawn, his complexion gray, as if he's aged ten years in the past ten minutes.

Jack shakes his head and turns to Max. "I'm hoping you can find some kind of digital fingerprint on it, though. I'm leaving it with you."

Max nods.

With a heavy sigh, Jack faces the rest of us. "We need to split up. They'll try to make our deaths look like an accident so there's no investigation. That'll be a lot harder to pull off if we scatter. And we need to stay off the grid."

Every day, the list of things we need to accomplish seems to grow. Now we need to add not being assassinated to the list.

13 Off the Grid

Bending down, I hug Liam and Quinn a little tighter than normal, breathing them in, trying to memorize everything about them. Liam's boyish smell, Quinn's soft curls.

"Ready?" Bryce asks, walking up behind me with our duffel bags.

I nod and follow him out. We make our way to the hotel room Eddie has rented in his name. The room where we'll all become someone else before quietly disappearing.

Bryce knocks on the door with the secret code we agreed on, but the peephole darkens anyway, as someone on the other side checks to see who it is. Colin swings the door open and we enter, Bryce tossing our bags on the bed. Lisa and Jack follow us in, carrying hair dye, clothing, and dark contact lenses for Bryce.

The room is beautiful, all light-colored linens and bright filtered sunlight through the privacy shades. Only the best for rock god Eddie McIntyre.

"Who's first?" Lisa asks.

I raise my hand. Might as well get this over with.

Jack rolls out a plastic drop cloth and I settle into the chair, tilting my head back. Lisa moves behind me, slipping on rubber gloves before applying bottled chestnut brown hair coloring. The sharp odor stings my eyes as she squeezes the goo onto my hair, massaging the color from the roots to the ends of my curls. While I wait for the color to take, Jack takes my spot in the chair and Lisa gets to work dying his blond locks black. She works quickly, next applying bleach to Colin's dark hair, before she sits so I can turn her dark blond strands a brilliant platinum.

Bryce pops in the contacts, turning his baby grays to a deep chocolate brown. It's not foolproof, but if hired killers are looking for a group of five, including a redhead and a light-skinned black guy with gray eyes, altering our appearances even a little might buy us enough time. Time to figure out who's after us and find a way to stop them.

Another knock at the door sends a shot of adrenaline through my central nervous system. Jack peers through the peephole and lets Eddie in. He scans the room, his gaze landing on me. He offers me a weak smile before handing a bag to Jack. Jack pulls out five newly-purchased tablets, giving them to Colin to configure.

Colin swipes for a while, types some stuff, and hands the first one to me. "I was able to hack it and make the AirNet address untraceable. Every time you log on, it'll send out a different random number. Still, you shouldn't use your real name. I set it up under your middle name, but you can change it if you want."

"No, that's good. We won't be spending a ton of time on them anyway."

While Colin works, Eddie hands a stack of prepaid debit cards to Jack. "These will automatically reload as needed so you can stay off the PrintPay system."

Jack takes a device out of his pocket and swipes each card through it, nodding his approval. "These are anonymous and untraceable."

Grabbing debit cards for me and Bryce, I realize there's nothing left to do. It's time. I walk up and wrap my arms around Lisa.

"I don't like this, Ev," she says. "I'm scared all the time. I hate living like this."

"I know, Lis, me too. I'm going to miss you. But when this is over—"

"When this is over, what? Nothing will ever be the same again."

"No, you're right."

Colin pulls me in for a long hug, and I burrow into his chest. I turn to Eddie last, not sure what to say. I've never given him a fair chance to make up for his earlier failings, and now it might be too late.

"Text Mom for me. Tell her I'm undercover. She knew it was coming, so it won't be a huge surprise. Let her know I'll contact her when I can." I step forward and wrap my arms around him, resting my cheek on his shoulder. He squeezes me so tightly, I can hardly breathe. "Thanks, Dad," I squeak out through his vice-like hold. His body stiffens, and it hits me this is the first time in my life I've ever called him Dad. He releases me without a word, looking away.

With a quick glance over my shoulder at my friends, I take Bryce's hand and leave them behind.

Sunglasses on, ball caps pulled down, we keep our heads lowered to avoid the security camera as we board the A-Train. Bryce leads me to the back of the train and takes the seat by the window, tugging me down next to him.

The trip back to the Eastern Province will take a little over a day. We talk in hushed tones even though no one is sitting near us. "Are you sure Colin, Lisa, and Jack will be okay staying here?" I ask.

"I'm sure. They're moving all the way down to the lower levels. I've spent plenty of time down there. Trust me, there's a lucrative underground industry catering to citizens who don't want to be tracked."

I chew on my lip, unable to relax. The only thing making me feel the slightest bit better is that they'll be working with Max to find out who's behind the memo. Whoever it is, Bryce thinks it's the big target we're looking for. The one they can use to stop the attack.

After talking for a little while longer, I can't fight the fatigue any longer. Laying my head against Bryce's shoulder, I close my eyes and doze off.

My eyelids flutter open, and I sit up, arching my shoulders to get the kink out of my neck. Small windows dot the side of the train, looking out onto a deep indigo sky.

"Are you hungry?" Bryce asks.

"Yeah," I say, my voice thick with lingering sleep. "What time is it?"

He glances at his watch. "Five-thirty western time, although I think we're in the Southern Province now."

"Wow. I guess I was tired."

"You were out for about five hours."

"I didn't drool or anything in my sleep did I?"

He laughs. "No, but you snored a little."

"I did not."

He laughs harder. "You did. A little, and it's cute."

I grab the sandwich from him, convinced he's messing with me, and tear open the wrapper. "Where'd you get this?"

"The attendant came by when you were sleeping. I took a chance on ham and cheese."

"Thanks."

The rest of the train ride is uneventful, and considering our lives lately, that's pretty much my definition of a perfect trip. We spend the hours talking about things that don't matter.

"If you could live at any time, past, present or future, when would you choose?" I ask.

He presses his lips together and glances at the ceiling. "Late twentieth century, I think. Seems like they had a long stretch of peace and prosperity, plus civil rights were a done deal. What about you?"

"Yeah, it's gonna have to be after the whole women's and civil rights thing and after the war, too. I don't think I'd like to live through that. So maybe early twenty-second century."

"If you could only take a dozen books with you to a deserted island, which ones would you want?"

"Why do I only get a dozen? Thousands fit on my tablet."

"What if it's a cave island without the sun to recharge it?"

"Well now you're being ridiculous." I smile, though, because I know he's trying to distract me. And it's been nice. For the past hour, I haven't thought about our impending demise.

We spend the rest of the trip dozing, eating, or talking about inconsequential things, arriving in the Eastern Province shortly before noon. After grabbing our bags, we head down to the lower levels where we're less likely to be noticed or run into anyone we know.

Bryce finds a hotel that doesn't require identification and gets adjoining rooms. This place is a dump compared to the one Eddie rented for us. My room has only one double bed and just enough room for me to squeeze between the bed and the wall. We're on the backside of the hotel, where daylight has never visited, giving the room a cave-like atmosphere similar to the desert island Bryce was attempting to create. The only window overlooks the hallway outside the door.

I set my bag on the mossy green comforter covering a firm mattress and sit. So this is how the other half lives. Life in the Ruins is better than this. At least they have fresh air and sunshine.

After a quick change of clothes, Bryce and I head out to grab lunch. Our sole purpose for being here is so I can meet with my uncle. I have no idea how I'm going to get in to see him without anyone noticing. If someone is looking for us, they'll be watching his apartment. That, coupled with the tight security already surrounding the Governor of the Eastern Province, and we've got our work cut out for us.

14 The Governor

We've been in the Eastern Province for a week and still haven't figured out how to get into my uncle's apartment. We stay in touch with the others through daily texts, only logging on long enough to communicate. Even though our tablets are safe, I'm still jittery about being connected to the AirNet.

Bryce paces between our two rooms, the door between them propped open with a chair. His nervous energy is making me even edgier. My tablet dings with the latest text from Lisa.

Lisa: C left.

Me: What do you mean he left?

Lisa: He took off. Went up to the NW.

Me: Why?

Lisa: Don't know. He wouldn't say, but I'm so pissed at him I could scream.

Shit. The three of them together was a bad idea, but now he's alone, and that's even worse. I pull up another text and start typing to Colin.

Me: Hey

No response.

Me: You around?

No response.

Lisa: Why would he do that?

Me: Don't know

Except I do know, but I can't be the one to tell her.

Me: Let me talk to B and try to reach C. I'll check back in tomorrow

Lisa: Stay safe

Me: You too

"Lisa said Colin left. Took off for the Northwestern Province."

Bryce stops his pacing and stands in front of the bed. "Well, I guess I'm not surprised, but I wish he hadn't."

"I just tried texting him, but he isn't responding.

"Keep trying. I'll text Jack and find out what's up."

While he texts with Jack, I take a quick shower. Being in this room makes me feel grungy, and I find I'm showering twice a day. As I towel dry my hair, Bryce glances up from where he's lying on my bed, tablet in hand. "Jack doesn't know anything more about Colin, and Max hasn't found anything useful yet."

"This sitting around is driving me crazy."

"Let's get out of here," he says, pushing up.

I toss my towel on the bed and let him lead me to a nearby park. Although we're now into late October, the warm afternoon sun makes it feel more like summer. Bryce picks a spot in the grass and lies on his back, one hand behind his head. He pats the ground next to him and I sit.

A sudden breeze sends colorful leaves swirling around us. Tipping my head back, I peer up at dappled sunlight filtering through trees trimmed in vermillion, gold, and crimson leaves, clinging to branches as if they're not yet ready to give up their tenuous grasp on life.

Bryce tugs me closer to him and I end up lying with my head propped up on his stomach. He plays absently with a piece of my hair as we talk about nothing in particular, before we cycle back around to what we're doing here.

"I'm starting to have second thoughts about talking to my uncle," I say.

"Why's that?"

"Everyone who learns the truth becomes a target. I don't want to put him in danger. I already regret telling Eddie."

He sits up, cradling my head, and turns me to face him. "Your uncle *is* in danger. This is about power. Those who want it will kill to get it, and those who have it will kill to keep it. Your uncle is a powerful man. Whether or not he knows the truth, he's probably a target."

"I can't believe I never thought of it in those terms before, but it explains why people in the Union would be working with Walker, arming the Ruins. I figured this was about the Ruins gaining access to our resources or seeking revenge or something."

"I might be wrong, but I've been trying to put all the pieces together. The Ruins doesn't have the infrastructure to pull this off. Even the Union doesn't have enough pissed off people to take on the whole country. I think they're using people in the Ruins to do their dirty work."

"I hate to admit it, but it makes sense. The Ruins have nothing to lose and everything to gain."

He pulls me back to his chest and rests his chin on top of my head, twisting one of my curls around his finger. Something about the way he's playing with my hair reminds me of another time in my life, sparking a memory. My breath catches, and I know how I'm going to get in to talk to my uncle.

"Are you sure about this?" Bryce asks for the tenth time as we walk briskly through the Borough to my uncle's apartment.

"Yes. I'm sure," I tell him for the tenth time. "I've done this before, only in reverse." I've never snuck into the apartment before, but I did sneak out once when I was fourteen. Halfway through my uncle's first term as Governor, I was making out with Avi, the son of his chief of staff, in the closet in the wait staff room. When we heard my stepfather, Joe, in the hall outside, Avi showed me a secret way out. I'd forgotten about it until yesterday when Bryce and I were in the park. The way he played with my hair was the same way Avi did. The boy who was my first kiss might just be responsible for saving my life and the Union along with it.

I stuff my hands into my jacket pockets and hunch my shoulders against the cold evening air. The only sound is our shoes scuffing against the sidewalk. When we reach the entrance to the alley behind my uncle's apartment building, Bryce grabs my hand and yanks me to a stop. "Where are you going?"

"To the back of the apartment."

"What about the security cameras?"

"What cameras?"

He shakes his head. "He's the Governor. There will be security. Trust me."

I roll my eyes. "I doubt it. If there were, I would've been caught sneaking out."

"How do you know you weren't?"

I stop trying to tug my hand away as dread washes over me and heat floods my cheeks. After that fateful day, we had very few opportunities for our secret make-out sessions. We were rarely at the apartment at the same time, and if we were, it was impossible to sneak away together. *Oh my god,* what if that was because our parents knew?

Shaking my head, I immerse myself in our present troubles. "So now what?"

He scratches the back of his head. "So now we scope things out."

Bryce peers around the corner, taking a few steps before signaling me to follow. I remain a few feet behind him, pressed up against the cold, gray bricks, my breath puffing out in a white cloud. Bryce slows, then stops, reaching back to take my hand. He points to a motion sensor and reaches down to pick up a rock, tossing it in an arc in front of the sensor. A camera pops out of the wall and swivels in the direction of the rock.

Well crap, this isn't good. I glance at him, wondering what we do now, and he motions back to the sidewalk. Retreating out of the alley, I refuse to give up. "Please tell me you have an idea."

"Not yet, but give me a few minutes to think," he says, taking my hand and pulling me to a nearby park.

Sitting on a bench while Bryce paces, the cold, wet air sinks deep under my skin until my teeth begin to chatter. I stand and move around, trying to warm up.

Bryce halts and the corner of his lip twitches up. "Come on, I have an idea."

"What is it?"

"We need something to distract the cameras long enough for us to get in." He stops in front of an electronics store. "Wait here, I'll be right back."

I watch from the sidewalk as he enters and talks to the sales clerk. The clerk disappears, returning a couple of minutes later with a box. Bryce pulls out the prepaid card Eddie gave him to pay.

Voices over my shoulder startle me and I pull my knit hat lower on my forehead, turning away from the door as they enter. A blast of warm air hits me before the door closes. I shove my hands deeper into my pockets and bounce on the balls of my feet until Bryce joins me a few minutes later.

Taking my hand, he leads me back to the park, where he opens the package and pulls out a wireless drone, looking remarkably like a pigeon.

"What—" I start to ask.

"We're going to keep the cameras busy for a minute or two. We won't have much time."

"How are we going to get back out?"

"Once we get inside, I'll disable the cameras."

"You can do that?"

He turns away from the drone and lifts an eyebrow, a cocky grin on his face. "I have many talents."

"I had no idea," I say, shaking my head

"I was a bit of a technogeek as a kid."

A smile splits my face. "Well aren't you full of surprises. And here I thought you were a jock."

He turns to me, both dimples on display. "I played sports, but was also a member of my school's robotics club." He fiddles with a few settings on the bird drone. "There. Done. Come on."

We head back to the alley, where Bryce lets the drone go. The electronic pigeon zips past my uncle's apartment, three cameras popping out of the wall to follow it. The bird drone flutters back and forth a few times as we run down the alley, stopping at the back wall.

"Right there," I whisper, "to the left of the stoop. See it?" A small lever juts out of the wall, looking like an ordinary loose brick. Bryce nods and moves closer. "Yank it forward."

A small door opens below the lever, revealing a dumbwaiter for food deliveries, but no one has used it as long as my uncle has been Governor. Well, except for kids like me and Avi to sneak in or out.

Bryce ducks his head in and pops back out. "You first," he whispers in my ear.

I climb into the cramped, frigid dumbwaiter. Apparently the builders anticipated a lot of power outages back then, because it uses a pulley system. I pull down on the rope and the box glides up to the wait staff room one floor above. When I reach the top, I peer out through the small round window into a dark and quiet room.

Pushing the door open, I pause and listen again. At the sound of silence, I hop down the three feet to the floor and push the release, sending the dumbwaiter back to street level. Bryce joins me a few tense moments later.

"Now where?" he whispers in my ear, taking my hand.

I point to a pantry on the right where we can change into uniforms, allowing us to blend in with the kitchen staff. My uncle will be in his study reviewing correspondence and the day's news. I used to think the way he stuck to a strict routine was boring, but now I appreciate his rigid schedule. In the pantry, I find a pair of black pants and white jacket in Bryce's size and another set for me. We turn our backs to each other and quickly change. I rifle around finding two low-slung white hats and stuff my hair up under mine.

"Here goes nothing." I open the pantry door and halt. Footsteps move across the tile floor in our direction. My heart races in my chest as I close the door. Thinking fast, I grab Bryce and push him up against the wall, pressing my lips to his.

He kisses me back, whether or not he suspects what I'm up to, he gets into his role, and I nearly forget where we are or why we're here.

The door jerks open and a startled female voice says, "Oh…Oh! What are you two doing in here? Never mind, I know what you're doing. Get out here. Now."

I pull away from Bryce and follow him out, head down. I don't recognize her voice, but I tilt my head enough to see her face to confirm I don't know her.

"What are your names?" she demands.

I manage to blink at her a few times.

"Michael and Delilah," Bryce says, using his first and my middle name.

"I don't recall seeing you on the schedule."

"We're last minute replacements reporting for community service," Bryce says. "We were changing for our shift. It's my fault. I wanted one last kiss before we started."

Community service. Brilliant. Wish I'd thought of that.

She narrows her eyes and waves us off. "Go report to Chef in the kitchen. It's time for evening coffee service."

I lead him around the corner and into the kitchen, bright with activity. Stainless steel prep areas occupy the center, and every inch of wall space is taken up with sinks, stoves, ovens, and shelving. Other volunteers as well as regular staff crisscross the black and white tile floor.

A tall guy with a sweat-covered baby face barks orders at a volunteer. "Smaller. Bite size. Do I have to do everything?" He notices us. "Are you here to work or watch?"

"We're reporting for our shifts," I say.

"Can you pour coffee into a cup?"

"Yes," I say.

"Good. Do that and deliver it to the Governor in his study. Do you know where that is?"

"Yes," I say again, moving to the cabinets where the cups are kept, unable to believe our luck.

"You," Chef snaps at Bryce. "Chop those vegetables for the omelets in the morning. Take over for Vance. And cut them small or you'll be washing dishes."

Bryce glances at me, one eyebrow raised. I nod, indicating I have this and grab the small square napkin from my pocket, containing the note I wrote earlier, setting it upside down on the saucer. After filling the cup, I head down the hall to my uncle's study and rap on the door.

"Come in," says a familiar voice that makes my breath catch. It's been so long since I've seen him, I wasn't prepared for the emotions surging through me right now.

I push the door open and step inside the large study. My Uncle David sits in his armchair, head down. The cup shakes, spilling coffee down the side and onto the napkin. I gulp in a calming breath and steady my hand. My eyes sweep the room, and satisfied he's alone, I move across the floor.

He doesn't glance up as I approach, which is good. I don't want him to react in case his place is bugged, which I assume it is. He holds his tablet in one hand, gesturing to the wooden end table next to him with the other.

I set down the coffee and lean close to whisper in his ear, "Uncle David, it's Evan."

His body stiffens and his head twitches. "Don't say anything and don't look up. I need to talk to you. It's urgent. There's a note under the cup." Standing back up, I say, "Do you need anything else, sir?"

"No. That'll be all, thank you." His words are smooth, but I know him well enough to detect the subtle underlying tension in his voice.

I rush back to the kitchen to meet Bryce, but he's not where I left him chopping veggies. Then I remember he was going to sneak into the security office to disable the cameras. Ducking out of the kitchen before I can be assigned to another task, I return to the staff room to pace and chew on my thumbnail while I wait.

After a half-hour passes and he's still not back, I go search for him. Stopping back by the kitchen to grab the coffee pot, I head toward the security office. If anyone stops me, I can pretend to be lost in the maze of hallways on my way to top off the Governor's coffee. I arrive at the security office without running into anyone and peek in the window. Only one guy is in there, sitting in a chair in front of the monitors, chin on his chest.

Turning back, I search for Bryce in the stock room and wash room before returning the coffee pot to the kitchen and heading back to the staff room. Where the hell is he?

Another fifteen minutes passes of me pacing the staff room waiting for Bryce. My pulse escalates with each passing minute, until I have to go look for him again or risk a heart attack. If he was caught, I'm sure I'd hear a lot more chaos in the house. Maybe he was sent back to the kitchen. I check every room I pass on my way, whispering his name loudly.

"Looking for something?"

My body jolts and I spin around, coming face-to-face with the woman who caught us in the pantry.

"Uh…I was looking for my friend, Br…er, Michael. Have you seen him?"

"No. And if I catch you two messing around in here again, I'll not only void your credits for today's community service hours, but ensure you're banned from the Governor's apartment."

"Yes, ma'am," I say and hurry to the kitchen.

He's still not there and I don't know what to do. Chewing my bottom lip, I give some thought to roaming the halls in search of him, but there are too many chances of running into someone who knows me. Instead, I go back into the staff room to wait. It's possible they have him off doing something other than kitchen work. As long as he's not in custody, he'll return here.

The door to the pantry cracks open, and a smooth brown hand reaches out, grabbing my arm and yanking me inside.

"Bryce!" The word comes out louder than I intended, but I'm just so damn glad to see him.

He puts a finger up to my lips to silence me. "We need to get out of here. Now," he whispers, handing me my clothes and pushing the door open.

He opens dumbwaiter and pushes me in, glancing over his shoulder before closing the door. I lower myself to street level and hop out to wait for him. Bryce emerges moments later, eyes darting around, a grim set to his mouth. He takes my hand and pulls me into the shadows around the corner and stops.

"Benton's here. I don't think he saw me, but I can't be sure. Did he see you?"

Alivia Benton's father, the mayor of our Borough, is in my uncle's apartment? They're definitely not friends, but they might be meeting on official business. If so, he'd have been in the study with my uncle, but he wasn't.

"*Evan*, did he see you?"

"No. At least I don't think so. I didn't see him, anyway. My uncle was alone when I delivered the note. Everything went according to plan until you disappeared.

"Benton was in the kitchen. He came in to talk to one of the staff."

"Why is he talking to my uncle's kitchen staff?"

"That's a damn good question."

"Do you think my uncle's in danger?"

"I don't know."

"What should we do?"

"For now, stick to the plan. Meet your uncle tomorrow morning. What we learn after talking to him might help us figure out our next move."

# 15 Next Move

The surf groans, echoing off the wooden boardwalk above, as I sit in the cool sand waiting for my uncle. This the same spot I once hid as a child, until my uncle found me and coaxed me out. A place only the two of us know about.

I was seven when my Uncle David moved in with us following a messy divorce. One day during the year he lived with us, we came to the beach for a family outing. I wanted to ride the Ferris wheel more than I wanted anything, but my half-sisters, Katie and Rachel, were throwing the monster of all toddler tantrums, demanding and receiving all the attention. When I begged one too many times, Joe snapped at me. I was crushed. He'd never even raised his voice to me until that moment. His short temper and harsh words were like a slap across my face.

I doubt he was even aware of my immediate reaction, what with the twin tornadoes doing their damage. But, being the young impulsive child I was, I took off down the beach and saw an opening under the boardwalk. I darted in and cried, hugging my knees, until I heard my uncle calling my name. He made a couple of passes before figuring out where I was.

He doubled back and poked his head in, "There you are, Pumpkin."

I stared at him through tear-filled eyes, snot running down my face, and wiped my nose with the back of my forearm. He crawled in and sat next to me, handing me a tissue.

"You know, your dad didn't mean it," he'd said.

I blew my nose and handed the snotty tissue back to him. "He loves Katie and Rachel more."

He took the disgusting snot-filled thing from me without hesitation. "No he doesn't."

"He does."

Uncle David wrapped his arms around me. "That's not even a little true. Parents don't always respond in the best way possible, but it has nothing to do with you and everything to do with a long day and a lot of tired people."

In my seven-year-old mind, I thought maybe he didn't know the truth. "Can I tell you a secret?"

"Of course, honey, anything you want."

"Joe's not my real dad," I whispered. "My real dad died. When Joe married my mom, he got me, too, but…I don't think he wanted me."

"Why would you think such a thing?"

"He didn't adopt me."

His expression didn't change as he studied me for a long time. Finally he said, "Do you know what real dads do?"

My eyes widened, wondering if I was missing out on something by not having one, and I shook my head.

"Real dads hug their daughters when they skin their knees, give them piggyback rides, and take them to the beach. They read to them at bedtime, help them with their homework, play dress-up, and drink tea made by their daughters. Real dads are there when you need them and even when you don't."

"But Joe does all those things," I'd told him.

He only smiled, then stood and reached down to pull me up. We walked to the Ferris wheel, where he bought two unlimited tickets and rode it with me until I couldn't stand another go around. It wasn't until years later I found out he hates Ferris wheels.

The soft brushing of footsteps in the sand outside where I sit alerts me to my uncle's approach. Uncle David squats and peers into the darkness under the boardwalk with eyes nearly as black as coal.

"Hi," I call to him.

He crawls in and sits next to me, wrapping an arm around my shoulder and kissing my temple. "Hello, Pumpkin." He pulls back and studies my now brown hair. "Although Pumpkin doesn't really fit any more. I might need to come up with something else."

"You'd better not."

Bryce slides in to join us. "I picked him up about a mile back. As far as I can tell, he wasn't followed." Bryce reaches out his hand. "Hi, I'm Detective Bryce Cooper with the Western Provincial Police Force." After shaking hands, Bryce takes the spot on my other side.

"Are you going to tell me what's going on?" my uncle asks.

With a deep breath, I launch into my story, bringing him up to speed on everything that's happened since I left home five months ago. My uncle shows no emotion as he listens. Years of being a politician helped him hone his poker face. Bryce fills in details I missed, explaining about his investigation of Peter Benton, and finally pulls out his tablet with the memo Jack found.

Uncle David is quiet for a long moment when he's done reading, letting out a heavy sigh and handing the tablet back to Bryce. "Things are beginning to make a little more sense now."

"What things?" I ask.

"Lost documents, sudden staff reassignments, conversations that stop when I enter a room. A lot of little things that don't seem to be a big deal in isolation, but when you add them up, it's clear something's going on. And if what you've discovered is true..."

"So you believe us?"

"Why wouldn't I?"

I scoop up a handful of sand, letting it sift between my fingers. "Because it's crazy as hell."

"I've known you for most of your life, Evan, and I trust you."

"What was Peter Benton doing in your apartment last night?" I ask, grabbing another fistful of sand.

"He came by to talk about business. It was a routine visit. Why?"

"I saw him talking to a member of your kitchen staff last night," Bryce says.

Uncle David's mouth is set in a grim line. "It's possible he knows someone on my staff, but in light of what you've told me, that's not a given." He glances at his watch. "I need to get going before anyone notices I'm missing."

"What are you going to do," I ask.

"I don't know yet. Give me some time to think about it."

He pulls me in for a hug then reaches over to shake Bryce's hand. "Thanks for looking after my niece." He begins to crawl out before turning back. "How can I reach you?"

"We have to assume all your communications are being monitored," Bryce says.

"Why don't we meet back here in a week," my uncle says. "With or without a plan we can at least touch base. Same time, same place."

"Be careful," I warn him.

We wait fifteen minutes before heading out ourselves, so if anyone is watching him, they'll be long gone before we emerge. We stroll along the beach, attempting to blend in with other autumn beach-goers.

I'm not sure why I thought my uncle would have some answers, but he clearly doesn't know any more than we do. Between the frustration and fear gaining a foothold inside me, my emotions are all over the place. I want to scream and cry, even though neither of those will accomplish anything, but I need to release some of this pent-up stress. Every time we make any kind of progress, we get knocked back down. This isn't two steps forward and one step back. It's one step forward and two steps back.

I don't see how we can do anything from inside the Union. It was worth a try. It's why I came back. But I'm beginning to think our only chance is back out in the Ruins, to join the revolution and find a way to stop it from within.

I glance at Bryce, his jaw working overtime as he's likely processing the worthless meeting we just had with my uncle, and wonder if there is any way I can convince him to come with me.

16 Two Steps Back

ryce paces the room like a caged wildcat, mumbling to himself, while I sit on my bed, pulling at the threads of the blanket, watching him. He finally stops his manic laps around the tiny room and faces me, both of his hands flying to the top of his head.

"I'm worried about your uncle."

"I thought you weren't."

"Benton's up to something, I know it."

I've never seen him like this and he's sort of freaking me out. "Okay…" I push off the bed and walk over to him. "What besides him talking to kitchen staff makes you think that?"

"Earlier this year, when I was investigating him, he was into all kinds of shit." He takes in a deep breath, his hands falling to his sides. "Small stuff that wasn't as important as the weapons smuggling. But what your uncle said, about people being reassigned…What if your uncle's a target? What if Benton's planting people inside his administration?"

"Yeah, that thought occurred to me, too. But at least now my uncle has a heads-up."

He shakes his head. "I need to follow up on this, Evan. I've got to find out what Benton's up to."

"Okay." I grab my jacket off the back of the chair.

"No," he says, putting his hands on my shoulders. "Too many people in this Borough know you."

"I'm not letting you go alone, Bryce."

"This is what I do, I'm a detective." He shrugs into his coat and makes his way to the door. "I'll be back in a few hours."

"Okay. But be careful." He gives me a look like I'd told him not to eat food he found on the sidewalk. "I get you know what you're doing, but people are trying to kill us."

He walks back to me and pulls me into his arms. "I will." He gives me a quick kiss and heads out the door.

After locking the door behind him, I flop on the bed and turn on the display wall. I flip through programs absently, my mind too wrapped up in what Bryce is doing and concern for my uncle to focus on anything else. Before long, this tiny excuse for a room, with its dank air and lack of sunlight, becomes even more cave-like until I feel as if the walls are collapsing around me.

I write Bryce a quick note, grab my jacket, and head outside to fresh air and open space. Dark gray clouds push in from the coast, threatening rain, and I tug my zipper up to my chin to ward off the wind gusting down the alley. A hot drink sounds perfect right about now. I make my way to the nearest cafe, pushing through the door, triggering a chime.

A middle-aged barista with dark hair and a nose ring glances up and smiles. "What can I get you?" she asks.

"Caramel latte, please."

I take off my jacket, draping it across the back of a chair, and turn when the door chimes again. A couple enters, their cheeks and noses pink from the cold. The barista delivers my drink before going to take the couple's order. I pull out my tablet and get engrossed in a thriller, losing track of time and place.

"Is someone sitting here?"

I glance up and see a boy about my age, indicating the chair across from me. "Oh, no. You can take it."

Although based on the overwhelming lack of people here, I'm not sure why he doesn't take a chair from an unoccupied table. Until he drops into the chair flashing a charming smile. He's cute and he knows it.

"Hi, I'm Simon." He thrusts his hand at me, his blue eyes alive with humor.

"Uh…hi." I take his hand, it's rough, calloused. "Delilah."

"Do people call you Lila or Dee for short?"

"Nope, just Delilah."

"Okay, De-li-lah." He drags out my name, making it sound like musical notes. "What're you reading?"

"Oh, umm…a book." I turn off my tablet and study him. Something about him seems almost familiar, although I'm sure I've never met him. "Where are you from, Simon?"

"Here and there. A little bit of everywhere, I guess."

I glance at his fingernails and they're ragged and dirty. He pulls his hands back, shoving them under the table. Chewing on my bottom lip, I try to put the pieces into place. He hides it well, but I detected a slight slow drawl when he spoke. Simon is rugged and evasive. He's from the Ruins.

As if sensing I've figured him out, he stands abruptly. "Well, I was supposed to meet someone, but I guess they didn't show." He flashes me another smile. "It was nice to meet you Delilah," he says before turning and striding out the door.

Does he know who I am, or was that the most random thing ever? I grab my jacket and rush out the door after him, needing answers. He's gone by the time I get to the sidewalk. Not willing to give up yet, I run to the end of the block, checking both directions, but the mysterious Simon has vanished. If he recognized me, he may tell someone.

Bryce is inside the cafe talking to the barista when I return. She points to me and he turns, scowling. "What are you doing here?" he asks, his voice tight.

"I was getting claustrophobic in the cave room. I needed fresh air."

He hands me my tablet and follows me out the door. "I expected you to have more common sense."

I whip around and glare at him. "Hey!"

We stare at each other for a few beats, both of us pissed. He drops his gaze first. "Look, that didn't come out right. I'm sorry. I was scared when I got back to the room and you were gone."

"I left you a note."

He runs his tongue across his teeth as he studies me. "I got it. And I know you're aware of this, but we're not on vacation."

"I know. Okay. You said I couldn't come with you. You didn't say I had to stay in that dingy room. It's not like I'm running around my old neighborhood. No one I know is down here. They wouldn't be caught dead in this part of the Union."

He takes in a deep breath and lets it back out, shaking his head. "Let's get dinner."

He picks up my hand, but I pull it back, still annoyed with him. We walk in tense silence for a couple of blocks before he scratches the back of his head and sighs. "I don't want to fight with you."

I don't want to fight with him either. In fact, other than the one blowup we had when he and Jack were interrogating me, we've never even had an argument. Cyrus and I argued all the time, but Bryce has always been so easy to be with. Which makes me wonder what's going on. This can't be only about me going to the cafe. "What aren't you telling me?"

"Benton's mixed up in something. A couple of guys went into his place, guys not from around here. I couldn't figure out what it was at first, but the way they carried themselves…I'm pretty sure they're from the Ruins."

"There was a guy in the cafe. We talked for a bit. I think he's from the Ruins, too."

Bryce stops, turning toward me. "What did he look like?"

I describe him, but Bryce says he wasn't one of the guys he saw. It can't be a coincidence they're all here in this Borough at the same time.

"The guys were in Benton's place for about an hour before leaving. One of them called out he'd be back tomorrow. Both of them seemed jittery, eyes darting everywhere, like they were afraid of being seen."

"What do you think they were doing there?"

"I don't know, but I'm going back tomorrow to find out."

We eat breakfast in silence, tension filling the air between us. Bryce is worried about my uncle and I'm worried about them both. There's no lighthearted conversation or playful banter. There is chewing and swallowing. And tension. Bryce glances at his watch and rises, pushing his chair back under the table. My heart drops into the pit of my stomach as he takes my hand, leading me out of the restaurant and over to the park nearest our hotel.

"I wish you'd let me come with you," I say again.

He doesn't answer me this time. Instead, he pulls me against him, wrapping his arms around my shoulders. "I love you," he whispers into my hair, and it comes out more like a sigh.

Why did he say that? Is he worried he's not going to come back? Fear and something else I can't identify seizes my chest as he releases me and walks in the direction of the train station. Watching him go, the tightness in my chest gives way to hollowness. I understand the fear, but this is different. Before I realize what I'm doing, I call out to him, "I love you, too," the words sticking in my mouth.

Bryce halts and turns back. Where the hell did that come from? I love Cyrus. I can't love Bryce, too, can I? Bryce's expression is blank as he walks toward me. Maybe he didn't hear, and yet, I want him to. These feelings I have for him are strong, but different from what I *still* feel for Cyrus, even after months apart.

When Bryce reaches me a smile spreads across his face, revealing two perfect dimples. "Say it again."

I lift my gaze to meet his, warmth spreading through me, and I greet his smile with one of my own. "I love you, too."

He takes my face in his hands and pulls my mouth to his. He kisses me deeply before wrapping me in a hug. "I really need to go," he says, releasing me.

I watch him walk across the park until he disappears into the train station then take my time returning to the depressing hotel room. Boredom is almost immediate, so I grab my tablet and text with Colin for a while. He finally texted me back after he arrived up in the Northwestern Province, and we've been texting every day since.

Colin: What r u doing?

Me: Nothing. Waiting. You?

Colin: Laying low. Bored.

Me: Write any new songs?

Colin: Nope. Not feeling inspired.

When even this gets boring, we log off, and I flip through channels on the display before changing into sweats and running shoes. I jog over to the park and do laps, hoping by the time I get back to the hotel, Bryce will be there. But he's not. The least he could do is text me. I take a shower to kill time as much as to rinse the sweat from my body.

Since I only picked at my breakfast, by dinnertime, I'm starving. I leave another note for Bryce and head over to the cafe to get something to eat. After finishing my sandwich, I nurse a cup of coffee and read, but as one hour fades into the next with no word from Bryce, I become convinced something's happened to him.

I've been trying hard not to think about what we said to each other in the park earlier, because it confuses me. But now, with thoughts of his safety front and center, I can't deny I care about him. Care deeply. And yeah, it's different than Cyrus. What I had with

Cyrus was intense and consuming and thrilling. Bryce is warm, comforting, like a hot latte on a cool fall day. I feel better when I'm with him, centered, needed, which only makes the fact he's not back yet that much more nerve-wracking.

Another couple of hours pass and Bryce has now been gone for more than eight hours. My stomach feels as if someone has taken an egg beater to it. I can't focus on my book, and I jump every time someone enters the cafe. When I return to the hotel, the note I wrote remains untouched. Grabbing his key, I check next door, but he's not in his room either, and there's no evidence he's been there since this morning.

I head down to the lobby and watch shadows winding through the park, trying to make out features as people pass beneath the lights. The urge to go find Bryce becomes overwhelming, and I run back upstairs to grab my jacket, figuring I'll start with Benton's place.

As I shrug into my sleeve, the sound of the door opening behind me makes me freeze before whipping around. Bryce walks in the door, and gallons of stress flood out of me. His mouth is set in a tight line, but his eyes brighten when they find mine.

Dropping my coat on the floor, I yell, "Bryce," and fly across the short distance to throw my arms around him. Relief overshadows my need to know where he's been or what happened. My lips press against his hard and desperate, communicating every jumbled emotion spilling through me.

He tugs me against him, kissing me back with equal emotion, if not more. Suddenly he pulls his mouth from mine, placing his hands on my shoulders and pushing me back, his gaze dropping to the floor.

"What's wrong?" I ask, unable to keep the tremor out of my voice.

He glances up and the pain in his eyes nearly tears me apart. "We should talk."

"Is my uncle okay? Are you okay?"

He nods, reaching out to take my hand and leading me to the bed. "Yes. He's fine, I'm fine. It's just…" He sighs and sits, pulling me down next to him, wrapping his arms around me.

"Bryce you're scaring me."

"There's nothing to be scared about. Well, nothing new anyway," he says with a sad chuckle, kissing the top of my head.

"Then whatever it is, it can wait, right?"

He doesn't answer, only pulls me tighter against him.

Thinking back to the park, how we left things, and how I was so terrified tonight something had happened to him, I reach up and press my lips to his. "Tomorrow," I say against his mouth.

He parts his lips and our kiss deepens, his hands sliding up my back, gliding beneath my shirt. His breath quickens when I unbutton his coat, easing it off his shoulders.

"Evansville," he moans and starts to pull back.

I grab his shirt and tug him closer. "Bryce, stop talking," I murmur.

And finally he does.

Bryce and I move together as one in silent communication, our bodies speaking without words. He crushes me against him and I hold on as if my life depends on it. His lips brush my neck, my shoulder, my cheek, my mouth.

I feel closer to him than I've ever felt to anyone, more connected than I thought possible. The darkness of our lives is temporarily replaced by something lighter and more wonderful. It pushes back the evil chasing us and drowns out the constant danger we never seem to be able to escape.

For one far too brief moment, nothing else exists except us.

17 Far Too Brief

My head rests on Bryce's chest, his arms around me, tethering me in the moment. He presses his lips to my forehead. "I love you, Evansville." His chest rumbles beneath my cheek, making me smile.

I tilt my head and gaze up at him. God, he's beautiful. His skin is so smooth, the color of my morning latte. Without his dark contacts, those mesmerizing gray eyes lock onto mine. "Can I ask you something?"

"Sure." The apprehension threading through his voice reminds me he wanted to talk about something. I want to savor this moment, make it last as long as possible, not deal with unpleasant topics. It's like we're on an island and if we can stay a few more hours, I'll be able to get through whatever's next.

"Why do you love me? You can have anyone you want, why me?"

He shifts beneath me and runs his hands up my arms to my shoulders. "First, it's a crazy assumption I can have anyone I want. Second, you're the only one I want, and I was sure I'd blown my chance with you. Third, you have a way of looking at the world that challenges my way of thinking. I think I started falling for you the day we had our first debate in English lit, months before I kissed you. Our first kiss only sealed what I already knew." As if to prove his point, he dips his head, pressing his lips to mine.

"And, finally," he says, his voice huskier, "you're kind of a badass. If I wasn't already crazy stupid in love, you jumping into a raging creek to save me would've pushed me over the edge."

I laugh and kiss his chest. Our island is safe and perfect for a little while longer.

I'm starting to doze off when his voice invades my hazy brain. "Why'd you give me another chance?"

I roll to my side and study his face. "At first, I fell for the beautiful, amazing boy from school everyone had a crush on. Turns out that boy wasn't real, but the man who risked everything to find me in the Ruins is, and he deserved another shot." I pause, blinking back sudden tears from the overwhelming emotions of the past few hours. "Tonight…I thought something happened to you, and I was terrified. I don't want to lose you, too." Oh shit, I didn't mean for it to come out that way. I drop my gaze and stare at his chest. We just had sex and I'm bringing up Cyrus. This is so wrong.

He clears his throat. "Evansville…" his voice is choked. I wait for him to continue, but I'm afraid to look at his face, to see pain I'm responsible for. He reaches for me, pulling me to him. "Why didn't you tell me?"

"Tell you what?"

He lifts my chin, his eyes searching mine. "That it was your first time. I just assumed…I mean after…"

"Oh." The emotion in his eyes hits me hard, and I glance away, unable to hold his gaze. "Because I didn't want to make it a big deal."

His lips brush my forehead. "It *is* a big deal, or at least it should be."

A nervous laugh escapes. "Maybe before. When hiding from people who want to kill me while trying to stop a rebel attack on the Union weren't the biggest concerns in my life."

"Well, I'm honored you wanted to share it with me," he says, his voice soft, like velvet gliding across my skin.

Even though it's wrong to think about Cyrus now, I can't stop myself. Memories of the night out in the Ruins, when I was ready to have sex with Cyrus and he left me, flood my mind. He believes everything happens for a reason, so there must be a reason that night didn't happen and this one did.

Pushing thoughts of Cyrus aside, I lean back, anchoring myself in the present. With Bryce. My eyes search his and I see something warring there, conflict or indecision, but only for a second before it's gone. He wraps strong arms around me, pulling me back to him and kisses my head. I reach up and let my lips find his.

With a quick roll, I'm beneath him, his kiss intensifying. I sigh and get lost in him again, in the here and now, where for a moment, we're free and safe and nothing else matters.

A long "mmmm" escapes my throat as I stretch and reach for Bryce, my hand hitting nothing but blanket. I glance at the clock. It's early, maybe he's in the bathroom. "Bryce…" My eyes drift to a torn piece of paper sitting on the nightstand.

"Evansville, taking care of something. Be back by ten. We need to talk."

With three hours until he gets back, I snuggle under the blankets for a few more minutes before hopping up to shower and dress. A light drizzle greets me when I step outside the hotel to get some coffee. The rain must have come down harder earlier, because puddles gather in low-lying areas. I know I shouldn't, but I take a commuter train to the back wall and head up to the top level to get my morning latte. Being this close to my family, knowing they're only an elevator ride away, is too tempting. If I can walk past the apartment, see it, maybe some of this ache in my chest will ease.

Joe will be at work, the girls in school, but home pulls at me like some sort of magnetic force. Stopping in the first cafe I come to, I take my coffee and stroll along the sidewalk, veering away from the buildings as I approach the apartment, staying near the park. My heart rate picks up as I get closer, a lump lodging itself in my throat. I stop across from the familiar place, remembering my life here. All the good and bad that went on inside those walls. Even my darkest days back then are shiny and bright in comparison to what's happened since I left.

The front door opens and my mom steps outside with Barklyn. I duck behind a tree to watch as she walks him toward the park. Toward me. Slipping around the other side, I slink in the other direction before Barklyn notices me. With my brown hair, cap pulled down, and sunglasses on, it's unlikely my mom will make a quick connection, since I'm not supposed to be here anyway. But dogs are not as easily fooled.

Following the path through the narrow strip of park, I head north to another park my mom would never come to. I sit on a bench as the drizzle gives way to rays of sun. The smell of damp earth and autumn mingle, and birds begin to come out of hiding. A young couple walks in my direction along the meandering path. The girl's arm is through his, their fingers laced. She stops and pulls his face down to kiss him, oblivious to anyone else around them.

I catch a glimpse of his face beneath his ball cap sending my heart to a screeching halt before it takes off at a manic pace. Alivia Benton is kissing Bryce. *My* Bryce.

My coffee slips out of my hand and hits the ground, hot liquid splashing my shoes and jeans. I stand and stare at them, as his hands run up her back to her shoulders. It's as if I can't look away, yet I don't want to see this. My stomach clenches, my pulse pounds, and I'm in danger of hurling. The boy I handed my virginity to on a platter last night has his tongue in the mouth of the girl who beat the shit out of me less than six months ago.

When she pulls back, he smiles down at her, then as if he senses me, his eyes rise and meet mine. His mouth drops open for a second before he shuts it, putting his arm around Alivia and steering her away.

White hot anger screams through my veins. The girl I hate most is with the boy I thought I loved. Seething with rage, I take a step toward them, ready to confront his cheating ass, but close my eyes and take a deep breath. Alivia can't know I'm here. Not if her dad's involved with whatever's going on. Unless Bryce was lying about that, too. Maybe Benton was never in my uncle's apartment.

Turning, I make my way back to the hotel where the bed we shared is a rumpled mess from tangled bodies and deceit. There's no way I can stay here. I throw my stuff into my duffle bag and slam the door behind me. With no clue where I'm going, I move quickly, putting as much distance as possible between me and Bryce.

My feet must know where I'm going, because they take me to the central train station. I buy a ticket to the Northwest, pulling my ball cap further down my head, avoiding the cameras. I shoot a quick text to Colin, letting him know I'm on my way and asking him to meet my train tomorrow afternoon.

Numbness settles in, taking root in my body, keeping me from feeling hurt or anger as the minutes tick by. But once the train arrives and I board, cracks in my foundation begin to form. When we pull out of the station, I head to the bathroom and lock myself in. The floodgates open and the tears fall.

Nausea builds until I have to lean over the toilet and retch. The betrayal stings, pierces my heart, but anger pushes in like an ocean wave, constructing a hardened shell around it. This burns hotter than what I felt after I was kidnapped and discovered he'd lied to me, more than when I discovered my mother lied to me about Eddie.

A knock on the bathroom door startles me. "Are you okay?" a female voice asks.

"Yes." The word comes out twisted like the wail of a tortured animal.

"There's a line out here waiting. If you're okay."

I blow my nose and look in the mirror. My eyes and lips are swollen, my skin blotchy. But I'm done crying over Bryce. Over anyone. I'm just...done. I open the door and ease past the several people waiting in line, returning to my seat.

At least I don't need to worry about getting pregnant. I took care of that at the women's health clinic before we left the Western Province. Life on the run sounded a lot easier without having to deal with my period for the next six months.

Logically, I know there's a very real chance Bryce is using Alivia again. He used her once before to get close to her father. But knowing that doesn't wipe what I saw from my brain. There's also a part of me that wonders how far he's willing to go to gain access to Benton's apartment. What if he slept with Alivia, too? I mean, up until last night, it's not like we were having sex, or doing much of anything else. He'd been sleeping in his own room every night, it would've been easy for him to slip back into his old fake relationship. Hey, it's just part of his cover, right?

Sure, he said we needed to talk, but he could've tried harder. He let me kiss him into silence. My stomach rolls again at the thought he could've slept with me not long after leaving Alivia. I bolt back to the bathroom and toss the remaining contents of my stomach.

Over the next day and a half, I force my thoughts away from Bryce and Alivia and focus on a plan. We've been flying by the seat of our pants since we returned from the Ruins, and that's gotten us nowhere. It's time for concrete planning, I'm done winging it.

When I check my tablet for a response from Colin, his response is a simple "K", but there's a text from Bryce.

I'm sorry, Evansville, but...

I delete it unread. I can't let him suck me back in with lame excuses or lies. From the night on the beach when we discussed plans, he and Jack wanted to investigate, follow protocol, do things their way. We tried it their way and it didn't work. It's time to try something different.

18 My Way

When I check my tablet an hour before we're due to arrive in the Northwestern Province, there's another text from Colin.

Colin: Hey I'm getting texts from everyone. What should I say?

There's also another one from Bryce. I delete Bryce's and respond to Colin.

Me: Tell them I'm fine. But that's all for now

Colin: K. Are you gonna tell me what's going on?

Me: Yes. Later

Once I'm in the Ruins, he can tell the others whatever he wants, but until then, I don't want anyone to know. They'll try to stop me, tell me it's too dangerous, but I'm not any safer in the Union.

I almost walk past Colin when I get off the train, forgetting he's now a blond instead of the dark-haired boy I'm used to. Colin smiles and swallows me in a hug. He smells of coffee and fresh air, familiar, safe. I've missed my best friend. He grabs my bag and slings it over his shoulder.

We make small talk about my trip and what life is like in the Northwestern Province while we ride the commuter train to where he lives. Everything is so green here, like a leprechaun threw up all over it. Colin leads me from the depot up two flights of stairs and down an alley to a long apartment building. The outside is weathered wood with richly painted trim and window boxes spilling with greenery. Colin unlocks a door on the second floor, opening into a small apartment. It's bare except for an old tan couch positioned in front of a large picture window, overlooking a nearby park.

He sets my bag on the floor. "Want some coffee?"

"Yes, please."

After messing around in the kitchen for several minutes, he joins me on the surprisingly comfortable couch, handing me a mug. "So…what's up, EvTay?"

I stare out at a stand of towering evergreens. The northwest boasts more parks than any other Province. From here, I can see at least four. "Can we go for a walk?"

"Sure. Finish your coffee and I'll take you to Pacific Park."

After taking a few more sips, I set my mug on the counter and head over to the door. Colin slings an arm over my shoulder as we walk. "Out with it," he demands.

I let out a long shaky breath. "I slept with Bryce. The next morning I saw him kissing Alivia."

"EvTay…" he starts, his face contorted as if he's in pain. But what can he say? Bryce is ass and I'm an idiot. Nothing he can say will change that.

"Did you talk to him?" Colin asks.

"No. He was with…I just….I couldn't face him after everything. I mean, I threw myself at him. He tried to stop me, said we needed to talk. What if he didn't want to?"

Colin chokes back a laugh. "Of course he wanted to. He's a guy. We *all* want to. Look, I don't know what happened, but I know Bryce cares for you. The way he was out in the Ruins, that wasn't out of guilt. And I saw his face when you were with Cyrus at the bridge. That wasn't the face of indifference."

"Then why was he with Alivia right after…we…you know?"

Colin blows out a slow breath and shrugs. "For some guys, it's all about the chase. Bryce's had it easy when it comes to girls."

"What about you? You've had your pick of girls. How many have you dated?"

"That's different."

It's not, though. He loves Lisa, and he isn't out with anyone else even though Lisa is with Jack. Bryce had me and left my bed before the sun even came up to meet Alivia, kiss her, and who knows what else.

"Tell me what happened, skipping the intimate details," Colin says.

I fill him in on breaking into my uncle's and why Bryce was investigating Alivia's dad.

When I'm done, Colin stops, turning me around to face him. "How do you know he wasn't using her again?"

"I thought about that, and I suppose it's possible, but that doesn't change the fact he was examining her mouth with his tongue. How convincing does he need to be? I mean he looked really happy with her."

Colin pulls me against his chest and hugs me tightly. "I don't know, but you don't either, because you took off without talking to him. You do that a lot, and you need to stop."

"You're one to talk," I say, pulling back from him. "You just up and moved here because you couldn't handle being around Lisa and Jack."

"Point made. Let's not think about Bryce or Lisa for the next hour, okay? Just enjoy the park. You're going to love this."

We follow a lazy stone walkway lined with moss and low-growing snow cap. As we approach the park, tall evergreens unlike any I've ever seen flank the entrance. The bottom ten feet of trunk is devoid of branches, but instead of bark, the trees are striped with bright shades of orange, indigo, yellow, and magenta. When we get closer, I realize the stripes are actually yarn. "Who knits sweaters for trees?"

Colin laughs. "Aren't they cool? A bunch of artisans up here make them."

"Who on earth has time for that? Although they are festive, I guess." The Ruins are so much a part of me now. I never would've considered this a waste of time before, but thanks to Draya and her comments on the abundance of my leisure time that allowed me to paint my toenails, I see things through more jaded eyes these days.

A gentle rain begins to drift down from above and we run to a covered walkway.

"Most of the parks here include covered paths," Colin says. "It rains a lot here. I mean a *lot,* like every day. I hated it when I first got here, but it's grown on me."

I hook my arm through his. "Are you hungry?"

He lifts an incredulous eyebrow as if he can't believe I asked him that. "Come on, I know the perfect place for lunch."

We walk to a sandwich shop, but I'm not hungry. I force down some soup and reach for a piece of sourdough bread. One bite and I'm in love. I've never had anything quite like this, with its crusty outer shell and chewy insides loaded with those spores, or whatever they are, that create the intense sour taste. I find enough of my missing appetite to scarf down two more pieces.

On the walk back to the apartment, I drop my bombshell. "I'm going back into the Ruins. After I'm gone, you can text the others where I went."

"Nope."

"What do you mean, 'nope'?"

"I mean, nope I'm not sending a text after you go into the Ruins. I'll send one before we *both* go. I am not spending another day by myself in this Province. I'm coming with you."

"So you can buy stuff out there?" Colin asks.

"Dude, you spent two months in the Ruins."

He shrugs. "Yeah, but Bryce and Jack took care of all that. I wasn't paying much attention."

I raise an eyebrow.

"Well, it wasn't like I thought I'd ever be going back."

I finish sewing up a pocket inside the waistband of my jeans and start on another one. We'll hide cash inside these in case anyone jumps us out in the Ruins. We've spent the past week planning our trip and making lists of everything we think we're going to need.

When Colin is done with his pants, we head out to purchase the rest of the supplies.

Rain pelts us as we step outside into the soggy wet northwest weather. I zip my coat up all the way and stuff my hands in my pockets to keep my fingers from pruning. After grabbing coffee, we slog our way over to a sporting goods store. Colin pushes through the door, and I follow him, trailing water across the stone floor.

A dark-haired teen wearing an Epic Vinyl T-shirt lifts his head from his tablet when Colin's shoes squeak on the wet tiles. "Need any help?"

"Camping gear?" Colin asks.

The boy walks around the counter and leads the way upstairs to a floor with nothing but camping stuff.

Like two kids in a toy store, Colin and I grab everything in sight. Tents, backpacks, sleeping rolls, canteens, and non-perishable food.

Colin picks up a small propane cooktop. "Hey, what about this?"

I love the idea of instant fire, but we can only take so much. "How much do you want to carry?"

"Good point."

"Why are these so heavy?" I ask, picking up a couple of flashlights.

Colin hands me a package of spare batteries. "There isn't enough sunlight up here to recharge them. See, they're not solar-powered."

"Seriously?"

"The weather you're experiencing right now? This is pretty much it. Maybe a little more sun in the summer."

"Okay, then."

We take our stuff downstairs and set it on the counter to be rung up.

"You heading out to the coast this weekend?" the kid asks.

"Yeah, we're thinking about going to the caves," Colin says.

I resist the urge for an explanation, but on the walk back, I need to ask. "The caves?"

"Yeah. They're really cool. There're a ton of caves here down at the beaches. People camp in them all the time."

"That's both creepy and pretty awesome."

Back at his apartment, Colin and I touch up each other's roots before packing. We grab Chinese takeout and sit on the floor in front of the couch to eat.

"Hey, do you know how to get out into the Ruins from here?" I ask.

He glances up mid-bite, and shakes his head. "No, I thought you did. This is your brainchild."

"I was forced out through a hole in the wall against my will. How'd you get out when you were looking for me?"

He swallows a mouthful of chow mein. "Bryce and Jack had a contact. He showed us."

"Okay, well…I guess we can go down to the lower levels and find a way out. How hard can it be?"

Warm maple syrup teases my nose as steam rises from the plate of fluffy pancakes in front of me. I pick up a strip of crispy bacon, dunking it into the syrup before taking a bite, my mouth flooding as the two very different flavors hit my tongue. Colin stabs his fork into a melon cube and pops into his mouth. We eat until we're stuffed, not knowing when our next hot meal will be.

"Okay, I'm sending them a text. How does this sound?" Colin asks. "'We're heading out. Not feeling safe here.' Do you think they'll understand that?"

"It's almost too cryptic."

"Fine, what should I say?"

I rub my forehead with the back of my hand and think through a number of ideas, but none is any better than Colin's. "What about, 'We're together. Going back, see what we can find out'?"

"How is that any different than what I said?"

"Well, it tells them why, for one."

"Why else would we go back there?"

I roll my eyes at him. "Just send it." Next I text Eddie.

Me: I'm OK. I need to do something tho. Don't worry.

I turn off my tablet before he has a chance to respond. If he starts asking questions, I'm either going to have to lie to him, or get into a big argument via text. Colin and I pay our bill, dropping a few dollars on the table for a tip, and head down to the ground level.

Instead of moving toward the trains like everyone else, we duck into the tunnels. Pipes traverse the walls carrying waste away from homes and businesses to be cleaned and recycled for use in agriculture. Conduit snakes its way overhead, delivering power from the solar, wind, and tidal grids throughout the Union.

"So, is this the plan?" Colin asks.

I give him a sidelong glance.

"What? I think it's a fair question. We just wander around hoping to spot a door leading into the Ruins?"

I shrug. "I figured there'd be doors here somewhere, but if you have a better idea, I'm all ears."

After another good long stretch of running my hands all over the walls without results, I'm beginning to wonder if I was wrong about doors to the Ruins being more plentiful.

A crack of light appears in the side of the wall fifty yards from us, and Colin grabs my arm, yanking me back. The crack grows as a door opens, and a body slithers in, closing the door behind them. Whoever it is peers down the tunnel in the opposite direction, allowing us to slip around the corner and out of sight. After a moment, Colin peeks his head out before reaching for my hand and dragging me behind him.

We reach the spot in the wall where the light was, and our hands explore. The pads of my fingers soon become raw from dragging over the rough concrete surface, but after running up, down, and across several feet, they catch in a narrow channel.

"I got it," I call softly to Colin who's exploring a few feet away.

Sliding the tips of my fingers along the channel until I find an indentation, I press. With a click, the line of light appears, and sunlight slips through from outside. I can't fight a smile as I push through the door and step out into the Ruins.

Book 2 – The Ruins

The Ruins

Soft undergrowth spreads out in front of us like a dark green ocean. The ground is a patchwork of moss, ferns, and a variety of plants I can't name, all coated with a light dusting of pine needles from above. Once the forest swallows us, the buzz of life we left behind disappears. The silence is both tranquil and unnerving after the never-ending hum in the Union. Our footsteps crunch as we walk, but the sound is dwarfed by the massiveness of nature surrounding us.

"Who do you think that was coming into the Union?" I ask Colin.

He shrugs. "We're not supposed to know the Ruins are inhabitable. Whoever that was knows a helluva lot more than the average Union citizen."

"When Bryce was staking out Benton's place, he was pretty sure some of the people he saw hanging out there were from the Ruins. Do you think people are coming and going freely?"

"Maybe."

If they're smuggling guns into the Union to start the attack from within, they might be bringing people in, too.

We hike for several hours without seeing evidence of other humans, although we come upon the remnants of life in the former United States when I literally trip over it. Colin reaches out a hand to catch me, but I slip, landing on my knee on what appears to be very old railroad tracks. Unlike the single sleek broad titanium track the Union trains use, these are narrow parallel steel rails with wooden slats in between. The rotted wood gives way, revealing squirming white bugs. I hop up and move back, brushing splinters, dirt, and insects from my jeans. Most of the slats are covered with moss, and vines wind their way up between them, wrapping around the rails.

With no better plan, we follow the tracks deeper into the Ruins. Rain continues to fall at a steady pace, but much of it is absorbed by the canopy above, with only a gentle mist reaching us. We stop for lunch, sitting on the damp ground, and Colin pulls out some trail mix.

"I can't believe this is the Ruins," Colin says.

"Right? I didn't expect it to be so different up here. The lies we were told were easier to accept when we were in the southwest, but here, life is…everywhere." A chipmunk darts across our path, as if illustrating my point.

"Should we continue to follow the tracks?" Colin asks.

"Well, trains used to lead to towns, and Cyrus said people still live in some of the smaller towns."

Saying Cyrus's name aloud sends a mixture of pain and longing spiraling through me. No amount of time or physical distance has taken the edge off my feelings for him. What if I never get over him? I thought finally with Bryce, I was starting to. Apparently not.

After hiking in quiet contemplation for a while, we lapse into comfortable banter the way we did back in school. He tells me what he'd been doing up in the northwest and I fill in more details about what Bryce and I were up to back east. Stuff we didn't share in our text messages.

"So, what about Cyrus?" Colin asks. "Are we going to look for him?"

"That's not part of our plan, and anyway, I don't know where he is. We could spend years trying to find him, and even if I found him, he's probably moved on. It's not like we agreed to wait for each other or anything."

"Mmm," he says.

"Maybe after this is all over, I can try to find him. But seeing Bryce with Alivia was brutal, seeing Cyrus with someone else might just kill me."

We don't talk any more about Cyrus or Bryce or Lisa for the rest of the day. We've probably covered close to twenty miles by the time the light fades, turning the sky a deep indigo.

"We should find a place to camp for the night," Colin says.

We survey the area for level ground to pitch the tent, clearing twigs, rocks, and pine needles from the spot. After setting up, we gather wood for a fire but everything is too damp from the rain.

Instead, we eat our nuts and dried fruit inside without hot tea before curling up in our sleeping bags.

I think I'm asleep the moment my head hits the ground. Until a loud noise outside awakens me. A noise that sounds a lot like a growl.

I bolt upright. "Colin," I whisper shout. "What was that?"

"Unk," he says, sitting up and scrubbing a hand across his face. The snuffling growl comes again, and his eyes widen, no longer half asleep.

All we have are a couple of hunting knives to defend ourselves. The strange animal noises are accompanied by rustling, and I scoot closer to Colin, my heart pounding. The clattering and grunting outside continues, and we sit huddled together until the sounds trail off. I blow out a breath I didn't realize I was holding. My shoulders drop, and I move toward the tent flap to investigate, freezing when I hear something sniffing…smelling *us*.

The silhouette of a giant paw pushes against the side of the tent and I swallow a scream. Colin grabs the heavy flashlight and holds it over his head, like he's going to beat the giant beast with it. I grip the knife tighter, but after more snuffling and some grunting, the sounds drift away again. We wait a few moments in case it comes back again, before Colin crawls to the opening and unzips a corner, peeking out.

"Shit."

"What?" My heart races into my throat as I crawl up behind him and peek under his arm.

"Whatever that thing was ripped our backpacks apart and ate all our food."

"You left the packs outside?"

"No," he says, glancing down at me. "*We* did."

"Crap," I say under my breath. I was so tired when I crawled into my sleeping bag, all I thought about was closing my eyes. "What are we going to do without anything to eat?"

"I don't know."

I sit in disbelief over our predicament awhile longer before realizing we can't do anything else until dawn and try to get a little more sleep.

Soft morning light filters through the beige canvas the next time I wake, filling me with a renewed sense of hope. Stretching and slipping outside without disturbing Colin, I survey the damage. One of the backpacks is destroyed, but the other one is salvageable. I stuff all the clothes that are strewn about into the one usable backpack. We still have our canteens, sleeping bags, and the tent.

Colin sits up, his hair rumpled, eyes still heavy with slumber.

"So what do you think we should do?" I ask.

He yawns and steps out of the tent, stretching. "We can't go back to the Union, people there want us dead. We can only hide out for so long. If we don't figure this thing out, we have no future. I say we push on. We can find stuff out here to eat, right?"

"Maybe…" I'm less confident than he is. At least in the Union we'd be able to get food, but Colin's right – eating and hiding out from whomever is trying to kill us isn't much of a life. Not to mention the impending attack if we can't figure out how to stop it.

Colin finds a way to attach both sleeping rolls to the one backpack, which he puts on, and I carry the tent and our canteens. We set off, following the train tracks again, and I scan the ground and trees for something edible, spotting a pinecone. Pinecones must have nuts, because I've eaten pine nuts. Picking it up, I smash it against a tree trunk until it splits open, but there are no nuts inside.

"You're the one who lived out here," Colin says.

"Yeah, but they grew their own food and hunted. I can set a snare, but we have to be willing to hang out long enough to catch something. And if we find a stream, we can fish."

"We'll look for water, then, and if we don't find anything by tonight, you can do the snare thing."

When we drain the last of our fresh water from the canteens, we refill them by capturing rain running off leaves. The day wears on and we make slow but steady progress. Colin is surprisingly upbeat. I expected him to be sulking and moody like he usually is when he's gone too long without food.

Darkness falls, and we decide to make camp to save our flashlight batteries. We may be able to trade them along with Colin's watch for something to eat if we can find a town. I drop the tent, and Colin begins to set it up, while I search for sticks to carve for the snare.

The scent of something familiar touches the air, like an escaping dream. I inhale deeply, trying to place it. Smoke. Wood smoke and something…cooking.

"Do you smell that?" Colin asks.

"I do."

He grins. "Let's go."

"Hang on," I say. He turns back toward me, brows drawn together. "Let's scope things out first, okay? Get a feel for the situation before we go barging in."

"Okay, but I'm hungry."

"Colin…" I shake my head. "Look, I get you probably had different experiences in the Ruins than I did, and I met some awesome people. People I love. But not everyone here is awesome."

We grab our gear and head in the direction of the heavenly aroma, picking our way with careful steps in the dark. Rounding a bend, we come upon a clearing with an ancient house sitting in the center. The small wooden dwelling is covered in moss. Vines climb the sides, curving up and over the eaves to join a cluster of dwarf pines that have taken root on the roof. A stone chimney perches on one end, smoke snaking up into the night sky.

Colin and I glance at each other, we can't be sure whoever's inside is friendly. With a quick shrug, Colin leaves the decision to me.

"Okay, let's do this," I say.

We approach the house, and Colin lifts his hand, rapping firmly on the weathered door. We wait a moment or two before Colin knocks again, harder this time. No one answers, but with a fire burning in the fireplace, someone must be home. Colin tries the door, twisting the knob, and pushing it open. "Hello…" he calls out.

No answer comes, but the fire is warm and inviting. And the house is dry.

"What do you think?" I ask. "Should we wait inside? Someone will be back soon."

He shrugs. "You tell me. What's the protocol?"

"I don't think there's a single set of customs governing the Ruins."

Before we can decide what to do, the distinct clicking of a rifle being cocked behind us, shuts us both up.

20 Protocol

"**S**hit," I mutter. "Don't move."

"Trust me, I'm barely breathing," Colin says through clenched teeth.

"Who are you and what are you doing here?" comes a raspy female voice behind us.

"Uh…we were passing by and were hoping to trade for some food," I answer.

"Turn around," she commands.

Lifting my hands above my shoulders, I turn to face a girl barely five feet tall, pointing a rifle at my chest.

"I'm Evan. This is my friend, Colin."

Her gaze shifts from me to Colin and back to me. "Evan did you say?"

I nod.

She tilts her head to the side, studying me. "That's an unusual name for a girl."

What's the deal with my name? The girl doesn't take her eyes off us, but mine drift down to gauge how tense her trigger finger is. Her shoulders drop and she slings the rifle over her shoulder. "It's okay," she calls out.

Three bodies materialize from the shadows and flank the first girl. Two guys and another girl.

"Well, are you going to go inside or stand out in the rain all night?" the raspy girl asks.

With another glance at Colin, I decide to take a chance and enter the house. The fire sends an orange glow dancing across the walls, snapping and spitting into the chimney. The raspy girl sets her rifle on a table. "I'm Rainey, and this is Ilona, Alexander, and Zak."

Colin reaches out his hand. "Colin."

I set our gear on the floor next to the door and step farther into the house, letting the warmth surround me. Rainey and Ilona, a tall girl with long hair hanging in wet ropes, light candles around the room. In the soft lighting, I get a better view of Rainey. She's quite pretty with wavy brown hair reaching the middle of her back, big dark eyes, and a smattering of freckles across her nose. A long scar starting above her left ear runs down to her jawline, giving her an almost fierce beauty.

"Have you eaten yet?" Ilona asks, her pale skin glowing in the candlelight.

"No," Colin answers. "Something got into our food last night, so we haven't eaten since yesterday. We can trade for supplies, though."

"Not necessary," Rainey says. "At least not right now. Have some stew and a good night's sleep. We can talk in the morning."

I turn to Colin, and he shrugs. His eyes are glassy as he fixates on the aroma coming from the kitchen area. We sit at the rough-hewn wood table surrounded by large stumps serving as seating. Rainey hands us each a spoon and a bowl of vegetable stew.

"Thanks," I answer for the both of us.

I close my eyes and let the rich gravy float down my throat, sighing with contentment. Colin, on the other hand, lets loose a deep groan that almost sounds dirty. God, he's embarrassing. I cut him a look, but he's oblivious, shoveling stew in his mouth as fast as he can.

Rainey chuckles and she and the other three rustle about the room while we eat. I want to make sure we communicate how grateful we are. One thing I know about people in the Ruins is they're very slow to trust outsiders, but generous once they do. I'm not quite sure why they were so quick to trust us, or if we should trust them.

Even though I thought I'd be pruned for life, the fire chases the last of the moisture from my hair and skin. Our sleeping bags are still damp, so Ilona brought us blankets. Colin and I stake out a spot in front of the fireplace to curl up for the night. The floor is hard, but that's my only complaint, and one I keep to myself. I close my eyes, and the events of the day roll through my mind like a movie until sleep takes me.

When I wake in the morning, Colin is out cold. Someone must have tended to the fire, because it's snapping and popping with a healthy vigor at the moment. I push up and fold my blankets. The house seems to be even older than I thought. Last night, there was sort of a charming warmth in the fire's glow, but in the light of day, it appears far less charming and more beat to shit.

I throw on a dry pair of jeans and long-sleeve thermal shirt hanging by the fire, letting the heat from them penetrate my chilled skin, warming me. Shrugging into my jacket, I head outside to look around. The house is the only building in the clearing, isolated from any other signs of civilization, which means we likely haven't stumbled upon the outskirts of a town.

"Morning. Sleep well?" Rainey says behind me.

I spin around. "Yeah. Thanks again for…everything."

"Sure." She cocks her head, studying me again. This is getting weird. She seems particularly interested in my hair. I reach up to tuck in a few out-of-control curls.

"Is something wrong?" I ask.

She smiles. "One thing there's never a shortage of out here is gossip. Word spread like wildfire about a redheaded Uni girl named Evan getting into some trouble with Walker." She tips her head to the side, taking me in from head to toe. "You're definitely a Uni."

I feel the color drain from my face and force myself to blink. "Wh-where did you hear about me?" I realize too late I just confirmed my identity for her.

"Where didn't I? Well, that's not entirely true. From what I can tell, no one up here has heard of you, but down south…" She moves next to me and leans against the house, glancing at me with an amused expression. "What I want to know, though, is why you're here. Why'd you come back?"

I chew on my lip and think how best to answer. I can't tell her the real reason. "It's a long story."

"I've got time."

"Wait, if you're from down south, what're you doing all the way up here?" I ask.

"Trying to stay ahead of the Uprising. Lot of people migrating up this way. But you didn't answer my question."

"No, I didn't." Lack of trust goes both ways.

"Tell you what. You tell me why you're out here, and you don't owe us anything for dinner last night."

I lift an eyebrow.

She holds out her hands. "Fair deal. You didn't eat much."

I'm not about to tell her we're out here to join the armed rebels so we can bring them down. So I blurt out the first thing that comes to me. "I fell in love."

She folds her arms across her chest and studies me. She nods as if she's decided to believe me for now. It might not be the reason I'm out here, but it is true.

"So do you live out here alone? Or are we near a town?"

"Here? No. We're passing through. This house is used by people like us. We heard about it from some others."

"When you say lots of people are migrating up this way…from where?"

"From everywhere. We're from the desert southwest. We fled the town where we grew up when the Uprising swept through and started grabbing everyone over the age of fifteen." That's the second time she's mentioned the Uprising and it's no coincidence. It's also no coincidence she mentioned Walker. "They used to only take volunteers. They'd offer six months' worth of supplies in exchange for able-bodied men and women over eighteen to join up."

"So, like a soldier of fortune?"

"In the beginning. At least that's how they made it sound. They said they were starting a movement to force the Union to open their doors to us. They call it the Uprising."

"You said they used to."

"I guess there aren't enough takers anymore. Now they take everyone they want. Girls and boys as young as fifteen, like a forced draft. And they don't even care if you believe in their cause. They'll beat you into loyalty if necessary."

I fight the shudder threatening to roll through me. "I lived out here long enough to know people don't love the Union. Why weren't there more volunteers? Seems like they'd have more soldiers than they knew what to do with."

"You'd think. It started out that way, but the Uprising isn't what they claimed."

"What do you mean?"

She gives me a strange look and shakes her head. "Let's just say their prime directive is a fluid target."

"I can understand why you're trying to avoid them."

"We're constantly on the move. Staying in one place too long will get you caught, and once you're in, there's almost no getting out."

I suck in a breath. What we're up against may be a no-win situation. If we go back home, we might survive the hit squad, but not the attack, and we'd never be able to relax and stop watching over our shoulder. But if we stay out here, join the Uprising, we may not get out alive. So what's the point?

"Are you okay?" Rainey asks. "You're all pale and shit. Not that you weren't before, but now you're even whiter."

I nod, although I don't feel okay.

"So where you headed?" she asks.

"I…I don't know."

"You came back out here to find a guy. Any idea where he is?"

I shake my head. "Last time I saw him, he was heading north."

"Lots of people migrating to the border. If they made it up this far without being caught, we can ask around."

"Wait. We?"

Her mouth twitches at the corners. "No offense, but you won't survive more than a few days on your own. You already let a bear eat your food."

"Why would you do that? You don't even know us."

"No. Let's just say I'm paying a debt."

"You don't owe us anything."

"No. But a stranger did something for me once, and the only thing asked of me was to pay it forward. All I ask of you is the same. Someday, you help someone else who needs it."

"Thanks, Rainey. I'm serious, thanks…" But the rest of my gratitude dies on my tongue as the full meaning behind her words sinks in. Could Cyrus and the others have made it up this far, and if so, can we really find them?

21 The Uprising

"**H**iking on the tracks is a good way to get caught," Rainey says as we pick our way along a narrow path through thick growth in a heavily wooded area.

Of course it is. Colin raises his eyebrows at me in silent acknowledgment of my own thoughts of how stupid we were. I thought the Uprising was this small, secret organization we'd need to figure out a way to get into. Turns out, we're damn lucky we're not already members. What the hell was I thinking? I guess I was thinking Cyrus said he believed in me, and his belief almost made me believe in myself.

Cyrus is too smart to think I'm capable of this, though. He must've been telling me what he thought I needed to hear to get me to go home. He probably figured out I was more effort than I was worth, or I was responsible for Lucien's death, and he couldn't bear to be with me anymore. Maybe he realized he didn't really love me. I mean that happens, right? I have no business trying to find him. This is a crazy, stupid plan.

"So where're we headed?" Colin asks Rainey.

"Up near the border. We should be safe there, and perhaps we can find your friends in the process."

Colin quirks an eyebrow in my direction. That's not what we came for, but I haven't had a chance to tell him about my conversation with Rainey yet. I shrug, trying to communicate we'll talk later.

Alexander falls in step next to me. He's tall, even taller than Colin, with a husky build. He looks like he could tear apart almost anything with his bare hands. His short, fuzzy hair and soft brown eyes make him seem less menacing, so I concentrate on those instead of his weaponized physique.

"Rainey tells me my reputation precedes me."

He smiles down at me. "Yeah, you're kinda famous."

"I doubt any of it's true."

He eyes me. "Perhaps not. For one, you don't have red hair."

I can't help myself, I bust out laughing. He eyes me like I might be insane, and before I can ask him what else he's heard, he drops back to walk with Ilona.

Colin waits for me to catch up, and we walk together in quiet conversation as the morning lapses into afternoon, stopping only for lunch. By early evening, the effects of walking for two days are taking their toll. Blisters bite the bottoms of my feet, and a slow ache climbs my calves. We didn't train for this during the lazy months spent back home.

Rainey freezes in place. "Keep quiet," she whispers, motioning for us to move back.

We duck into the nearby undergrowth, the constant rain helping muffle our movements. Rainey pulls her rifle down from her shoulder and cocks it, slipping behind a tree before joining us on the ground. Voices grow louder as they near.

Through parted leaves, I watch a large group of people march by on the path we were on only minutes ago. They're led by a girl not much older than me and a boy about my age or even younger, dressed in military fatigues. They're followed by boys and girls of various ages, some seeming to enjoy themselves, chatting and laughing. In the center of the group are some kids who appear quite young, their faces drawn, and a few have their hands bound in front.

Bringing up the rear are two men at least a decade older than the others. They're also wearing fatigues, rifles at the ready, eyes sweeping the area. In the middle of the pack is a young girl with dark blond hair, who can't be more than twelve or thirteen. The terror in her eyes causes my heart to skip a beat. Then those large brown eyes zero in on mine. Somehow she sees me. I pull back further into the foliage and suck in my breath, hoping she doesn't say anything.

After they pass, we come out of hiding and continue on, well off the path. In the time I've been gone, the Ruins has morphed into something even more dangerous. The idea of finding safe harbor among this wild beauty seems remote. I'm beginning to believe there's nowhere we'll ever truly be safe.

Once darkness falls and continuing on is more hazardous than not, we make camp for the night. Rainey picks a spot in a heavily forested area far from the trail, not risking a fire. There are four tents between the six of us, but we separate into only two — one for the girls and one for the boys. With three of us in a tent designed for two, it's cozy, although the temperature will drop as the night wears on.

Lying on my back, staring up into darkness, I finally unleash my questions. "Where are they taking them, those kids?"

"To the closest Uprising camp," Ilona says.

"They'll separate them," Rainey says, "taking the enthusiastic ones to the training camps and teaching them how to kill. They don't tell them they're probably all gonna die. The others will be taken to the indoctrination area where they'll be taught to embrace the Uprising."

I roll onto my stomach, propping my chin up on my fists. "I don't understand something. When I was out here over the summer, we didn't see any of this. No one knew anything about an Uprising."

"They're ramping up operations, expanding into new areas, like they're approaching some sort of deadline," Rainy says. "They're becoming less organized and more frenzied and frantic."

"That seems like the opposite of how things should be. Shouldn't they be getting more organized?"

"They're training children. How organized can they be?" Ilona says.

She's got a point. A horrible, disturbing point. "What are they hoping to do then?"

Rainey fingers the zipper on her sleeping bag. "When the Uprising first started, they talked about doing great things for the Ruins. It wasn't so much about a war as about negotiating. But those without power don't have much leverage to negotiate with those in power, so arming people made sense. They made it sound like they were putting together an army to force the Union to meet at a bargaining table.

"At first, they were selective about who they'd take. They claimed to only want the best of the best — smart, educated, strong young people who vigorously believed in the cause. Now they're taking everyone. They used to train people to fight, stressing they didn't think it would even come to that. Now they're getting these kids ready to, I don't know what, but not fight to win. It's almost as if they expect most of them not to come back."

I push back at the chill running through me, threatening to steal my thoughts and plunge me into a terror-fueled panic. "If they don't want to negotiate, what do they want?"

"That's the thing," Rainey says. "I don't know. The group today…some of those kids were younger than fifteen. And they're promoting anyone with even a hint of leadership abilities. It's like they're creating a massive killing machine. I'm not sure what they think they're going to accomplish anymore. None of this makes sense."

Is this a change in strategy or was it always the plan? They might've figured out they can't get the Union to sit down to negotiate, leaving them with no choice but to attack. Or it's possible they always planned on bringing down the Union. A thought strikes me. "Rainey, how do you know so much about this?"

"Because," she says, sliding her shirt off her shoulder revealing a tattoo. "I used to be a Commander in the Uprising."

Rainey's shoulder is inked with an intricate design. The letter U sits in the center of a circle, surrounded by ornate filigree and flourishes. "I thought you said no one gets out."

She pulls her shirt back up and shrugs. "I said almost no one. As Commander of the training camp, I had a lot more freedom than most, plus access to an arsenal of weapons. It isn't hard to escape when you're in charge of an entire camp. I told the guards I was going to check on something and never went back. That's why we can't stay put. If they find me, I'm dead."

"You keep saying, 'they.' Who are 'they'?"

"Each camp has its own Commander and a team of leaders, but at the top of the ugly monster is another organization pulling all the strings. I don't know much about where the orders come from, but sitting at the controls is a guy named Walker. The name familiar?"

The tent spirals around me as the oxygen leaves my lungs. The guy who kidnapped me and Colin, who tried to kill us, is orchestrating this whole thing?

"Yeah, figured that'd ring a bell. You wonder why you're famous? Now you know."

I pull on my gloves and scrunch a knit cap on my head, my curls fanning out underneath. Colin and I drop back as we walk, our breaths hanging heavy in the moist air.

"Interesting conversation in our tent last night," Colin says quietly.

"Same here."

"This thing is bigger and bolder than we thought," he says, tension lacing his voice. "What the guys told me sounds like they're recruiting for something more than a loosely organized rebellion."

Then I tell him what Rainey shared with me last night.

"Walker? You're sure that's what she said?" His breathing becomes shallow as he absorbs the news.

I lift an eyebrow in his direction.

"Fine, I get it. You're sure. *Shit.*"

"Yeah, and he's in the Union right now, Colin."

"What do you think that means?"

"Rainey thinks they're training an army of kids to die fighting."

"She might be right," he says, hunching his shoulders and adjusting his backpack. "It might've been the plan all along."

"Do you think Walker's from the Union or from out here?"

"No clue, but we do know he's working with people inside the Union."

"But is this being orchestrated by people out here or in the Union?"

"The Union has the money, which means they probably get a lot of say in how it's spent. But if you think about it, the ones who have the most to gain or lose are the people of the Ruins."

A sudden thought enters my head. "Colin, what if it's neither?"

"What do you mean? Who else would it be?"

"The group we saw go by were wearing fatigues and carrying weapons. Those military supplies aren't made in the Union. Sure Union money can buy them, but they need to get them from *somewhere*. What if this is being driven from the north?"

"Like the Northern Territories?"

"Yeah. I mean if you can believe history, and I'm not sure we can anymore, when Canada fell apart after the Second Civil War, so many people suffered. The Territories didn't close themselves off from most of the world like we did. With all the refugees fleeing up there during the war, a lot of the Territories' citizens must be descendants of those refugees. They might be pissed enough to want to help the Ruins. Plus Rainey said people are migrating up to the border because it's safer. Makes sense if they're behind this. They wouldn't be taking their own people."

"Why would they let potential soldiers hide out up there?"

I shrug. "Maybe they're only funding it, but manning it isn't their concern."

Colin shakes his head. "That sounds pretty wild, but then this whole thing is crazy."

We walk on through the morning only stopping for a quick lunch. The forest around us gives way to more open land spotted with clusters of trees rather than thick groves of them. By late afternoon, we approach a small single-story concrete structure.

"Are you ready to go for a little ride?" Rainey calls back to us.

Inside the building is a large wagon with titanium wheels and rubber tires. A couple of guys are nearby, grooming a pair of horses. They stop and turn toward us, stiffening.

Rainey pushes past the rest of us and approaches them. The one with the beard smiles broadly. "Rainey. Been awhile."

They exchange a few words before she returns to us, pulling me and Colin aside.

"Do you have any Union money on you?"

"Uh…" I'm not sure I'm ready to reveal that.

"Union dollars are the easiest and most valuable thing to trade if you've got them. If not, we can trade supplies."

Colin and I exchange a glance before he turns and pulls out a few bills, giving them to her. Rainey hands the money to the bearded guy, and he signals for us to climb in the wagon.

"Lie down," the clean-shaven guy says.

They pile our stuff around us, adding crates of their own, and draping tarps across the top of everything, with only thin gaps allowing fresh air in and narrow views out.

Once we're underway, Colin asks, "Where are they taking us?"

"To the nearest town," Rainey answers.

"How far?" I ask.

"We should be there about this time tomorrow."

"Why are we hiding?" I ask.

"They're businessmen. They carry people and products for whoever's willing to pay, including the Uprising. It's best if their human cargo is under wraps. If the Uprising starts nabbing paying customers, they won't be in business very long."

We ride in silence, jostling about like a tossed salad, on a rough, unpaved road, rutted from rain and heavy use. We pull out some rations and eat dinner as darkness settles in. The drivers stop to switch and allow us bathroom breaks before driving on through the night.

Despite the bumping and rocking, I drift off, waking in the morning before the others. Stiff and sore, I twist to dislodge my limbs from those around me until I can sit up and stretch. I poke my head through the opening and look around. The terrain has changed dramatically. Tall grass stands at attention around us, and steep cliffs with snowcapped mountains rise up in the distance.

When everyone is awake, we eat a breakfast of granola bars washed down with water. Rainey nods her head toward the east where the dilapidated remains of a huge city sit. What must have once been tall majestic buildings are now steel skeletons with jagged glass panels hanging on for dear life, while crumbling brick and stone sprinkle the ground below. A mess of rubble and overgrowth spills around shorter buildings, bowing down to the skyscrapers like loyal subjects.

"Is that where we're going?" I ask her.

"No. Not many people live in the old metropolitan areas. Those tall buildings require too much work to be made safe. And the shorter ones are in the path of falling debris from the tall ones. The only people who venture in anymore are isolationists and gangs."

What a waste. All because our ancestors couldn't agree on the cause of rising temperatures or a way to solve their problems. Instead they killed each other to prevent the other side from implementing a solution. Then again, we're no better. With the Uprising planning to attack the Union and members of the Union willing to sacrifice innocent life in their quest for…I have no idea what. What makes someone turn on their own people?

"Things weren't always like this, you know," Rainey says, breaking into my thoughts. "Our parents and grandparents all passed down stories about life after the war. Rape gangs roaming freely with no one to stop them, neighbors turning on one another in order to survive. People who'd always had easy lives, suddenly in a daily fight for survival."

Leaning against the side rail, I study buildings in the distance, trying to picture them in their glory days and wondering who would choose to live there now.

"Down in back," the bearded guy calls over his shoulder.

We all drop and bury ourselves beneath cargo. My heart races and I reach for Colin's hand. He gives me a reassuring squeeze while we wait to find out what's happening.

"Whoa…" one of them says, and the wagon slows before coming to a stop.

I hold my breath, straining my ears.

"Where you headed?" asks a male voice I don't recognize.

"Up a ways to do some trading."

"Got any coffee?"

"Not this trip, maybe next time. Check with the trading post in Okanogan next week."

"Will do. Thanks for stopping."

The driver clicks and the horses start moving again.

"You can sit up again," one of them says. "We should be there in about an hour."

We're no longer on a rutted dirt road, at some point we transitioned to pavement, but the ride isn't much smoother. We stop at the outskirts of a town with rows of neat little houses in decent shape. After climbing down, Rainey thanks our drivers and heads back to where we've gathered behind the wagon. She picks up her pack and starts walking.

"There'll be a gathering place of some sort in the center of town. We can ask if anyone's seen your friends."

My heart catches. There's a chance I could see Cyrus tonight, and I'm not sure if that's a good thing or not.

22 Gathering Places

The streets and sidewalks through town are wrecked from more than a century of neglect, but the houses are in incredible condition. It looks like they've been repaired with materials from the immediate surroundings, resembling the patchwork quilt my great-grandmother made that's draped over the foot of my parents' bed.

Colin dropped back and is now chatting with Ilona, leaving me and Zak to walk in awkward silence, although I catch him eyeing me from time to time. Finally he mumbles something I can't make out.

"I'm sorry, what?"

"What're you gonna do after you find your friends?"

I tip my face up to meet his dark eyes that are nearly as black as his hair. "I don't know. When I left, they were in danger because of me. I need to see for myself they're okay. After that, I'm not sure."

He gives me a sideways glance, as if he wants to ask something else.

"What?"

He shrugs. "You're just different than I thought."

"Um…should I be offended?"

He smiles, revealing dimples in his lower cheeks, right above his jaw. "No. Being a Uni and all…I guess I didn't expect you to care about people out here."

"People are people, Zak. I love them. Where they were born doesn't matter." Whether he meant it that way or not, his statement *is* kind of offensive. "Look, you all got a raw deal out here after the war, but most people in the Union don't even know anyone lives out here. It's not that we don't care."

We lapse back into silence for a few minutes before he says, "I think that's cool of you. I don't think I would've done the same."

"You kinda are, though, aren't you? You and your friends are risking a lot to help a couple of total strangers. And right now, a handful of people in the Union are risking everything trying to protect everyone out here."

The late afternoon sun is at our backs when we stop in front of a bar with solar panels on the roof. Unease winds through me as I try to understand how they have access to all this technology. I'm on heightened alert as Rainey opens the door, and we file inside. She walks up and leans across the counter to talk to the bartender while the rest of us stay close to the door.

Most of the tables are taken, and at least a dozen people sit at the bar. A combination of reclaimed furniture from before the war and items thrown together from whatever materials could be found fill the large space. The counter, stretching the width of the room, is constructed of a long piece of wood perched atop rusted metal kegs. Shelves lining the back wall are stocked with an array of liquors that would rival any nightclub in the Union. The solar panels are powering an eclectic mix of lights, which are supplemented by candles, creating a warm, inviting glow. A low steady hum of conversation fills the air.

Rainey returns to us after a few minutes. "He said lots of people are migrating up here from the south. Can you give me a description of your friends?"

"Umm, yeah. Cyrus is tall, like six feet, wavy short brown hair. Marcus is taller, black, always smiling. Sonia's beautiful, not the kind of girl you overlook. She's kinda exotic with dark skin and light brown eyes. Will's fifteen-ish and Ally's a year or two older than Will. Blonde, blue eyes. Then there are three little boys, age eight, six and four."

"Okay." She talks to the bartender for a few more minutes before heading back to us. With a nod toward the bar, she says, "He said he thinks they came through about a month ago, but they didn't stay. Moved on not long after arriving."

My heart skips in my chest. Disappointment at not finding them is soon replaced by budding hope. Up until now, I didn't really believe we'd find them. That's a lot of distance to cover in a few months, but if they managed to trade for wagon rides, they could've made it up here sooner. Even if they only walked, if they hiked twenty miles a day, it would've only taken them sixty days to make the twelve-hundred-mile trek.

"It's late enough now, we should plan to stay here tonight," Rainey says. "There are rooms for rent upstairs if you have any more Union money."

After checking in, I flop down on one of the beds, exhausted and a little numb.

Colin pokes his head out of the bathroom. "Nothing works in here."

"I think there's some outhouses out back. Oh, and I'm pretty sure I saw a sign for baths as well. It's sort of like those old Westerns you like so much."

We get cleaned up and change into fresh clothes before meeting the others downstairs. A restaurant sits across from the hotel. Eating at a restaurant in the Ruins is surreal. But strangely affordable. The total bill for the six of us is less than the cost of one meal in the Union.

"How does this whole Union money thing work?" I ask Rainey. "Why is food and a hotel night so cheap but the ride to get here would buy us a month of stays? The prices seem to be all over the place."

"It's about perceived value. The more dangerous a service is to provide or the harder a product is to acquire, the more valuable it is. That's why covert transport costs more than a bed for the night."

We head to the bar after dinner, and I grab a beer, sitting with Rainey, Alexander, and Zak. Colin and Ilona are deep in conversation at a table in the corner, where I watch Colin downing one beer after another. When he orders his fifth bottle, I make my way over to check on him. Ilona excuses herself, rejoining the others.

"Hey, Col. What's going on?"

"Whaddaya meeeeeeen?"

"I mean you're drinking beer like it's water and we're in the desert."

He sighs dramatically and slumps back, running a hand through his hair. "Don't you ever wonder if there's any point to it?"

Oh joy, he's a sad drunk. "Any point to what, Colin?"

"All of it. It's just pointless. We live here in danger, we live there in danger, the people we love, love someone else..."

"Okay, you're done, time to go."

He grabs his beer off the table as I pull him up by his arm. I take the bottle from his hand, setting it on the table next to Rainey as we pass. "I'm going to put him to bed, I'll be back."

Colin drapes an arm over my shoulder. "Those lights look funny."

I roll my eyes and drag him up to our room. The door unlocks with a metal key, something I didn't think even existed anymore, and I pour Colin onto one of the beds.

"EvTay, can you take my shoes off?"

With a heavy sigh that sends a piece of hair flying out of my face, I lean over and tug off his boots, dropping them on the floor with a clunk.

"Love sucks," he says, closing his eyes and laying his hands across his chest.

It does, but I'm getting a little tired of his unrequited love routine. "Col, I'm sorry. But why not try to move on? Ilona seems like she's into you."

"Yeah, but Alexander likes her. And I'm not going to be that guy."

"What guy?"

"Jjjjjjjjjack."

I turn to leave the room. "Goodnight, Col."

"I'm going to tell her. When we get back, I'm gonna tell Lisa I love her."

I halt and spin back to face him. "Colin, you can't. That's not fair, she's with Jack now. You had your chance, and you didn't take it. You had your reasons, I get that, but you don't have dibs on her. She loves Jack, and he loves her."

He sits up and stares at me. "Yeah, well you slept with a guy who kissed your arch nemesis as soon as he left you. And now you've got us running all over the Ruins chasing after some other guy you aren't even sure still loves you. Excuse me if I don't take your stellar romantic advice."

My hands ball into fists and I clamp my jaw to keep from saying something I'll regret. "Whatever, Colin."

"Hey, Ev, I'm sorry. I didn't mean it like that."

But I know that's exactly how he meant it, so I keep walking out the door.

Back in the bar, I grab Colin's beer and take a long pull.

"Is Colin okay?" Ilona asks.

Setting the bottle on the table, I spin it around, examining the artwork on the label. "He's fine. He's not much of a drinker, though. Neither of us is."

"Yeah," Rainey says. "I guess when you live in Utopia, there's no point in drinking until you're numb."

"There's some truth in that. But also, the drinking age in the Union is eighteen, and we haven't been of age for very long."

The four of them exchange a look, as if a drinking age is absurd, and out here, I suppose it is.

"So, you came out here for the love of your life. What's Colin's story?" Rainey asks.

"Unrequited love." I peel back a corner of the label on my bottle. "So what are you guys going to do after you're rid of us?" I ask, changing the subject. "Where are you headed next?"

"I don't know," Ilona says. "I can't go home. When the Uprising came through, they grabbed my brother. My mom tried to stop them, and they shot her. I ran, but my dad's still there. I hope they don't hurt him because of me. I...I can't kill innocent people, no matter how self-indulgent they are." She glances at me and winces. "Sorry."

"No need to apologize. I mean, it's kinda true," I say with a shrug. "So, where will you go?"

"Being on the run is getting old. I wouldn't mind settling down in a town like this."

Alexander sneaks a peek at Ilona. "I was thinking the same thing."

Zak leans back in his chair and takes another swallow of his beer. "I wanna at least try to go back home. I have four siblings who're still too young to be drafted, but I still worry about them. I don't want them to be punished because I left."

"What do you mean?" I glance up from the little pile of label debris I'm creating on the table. "They keep track of that?"

He shakes his head. "No, but someone else might turn my family in to protect their own."

"How can they use your family to get to you if they can't find you?"

"They can make his family an example for the others," Rainey says.

"Oh," I say, taking another sip of beer, letting that new piece of horror sink in.

The lights dim as the battery runs low on stored power, and the bartender brings out more candles. The darker it gets, the more crowded the bar becomes. The heat from all the bodies and the soft glow from the flickering candlelight, along with the hum of conversation, make me warm and cozy in a way I didn't think possible in a foreign place surrounded by strangers. Although the beer might have something to do with it.

My battle to keep my eyelids open becomes a losing one, and I take that as my cue to call it a night. I hand a couple of bills to Rainey to pay for the drinks and stand to go upstairs.

Rainey gives the money to Alexander. "I'll walk up with you."

As we climb the stairs, I ask Rainey, "So what's your story? Why'd you join up only to leave?"

"I had no love for the Union, but didn't hate them enough to join the Uprising. My sister signed up, so I joined to keep an eye on her. They used her as leverage, promising me they'd keep her safe if I did what they wanted. But when she died…" She shrugs. "They had nothing to hold over my head anymore, so I left."

"Shit," I say under my breath.

She continues as if she didn't just share one of the most painful experiences of her life. "After leaving the Uprising, I went back home, but my family had moved on. I don't even know if they're still alive. This last time the Uprising swept through, I knew if they caught me, I was dead. They're not big on second chances."

We turn and make our way up another flight in silence. Rainey opens the door into the hallway, and when we reach my room, I ask, "How far to the next town?"

"Forty miles. The bartender said there's a handcar outside town which'll cut down the travel time significantly. We'll be able to get there in a day."

"A handcar?"

She smiles. "You're in for a treat. See you in the morning."

23 Handcars

oud thumping drags me from sleep, and I open one eye.

Colin's shuffling around the room. "Hey, EvTay, are you ever going to get up? I'm starving."

With the sting of his words from last night still fresh, his stomach isn't my biggest concern. I grunt and pull my pillow over my head, blocking out the sunlight streaming across my face. Colin grabs the pillow from my head and tosses it onto the foot of the bed.

"What is *wrong* with you?" I snap.

"It's almost ten o'clock, let's go."

"What?" I bolt out of bed and check the clock. With the possibility of Cyrus being only a day's journey from here, oversleeping wasn't on my agenda. When I'm dressed, we go get the others.

Ilona answers the door, her eyes hooded. "What's going on?"

"We're going to go get breakfast," I say.

"What time is it?" she mumbles with a yawn.

"Like ten fifteen."

She blinks and calls over her shoulder, "Hey Rainey, it's late. They wanna eat." She turns back to us. "Kay, we'll meet you at the restaurant."

After waking Zak and Alexander, Colin and I head across the street to get a table.

"You're not supposed to be this…bouncy after so many beers last night," I say.

"Why? I didn't drink that much," he says as we turn the corner and walk down another flight of stairs.

"You had at least four in forty-five minutes."

"Oh, yeah…" The smile slips from his lips and his mouth falls open.

"It's all coming back to you, isn't it?"

"Oh, hey, Ev…I'm sorry about what I said."

I push open the door and we exit the stairwell into the lobby. "Yeah, well, you might be sorry, but you weren't wrong," I grumble.

"No, I was. Look, I get your shit's complicated, but I thought about what you said…about moving on. It hurts to love someone who doesn't love you back, and I don't want to hurt anymore. It sucks."

He may only be trying to smooth things over, but he sounds genuine. Even though I'm the one who told him to suck it up and get over Lisa, I know it's not that simple. Because if it was, I'd be over Cyrus already.

The walk through town is at least a couple of hours, and with every step I take, my heart reacts to being one step closer to finding my friends. Finding Cyrus. Anxiety scrambles my stomach, but not knowing how Cyrus will react when he sees ratchets it up.

On the other side of town, a small gray building sits in front of a set of railroad tracks similar to the ones Colin and I found on our first day out here. Except these aren't rotted, covered in moss, or bug-infested. Neat gravel fills the spaces between the slats instead of untamed grass, and the rails, while tarnished, are not rusted and flaking.

Rainey leads the way up to the building and slides the door open. Once my eyes adjust to the lower light inside, I can make out a dozen or so wheeled platforms.

"Handcars," Rainey announces.

Each handcar is a rectangular platform mounted above four titanium wheels with a pole jutting up through the center, a crossbar atop it. Alexander and Zak push a cart out of the barn and position it on the tracks. They return and do the same with a second cart.

Rainey nods to me and Colin. "Hop on."

With a quick glance at me, Colin climbs up on one side, and I get on the other, the platform wobbling as our weight transfers. Rainey stands next to me while Alexander, Zak and Ilona get on the cart behind us.

"Put your hands on the bar and push down," Rainey says to Colin, kicking a lever with her foot.

Colin does as instructed, and we begin to move away from the others. Our side of the handle goes up, and Rainey grabs on, pushing the bar back down, propelling us forward. I join her and we repeat this process, going faster and faster. The wind caressing my face, my hair whipping behind me, I can't stop a little squeal from escaping.

Rainey laughs. "You two are like a couple of kids with a new toy."

Colin and I exchange a look and our grins only grow wider.

The trip across the tracks is surprisingly fast, and we're at the other end, more than twenty miles away, in less than an hour. After parking the handcars in the shed, we pick up our gear and begin hiking. By late afternoon, we're passing houses on the perimeter of town. These houses are in better shape than the last town, many with tidy gardens and manicured lawns.

A sudden gust of wind sends more leaves dancing around us in an autumnal shower, illuminated by the soft glow of lights from shops, restaurants, and bars, creating a charming village atmosphere straight out of an antique painting. The sun hugs the horizon as we reach the center of town and that's when it hits me — it's not only businesses with solar panels, but more than half of the homes, too.

"It's too late to do much except find a place to stay for the night," Rainey says. "We should scope things out before we draw a lot of attention to ourselves."

Disappointment washes over me like a dark wave. "Yeah, okay." I try to keep my mood from coloring my words.

"This town is like nothing I've seen before," Rainey says. "It's too clean and there are too many solar panels. I want to make sure that's not because of a strong Uprising presence."

I nod. She's right, of course, but being so close to Cyrus is gnawing away at me, making me edgy. I try not to dwell on it. Either Cyrus still loves me or he doesn't. I guess I can wait another twelve hours to find out.

Rainey stops at the first bar we come to. "Let's observe before asking questions. Zak, Alex, come with me. You guys walk down to the end of the block before coming in," she says to the rest of us.

Colin, Ilona, and I stroll down the sidewalk to the corner, peeking into shop windows before turning and heading back to the bar. Voices and clinking glasses greet us as we enter, grabbing a table near the door.

A guy in an apron makes his way over to us. "What can I get you?"

"Uh, three beers?" Colin asks, glancing around the table.

Ilona and I nod, and the waiter disappears, returning with three bottles. My beer is cold. A lot colder than the ones we had last night, further proof they're powered. A group of rowdy guys are in a heated game of darts in the corner, and on the other side of the room is a small-scale pool table with a line of people waiting to play.

Colin nudges me and points to the back wall where a small stage sits with an old upright piano and an acoustic guitar.

"No way," I hiss. "What part of 'don't draw attention to ourselves' didn't you understand?"

I glance at Rainey across the bar, watching us with interest. She makes her way over to us. "What's going on guys?" she asks.

"I'm itching to get my fingers on that guitar," Colin says.

Rainey glances around. "Hang on a minute. I think it's okay, but let me check it out a little more."

She heads over to chat with the bartender, then does a quick lap around the room, talking to a handful of people, mostly guys who flirt with the pit bull disguised as a harmless pixie.

When she returns to our table, a smile lifts the corner of her mouth. "Seems we're a lot closer to the border than I thought."

"Border?" Colin asks.

"Yeah. The Northern Territories are only about two miles north of here. They've got a steady influx of migrants trying to stay a step ahead of the Uprising. New people are a dime a dozen. We're not likely to draw much attention, at least no more than anyone else, so if you want to play music, go for it."

"Come on, Ev, it'll be fun," Colin says. "Just like in my bedroom back home."

I haven't played in a long time, but after finishing my second beer, I'm feeling more adventurous. Colin exchanges a few words with the bartender. The cute brunette has been eyeing Colin since we got here, so I'm not surprised when she tells him to go for it.

He heads to the stage and picks up the guitar, tuning it. I sit at the piano, and play a few notes. It hasn't been tuned in ages. The white keys are chipped on the edges, and the black ones are rubbed smooth. I've never played a stringed piano, and the action is sluggish. After fingering the scales once or twice, I get a sense of which notes are the most out of tune so I can avoid them if possible.

There's something almost liberating about playing again. My fingers know what to do, the muscle memory returning with glee. Colin strums a slow, gentle melody I don't recognize at first. By the time he hits the chorus, I smile, realizing it's one of Eddie's, although Colin's slowed it down, turning it into a ballad.

Applause erupts when the song is over, reminding me we're not sitting in Colin's apartment. Most of the girls in the bar are openly staring at Colin with admiration, including one in particular. Standing near the door, holding an empty tray against her hip, is a small blonde with big blue eyes locked on Colin.

Ally. My heart stampedes in my chest as I rise and push my way over to her. She shifts her gaze from Colin to me, and recognition flickers across her features. A smile lights up her face, and she throws her arms around me.

"Evan! What are you doing here? Oh my god, your hair!"

I laugh and squeeze her against me. The last time she saw me I was blond, and when I met her I was a redhead. "I came to find you guys." Her eyes move beyond me, checking out Colin again. "C'mon," I say, taking her hand and dragging her to the stage where Colin is putting the guitar back in the stand. "This is my best friend, Colin. Colin, this is Ally. She's one of the people I lived with over the summer."

Colin smiles at her in a way I'm not entirely sure I'm happy about. Ally is fragile and doesn't need Colin to mess with her heart. She gives him a shy smile before staring at her feet.

"So, Ally, how is everyone?" I pause, swallowing hard. "Cyrus?"

Her head jerks up, pain etched into her features. "Cyrus is gone."

I take a step back, air abandoning my lungs.

"Oh, god, no, not like that. I'm sorry." She reaches out and touches my arm. "I just mean he left."

Relief mixes with soul-crushing disappointment, and my voice cracks with emotion. "Where'd he go?"

"I don't know." She shrugs and drops her gaze again. "He was just gone one morning when we got up." The way she stares at her shoes, unable to look at me, I know she's hiding something.

"Did you look for him?"

"We did, but…Evan…" She pauses and swallows. "After Lucien died and you left…it kinda messed him up. We figured he needed to be alone for a while."

Her tone is apologetic, but I'm the one who should be apologizing. I never should have left them. Everything turned upside down when I landed in their lives and again when I walked back out. But Cyrus…he lost me and his brother that day, Lucien *because* of me. The ache in my chest tightens. Ally finally lifts her eyes to meet mine, pleading. She didn't do anything wrong. I reach over and pull her into a hug. "It's so good to see you. What are you doing here, though? In a bar by yourself?"

Her expression relaxes into a smile. "Oh, I work here. In fact, I'm going to be late for my shift. Hey, you need to come home with me tonight. Wait for me, okay?" She glances past me to Colin before rushing behind the bar.

When I turn to Colin, he's watching Ally walk across the room. Could he actually be interested in her? Colin doesn't really have a type, and as far as I know, Lisa's the only girl he's ever shown any interest in. I wanted him to move on, but not with Ally. He could shatter her already damaged heart.

Ally is finishing up her shift when the front door opens, and a tall guy with messy blond hair enters. It takes me a second to recognize Will; I swear he's grown two inches since I last saw him. His eyes adjust to the lower light, then widen, and a smile blooms across his face. He crosses the bar and pulls me into his arms, lifting me up off the floor.

"Evan! When did you get here?"

"Earlier this evening." I kiss him on both cheeks and hug him back.

He sets me down and his eyes take in the rest of our group. I make quick introductions, and he stops when I get to Colin. "I've seen you before," he says.

"Yeah," Colin says. "At the other place. I stayed outside though."

"Right. You were the guy on the rock." Will tilts his head. "But you had dark hair."

"Yeah."

Ally joins us, and we head out into the crisp night air.

"How far is the house from here?" I ask Will, shoving my hands deep into my pockets.

"Not far. Couple miles."

The temperature dropped while we were in the bar, and the wind is like a knife, slicing through my thin layers of clothing. Will takes off his coat and hands it to me.

"Oh, no. I mean thanks, but I can't take your coat."

"Yeah you can. You're turning blue."

"Thanks," I say, shrugging into it. He drapes an arm across my shoulder as we walk and asks how we ended up here. I fill him in on meeting Rainey and the others and our adventures since arriving in the Ruins. I glance behind me to ask Colin if wants to weigh in, but he and Ally are in their own private conversation, several yards behind us.

Before I can ask Will how everyone else is doing, he leads us up to a small, well-maintained house. A large picture window is nestled in a wood siding-covered front wall, above neatly trimmed hedges.

My pulse quickens, then skips a beat as he unlocks and opens the front door.

Ally grabs my arm. "Oh, there's something I need to tell you first."

Before she can say more, I spot Sonia and burst inside to hug her. Her eyes widen in surprise, then she folds her arms across her chest, her expression molding into a scowl.

"What are you doing here?" she demands, her pale brown eyes narrowing further.

"What?" I halt and take a step back. "I-I wanted to see you guys."

"Well, you can just turn yourself around and go right back where you came from." She storms out of the room.

"Sonia…" Marcus says, but turns to me, a huge grin lighting up his face, all white teeth against dark skin. "Hey, Evan, it's really good to see you." He pulls me in for a long, tight hug and I sink into him, sighing. Damn, I've missed these people.

When Marcus releases me, Sonia marches back into the room. "You have a lot of nerve showing up here."

Moving away from Marcus, I turn to Sonia, remembering the day I left. She gathered everyone up to leave their home because Walker knew where they lived, and he'd be back. She invited me to join them, but at the time, she didn't seem to care if I did or not. A hollow feeling pushes away the warmth that had been blossoming, and I clamp my teeth down on my bottom lip to keep it from trembling.

Sonia moves toward me, her fists clenched. "You left and *we* had to pick up the pieces. You weren't the one holding Ty as he cried himself to sleep every night. You weren't the one who had to deal with Cyrus and his attitude. I told you he cared for you, warned you not to hurt him."

He'd just lost his brother, the only person remaining in his family, my leaving was hardly the sole source of his pain. "Cyrus told me to go. And as far as Ty goes…I feel like shit. I promised him I wasn't going anywhere, but I didn't plan on leaving like that."

Sonia closes her eyes and blows out a slow breath.

"Sonia—"

"You have *no* idea the mess you left." She storms out of the room, stopping at the hall and turning back to face me. "You were my best friend."

"I'm sorry," I say, moving toward her.

She puts up a hand to stop me and disappears down the hall, Marcus following her.

"That's what I needed to tell you," Ally says. "Sonia's really mad at you."

"No shit," I say, dropping to the couch with a heavy sigh. I get Ty is hurt, Ben and Connor, too. But Cyrus practically forced me to go. She can't blame his crappy attitude on me. The boys…well that couldn't be all me either. It was everything. Losing Lucien, and Draya, their home, and…okay, maybe me, too. *Damn.* I left them after everything they'd lost. So leaving them that day may not be the sole cause of their pain, but maybe it was one thing too many.

I run my hands through my hair and blow out a slow breath. Sonia probably won't even talk to me anymore tonight, but I need to fix this. I only wish I knew how.

Fixing Things

A dull ache in my back drags me from a deep sleep. I pry one eye open and stare at the ceiling, forgetting for a moment where I am. At least until last night's events come back to me with depressing clarity. Sighing, I close my eye, trying to return to a dream world where Sonia doesn't hate me and Cyrus is here.

The hard floor pressing into my shoulder makes falling back asleep impossible, so after a few minutes of wishing and hoping, I give up. This time when I open my eyes, three little pairs of eyes are staring back. "Ty, Connor, Ben," I squeal, reaching my arms out to them.

Ben and Connor both smile, snuggling in next to me on the floor, but Ty pulls back. I inhale their little boy smells, making my heart soar in a way I wasn't sure possible only moments ago.

Ben nestles his curly head under my arm, staring at me with dark unblinking eyes. "Are you really here?"

"Yeah, buddy, I am."

"I knew you'd be back, I told them," Ben says, nodding at Connor and Ty. At eight, he's the oldest of the bunch and never lets them forget how much wiser that makes him.

Connor climbs over me, jamming a foot in my ribs as he goes. Wide blue eyes, the same color as his sister's, take in my face and hair. "How come you left?" he asks.

"My friends came for me, and I needed to go back to take care of some things. Cyrus was supposed to tell you." I glance at Ty to make sure he's listening.

Fat tears pool in Ty's eyes, spilling out and running over round cheeks. I'm the worst kind of person — making a little kid cry.

"Ty, I know I told you we'd talk before I left, but I couldn't, and that wasn't fair to you. I made you a promise and I didn't keep it. I'm so sorry."

He turns away from me, and I realize this is going to be harder than I thought. Sonia's anger is one thing, but this rejection coming from a four-year-old is ten times worse.

Morning light streams through the window across the living room, making bright rectangles of sunshine on dark wood floors. Outside, brittle leaves skitter along the sidewalk. I stand and stretch my arms to work out the kink in my shoulder.

Ally and Colin are at the table, talking over steaming cups of something I sure hope is coffee. Footsteps approach from behind as I reach the doorway into the kitchen, and before I can turn around, two small arms wrap around my waist, and a face buries itself in my back. Relief fills my soul, and I twist around to scoop Ty up, squishing him against me.

I groan inwardly when I discover Ally and Colin are drinking tea and not coffee. Seriously, they're just beans. How hard can it be to get coffee here? I grab myself a mug and join the others at the table. Their morning routine is so different here — no cows to milk, chickens to feed, eggs to collect.

The boys head down the hall, disappearing into their rooms, doors slamming shut behind them. I keep going, stopping at a door at the end leading to the bedroom where Colin slept last night, Cyrus's room. Ally offered it to me, but I couldn't sleep in there, not without him.

The bed is up against the wall, beneath a window overlooking the backyard. The blankets and sheets are rumpled. Seriously, Colin? You couldn't spend two minutes making the bed? Beside the bed is a dresser, the top bare. I wonder if Cyrus cleared out all his things when he left.

Hoping for something of his to make me feel close to him, I pull open the first drawer. Inside are a few T-shirts and condoms. I slam the drawer shut, my stomach twisting, wondering if he used them here, in this room, in that bed. Tears fill my eyes and I turn to leave, but stop before I reach the door. Turning back, I open the drawer again and grab one of his shirts. The blue cotton is soft, worn, and I hold it up to my nose, breathing deeply. I can still detect his scent, a combination of earth and the natural soap he uses, like sunshine and sage that is all him.

"There you are," Ally says, startling me.

I whip around, the shirt still in my face. Dropping my hand, feeling a little like a deranged stalker, my mouth falls open and I stammer, "I was just…I mean…I…I just miss him."

She gives me a sad smile and wraps her arms around me. "He misses you, too. I know he does."

I stare at the shirt in my hand, thinking about keeping it, but end up putting it away and padding down the hall after Ally, back to the kitchen. Someone knocks on the front door.

"I'll get it," Connor singsongs, skipping through the living room.

A guy walks into the front room and unwraps a scarf from his neck. He's tall, not much older than me, and is wearing glasses. I realize I'm staring at him, but he's the first person I've ever seen wearing corrective glasses. Vision problems are fixed as soon as they're diagnosed in the Union.

The guy heads into the dining room and sets his bag on the table with a solid thunk before pulling out a stack of books, papers, and pencils.

Ally places a mug of tea on the table in front of him. "Alphonse, these are my friends, Evan and Colin."

Alphonse nods at us before resuming his work, not even a little interested in us or why we're here.

"They have schools here," Ally says. "But the boys are so far behind the other kids their age, Alphonse is tutoring them to help them get caught up."

"Wow, that's awesome."

Ty and Ben bound in and join Connor, taking seats at the table, reaching for books and pencils, ready to work. A small pang of jealousy threads through me, watching someone else teaching my boys. If I hadn't gone back, would I be the one tutoring them? Or would I be working at a bar like Ally to help with expenses?

Rainey, Zak, Alexander, and Ilona walk through the front door, cheeks and noses pink from the cold. The boys' heads pop up and turn to stare at them. Alphonse clears his throat and glares at the new arrivals. We're clearly a distraction, so I pull Colin into the kitchen with me to make more tea, and drag everyone except Alphonse and the boys into the backyard.

"Ally, is there a store in town where we can get some warmer clothing?" I ask, handing one of the mugs to Rainey.

"Yeah. We can all go this afternoon after Alphonse leaves."

"We just got back from looking at a few places to rent," Alexander says. "We're thinking of staying here for a while. We saw a few help wanted signs, too."

"Really? You're staying?" I ask.

"Well, Alexander, Zak, and I are," Ilona says. "Rainey's not so sure yet."

Rainey just shrugs.

We spend the morning on the steps of the deck, sipping tea and talking. Well, I mostly listen to the others making plans to settle down here. Soon the voices become background noise and my eyes wander around the backyard.

The wooden deck comes off the back of the house, taking up a third of the yard, with grass filling the space between the deck and raised planters that house their small garden. A well-used brick oven sits in the corner next to the garden, against the house. Although not lushly landscaped like in the Union, it's practical. It's large by Union standards, but much smaller than the land they lived on down south.

If they hadn't rescued me, would they still be there? Or would they have fled up here like so many others to avoid the Uprising? The house, the yard, their lives, it's all so different from what I knew before, proving the Ruins are not a single entity, but as varied as the people who live out here.

After lunch, Ally and the boys accompany me and Colin into town to the same store-lined street we were on last night. We enter the first shop we come to that sells clothes.

Colin dons a cowboy hat and turns to Ally, waggling his eyebrows.

She laughs. "I like it. It's a good look."

He grins at me, and I shake my head. "I'm not sure you can pull it off, plus, it won't keep you warm." I toss a knit cap at him. "This is what you need."

He sets the ten-gallon hat back on the shelf and grabs some gloves before choosing a thick wool coat. I find a navy pea coat, hat, and gloves for myself, making the walk back to the house much more comfortable. We pour through the front door, and the aroma of something incredible, spicy, meaty, fills my nose. Alexander, Zak, Rainey, and Ilona are in the kitchen, chopping, sautéing, and stirring, while some sort of sauce simmers on the stove.

"Tamales," Rainey says, turning back to stir a pan of heavenly smelling meat.

"How can we help?" I ask.

She nods toward the prep table. "You can help assemble."

We're given quick instructions on spooning masa onto corn husks, filling them with meat and cheese, then rolling and tying them. When we're done, my back aches and my stomach is ready to devour itself, but Rainey says they still need to be steamed before we can eat them. Ally drains a pot of pinto beans, handing them to Rainey, who mashes and fries them in a hot skillet.

The boys and I set the table, and my hunger pangs are replaced by knots. It's been so relaxed and fun around here the past few hours, but that will change once Sonia gets home. For everyone's sake, it might be better if I didn't stay here longer than necessary.

I approach Ilona. "Hey, ummm, would it be okay if I stayed with you at your new place for a while? Just until I figure out what's next. I can help with the rent."

"Fine by me," Ilona says, looking to Alexander and Zak.

"Sure," Zak says. "What about Colin?"

I glance out to the living room where Colin and Ally are sitting entirely too close on the couch. "I'm not sure, but I'll ask him what he wants to do."

The front door opens and silence crawls across the room like long fingers. With a deep breath, I turn to face Sonia.

"Can I talk to you outside?" she asks.

Good thing I've got someplace else to go soon. I grab my new coat and follow Sonia out to the porch, closing the door behind us.

"Look, I'm glad you're back for the kids' sakes, but this doesn't change anything."

Her reaction cuts through me, but I work to keep my feelings from showing. "I've made arrangements to stay elsewhere, and I can go to a hotel tonight if that would be better."

Her eyes snap with anger. "So you're going to abandon the boys again?"

"What the hell, Sonia? You just got done saying…" I huff out a breath and shake my head. "I didn't abandon you. I went home with my friends, because I felt I needed to. Get over it."

She turns her back, and I wait for her to walk away, but instead, her head drops, her shoulders quivering. Oh god, she's crying. I put my arms around her and rest my head on her back while her body quakes.

She sniffs and wipes her eyes. "I don't know how to deal with what I'm feeling. There's just been *so much* lately. It gets overwhelming at times, and I get angry."

I sigh and hug her tighter. "Yeah, that's something I can understand."

"I didn't think I'd ever see you again, and I couldn't believe you left without saying goodbye. And Cyrus…I know he was dealing with Lucien, it wasn't fair to throw that all on you. I don't even know where he is."

My heart contracts, curling into a tight ball in my chest to protect itself. I pull my arms from her and wrap them around my body. "He said I had to go, that it was my destiny," I say more to myself than Sonia. "I didn't want to leave him, but he made it sound like…it doesn't matter now.

She turns to face me. "That doesn't mean he was happy you were gone."

"It's definitely complicated with us, especially after everything that happened. When did he leave?"

"About a month ago."

"I don't get why he left. I thought the reason he wouldn't come with me was because he needed to stay with you, but I guess that was never it."

She stiffens and turns her face to glance down the street. She's holding something back. Does she know the real reason he didn't come with me? I can't do anything about me and Cyrus now, but maybe I can fix things with Sonia.

"I'm sorry, Sonia. Everything happened so fast, the water in the river was rising, I didn't have time to say goodbye. Do you think you can ever forgive me?"

She sighs and a small smile graces her lips. "I think I already have."

25 Forgiveness

The last few weeks passed in a blur. Rainey and the others moved into a small apartment in town. Everyone else in the house has a job, relegating me and Colin to babysitting duties. We help out in other ways, too, doing all the house and yardwork. The way everyone has embraced Colin as part of the family, and the way he's stepped up to fill that role, reminds me why I love all these people so much.

Life up here is like a cross between Union life and the life in the Ruins I experienced over the summer. The neat cookie-cutter houses, access to power, schools, and jobs are more like the Union than the Ruins. But my friends don't have solar panels yet, there's no indoor plumbing or public transportation, and daily activities still focus primarily on survival, but they have more time for recreation.

The boys are inside with Alphonse, and Colin and I are working in the front yard. With winter coming, the grass isn't growing much, but Marcus wants one more cutting before it goes dormant. Colin pushes a bladed mower across the lawn, the clippings littering the ground behind him. I follow him, raking them into a pile to throw onto the compost out back.

"What's up with you and Ally?" I ask.

He glances over his shoulder and shrugs. "You know."

"I know you walk her to and from the bar every night, and you guys are always talking. She isn't like the girls from the Union."

He stops and turns to face me. "What, she has a tail and horns? She seems like a sweet, normal girl, and I like her. I thought you wanted me to move on."

"I did…I do, but…she's been through a lot already, and a Colin-induced heartache is more than she needs."

"Why do you assume I'm going to hurt her?"

"You haven't noticed the way she looks at you? Just be careful with her, okay?"

He throws an arm over my shoulder and grins. "I'm always careful. Look, I like her, she's a bit of an old soul."

Maybe he's changed his mind about coming with me. The thought of joining the Uprising alone is about as appealing as an intimate dinner with Walker, but if Colin wants to stay with Ally, I can understand. If Cyrus was here and still loved me, I might be reevaluating my plan as well. I glance at Colin out of the corner of my eye. "Okay…"

"Okay. Now get back to work before it gets dark. I swear the days are only like seven hours long up here."

Bundled in layers of clothing, Sonia and I sit on the bench on the front porch watching the first flakes of winter fall from the sky. "I need to leave soon," I tell her.

"You've been restless since you got here. With Cyrus gone, I guess I knew you weren't staying."

"It's not like that. Yeah, being here without him makes me lonely in an entirely new way, but I came out here to join the Uprising, I have to see it through."

Her mouth drops open and she grabs my arm. "Evan, you can't."

"There's so much I still haven't told you. I know joining is dangerous. And probably idiotic. Maybe the dumbest thing I've ever done, but I can't go back home either."

"Then stay here."

"Sonia, the Uprising has to be stopped." I take a deep breath and fill her in on everything that happened after I left. About Colin's kidnapping, the memo, even what went on between me and Bryce.

She stares unblinking into the darkness for several long moments before turning to me, searching my face. "I hope you know what you're doing."

"I have no idea what I'm doing, but I have to at least try. When Lucien first suggested joining up, I thought he was crazy, but now…maybe he was onto something. Nothing else we've done has gotten us anywhere. This may be the only way."

She sighs and gives me a sad smile. "You'll figure something out. You usually do. I just hope it's the right thing this time."

"Me too."

Ally and I tuck the boys in after dinner then return to the dining room to talk. With Colin's help, I fill the others in on what happened after we returned to the Union, the stuff I told Sonia on the front porch earlier, adding more details.

"So the guy who kidnapped you is calling the shots, but is he financing it, too?" Marcus asks.

"We're not sure," Colin says. "But this plot, or whatever it is, involves the Union government. Just how much is anyone's guess." He turns to me. "And Evan thinks the Northern Territories might be funding it."

"Why do you think that?" Will asks.

"The Ruins, smuggling aside, doesn't have that kind of money. So I was trying to figure out who does, and the Northern Territories came to mind."

Marcus and Sonia exchange a look.

"What?" I ask.

Sonia shakes her head. "Nothing."

"No, it's something. If it was nothing, you two wouldn't be looking at each other like someone killed my puppy. What aren't you telling me?"

Sonia sighs and drops her head before glancing up at me. "When we first got here, Cyrus was hanging around with a group of people from the Northern Territories — a couple of guys and a girl. He was spending a lot time with them, and after Cy left, I haven't seen the others around." She and Marcus exchange another look, but he shakes his head.

"Do you think they took off together? Is Cyrus in danger?"

"I don't think so," Marcus says. "I didn't think much of it at the time. In fact, he was kind of..." he looks away and swallows. "He was involved with the girl. Bridget." He shrugs, "But maybe there was more to it than that."

A sharp pain slices through my chest as my heart shatters into a thousand tiny pieces. Even though I've been preparing myself for this, hearing he moved on, giving her a name, is so much more painful than I imagined. And yet I have no right to feel this way. Who am I to say he should've waited for me? I sure as hell didn't. But god, it's like someone's driving nails into my chest and stomping on them with heavy boots.

"Evan," Sonia says. "He loves you. I have no doubt about that."

"He used to," I whisper.

"I think he still does," she says.

I'm less sure. He said he did, he kissed me like he did, but he sent me away with no hope of ever seeing him again. It's not fair for me to wish him to be lonely, but this pain is searing, as if my insides have been ripped out and torched.

The weather turned bitterly cold in the last week, colder than I've ever experienced. The sun dangles low in the southern sky even through mid-day. The squash I'm trying to tug loose from its vine holds tight like a stubborn toddler. I grab the vegetable with both hands, pulling until it yields and place it in the basket with the others before moving on to the next one. A few feet down, Colin's busy wrestling with his own plant.

Shoving my hair out of my eyes with the back of my wrist, I take a deep breath and dive into the conversation I've been putting off way too long. "Colin, we need to talk."

He stops and turns toward me, eyebrows drawn together. "Uh-oh. The whole 'we need to talk' thing never ends well."

I sit cross-legged on the ground and look up at him. "I'm leaving soon."

"I know." He shrugs. "I'm coming with you."

"Still?"

"Well, yeah. I came out here with you to join up. Nothing's changed that."

"But what about Ally?"

"She understands. We've been talking a lot, and she knows everything. About me and Lisa, about why I came out here, and that I'm going with you." He glances inside where the boys are studying with Alphonse. "I think if it wasn't for her brothers, she'd come with us."

I still worry Ally's going to get hurt. So many people have abandoned her — her dad, Draya, me…but I guess if Colin's been upfront with her, she knew what she was getting into. "I'm glad she's staying here. You realize there's a chance we're not coming back from this, right?"

His brow creases. "Yeah. I know."

The Ruins doesn't celebrate Thanksgiving, but that doesn't stop me and Colin from planning a good old-fashioned, Thanksgiving-style dinner, inviting Rainey and the others to join us. We missed the traditional date and celebrate in early December instead. There's no turkey, but Ally and I made pumpkin pies in the brick oven this morning, and Colin and I roasted the vegetables we picked yesterday. Marcus brought a ham home last night and Sonia made mashed potatoes.

Squeezing thirteen people at a table designed to hold eight is cozy and energetic. Voices and laughter fill the small dining area as bowls are passed around, metal serving spoons clinking against ceramic. For a few short hours, I lose myself in these people and this moment. Between the rich aromas and intense flavors mixing with the company at hand, the hole in my heart caused by the people who aren't here is a little smaller.

When the last bite has been eaten, Ally and Colin clear the dishes. After indulging in a couple minutes of a food hangover, I get up to help. Carrying the empty mashed potato bowl, I walk into the kitchen and stop in my tracks. Colin has Ally pressed up against the sink, kissing her.

"Whoa," I say, spinning and heading back into the dining room, the bowl still in my hands.

"Is everything okay?" Sonia asks.

"Yep." I say, sitting back down in my spot at the table.

Ally's eyes are red when they return several minutes later, and she excuses herself, leaving the room. I raise an eyebrow in Colin's direction, but he won't meet my eye. Damn it, this is exactly what I didn't want to happen. Ally doesn't rejoin us for dessert, and I think about going to look for her while the others do the dishes, but I suspect she wants to be alone.

"We need to get going," Rainey announces when the clean dishes have been put away.

I walk them to the door, giving each of them a hug goodbye, holding on a little tighter than necessary, unsure when or if I'll ever see them again. Locking the door behind them, I turn around and announce, "We're leaving in the morning."

"I know you said you were going, but the longer you stayed, the more I hoped that meant you'd changed your mind," Sonia says.

"With Cy gone, I guess it makes sense," Marcus says.

"Sonia said the same thing, but it's more than that. I didn't come out here looking for you, I never thought I'd see you guys again," I admit. "Although it seems like dumb luck we found you, it's probably not as random as that. Not with so many people settling up here from down south." Cyrus's theory of everything happening for a reason comes to mind, and I wonder if he still believes that.

"Colin and I came out here to do something, and yeah it might be crazy, but I'm not sure what else to do. I'm not going to pretend that…" I pause, taking a deep shaky breath as unexpected tears burn my eyes. "I can't pretend Cyrus moving on doesn't hurt like hell. If he was here and things were the same between us, I'd be tempted to stay, try to forget what's going to happen in the Union. So it's better this way, you know?"

Marcus shakes his head and studies me. "Evan…" His mouth moves, but no words come out. He glances at Sonia before continuing. "I guess I can understand why you have to do this, but damn, I wish you weren't. Just be careful, okay? And whatever you do, don't tell them where you're from."

I smile and wipe the few escaped tears with my fingertips. "I'm not a complete idiot."

He smiles a little before giving me one of his bear hugs.

"I need to tell the boys," I say, resigned.

This isn't going to be pleasant. I find Ben in bed in the room he shares with Will and sit on the edge next to him. Reaching over, I tuck the blankets around him. "I have to leave tomorrow."

Big dark eyes meet mine, his bottom lip quivering. "I know, I heard you talking. I wish you could stay longer."

"Me too." I lean over and kiss his forehead. "But as soon as I can, I'll come back. And the next time, I want to stay a lot longer."

"Forever?"

"We'll have to see." Being here without Cyrus has been painful, like a constant dull ache. Having him here with Bridget would be like knife blades carving gaping wounds in my heart. I stand and cross the room, stopping at the door, my hand on the doorknob. "I'm sorry, Ben. About leaving like I did last time and about coming back only to leave again. I love you, you know that right?"

He nods and turns onto his side, his back to me. I close the door and take a deep breath before going into the next room to have the same conversation with Ty and Connor. They take it about as well as Ben did.

Back in the living room, I plop on the couch next to Ally, who's nestled in Colin's arms. "They're not happy, but they're all right," I tell Ally and Will. "And I really am sorry about how I left last time."

"I understand," Will says. "Be careful, okay?"

"Yeah. We'll see you soon. I promise." I'm not sure why I said that. It's not a promise I can keep, and Will's tight smile tells me he knows it's bullshit.

"We put the rest of the money we brought in the top dresser drawer in your room, Ally," I say. "Buy solar panels and a generator. Or whatever you need. It's a lot. You'll have plenty to last for a while."

"You don't have to do that," Sonia says quietly.

I turn to see her standing in the door frame. "Maybe not, but we want to."

She gives me a sad smile. "I'm going to bed. I'll see you in the morning."

"G'night, Sonia," I call.

Alone, on the couch, I stare at the ceiling, no longer able to fight the tears. They spill from the corners of my eyes, sliding down my temples and curling into my ears. I sniff and roll over, my cheek brushing against soft fabric, reminding me of the last time I slept on a couch in the Ruins. The night after I was nearly eaten by a mountain lion. When the boy I love held me in his arms all night. The boy I love so completely, he both fills my soul and destroys me. Because he isn't here. Because he's with another girl.

26 Leaving

The inky sky wraps around us, the cold cutting through our new, thicker coats as we close the front door behind us. Colin slings the backpack with our stuff over his shoulder and heads down the steps with me on his heels.

"So, you were just going to leave without saying goodbye?" calls a familiar raspy voice.

"Shit, Rainey!" I say. "You scared the crap out of me."

"Good. You should be scared." She steps out of the shadows, arms crossed.

"Rainey—"

"Save it. You were going to sneak out without a word."

I shrug. "I figured you'd try to talk us out of it."

"You're right. This is a suicide mission. You have no idea what you're getting yourself into."

"How did you know?" I ask.

"I've been watching you since we met. And while it's pretty clear you had something going on with Cyrus, I don't think you actually came out here to find him. You came into the Ruins a thousand miles from where you last saw him." She shakes her head. "Something always felt off there. Then all of your questions about the Uprising…it doesn't take a genius to put two and two together."

"Well, it's not the sort of thing you go around announcing to people you just met, especially after you find out one of them used to be a Commander."

She's quiet for a few minutes, studying us. "Well, if you're stupid enough to go through with this, the least I can do is help you. You're a walking advertisement for the Union. They'll spot you coming a mile away."

"What do you mean?"

"The way you're dressed for starters. That we can fix. The way you speak and carry yourselves is harder to hide, but maybe you can pass."

She hands Colin a backpack.

"What's this?" he asks.

"Clothes. You need to change. You can't show up at a recruiting center wearing designer clothing."

Colin pulls out two pairs of jeans, a couple of shirts, socks, and boots. Everything is used, worn, comfy looking.

"Go change. We can talk on your way out of town."

Colin and I slip back inside, dressing in the old clothes, leaving our Union stuff folded on the floor by the door.

Rainey is waiting for us on the front porch. "Leave the backpack, too. It screams Union. Take these."

She hands us each a frayed canvas backpack. We transfer our food and water to the old backpacks and hand ours to Rainey.

"How'd you know we were leaving this morning?" I ask Rainey as we make our way down the street.

"Last night's dinner was obviously a farewell feast. Coupled with Ally's crying, I figured it was going to be fairly soon. I thought you might sneak out after we left and wandered back here late last night."

"You're nuts, you know that?" Colin says.

"So," she continues, ignoring Colin. "What are you planning on telling them when you get there?"

I glance at Colin and we both shrug.

"That's a problem. Recruiters will be curious why you're volunteering. You need a believable story."

"I thought they were so desperate, they're taking anyone," Colin says.

"True. But they're still going to ask why you're joining up. You don't want to say anything to make them take a closer look at you."

"So we can't just say we believe in the cause?" I ask, tripping over a rut in the road. Colin reaches out a hand to steady me.

The look Rainey gives me after I right myself indicates I'm about as prepared for this task as I am to perform brain surgery. "No, you can't. Everyone here has a story. Good or bad, but no one believes in the Uprising cause without a reason."

"What do you mean?" Colin asks. "Since I've been here, no one has anything good to say about the Union."

"Right, but do any of them look like they're ready to go to war for their opinion?"

"No, probably not," he says.

"So, what makes someone willing to die for a cause?" she asks.

Colin shakes his head, but I get it now. "People you care about. Walker's goons killed Lucien. I'd do anything to take him down," I say quietly.

"That's what I mean," she says.

"Why'd your sister join up?" I ask before I can stop myself.

"My mom got sick. My dad tried getting medicine from the Union, but the drugs were too expensive. When she died, he drank himself to death. My sister blamed the Union for both of their deaths." I have nothing to say to that, and she quickly turns the conversation back to us. "Stick with the death of a loved one at the hands of the Union. You don't need a big elaborate story. Keep it short and sweet."

When we get to the edge of town, Rainey stops. "This is where I get off." She reaches out and hugs me stiffly, then Colin. "Be careful." She turns and starts walking back before we can thank her.

"She's a little unusual," Colin says.

"Yep."

We hike at a good pace, eating as we walk. Morning drifts into afternoon and we've exhausted all other topics, so I finally broach the subject of Ally. "So, how was she this morning, really?"

"Fine. I mean, she was sad, and so was I, but she's okay. She understands." He gives me a lopsided grin. "She's amazing. I know she's younger than me, but she seems so much older, more mature. She's been through a lot." He pauses and his smile broadens. "And I *really* like her."

"Wow." I didn't expect Colin to develop such strong feelings for her so quickly.

"I didn't mean to fall for her, but she's special."

"I know she is, but...I also know how you feel about Lisa. It's only been a little over a month since you were drowning your broken heart in beer. I'm just a little skeptical of the depth of your feelings."

He stops so suddenly, it takes me a few seconds to realize it. "This coming from the girl who was whining she was in love with two guys at the same time."

"That's different—"

"It's not and you know it."

"Fine. You're right. Happy?"

He sighs, running a hand through his messy hair. "Ally really is okay, I promise. I didn't break her heart. I'm gonna go back as soon as I can. I want to bring her and the boys back to the Union someday, and the only way to make that happen is right here with you, doing what we're doing."

"Well, I guess that answers my next question."

"What's that?"

"If you were so crazy about Ally, why would you leave her to come with me on this suicide mission? I thought it meant you weren't that into her."

He stops again, turning to face me, putting both hands on my shoulders. "Evan, you saved my ass. If it wasn't for you, I wouldn't even be here right now. What kind of friend would I be if I let you go off on this half-baked mission from hell alone?"

"If it wasn't for me, they never would have kidnapped you in the first place, but thanks, Col. I know I said you didn't have to come with me, but I'm glad you're here."

The sun hugs the horizon, painting the sky tangerine and pink above silver clouds. We crest a hill and peer down at a large khaki tent with dozens of fatigue-clad bodies milling around, some armed with menacing weapons. My pulse quickens, and I give a fleeting thought to turning back.

"It's not too late to find another way," Colin says, as if reading my mind.

"There isn't a better way. Knowledge is power, and right now this is the best way to get the knowledge we need."

He blows out a slow stream of air and rubs his hands together. "Okay, let's do this then."

Colin begins making his way down the rocky slope toward the tent. I take a deep breath and follow. By the time we reach the bottom, the sun has dipped behind the western mountains, turning the sky cobalt.

We're immediately flanked by two armed soldiers. "This way," a guy with scary-broad shoulders says.

My heart beats a staccato rhythm as we cover the short distance. I wipe my palms on my jeans, and wait while one of the soldiers pushes the flap out of the way for me and Colin to enter. The tent is dark inside, lit only by candles. A woman sits at a desk in the center, staring at a tablet. This strikes me as odd. Even with solar power to charge it, I don't think there's a data network out here.

She glances up, noticing us, and sets the tablet down. Two other soldiers materialize, one a teenage boy, the other a woman in her early twenties. The woman at the desk stands, waving them off, and they retreat back into the shadows.

With another wave of her hand, our two escorts duck back outside, leaving us with the woman. A handful of empty desks are arranged inside the tent, and a half-dozen soldiers are busy packing boxes, folding chairs, and stacking crates. The woman walks toward us, her dark hair pulled into a severe bun at the nape of her neck. The fine lines etched around her mouth are the only indication of her age.

Adrenaline pumps through me, and I clench my fists to keep my hands from shaking.

"Can I help you?" she asks.

"We'd like to join," Colin says.

She crosses her arms over her chest and narrows her eyes. "What are your names?"

"I'm Colin and this is…E…uh…Delilah."

"Where are you from?" she asks.

"Down south." Colin says.

The woman tilts her head. "Why are you here?"

"Where we lived before, our neighbors, our friends," I start, telling her the story of Will and Ben's parents killed at the hands of the Union so the Union boy they rescued wouldn't talk about what he saw in the Ruins. As my story unfolds, it's easy to conjure legitimate emotion.

She studies us for a long time when I finish, and I concentrate on my breathing and trying not to squirm. Finally, she calls over her shoulder, "Eight, Sixteen, we have two new recruits. Get them outfitted and send them with the group going to Northwest Seven."

The two who disappeared into the shadows earlier return. "Yes ma'am," says the woman with a number eight on her shirt.

Colin turns to me, eyebrows raised. People are reduced to numbers? Talk about dehumanizing.

We head out the back and into a flurry of activity that was hidden from view when we entered. Several smaller tents butt up against the main tent, while others are in the process of being torn down, folded, and loaded onto pallets. A fleet of flatbed trucks are loaded with crates and our fellow recruits.

"Follow me," Eight says. We start after her, but she cuts her eyes to Colin. "You, go with Sixteen."

Colin and I lock eyes for a few beats before he turns and catches up to Sixteen.

"In here," Eight says, entering one of the small tents. "Take everything off." When I don't move fast enough, she claps her hands. "Now."

I strip down to my underwear, feeling exposed.

"Everything," she snaps.

My face heats up as I remove my bra and step out of my underwear. She examines me in a way that makes me feel like livestock up for auction before handing me a pair of khaki boxer briefs, sports bra, fatigues, T-shirt, socks, and boots.

"Tell me if the boots don't fit," she says.

Apparently she doesn't care if anything else fits. I glance at my shirt and see I will now be known as 172. My shirt is too small, pulling tightly across my chest, making me look like a cocktail waitress from Melons bar.

"Can I get a bigger shirt?" I ask.

Eight looks at me as if I'm Oliver Twist asking for another bowl of gruel.

"Guess not," I mumble.

"You'll get another set of clothing and winter gear when you get to your training camp," she says, opening the flap for me to exit.

I head outside to wait for Colin. He pops out of the other tent and looks me up and down. "Nice," he says, his gaze locking onto my chest.

"Hey, eyes up here."

He grins. "Sorry. You may be my best friend, but you're still a girl."

I roll my eyes.

"This way," Eight says, motioning for us to follow.

She leads us to one of the flatbeds loaded with people. The evening air is thick with moisture, making me shiver. I wish I had my winter gear now, but none of the other recruits has a jacket. They're all huddled together in an attempt to keep warm, and a failed one at that based on the number of chattering teeth.

Colin hoists himself onto the back of the truck and reaches to pull me up. We're the last on, and I feel everyone's eyes on us. Colin sits with his back to them, feet dangling off the end of the platform, and pats the spot next to him. I sit and lean against him for warmth.

Within minutes, we start moving, large knobby treaded tires help the truck move over the unpaved roads. As we pick up speed, the high-pitched whine of the electric motor creates white noise. Between the gentle rocking of the truck as it jostles along and a long day of walking, when I rest my head on Colin's shoulder and close my eyes, everything fades away.

I jerk awake when we slow and come to a stop in a densely forested area, thick with evergreens. Clouds hug the ground so heavily, I can only see fifty yards in any direction. The air smells of fresh pine and earth. Colin and I hop down, huddling close to each other until everyone is unloaded.

A dark-haired girl and a guy with a blond buzz cut approach us. "We're your Group Leaders for the next four weeks," the girl says. "Separate into two groups. Women, follow me, men follow Five."

The anxiety in Colin's eyes mirrors my thoughts. This is the first time we'll be apart since he picked me up from the train station in the Northwestern Province. He's been my anchor, so when he follows Five in one direction and I trail after the girl, Seven, in the opposite direction, I feel adrift.

I watch the boys disappear into the fog, before jogging to catch up with my group. There are fewer women than men, and I'm one of the oldest new recruits. The terms "women" and "men" can only be used loosely — some of the girls aren't much older than my sisters, Katie and Rachel. So much for only taking those over the age of fifteen. Seven leads us to a row of tables where a change of clothing is shoved into my hands. We file past, stopping at each station to pick up a heavy coat, a pair of gloves, a knit hat, a comb, toothbrush, and some lip balm. Holding my possessions to my chest, I follow the line.

"Laundry's twice a week. You're expected to wash your clothes every laundry day," Seven says, leading us across the compound to a long tent. "This is where you'll sleep. The bunks are marked with numbers with a corresponding locker at the foot of each bunk. Find your bunk and get some sleep. Your day starts in three hours."

Someone groans behind me and Seven stops, turning to identify the groaner. She spots the guilty party. "Number 164, follow me."

A young girl with a round face and wide, terrified eyes follows Seven while the rest of us file into the tent. I locate my bed, put my clothes and toiletries inside my locker, and climb the ladder to the top bunk.

Lying on my back, staring up into darkness, I'm second-guessing, or maybe third- or fourth-guessing, my decision to come here. I close my eyes and try to sleep, but thoughts of Cyrus invade my mind, betraying me. Does he miss me at all anymore, or is he over me and happy with a girl named Bridget? Tears slip out the sides of my eyes, and I angrily push them away, rolling onto my stomach and shutting down all thoughts of Cyrus.

The next thing I'm aware of is someone yelling for us to get up. The day has begun.

Book 3 – The Uprising

27 Day One

My eyelids are at half-mast as I drag myself out of bed and dress, blindly following the others to the mess tent. Breakfast consists of overcooked scrambled eggs, soggy toast, and…sweet mother of all that is holy, they have coffee. It tastes like it's been strained through an old gym sock, but at least it's not tea.

We're corralled outside the minute we finish eating and divided into groups of twenty, based on our numbers, which means Colin and I are together. Our group is the last and smallest with only eighteen.

"You'll rotate through various activities throughout the day," Five says, his voice higher-pitched than I would've thought for a guy of his size. At well over six feet, I'm guessing he's been through puberty, but his voice along with a surprising lack of facial hair leaves some doubt. "Your first rotation is the tattoo tent."

With only a handful of tattooists, I get to watch everyone else squirm and bite their lips as they get marked while waiting for my turn. Colin goes before me and does his best not to flinch while the girl injects ink under his skin. Finally I'm up, and I take off my T-shirt before laying face-down on the table in my sports bra. The tattooist swipes an icy gauze pad soaked with sanitizer across my shoulder, making me suck in my breath. She grabs a wooden stick and burns the tip in the candle flame until it's black and sketches the Uprising U on me with the soot.

I bite down on the inside of my lip to keep from screaming as she pierces my skin. My teeth clamp together, drawing blood. Holy shit this hurts. Just when I think this torment will never end, she applies an antibiotic gel and covers my new tattoo with a bandage.

Although the sun is up by the time we head to our next rotation, low-lying fog creates an eerie atmosphere. A muffled popping comes from the distance as we follow Five along the path. He stops at a tent and holds the flap for us to enter. Inside, tables with piles of firearms line either side. Above each table is a sign with a range of numbers.

We locate our table and I'm handed a long, rifle-type gun with 173 stamped on the side. It's large, but lightweight, made from a sleek composite material. The rifle has two barrels, one shorter than the other. These are the same type of weapons I saw by the power station over the summer. The night I first overheard a plan to attack the Union.

Five leads a half-mile hike to the firing range. The closer we get, the louder the pops are. "Have a seat," he says, pointing to a series of stumps arranged in a semicircle. "Over the next four weeks, you'll learn to clean, load, and fire your weapon until it's second nature. You have one prime objective — to invade the Union and kill as many of those commies as possible. You'll be trained to fulfill this objective."

Someone to my left raises their hand.

"Yes, 167?"

"Um, aren't we going to live in the Union after this is over? Shouldn't we leave like doctors and nurses alive so they can help us?" asks a boy with long hair pulled back into a ponytail at the base of his neck.

Five turns and waves his hand at someone outside the circle. Two other leaders approach and Five says something quietly to them. They walk up to 167 and pull him to his feet.

"What did I do wrong?" he asks as he's led away.

"In order to fulfill your prime objective," Five continues, narrowing his dark blue eyes at the rest of us, "you'll learn to take orders without question. Stopping to seek answers can get you or one of your fellow soldiers killed."

I chance a look at Colin. They're worried about communists in the Union all the while training an army of obedient killing drones?

By the time we're released for lunch my fingers are sore after spending two hours jamming bullets into cartridges and cartridges into and out of my weapon, until I was able to master both tasks while blindfolded.

I scan the mess tent for 164 and 167, the groaning girl from last night and the boy from this morning, but don't see either one. Our next rotation is kitchen duty, and we gather around a short, stocky guy with the number twenty on his shirt.

"Right now, I need you to fetch water," he says, pointing to a wheeled cart with a couple dozen large buckets.

A handful of recruits head up front to pull, while the rest of us push the cart over bumpy ground to the river. We fill the buckets with water and hand them up to Seventy-Six, a freckled, sandy-haired boy with rosy cheeks, before returning to the kitchen to unload them.

"Half the buckets go here," Twenty says, inclining his head toward a pole suspended above an open fire, a lock of dark hair falling into his eyes. "The rest of the water goes into the pots on the stove."

I work with Colin and Seventy-Six to hang the full buckets over the fire to heat.

"Here," an apron-wearing girl says, thrusting a paring knife in my hand and pointing at a pile of potatoes. "Get busy."

I'm used to doing this with a specially-designed peeler at home, but I grab the knife and a potato, doing as instructed. Lack of sleep and bone-weary exhaustion take their toll, and I slice my index finger. I swear and shove my finger into my mouth, sucking the blood, too scared to seek medical attention, if there even is such a thing. Colin grabs my hand and pulls my finger from my mouth, wrapping it in his bandana and applying pressure.

Colin and Seventy-Six finish the potatoes and I go help the others with placing pinto beans into pots of water to soak. My back is killing me and my arms are so sore, I feel like I can't lift them by the time we're released to our bunks to clean up for the evening meal. I glance up at my bed and put my foot on the bottom rung to climb up. Maybe I can lie down for a minute, even take a short nap.

"Don't do it," says a girl behind me.

I turn around and come face-to-face with a pretty blonde with pale green eyes and the number Seventy-Two on her shirt. She opens her footlocker and grabs her jacket.

"Trust me, if you go up there, you won't come back down until tomorrow and will miss dinner. You'll need every meal they serve here if you want to get through Basic."

She's probably right. I sigh and grab my jacket, following her outside.

"Where're you from?" she asks.

"Down south. You?"

"From a town northeast of here." She turns to face me and thrusts out her hand. "I'm Emmali. Like Emma and Li smashed together."

I shake her hand. "Nice to meet you. I'm…Delilah."

She stuffs her hands into the pockets of her coat. "I saw you sitting with 173 at lunch today."

"Yeah, we're from the same town."

"He's hot. Are you two, you know, together?" Her tone is a little too casual.

"Not officially."

"Well, no one is officially together here." She laughs, a big throaty one, head thrown back and everything. I like this girl already. "There's a make-out spot inside the trees that's heavily used. I mean, relationships are frowned upon, but mostly they look the other way, as long as you don't get into any trouble."

"Trouble?" I step around a puddle from a rainstorm that passed through an hour ago.

"Yeah, you know, like guys fighting over a girl, or girls over a guy. That kind of thing will get you sent to the Hole. And pregnant girls disappear."

I want to ask what the Hole is or how many girls have disappeared, but we've reached the mess tent, and I'm not sure if we're supposed to be talking about this.

"Avoid all public displays of affection," she whispers, "and you'll be fine."

We grab trays and stand in line to get our dinner. I glance around for Colin and find him sitting at a table with Seventy-Six. A lump of mashed potatoes hits my plate followed by a spoonful of runny pinto beans, making me wonder why I bothered to stay awake for this. Emmali and I walk over and join the boys.

"This is Emmali," I say. "And this is Colin."

"This is Jefferson. Jefferson, this is Delilah," Colin says.

Jefferson grins broadly and his smile totally transforms him from homely to almost adorable. He should smile more.

"Do you two know each other?" I ask Emmali.

"Yeah. We went through Basic together," she says.

We make small talk as we eat, but the effects of the long day are hitting me hard, and soon I'm only listening to the others. After dinner, I say goodnight and drag myself back to our tent. I barely make it up the ladder with my eyes open, and they're closed by the time I roll into my bunk.

My bladder nudges me from a deep, dreamless sleep. I climb down and stuff my feet into my boots, throwing on my coat before stepping out into the bitter cold. With my hands jammed into my pockets, I rush to the latrines, which are a good five-minute walk away. My breath curls in a white cloud in front of my mouth, encouraging me to move a little faster.

I sit down and I'm jolted fully awake when my butt hits metal. For the love of god, why would anyone put a metal seat on a latrine somewhere it gets this cold? I swear the pee runs back up inside trying to find warmth. Instead, I perch over the opening and do my business so I can hurry back to the semi-warmth of the tent. On my way back, the soft pop, pop, pop of someone firing their weapon echoes through the night air.

What a strange time for target practice, although on second thought, I doubt there is a strange time. We'll probably practice at all hours of the day and night as part of our training.

"Oh good, you're back," Emmali says when I'm halfway up to my bed. "I heard the shots. I was worried you ran."

I climb back down. "What do you mean?"

"Those shots. Didn't you hear them?"

"Well, yeah, but…" A sudden chill works its way through me.

"That's the sentry," she says, her voice still groggy with sleep.

My eyes widen as the meaning of her words sink in.

She rolls her eyes. "Did you think this was something you could just walk away from if you changed your mind?"

The morning wake-up call comes far too early once again. Seven is standing inside the tent when I crack my eyes open, her dark hair pulled into a high ponytail, looking way too alert.

"Today is laundry day," she announces. "For new recruits, that means you strip down completely, dress in your change of clothes, and put your soiled clothing in here." She holds up a mesh bag.

After changing and dropping my dirty stuff into the bag, I'm ready to go to breakfast. But apparently that's not the plan for today.

"Pick up the laundry bags and come with me," Seven directs.

I wave to Emmali and follow my fellow recruits to a tent next to the mess tent. We file in and set the bags down.

"You'll work with Twelve here to sort and start laundry," she says before turning and leaving us in the hands of a large, oafish guy with an upturned nose and a unibrow. The clenched jaw and tight-lipped expression says he won't be cracking any jokes this morning.

"Dump everything out," he says. "Underwear and socks in one pile, fatigues and shirts in another."

We spend the next couple of hours fetching water, washing other people's sweaty shirts and underwear, and hanging them to dry, making yesterday's mess duty seem like a vacation. We're finally released and told to return in two hours to fold and sort the clothes. Everyone else has eaten and moved on to their morning activities, and the breakfast that's left is cold and even less appealing than yesterday's. Colin and I grab our food and eat, not bothering to talk between bites before being rushed to the firing range to practice.

Emmali's words from last night are front and center in my mind while I stuff bullets into the clip. Will we be expected to shoot our fellow soldiers, our friends, if they try to escape?

After delivering the folded laundry to their proper bunks, we're released to the mess tent for lunch. Colin and I take our trays to the corner table where we're alone for the first time today, and I share what Emmali told me about the make-out spot.

"We should plan on meeting there periodically," I say.

He waggles his eyebrows and smiles.

I kick him under the table. "Not to make out, you douche. To talk. Privately."

His smile doesn't falter. "So, when you want to meet up, you should twirl your hair and give a come hither look."

"How about if I slug you instead?" Even though he's just messing with me, it's getting on my nerves, until I realize he's trying to cheer me up. My irritation fizzles, and I give him a small, grateful smile.

Lunch is abbreviated due to our late breakfast and laundry duties, and we're herded outside before we've even finished eating. Colin stands, shoveling food into his mouth even as he steps away from the table.

Seven leads us into a clearing a good twenty-minute hike from camp. The clearing is ringed with stumps, and in the center is a maze outlined with hundreds of those wooden spring-loaded mouse traps. Dozens more are scattered throughout the maze.

"This is an exercise in trust. The goal is to learn to follow your leaders' orders without question," Seven says, indicating Two, Nine, a couple of other leaders I don't recognize. "173, you'll go first."

Colin walks over to stand next to Seven, towering over her.

"Take off your boots and socks," she says.

Two, a tall, slender girl, places a black hood over Colin's head. "Can you see?"

"No."

To make sure, she waves her hands in front of his face and then acts as if she's going to slap him, watching for a reaction. When he doesn't flinch, she appears satisfied.

"The way this works," Seven says, "is your leader will give you verbal commands, guiding you through the maze. You may be tempted to not listen based on various external stimuli. But if you obey, you won't be hurt. Don't listen, and you can expect some pain."

Two sits outside the maze and begins instructing Colin to take one small step to his left, two long steps right. Stop, turn left, squat. He follows the directions well until things get chaotic. Out of nowhere, a small quadcopter, no larger than my fist, buzzes Colin's head. He whips around, searching for the source of the hum.

Two continues with her commands, but Colin's distracted now. He swats the air around him, losing his footing and steps on a trap. The metal snaps, and he yanks his foot up, swearing loudly. He loses his balance and falls, hands first, catching his pinkie in another trap. He utters a few more choice words, but keeps going. Pushing himself up, he shakes his hand and waits for his next instruction.

"Only pay attention to my voice," Two says. "Tune everything else out."

The quadcopter continues to buzz him, and he's doing everything he can to ignore it, but I see the muscles in his shoulders tense. He rounds the last corner and it looks like he's going to finish easily when Nine approaches with a huge dog on a leash. Colin is oblivious until the beast snarls at him. He halts even though Two hasn't told him to, and because he paused, she pushes two mouse traps into his path with a long stick. Colin steps down and both traps snap onto his foot. He lets loose a steady stream of profanity as red welts form on his ankle where one of the traps flung up and struck him.

He finishes the course without further incident, but rips off the hood as he storms over to sit next to me. As pissed off as he is, he doesn't grumble or complain. We're all acutely aware 167 hasn't been seen since yesterday morning.

28 Mazes and Traps

While waiting for my turn on the maze, I remove my boots and peel off my socks. Nine, a stocky guy in his mid-twenties whose neck is like an extension of his head, will be my leader. The cold, hard ground beneath my bare soles cramps the muscles in my feet. I studied my fellow recruits going through before me, so I almost feel ready. What I'm not ready for is the disorienting sensation of being plunged into total darkness.

The hood over my head not only blocks my vision, but also filters my other senses, sending me reeling back to the cargo train when my kidnappers used a similar hood. My breathing quickens and sweat beads on my forehead. Closing my eyes, I remind myself I'm not being kidnapped. I'm just — idiotically — in an Uprising training camp with Walker at the helm. Yeah, that's not helping. I thought I was prepared, but nothing could've prepared me for this sensory deprivation.

Fear licks at my skin like flames, and I gulp in air that is rapidly becoming stale. Wind moving through the trees brings the sweet scent of fresh pine, reminding me of our apartment at Christmastime. Thoughts of my mom, Joe, and my twin sisters edge out reminders of Walker and kidnappings and kids being shot in the middle of the night trying to escape. My breathing regulates and my heart rate gradually returns to normal.

Still no instructions come, and my fellow participants are so quiet, I begin to think they've all left. Minutes tick by with nothing happening, and I grind my teeth together to keep from losing it again. Maybe this is all part of the training, to see how long I'll wait. I count the seconds in my head until another five minutes of complete isolation passes. My breathing is loud in my ears as I strain for the sound of anyone who might still be here.

My fingers itch, wanting to reach up and rip the hood off my face, but the still-missing kids, 164 and 167, keep my hands at my sides.

"Take one small step forward," Nine's muffled voice says.

My hands shake, and my nerves are on edge as if they've been jolted by electricity. Blowing out a cleansing breath, I take a step and wait for my next instruction, adrenaline still running through my veins at a manic pace. After the initial waiting, things go smoother, and I start to relax, getting in the zone. I follow directions, winding my way through the maze until a swarm of bugs surrounds my head. *Just ignore them, pretend they're not there.* One gets under the hood, buzzing my ear, and I shake my head to get it out. That movement causes me to lose my balance, and I fall back, a sharp thwack stinging the fingers of my right hand.

"Ow, shit," I say, yanking my hand back. Squeezing my eyes shut against the pain, I push myself up, and square my shoulders, determined to not let that happen again. *Ignore everything except Nine.* More instructions come, and I continue, step-by-step. Something pokes my leg, and I start to jerk away but remember what happened to my fellow recruits and ignore it. When something tickles my arm, I suck in a breath. Nine shouts directions at me at a rapid-fire pace, and I focus only on him, managing to block out a few more pokes and a voice that isn't Nine's trying to distract me.

The giant monster dog growls in close proximity, and an involuntary scream escapes my throat.

"Take a step forward," Nine says.

Yeah, I have no interest in getting any closer, but I don't have a choice. I place my right foot on the ground in front of me, my rapid breaths filling the space inside the hood. A loud scream to my right that sounds an awful lot like Colin in pain nearly undoes me.

"Take a small step to your right," Nine says.

I don't move.

"172, take a small step to your right."

As I reach up to rip the hood off, I'm hit with a sudden moment of clarity. This is the test. They found my weakness and are trying to exploit it. But what if it's not and he's really in pain? The others would do something for him if that was the case, right? When I drop my hand back to my side and take a small step to the right, Colin stops screaming, but a trap snaps my toes. I bite down hard, swallowing a yelp. It's not like I didn't know that was coming. I finish the maze without further incident, and rip off the hood, my sweaty curls matted to my head. Colin's waiting for me at the exit with a lopsided grin.

Seven steps into the center of the ring while I'm lacing up my boots. "All in all, you did well for your first time. This exercise will be repeated often, and by the end of your training, you'll have mastered it." She zeros in on me. "172, can I see you for a minute?"

After I finish tying my second boot, I walk over to her. She leads me away from the others, ratcheting up my anxiety. Is this about me and Colin? We've been so careful, but they must be aware of how important he is to me if they used him to try to break me.

"You did well."

"Thanks." I didn't do better than anyone else, though, and worse than some, so that can't be the reason she singled me out.

"I'm curious what you were thinking at the beginning of the exercise." My panic attack comes to mind, but I'm not willing to reveal that.

"Well, at first I thought everyone left. Then I wondered if it was part of the test, like maybe you were testing my patience or something."

"Interesting," she says, tapping her chin with her finger. "It was actually a technical glitch with some of the external stimuli."

"Why didn't anyone tell me?"

"Your role is to listen and obey. Nothing more." With that she turns and walks away.

Okay... I head back to Colin, who's watching me with an amused expression. "Why'd you scream like that? What did they do to you?"

"Nuthin'. It was my idea."

"You scared the crap out of me. I thought something happened to you."

"Yeah, but only for a moment. I knew you'd figure it out. Nine was gonna get one of the girls, but I told Seven I'd be a bigger temptation."

"What the hell, Colin?"

Several people turn our way, and Colin leans in and whispers in my ear, "Meet me in the woods tonight."

My tentmates stir around me, but with less vigor as they begin to settle down for the night. When the only sounds are deep and even breathing, I swing my legs over the side of the bunk and climb down the ladder, doing my best to avoid waking Emmali.

No such luck. "Where are you going?" she asks with a groggy voice.

"To meet Colin"

"Be careful," she whispers. "Don't get caught."

"I thought you said they don't care."

"They don't go looking for violators, but if they stumble across one, they can't look the other way. If they catch you, though, they might make an example out of you, because you're so visible."

My breath stalls. "Wh-what do you mean?"

"People are noticing you and Colin. Just be careful, okay?"

"Yeah, okay. Thanks." *Crap.* Being visible is not what we wanted.

I look both ways when I exit the tent, something I didn't even think of doing when I went to the latrine last night. Now I'm on edge as I rush to the rendezvous spot. Colin's not here yet, but plenty of other couples are, and based on some of the noises, a lot more than making out is going on.

Colin lopes over to me a few minutes later, giving me a lingering hug for appearance sake. He sits down and stretches out one lanky leg in front of him, bending the other at the knee. He pats the ground next to him, and I sit facing him, our hips pressed against each other. He wraps his arms loosely around my waist, and I turn to face him, my cheek resting on his shoulder, as if we're going to kiss.

"You were awesome today," he says quietly. "Everyone is talking about you."

I jerk my head up and almost bash his chin. "What do you mean everyone's talking about me? We're supposed to blend in. If people start looking into who I am and where I'm from, we're both in danger."

He rubs his hand up and down my arm. "Calm down. No one can look into your history because there aren't any records out here, remember? Plus, I don't think they care where any of us are from as long as we follow orders."

My heart rate begins to normalize, realizing he's right. "Why'd you scream like that today?"

"Because I want people to notice you. It's important. Can't you see what they're doing?"

Another couple enters the woods and glances our way. Colin leans his forehead against mine. "They're training an army of drones. They want soldiers who'll do their bidding without asking questions. There's no way the drones will ever find out the information we need. The only way to get it is to be in leadership positions. I'm helping you reach your true potential."

I roll my eyes, but I understand what he's saying, and it makes sense. Rainey said they were promoting anyone with leadership abilities. "Before I came out here, Emmali said to be careful. Because we're so visible, they might want to make an example of us if we get caught."

We waggles his eyebrows. "Then let's not get caught."

"Let's go. Up and at 'em!" Seven calls way too loudly for the middle of the night. No one is stupid enough to complain, though. Instead, we dress in silence and meet her outside. "You've got five minutes to stretch and warm up before a five-mile run."

I drop to the ground and begin my old cross-country pre-run stretching. I haven't run in way too long, something that was once a part of my daily routine. We take off, following Seven's swinging ponytail as she sets a slow pace. The cold air piercing my lungs invigorates me, and soon I'm itching to break free. At the two-mile mark, endorphins flood my system, giving me an extra kick, so by the time we finish our run, I'm pumped. No post-run shower for us, though. We're released to eat breakfast before reporting to the shooting range.

"You'll be doing target practice today," Five says, his pubescent voice cracking. "Load your weapons the way you learned yesterday, practicing proper gun safety."

Once again, Colin and I are in the back of the line and watch as 151, a girl with short spikey hair and buckets of attitude, is instructed on how to flick off her safety, hold, and fire her weapon at the target. The morning passes quickly, with each of us taking a turn. This gun has much less kick than the rifle I learned on over the summer, but it's also a lot less accurate. I'm forced to concentrate on so many things at once, I finally get what Cyrus was trying to explain to me about my breathing.

After lunch, Seven and Five line us up outside the mess tent, marching us to another clearing about a mile away. This one is bigger than the other two combined and houses an obstacle course.

"Today we're working on agility," Five says. "You'll be expected to master each obstacle over the next four weeks. Some of you will accomplish this sooner than others, so if you find yourself experiencing difficulties with any of the obstacles, you can plan on clocking extra time here."

I'll be one of those people. Looking at the rope I'm expected to climb and the wall they want me to scale, I know I'm in trouble. I've never had much upper body strength, but hey, if extra practice gets me out of laundry duty, maybe it's not all bad. Seven divides us into groups of five, and each group is assigned to work on one obstacle. My group starts with the rope climb. Colin and the two other guys in our group climb up and slide back down in under a minute. It's only eight feet high, but it might as well be eighty.

Colin hands me the rope, and I take a deep breath, grabbing on with both hands. I pull myself up, wrapping the rope under one foot and over the other, anchoring myself the way the guys did. With my right hand, I reach up and grip tightly, then move my left hand above my right, scooting my feet up. The boys made it look so easy, but the rope slips out between my feet and I scramble to get a hold of it again, my biceps and shoulders burning as I hang on with everything I am.

Perspiration beads on my forehead, dripping into my eyes and making them sting. Bending my neck, I wipe my face across my sleeve, then pull myself up another six inches. At least five minutes passes before I arrive at the top, my arms quivering like they're made of Jell-O. I slide down, breaking open one of the blisters on my palms I developed on the way up. With a sigh of relief and a sense of accomplishment, I put shaky feet on solid ground.

We rotate to the next obstacle where we're required to crawl on our stomachs under a rope mesh. This one is easier, although my arm and back muscles are shot, so I'm the last in our group to finish. Low hurdles are next. They range in height from a few inches to two feet, and thanks to the season I ran track the year before I discovered cross, I breeze through this obstacle.

When we reach the wall, I silently curse the nearly vertical obstacle. I'm up first this time and get a running start, flinging myself up, my feet scrambling to find one of the few holds while my nails scrape down the wall, searching for a handhold. All they find is a splinter as my hands slip off, and I fall to the ground. Lying on my back, I stare up at the sky, playing hide-n-seek with the clouds, and take a few deep breaths before getting back in line to try again.

My second attempt isn't much better than the first, well except this time I'm smart enough not to get another splinter. It's time to rotate before I get over. I follow my team to the balance beam. When it's my turn, I step onto the narrow wood plank suspended between two stumps and angle my feet in the hopes it'll provide more stability. Holding my hands out to the side, I move one foot forward, pivot and lose my balance. No amount of arm waving will save me as I land on the grass.

"Back of the line, 172," Five calls.

The guys in our group, with their higher centers of gravity and wider feet, have a tougher time with balance than 151 and I do. Finally something I'm better at than they are, but I still have a long way to go.

29 My True Potential

Emmali hooks her arm through mine as we walk back to our tent together after dinner. "So, I've been wondering," she says. "Why did you sign up? I heard you enlisted."

"Who told you that?" Is that kind of information shared? They seem pretty tight-lipped about everything else.

"Just talk. A lot of people are talking about you."

So I tell her the same story I told the recruiter about Will and Ben and their parents.

"Oh. That makes sense." Her voice holds a hint of disappointment. "I was hoping for something more…epic."

"Sorry, nothing epic about me. What about you?"

She lets out a long sigh. "They came through our town seeking recruits. Even though they said they were looking for volunteers, it didn't come across as optional, so basically I signed up so they'd leave my family alone."

"How long have you been here?"

She glances up at the sky. "About seven weeks. I finished Basic and now I'm learning my specialty."

"Your specialty?"

"Yeah, after you get through Basic training, they assign a specialty based on your natural abilities."

"What's yours?" My foot lands in a gushy mud puddle, and I wipe my boot on pine needles to clean it off, holding on to Emmali for support.

"We're not supposed to say. They don't want the new recruits to know what the specialties are until after you're tested. They're afraid you might perform differently, trying to land the one you want. They want to place you according to what you're good at, not on what you think would be the most fun."

"That makes sense, I guess."

"Are you meeting Colin tonight?" The sudden change in subject is jarring. She seems to have an unnatural obsession with my love life, or maybe a natural obsession with Colin.

"No. We talked about what you said the other night, and we aren't sure we want to risk it."

"Well, I just wanted to warn you. There are rumors going around about rapes. You shouldn't be out alone after dark."

I stop and turn to her. "Rapes?"

"Yeah. No one's reported anything, so they're just rumors, but I think they're true. The girls are probably more worried about what'll happen if they report a rape. You know, having to explain what they're doing out of bed in the middle of the night."

It's as if I've entered a portal and taken a giant step back in women's rights. Back to when women would rather be silent than be called a liar, a tease, or worse.

"So…I just thought you should know. If you change your mind and end up going to meet Colin, buddy up with someone." She glances around before leaning in and whispering, "I saw 151 sneaking out last night after you left, so you might be able to walk with her."

I decide she's being genuine. "Thanks, Emmali. Really."

After our morning run and breakfast, we're sent to the firing range, but instead of being handed our weapons, we're directed to sit. A tall, muscular guy with an olive complexion and dark eyes enters the clearing. He's both striking in looks and build. His shirt fits like a second skin, revealing every ripped muscle in his upper body, and I'd bet money he sweats testosterone.

Ever girl inhales sharply at the sight of him, me included. Colin cuts his eyes my way before rolling them. The guy walks to the center, folding his massive arms across his chest just under the number three printed on his shirt. He glances around the group, and when his gaze meets mine, warmth floods my cheeks. There's something dangerously sexy and a little terrifying about him.

Three pivots on his back foot, swiveling his head to lock eyes with each of us as he turns. All of a sudden, he whirls around, his hand flying away from his body in a blur. A thwack echoes through the clearing, and a knife is lodged in the trunk of a tree at least a hundred feet away.

Three turns back to face us, and Five moves to stand beside him. "You're all progressing well with your assault weapons, and you'll continue to practice with them, but there will be times when you'll need a silent attack method. Each of you will be issued a knife and taught how to throw with accuracy as Three here demonstrated." Next to the raw male massiveness that is Three, Five looks like a boy.

"Right-handed people on the right, lefties on the left," Three says. "Extend your dominant arm with your palm up." Three walks down the line, placing knives in our open hands.

I study the six-inch titanium baton-like knife. On one side is a wooden plate with two smooth round buttons, one slightly smaller than the other. The other side is plain metal. What I don't see is a blade.

"Make sure the side with the wood is up," Three says. "Notice the opening along the length of the handle. That's where your blade is located. Make sure that faces away from your body." Upon closer inspection, I locate the blunt edge of the blade tucked inside the handle. "Curl your fingers around the metal underside but *do not* wrap your fingers over the opening. Now, gripping the knife firmly, press the larger button with your thumb."

A series of clicks rushes across the clearing as eighteen blades launch out of handles simultaneously, followed by a chorus of "whoas" and "cools" as we fawn over our latest instrument of death.

"The other button allows you to close the blade. Pressing it will release the catch, so you can fold the blade back in."

We practice opening and closing our knives a dozen times until we're released for lunch.

I climb down from my bunk and slip over to where 151 sleeps, hoping the two of us can sneak out together tonight, but she's already gone. Ducking out of the tent, I look both ways and hurry to the rendezvous spot, never letting my guard down. I keep my eyes peeled and my knife ready. By the time I enter the woods, I'm on edge.

Colin stands and puts his hands on my shoulders. "What's wrong?"

"Nothing, I'm okay." Then I tell him about the rumors of rapes. "Emmali said if the girls are caught out, they're sent to the 'Hole.' Have you heard of that?"

He nods, a shadow crossing his eyes. "Yeah. Today. Apparently they take reluctant recruits outside the perimeter where they have isolation cells in the ground. They starve them until they're so broken they'll do whatever they're asked. But it sounds like they use the Hole for more than new recruits."

A knot twists in my gut, and I'm in real danger of losing my dinner. "Do you ever wonder if this is worth it?"

He sighs and picks up my hand. "Sometimes I think it'd be easier to head back to the border and ride it out up there with Ally. But then I think about my family and Lisa, and I can't just run away and do nothing."

"Yeah, you're right, I feel the same way. But sometimes I wonder what we can do anyway. We're only two people. Who are we to stop a war? I mean, how arrogant, right?"

He shakes his head. "Maybe not alone. But we came out here with a goal, we should try to see it through."

"So, you wanted to meet," I say. "What did you want to tell me?"

"Oh, right. So, I'm getting in good with some of the guys who've been here longer. They're including me in conversations, telling me stuff they don't share with the other new recruits. Anyway, our camp Commander is leaving in a couple of weeks, and we're getting a new one. Someone newly promoted from a nearby camp."

"Okay. And?" I say with a shrug.

"The Commander sets the rules for the camp, like when they use the Hole, for what infractions, how long they have to stay in, enforcing the perimeter, stuff like that. Things are gonna change, and everyone's nervous. No one knows anything about the new Commander, but they say the ones who are recently promoted have the most to prove, so they think things are gonna get more locked down here."

I glance up at him and wonder if we should switch strategies. "What do you think we should do?"

"Well, the other thing I heard is the attack will happen before summer, after everything thaws out. That gives us maybe five months at most. I'm worried we still don't know anything. If we want to get out before then, we need an exit strategy. We need to start planning."

"Let's wait until we're done with Basic and get our assignments." I fill him in on what Emmali told me about specialties, which granted, isn't much. "We might get good ones with access to more information."

He scratches a hand through his hair. "Maybe. But if neither of us gets into a good specialty, we'll need to get out fast."

I nod. "Okay. So we both need to work on figuring a way to get out of here without being shot."

My feet pound the ground, and cool air fills my lungs. I just wish I had my running shoes instead of these boots. Morning runs are the only time I feel normal. For an hour, I can let go, forget why we're here, breathe in the clean scents, feel the wind whipping my hair, cooling my cheeks.

A blur of green flies past as I dodge pine boughs, sidestep roots, and leap over rocks. This is nothing like cross-country back home, running through the planned and cultivated park paths designed to mimic nature, but not quite nailing it. I didn't know that then, but I sure as hell do now. Nothing in the Union compares to the raw beauty of nature doing what it does best — living unchecked.

I come upon a group of recruits I've never seen before. They must have started the run before we did, but we're about to lap them. Most have numbers lower than ours, in the 110s and 120s. They all seem to move without purpose, like zombies or…oh crap, they must be the Hole kids. A shudder rolls through me, and I pass several before I nearly collide with a girl with scrawny arms, bent at the waist, hurling. I stop and Colin pulls up next to me.

"Are you okay?" I ask the girl, reaching out to touch her arm.

"172, 173, get going," Fives yells.

The girl gives me a quick nod, wiping her mouth with the back of her hand. Colin and I take off, but I glance over my shoulder one last time as she and the other Hole kids disappear from view. We finish our run and head to the mess tent for breakfast, keeping one eye on the entrance for the Hole kids in general, and 164 and 167 specifically. If they were sent to the Hole, they might be part of that group. Neither one makes an appearance this morning, but my heart slams to a stop when I spot someone I do recognize. A young girl with long blond hair and large dark, haunting eyes.

She's the girl I saw when we were walking through the Ruins with Rainey, the one who spotted me hiding in the bushes. She turns my way, her eyes unfocused, glassy, but when her gaze meets mine, something flashes across her face and her eyes spark to life. The zombie-like stare morphs into something far more chilling — expectation. Why is she looking at me like that?

Colin spots Jefferson and some of the other guys and leads me to their table. I'm just digging into my breakfast when Emmali sits down next to me. "Hey."

"Morning," I say, swallowing the lumpy glue they try to pass off as oatmeal.

In my peripheral vision, I notice the Hole girl standing near our table, holding her tray and watching us. I motion for her to join us, and she takes a few tentative steps toward us before stopping. Trying again, I wave with more vigor until she shuffles up, sitting at the end of the table, several spots from the closest person. Emmali shoots me a wide-eyed look and shakes her head.

Turning to the girl with the number 108 on her shirt, I say, "Hi, I'm Delilah, and this is Colin, Jefferson, and Emmali."

No one else says anything, and I cut my eyes to Colin, hoping he'll introduce the rest of the guys, because I don't know their names. He won't look up though, and seems unnaturally obsessed with his bowl of gray slop.

I roll my eyes and turn back to 108. "What's your name?"

She swallows hard and looks up at me, whispering something.

"I'm sorry?"

"Willow," she says, a little louder this time.

"Hi, Willow. Nice to meet you."

I'm about to ask her something else, but she inhaled her breakfast and is getting up, her tray in hand. If she's been in the Hole, it's probably the first food she's had in a while.

When she disappears outside, I turn to the others. "What the hell is wrong with you? You couldn't even say good morning or tell her your names? She's just a scared kid, not diseased or anything."

"You shouldn't have asked her to join us," Emmali says, her voice low. "We're not supposed to associate with Holers."

I glance around the table. "Are you serious?"

"Hey, we didn't make the rules," Jefferson says.

"There are rules about who we're allowed to eat with?"

"Well, not so much a rule," Emmali says, "more like… common knowledge."

"Not common enough if not everyone knows." I slam my spoon on the table, my voice louder than I intended. "You guys know we're being trained for *war*, right? Do you think the 'Holers' will give two shits about saving your ass if you treat them like crap while we're in camp?"

They're all staring at their food as if it's the most interesting thing ever. Disgusted, I grab my tray and dump it with the rest of the dirty dishes before storming outside.

30 Trained for War

My shoulders ache and my arms quiver as I sit on my foot locker, untying my laces. I spent two hours on the obstacle course after dinner practicing the rope climb and the wall. All I want to do is crawl into my bunk and sleep for days. A shadow falls across my feet and I glance up to Willow's big dark eyes boring into mine.

"Uh, hi, Willow." She gives me a small wave but doesn't say anything. Stuffing my socks inside my boots, I set them aside, waiting to find out what she wants. "Do you need something?" She shakes her head, but still makes no move to leave, those enormous brown eyes of hers watching and unnerving me. "Are you sure you don't want anything?"

"Thank you." The words are barely above a whisper.

I lift my brow. "What for?" Maybe she heard how I stood up for her in the mess tent the other night.

"For finding me."

"I-I…" I start to say I didn't come here for her, but with the way she's looking at me, I can't bring myself to. What if hope is the only thing keeping her going? Instead I shrug my shoulders. "Sure."

She throws her arms around me, pinning my arms to my sides before scurrying back to her bunk. I climb up and lie on my back, staring into darkness. Is this what Rainey meant about paying it forward? She helped me. Am I now supposed to help Willow? I can't, though. Hell, I can't even help myself. Emmali crawls into bed below me, the bunk rocking as she settles in. Soon, her breathing becomes rhythmic, but as exhausted as I was five minutes ago, sleep doesn't come for me.

My mind races with thoughts I can't control. I'm in over my head, and even if Colin and I manage to land the best specialties and learn everything about the Uprising, what can the two of us possibly do to stop them? Even with help from the others, how can we save the Union without putting everyone in the Ruins in danger of retaliation?

The next few weeks unfold at a steady, consistent pace. Our routine consists of morning runs on non-laundry days, eating, training, and kitchen duty. Willow and a few of the other Hole kids join us for meals. A couple are even opening up and talking a little, but most of them still keep to themselves, way too damaged by their experiences to ever feel like they're a part of us.

Even though the new Commander is here, so far nothing's changed. Still, just to be safe, Colin and I only meet at the make-out spot if there's something we absolutely need to talk about without anyone overhearing us.

We've been here over a month now, and Colin's roots are starting to show. Mine are more subtle, and since we don't wash our hair every day, my color hasn't faded much. Still, we both wear our knit caps most of the time.

Clouds crept in over the course of the afternoon, bringing cooler temperatures. But the brisk air is perfect for this last knife training session before our testing begins tomorrow. Three calls my number and I walk to the middle of the throwing ring. I close my eyes, inhaling his masculine scent as he ties the blindfold. Damn, he even smells hot. His fingers brush my temples as he adjusts the material, and I have to force myself not to sigh, because every part of my body is reacting to his touch.

Three grabs my shoulders and spins me around. Breathing in slowly, I count to three, inhale, exhale, getting in the zone. My senses are on alert, listening for the signal. The click comes and I grab my knife, flicking open the blade. With a snap of my wrist, I send it sailing in the direction of the sound, hitting with a thwack.

I take off the blindfold, and I see I hit the target. The corner of Three's mouth curves up in a subtle smile. My smile is not subtle. Colin and I are naturals at this after years of playing darts in coffeehouses in the Union. The fact that I get to work with Three only makes it that much better. When he praises my skills, I turn girly. I know it's ridiculous, I mean I'm still pissed as hell at Bryce, I'm not over Cyrus and may never be, but Three is just all kinds of sexy.

On the way back to camp, Colin pulls me aside. "What is it about guys like Three that makes girls go all stupid?"

"What do you mean?" My voice is even, but my burning cheeks give me away.

He cuts his eyes to me. "The guys are giving me shit, saying I'd better be careful or you're gonna dump me."

"You know you're not actually my boyfriend, right?"

"Yeah. But they don't know that. Can you maybe take the panting down a bit? I have my reputation to protect."

"Seriously?" I roll my eyes.

"Hey, being in the inner circle is helping us get information. I'd like the conversations to be less about my girlfriend ogling the man candy and more about what the Uprising is doing."

"Fine." It's a pointless attraction anyway. Inappropriate thoughts about a shirtless Three might keep me awake at night, but he's the enemy. If he ever found out who I really am… I shudder. *Those* thoughts will keep me awake tonight for a completely different, totally not good reason.

"Nervous?"

"Yeah," Colin says. "You?"

I nod and chew on my lip as we wait. "At least by this time tomorrow, we'll know our specialties. Let's meet in our usual spot tomorrow night."

He pulls his right arm across his body, stretching his triceps. "Yeah, good plan."

Our first test is a timed five-mile run, and I'm feeling pretty confident. I'm the fastest girl and usually finish about mid-pack with the boys. Looking around, I realize the Hole kids aren't here, so maybe they're not being tested yet. They're clearly not ready. Somehow this thought comforts me a little, like maybe not everyone in charge here is pure evil.

Seven arrives, tablet in hand. "Line up by number, in rows of four across."

Colin and I are in the back row behind a sea of khaki shirts with olive numbers. I bounce on the balls of my feet to get my blood pumping. Seven fires a handgun in the air, signaling the start. A light drizzle makes the trail slippery, and several of my fellow recruits wipe out in front of me. I sidestep the muddy bodies, cutting around the first turn as the ground changes from earth to pine needles, providing much-needed traction. This is my thing, and I get in the zone, running at a steady pace, passing others as their stamina wanes, and ending up first among the girls and in the top third of the boys.

Fog kisses the tips of the grass as we hike after breakfast to the shooting range, where we're tested on cleaning, loading, and firing our weapon, then retested while blindfolded to simulate darkness. When we're done, knife throwing is next and I'm pumped. Three is waiting for us when we arrive. Colin and I take a seat on the stumps outside the circle and wait our turn.

When Three calls my number, I step forward, shaking out my shoulders and rolling my neck. I'm ready for this. He blindfolds me and spins me around, placing a knife in my hand. At the first click, I spin, extending my arm, and release with a flick of my wrist. Another knife appears in my hand, and I wait for the next sound, repeating the process until I'm out of knives. Three removes my blindfold and I can't keep the stupid grin off my face when I see I've hit all five targets. Because yeah, even though I'm not really training to attack the Union, I can't help feeling a sense of pride that I'm good at this, better than anyone, Colin included.

After lunch, we report to the maze for our trust test. As we enter the clearing, a murmur rises above the otherwise still afternoon. We've been practicing on the same course over the past month, but for our final, they changed it. Up until now, we've been using a combination of verbal commands and memory, knowing where the maze goes. But now, we'll need to rely solely on the directions we're given.

Five walks to the center and stands with his hands behind his back. "For your test, you will not receive direction from your Leaders, but from your fellow soldiers. You must trust each other at least as much as you trust your Leaders. Your team may be the only thing standing between survival and death."

I am not sure about this. What's to keep our teammates from sabotaging us to get a better specialty? Although they're probably watching for that. Part of the goal might be to figure out who'll make good Leaders.

"The way this will work," Seven says, "is 142 will guide 141, 143 will guide 142, and so on."

This means Colin will guide me, and I know this test is also in the bag. At this moment in my life, I trust Colin more than anyone else on Earth. It's a long wait as we watch the rest of the recruits take turns navigating the maze, some falling and getting snapped, but most get through with very few errors.

By the time my number is called, I'm a wreck, but when I turn to Colin, the jitters evaporate. A calming force flows through me, filling the spaces where anxious energy bit into my nerves. He gives me a thumbs up as Five steps behind me with the hood. I listen to

Colin's instructions and follow them exactly, ignoring everything from quadcopters, buzzing insects, stick pokes, loud noises, and dogs. Even new ones, like the sound of gunfire next to my head. As long as Colin continues to give me directions, I know none of the external distractions are worth worrying about. I finish with the best time of the day, and when I take my hood off, Colin's waiting for me with the biggest shit-eating grin.

Colin's up last, and I realize I don't know who'll guide him. It won't be me, because I guided 171.

"141, you're up," Seven says.

Right. She hasn't had a turn yet. Her name is Liza, and she's a tiny little thing with pale blond hair and almond-shaped blue eyes. I've seen her at the make-out spot with 156, a guy named Beckett, but I don't really know her all that well. She's not strong, but she's wicked smart.

Colin steps up to be blindfolded and I shake my hands at my sides, my nervous energy back in full force. Liza directs him through the maze like an expert. He only falters a few times but never falls. He trusts her enough to get to the end, maybe not in record time, but a solid performance. I'm beginning to think we really can do this, all that stands in our way is the damned obstacle course.

Seven leads us from the maze up to the clearing on the other side of camp, where we gather together in the late afternoon haze, the sun never bothering to make an appearance today.

"The run order will be based on your performance so far. However, we'll group you with other recruits, and you'll be tested as a team."

Okay, maybe I stand a chance after all. Sure, I'll be a major drag on the rest of the team, but they might be good enough to negate my suckage. Everyone glances around, sizing each other up. No one wants to be teamed with me, and I try to pretend I don't care, but I swear this is like grade six P.E. all over again. Yeah, I'm a wicked fast runner and I've got good hand-eye coordination, which makes long-distance running, knife throwing, and playing the piano a breeze. Climbing ropes and scaling walls, not so much.

When my number is called, I stifle a groan and wonder if they're setting me up for failure. My team consists of two others; when added to me, make the worst team possible. My teammates, Liza and Summer, a shy girl with short dark hair, look as glum as I feel, making it clear I'm not the only one who realizes this fun fact.

"This is a test of teamwork and speed," Seven says, taking a stick and drawing a solid line in the mud at one end of the obstacle course. She walks past all the obstacles to the other end and draws another before returning to us. "You will be tested on how well you can work together to develop a strategy and make it from the start line here to the finish line there."

No surprise, we're the last group to go.

"So, what order should we do the obstacles?" Summer asks.

"Let's get our weakest events out of the way first," I suggest.

"Is anyone good at any of them?" Liza asks.

"I don't totally suck at the balance beam," I say.

"The crawling thing isn't too bad," Summer says.

"Maybe we should all start on a different obstacle and cross paths, rather than following each other," I say.

The gun fires and the first team takes off. We watch them, abandoning our conversation for the moment.

"Oh hell. We're in trouble," Liza says as 163 flies up the rope and slides back down like he does this for fun.

"There's no way we're not coming in last," Summer mumbles.

Seven enters their times in her tablet and calls the next group.

"Hey, listen," Liza says. "What were her exact instructions?"

"Work together as a team to complete the obstacles?" I say.

"No," she says, a small smile tipping up the corners of her mouth. "She said, 'develop a strategy to go from start to finish.' She never said we had to do the obstacles."

I stare at her, because she's crazy. "If we don't do the obstacles we'll be disqualified."

"What if this test isn't *only* about strength or agility, but also about being creative? I mean, they know the three of us are terrible at this. Why put us together unless they want us to find a way to win?"

Liza is easily the smartest of all the recruits — maybe they expected her to figure this out. "I don't know. They didn't make us spend the past month training here only to trick us at the end."

"No," Summer says. "But what if it's another option rather than a trick? We're being tested on our natural abilities, right? They know we're not naturally athletic, so let's show them what we are good at, using our brains."

Liza gives me an impish grin. "What's the best that can happen if we do all the obstacles?"

"At this rate, come in last," I say.

"And what's the worst if we *don't* do them?"

"Be disqualified?" I guess.

"Which is worse?" Liza asks, "Being disqualified or coming in last?" Her grin has now grown into a full smile. Maybe it's not such a crazy idea after all.

When they call our group, the three of us toe the line next to each other. The rest of the recruits watch with varying levels of interest, most expecting us to fail. I would if I were them.

The gun fires, signaling the start, and I push off, racing past every obstacle to the finish fifty yards away. I reach it first, running past the line before slowing and turning around to greet my teammates as they join me seconds later. Across the course, the others stare at us with dumbfounded expressions, laughter, or in Colin's case, horror.

I drape my arms over my teammates' shoulders and hug them. We worked together as a team, and no matter what else happens, that feels pretty damn good.

"You're released," Seven says. "Go get ready for dinner and assemble behind the mess tent after you've eaten."

Colin slings his arm across my shoulder and walks with me, Liza, and Summer. "What was that all about?" he asks.

"We figured we were going to lose anyway, so we thought we'd try something different," I say.

"Yep," Summer says, beaming. "It was Liza's idea. If it works, it was brilliant."

"And if it doesn't?" Colin asks.

"Then we're in last place. Pretty much where we would've been," I say.

We stop in our tent for a few minutes to change out of our sweaty shirts. Then Summer, Liza, and I lock arms and walk to the mess tent as a team. Everyone stops talking and turns to stare at us as we enter.

Emmali marches up to us and throws her arms wide. "You guys rocked it! No one's ever done that before. At least not since I've been here. You'll be legendary."

The four of us join Colin, Jefferson, and Beckett at their table and have a rowdy meal in which we rehash every detail of our day. None of this has anything to do with why Colin and I are here, but for a little while, it feels good.

31 Feeling Good

S oft puffs of white escape my mouth while standing outside the mess tent after dinner waiting for Seven and Five. My toes ache, and I'm beginning to wish I'd put on both pairs of my socks. Buttoning my coat up all the way, I shove my gloved hands into my pockets. Colin's on my left, bouncing on his feet, trying to keep from freezing.

When our Group Leaders arrive, we follow them through the camp, far from our usual stomping grounds. Seven stops beside a spacious tent and lifts the flap. Solar-powered heaters border the perimeter warming the space to a cozy temperature. Seriously? The Commander could settle for two less heaters and let each of us have one in our tents to at least keep the icicles at bay.

"Line up by number in rows of ten," Seven calls out.

Colin and I are in the back, as always. While we wait, I glance around. The tent is divided into smaller rooms on the inside, with flaps leading to other areas. Soft lighting is also courtesy of solar power. It pays to be the Commander.

"You're no longer recruits, but full-fledged members of the Uprising," Five begins. "And as such, will be inspected by the camp Commander. He'll come in, introduce himself, perhaps offer a few words of encouragement, and then you'll be dismissed. Tomorrow morning, you'll receive the next part of your tattoo, signifying your full membership in the Uprising. Then you'll report back here for your specialties."

I stare down at my toes, willing them to warm up. Colin nudges me with his shoulder, and I glance up as Three comes in. My cheeks heat and my pulse quickens. God, I'm such an idiot.

The Commander walks in behind Three, and my breath stalls in my lungs. My eyes freeze open, and I lock my knees to keep from collapsing. My heart is thundering so hard, I'm afraid I'm going to go into cardiac arrest. Emmali said the new Commander was hot as hell, but that was an understatement.

He scans the room, surveying the new graduates with an expression of utter boredom, as if he'd rather be anywhere but here. His eyes rake the back row and halt when they get to me.

My heart stops its manic galloping and my windpipe slams shut. Cyrus's eyes bore into mine, pinning me in place, otherwise I'm sure I'd collapse. He gives no other indication he recognizes me. No warmth nor surprise colors his eyes, and his face holds the same bored expression when he finally tears his eyes away. My breath escapes in a whoosh, and I see Colin turn to stare at me out of the corner of my eye, but I can't take my eyes off the Commander.

Cyrus steps back and addresses the group, my body responding the way it always does to the deep timbre of his voice. "Today, you've officially joined the ranks of the Uprising. You've been trained for a difficult mission against a formidable opponent, but you *are* ready. You'll receive further training to prepare you more fully for the task ahead, but I believe you will all serve the Uprising proudly." He scans the group again, avoiding me completely this time, before turning to leave.

As soon as he's gone I lean over and whisper to Colin, "I need to talk to you. Meet me tonight."

"I thought we were meeting tomorrow," he whispers back.

"Tonight," I say through clenched teeth.

He rolls his eyes, but I know he'll be there.

Seven steps forward again. "Before I release you, I want to tell you all how proud I am of all of you. It's been a pleasure serving as your Group Leader over the past four weeks, and I have no doubt you'll all do well in your next assignments."

My mind is a scrambled mess on the walk back to the sleeping quarters with the others. Why is he here and how did he get to be a Commander?

My brain whirls, slicing and chopping, disintegrating my thoughts like a blender on high. It's taking forever for the rest of the girls to fall asleep. Cyrus joined the Uprising. Why didn't he tell the others what he was doing? Was he worried they wouldn't approve or was he trying to protect them? And where is this Bridget chick? Does he love her now instead of me? I have no right to be jealous, but I can't help it. The thought of him touching another girl, kissing her, rips up my insides, tears them apart, and skewers them.

When the rustling around me finally dies down, I climb down and pull on my boots, not bothering to tie them. Grabbing my jacket, I rush to meet Colin, not paying any attention to my surroundings as I pass the vehicle depot. Someone grabs my arm and pulls me into the dark shadows where two tents come together. Emmali's warning about the string of rapes sends fear sliding down my spine, and I reach for my knife.

Before I can get my hand into the side pocket of my fatigues, my back is pressed against the tent post, and I'm staring up into amber eyes. My heart stutters, my lungs fail. Cyrus's face is a mask, devoid of emotion, but I still search his eyes for any clue to what he's feeling. Is he surprised I'm here? Happy? Pissed? His gaze drops from mine, drifting to my mouth.

Released from the intensity of his stare, I take in the rest of his face, a face I thought I'd never see again. The high cheekbones, strong jaw, full lips, and masculine stubble that makes my knees turn to jelly. My breaths come faster now that my lungs have restarted, making it abundantly clear what his nearness does to me.

He lifts his gaze back to mine, and for a split second, his walls crumble, and I catch a glimpse of something deep and intense. His eyes close, shutting me out, but when his warm, soft lips press against mine, everything I just saw in his eyes is in this kiss. The world falls away as our mouths communicate so much without uttering a single word. His hands snake behind my head, his fingers tangling in my hair, tilting my head back so he can deepen the kiss.

Whiskers rake across my cheek and I gasp. His tongue slides between my parted lips, twisting with mine. Every inch of my skin tingles as my toes curl inside my boots. Grabbing his T-shirt, I pull him closer, wanting to crawl inside him, be a part of him. His kiss ignites me in a way I forgot was even possible, engulfing me in an inferno of emotion and need. I pour all the longing, passion, and desire I've kept bottled up over the past four months into this moment.

He slides his hands to my hips, digging his fingers in and tugging me against him until there's no space separating us. Where he ends and I begin, I can't tell, I only know I want him to kiss me like this forever. He steals my breath, my heart, my soul, and I don't care. His heart pounds beneath my palm, his breathing becoming ragged, too. When he draws back, chilly air settles in between us where fire raged only seconds before. My eyelids drift open and I stare into irises sparked with raw emotion.

Cyrus presses his forehead to mine for a moment while we both catch our breath before he steps back from me, holding me at arm's length. "What are you doing here?" he asks, his voice rough. "Do you have any idea how much danger you're in?"

I blink a few times, trying to recover, transitioning from the hottest kiss I've ever had to conversation. "I...uh..." My voice cracks, and I clear my throat. "What are *you* doing here?"

He lets out a sigh and rubs the back of his neck. "It's a long story."

"Same here."

"You can't stay here, Ev. If they figure out..." He shakes his head. "I'll get you out, but I need a little more time."

"For what?"

He lifts his head and stares beyond me, as if he's seeking the explanation over my shoulder. I want to ask if it has to do with Bridget, but I'm afraid of the answer.

"My contact. He's getting me Union credentials."

My head snaps up. "Wh...what? You were getting Union credentials? Oh my god...were...were you coming to find me?"

His chin tips down, warmth filling his eyes. He pulls me to his chest, wrapping his arms around my shoulders. "God, I've missed you."

Heat curls through my insides, knowing he didn't give up on me, on us. I don't understand how that led to us both standing in the same Uprising camp at the same time, unless... "Wait, did you know I was here?"

"What? No." He takes a step back, his eyes intense. "What *are* you doing here?"

"I was trying to find out what's going on."

"Are you insane? Do you have any idea what you've gotten yourself into?"

"Actually, I think I do," I say, chewing my lip.

"I need to get you out of here."

"How?"

He runs a hand through his hair. "I don't know yet. Damn it, Evan, you..."

I close my eyes, sensing his frustration, and realize I'm about to frustrate him further. "Uhh, Colin's here with me and there's this girl, Willow..."

"Colin?"

"Yeah. He was one of my friends at the bridge the day I left. Anyway, he came out here with me, I won't leave him behind."

He blows out a long breath through his nose, his jaw working overtime. "And the girl?"

"I met her here. She's really young, and she spent a bunch of time in the Hole."

"You can't save everyone," he says, closing his eyes and sighing.

"She's just a kid, Cyrus, and she looks at me with these big eyes, like I'm here to save her."

"Colin came with you, so I'll get him out, but the girl's fate lies here."

"But—"

"This is risky enough. Another person only makes it more dangerous for everyone."

"Cyrus—"

"Ev…" He shakes his head. "Please." The set of his jaw tells me he's done talking about it.

Willow's counting on me, but arguing with him when he's like this is a complete waste of time. I'll have to figure out something later. "Fine," I say, crossing my arms.

"I want to give my contact a chance to show up with the credentials, but at the first hint you're in danger, I'm getting you out of here."

"Okay."

His eyes search my face, as if he's trying to read something there. He cups my cheeks with gentle hands and kisses me. The last one was hot and desperate, but this kiss is soft, slow, deliberate, the way he used to kiss me when we had all the time in the world. His fingers trail along my neck, his thumbs skimming my collarbone. I let out an involuntary sound as the bones in my body turn to mush.

My hands run up his chest and around his neck, tugging him closer. My mouth responds as if he's water and I'm the desert floor in the middle of summer. He both quenches my thirst and fuels it because I can never seem to get enough.

Too soon he draws his lips from mine and wraps me in a tight hug, resting his cheek on top of my head. "Be ready to go at any time." With a quick kiss on my forehead, he's gone.

I can still smell him, his scent lingering, and I want to bottle it up, pour it on my pillow so I feel like he's with me when I crawl into bed. Suddenly I remember I was on my way to Colin and take off at a run to meet him.

Colin is pacing when I finally reach him. He rips the knit cap off his head and thrusts a hand through his hair. "What the hell? I was just about to go look for you."

"Shhh." I glance over my shoulder at the handful of couples still brave enough to venture out with the new Commander here. I pull Colin to the ground. "I'm fine. I got…sidetracked."

His brow furrows and his face darkens.

The rumors of camp rapes have only escalated in recent days. I grab his arm and shake my head. "Not like that. I'm okay, I promise." A smile slips out despite my efforts to hide it. "It's Cyrus. He's here. He's our new Commander."

His mouth drops open. "What?"

"Cyrus is the Commander. You didn't recognize him? From the bridge? The day you guys came to get me?"

"No, but he was wearing a rain slicker, and I was focused on you."

"I ran into him on the way here, or he ran into me. Anyway, we didn't have a lot of time to talk, but he's going to get us out. Soon."

"I don't understand."

"Neither do I, Colin, not really, but there's no specialty that will give us access to more information than what he already knows. We can leave."

Understanding dawns for a moment, before his expression darkens again. "He's a Commander, EvTay. You don't get to be that without doing shit. Are you sure we can trust him?"

I roll my eyes. "I'm sure."

"What about the girl from the Northern Territories and…everything else?"

The mention of Bridget makes me flinch, but I get why Colin's concerned. "Rainey was a Commander and we trusted her. He'll tell me everything when he can, but for now, I trust him with my life, and more importantly, with yours." His brows are knotted together as if they're wrestling with the rest of his face for control. "If he wanted to report us, he would've done it as soon as he saw me."

Colin is quiet for a long time, his face contorting as he processes everything. "You really trust him?"

"I really do."

He nods. "When do we leave?"

I shrug. "He said to be ready to go at any time."

We talk a little while longer, and then he walks me back to my tent. I climb up into bed and lie down, but I can't sleep. A smile pulls at my face — Cyrus is here. I don't need to wonder where he is or worry that something's happened to him, or hope he still loves me. Because oh my god, that kiss…his lips erased all my doubts, and he's getting us out of here.

I roll to my side and my eyes drift toward Willow's bunk, my smile fading. How can I let her down? Even though I never made her a promise, I know she's counting on me. The thought of leaving her behind, those big eyes of hers filling with tears when she realizes I'm gone and she's not, tightens my stomach, washing away all the giddiness.

32 Specialties

"Come on, sleepyhead. Get up or you're gonna miss breakfast."

I groan and roll over to see my bunkmate staring up at me, a grin plastered on her face. "What time is it?"

"Umm, six, I think. But you're not a recruit anymore. No more running or laundry duty. Now you get to go straight to the mess tent, but if you're not there before 6:30, you don't get to eat."

"Mm," I grunt, rolling over and rubbing sleep from my eyes. I meet her on the floor and finish dressing.

Emmali locks her arm with mine. "I can't wait to find out what your specialty is. Maybe we'll end up together."

"So what's yours? Can you tell me now?"

"I'm in Special Operations with Edison, he's Fifty-Five, and Leslie, and Nico. They're Forty-One and Thirty-Seven. We're learning how to get in and out of places quietly, gather information, that sort of thing. If you're smart and good with the knife, which you and Colin are, you usually get put into Special Operations."

"Cool." Twenty-four hours ago, I'd have been thrilled with that assignment, but now it doesn't really matter.

We grab breakfast and head over to sit with Colin, Jefferson, Liza, and Beckett, plus the two guys who were on Colin's obstacle course team. My eyes sweep the mess tent for Cyrus, even though before last night I hadn't seen him. He probably eats with the Leaders and not the riffraff, but I can't stop hoping to catch a glimpse of him.

I'm stuffing the last bite of stale bread in my mouth when Five approaches our table. "Graduates, report to the tattoo tent when you're finished eating."

Willow and the other Hole kids, along with what appear to be new recruits, enter the mess tent as we get up. Her eyes light up when she spots me, and she gives me a small smile.

The tattoo tent is bound to have a long line this morning, so I grab another cup of coffee and move to join Willow. "I'll meet up with you over there," I call to Colin.

We sit in the corner, far from the others. "I don't think I can do what they're training me for," she says, barely above a whisper.

My mug stops halfway to my mouth, and I stare at her. Even though she was quiet, she needs to be careful about what she says, especially in front of others. "Willow…"

"I can't shoot anyone, and if I don't do what they tell me, they'll kill me."

How the hell am I supposed to just leave her behind now?

"They're not bad, you know," she says.

"Who?" She just told me they're going to kill her for not following orders. How is that not evil?

"People from the Union. They're like us, except they live differently."

My mouth drops open. "How do you know that?"

"A girl from the Union lived in our town for a while. She escaped from her dad who was," she lowers her voice even more, "doing things to her he shouldn't." Sex abuse doesn't happen often, but when it does, it's handled quietly. I had no idea some kids went into the Ruins to escape. "She said people in the Union don't know anyone lives out here, and they don't even have weapons. I can't shoot them."

Oh god, she's killing me. "How did you end up in the Uprising? You're the youngest person here."

"My parents got sick last winter, and they…they never got better." She pauses and stares at her plate. "My older brother, Dakota, was gonna join. Every family was s'posed to send one volunteer, but after our parents died, Dakota said I was too young to take care of Sequoia, 'cause she's just a baby. So they took me instead."

"Your brother let them take you while he stayed behind?"

"It's not like that. He cares about us, but I can't care for Sequoia. Not really. I can't hunt or anything. So if he left us, we'd both die. This way, at least she has a chance."

That's totally twisted logic. What kind of brother lets the Uprising cart off his little sister? Cyrus believes everything happens for a reason, he can't deny fate brought me and Willow together. She saw me hiding in the underbrush when no one else did, we wound up at the same camp, and now she's telling me her tragic story after Cyrus said we can't help her. There's a reason for all of this, and the feeling she's the one I'm supposed to help is only getting stronger. I need to find a way to get her out of here.

As usual, Colin and I are last to get our tattoos thanks to our high numbers. Waiting to get stabbed with that damn needle again only amps up my anxiety. When it's finally my turn, I lie on the table, gritting my teeth as the tattooist inks a circle around the outside of the U, signifying our status as graduates.

"When you get your specialty, you can come back and add something meaningful to you. Most pick something relevant to their specialty," she says, as if it's a privilege to choose my own markings. I tug my T-shirt over my head and follow Colin back to our sleeping quarters until we're summoned.

Liza and Summer are standing all tense and rigid in between the boys' and girls' tents with Beckett, 153 and 170.

"Hey," Beckett says, and Colin grunts a response.

Five and Seven approach and lead the way across the compound to join the rest of our graduating class at the Commander's tent. The Commander. Cyrus. My cheeks warm at the thought of being near him again. This isn't good. Everyone's going to figure out how I feel about him if I can't get my emotions under control.

We file in behind Seven, and I wait for my eyes to adjust to the lower light levels before looking around. My fellow graduates are all fidgeting, nervous about finding out their specialties. I'm only anxious about one thing — seeing the boy I love.

I study the toes of my boots to keep from staring at the corner where he'll enter. Everyone around me stills, and the air thickens. I lift my head as Three walks in, holding up the flap. Cyrus ducks under it and moves to stand in front of us.

My breath catches as I drink him in. Shock kept me from studying him last night, but now I can't take my eyes off him. He's different, a little bigger than over the summer. Maybe taller, but definitely more muscular. Then again, so am I. This place'll do that to you. And his hair is shorter. But what stands out the most is a hardness that wasn't there before. How much is the loss of Lucien, and how much is from time spent in the Uprising?

Cyrus rattles off numbers, and those called step forward, including Beckett. "You're being assigned to sentry duty. Report to Six outside the firing range." He shakes their hands and moves on to the next group. This continues until only Colin, Summer, Frank, and I remain.

Cyrus's gaze travels over our little group, avoiding my eyes. "You've been selected for our Special Operations program. You'll be working with Three over the next several weeks before being relocated to other camps when your training here is complete. Congratulations."

He shakes hands with each of us, but he barely glances at me when his palm touches mine. I, on the other hand, stop breathing and my skin grows hot, electrified, every place our hands meet. With the complete lack of reaction on his part, he might as well be shaking hands with a stranger. When he turns to leave, my heart drops into my stomach, swimming in a sea of rejection. I tear my eyes away from his retreating form before anyone notices me staring at him, my face dripping with longing and heartbreak.

"Welcome to my team," Three says.

Swallowing my pain, I turn my attention to Three. He leads the four of us out of the tent and up to the clearing where we first learned to throw the knives.

Colin falls in next to me, bending down to whisper in my ear. "So that was Cyrus?"

I glance up and nod.

"Dude's got the best poker face ever. I'd never have guessed." I decide not to air my insecurities for the moment. It was hard enough last night getting Colin to agree to trust him. "He squeezed the shit out of my hand, though."

"Being in Special Ops is more than throwing knives," Three says, before I can ask Colin anything more. "You'll learn how to move silently, use the advantage of surprise, and how to kill using only your bare hands." A chill rolls through me. "When your training is complete, you'll be sent to other camps where you'll teach other recruits. You are among the best in camp and will be promoted to the position of Leader at the conclusion of your time here."

Emmali, Edison, Leslie and Nico enter the clearing.

"This is your team over the next several weeks," Three says. "You'll be spending a lot of time with each other. Get to know one another, socialize and eat together. You'll rely on each other to save your asses in the coming months."

Emmali hooks her arm through mine as we walk to lunch after morning orientation. "So, what do you think?"

"Um, we're being trained to do really horrific things to people?"

"You can't think about it that way or you'll never survive."

I nod in agreement and decide to adopt her strategy for now and start by changing the subject. "Is there a girl in camp named Bridget?"

She scrunches up her face. "No, I don't think so. Why?"

"Just curious. I thought I heard someone mention her."

"Not that I'm aware of, but I don't know everyone. So…" she says, changing the subject yet again, "what do you think of the divine piece of man candy we call Commander?"

I choke on my spit and she slaps me hard on the back. "Thanks. Yeah, he's definitely…um that."

"Some of the girls who've been here longer were trying to get the details on his status."

"Status?"

"Yeah, you know, if he's got a girlfriend or anything."

"Are Commanders allowed to date?"

"I don't know the rules, but from my experience, they pretty much do whatever they want. The last Commander had something going on with a couple of different guys. She thought she was being discreet, but they all like to brag."

I roll my eyes. Of course they do. "So what's the word? On the new Commander, I mean?"

"Leslie said that girl, Jessica, number eighty-nine, snuck into his tent and waited for him the other night. In his bed."

Oh god, I do *not* want to know this. Why did I ask? "And?" I croak, apparently incapable of keeping my mouth shut, even for my own stupid sake.

"Still got something stuck in your throat?" She turns to me, concern on her face.

"No." Why can't she just answer the question? "So, Jessica?"

"Oh, yeah, so nothing. She says he was nice about it, but kicked her out. Someone else said he has a girlfriend, but she's not here. Maybe back home or his old camp or something."

He wasn't even aware I was here until last night, so it must be Bridget. She's probably at his old camp, I should've thought of that. My mood takes an even darker turn as we head into the mess tent to get lunch.

"Let me see yours," I say to Colin.

He lifts his shirt enough for me to check out his tattoo. After we got our specialties, he ran straight back to get more crap inked on his shoulder. I run my fingers lightly over the design, his skin still slightly raised and red. Music notes dance around the outer edge of the circle, a guitar slashing through the center like a knife.

"What does that have to do with Special Ops?"

He shrugs, the hem of his shirt falling back to his waist. "Nothing, but Rainey's had weeds and spirally shit, so I figured I'd get something personal."

That gives me an idea. We still have an hour before we need to be to our first training class. "I'll catch up to you later," I call to Colin over my shoulder and head to the tattoo tent.

"Hi," says Fourteen, a brunette with tattoos covering both of her arms like sleeves. "Did you decide what you want?"

I nod, and explain what I have in mind. She inks a series of neat, ordered dots, equally spaced up the left side of the circle, and wild, rambling leaves and vines on the right, representing the two halves of me — my organized, controlled Union half and my crazy, untamed Ruins half.

The week is filled with anatomy lessons and practice as we learn how to subdue our enemies and kill them more efficiently. Any initial attraction I felt toward Three vanishes as he demonstrates new and heinous ways to disable or execute another person. Colin and I are biding our time until Cyrus says it's time to go. But this means we have to go to class every day and participate like we care, as if we enjoy learning how to properly knife someone at the base of their skull to ensure a quick and silent death.

Even though I'm only going through the motions, all of this training has brought on nightmares. The kind that leave me drenched in sweat, my heart racing. In these new versions of my recurring nightmare, I slice Dantel's throat, or break his neck. The past two nights, Emmali had to wake me because I wouldn't stop screaming. Lots of girls whimper or cry at night, but most of the screamers are the Hole kids.

Colin and I learned anatomy in school, but no one in the Ruins has had much education on the subject. Emmali's struggling with it, so she's still in the rudimentary class with us newcomers. Colin and I try to hold ourselves back, because there's no logical reason for us to know as much as we do. We pay quiet attention, ask appropriate questions, and blend in. Half our time is spent in the classroom, and the rest in the clearing, practicing chokeholds, locating the carotid artery, and flipping each other. Three also teaches us how to move stealthily, and we practice until we can sneak up on one another without detection.

What we aren't learning, is anything about the master Uprising plan. With Cyrus here, in his role as Commander, this isn't as important as it once was, but it makes me realize how stupid we were to think they would tell us anything if we joined up.

The last time I saw Cyrus was the morning we learned our specialties, furthering my assumption Bridget is the rumored girlfriend. Since Colin and I haven't met recently, there's no one to talk through all my issues with. Instead, my insecurities and paranoia are all bottled up, stewing in my belly, leaving me unsettled and tense.

Staring at a drawing of the human circulatory system, my eyes threatening to close, Seven motions to me. "The Commander would like to see you." With a nod at Three, she leads the way across the compound.

"Is this normal? To summon people, I mean?" I ask.

"Yes."

Nothing stopped him from asking for me days ago, which means he probably needs to talk to me about something specific, like getting out of here. Suddenly, I'm not sure what to say to him. Should I ask him why he kissed me? Or about Bridget? Is she coming with us? By the time we get to his tent, my stomach is a twisted mess. I follow Seven to a smaller enclosure in the back corner.

Cyrus sits behind a solid wood desk and glances up when we enter. My heart hammers in my chest with equal parts anticipation and apprehension. He rises and walks around his desk, leaning against the front edge, and points to a canvas folding chair for me to sit on. My legs are all gooey as I take the several steps required to cross the room and take a seat. I stare at my hands twisting in my lap, too afraid to look at him because I'm sure Seven will see my feelings for him plastered all over my face.

"You may go," Cyrus says.

I jerk my head up. "But I just got here."

The corners of his mouth quirk up for a split second. "Seven, wait outside, please."

"Yes, sir," she says.

I watch her leave before turning back to Cyrus. His eyes are bright in the light, but reveal nothing. My knees are only inches from his, and heat radiates in the small space between our bodies.

"Why did you kiss me the other night if you have a girlfriend?"

"What?"

I lift an eyebrow and cross my arms over my chest. "You kissed me."

He looks over my head, and I twist around, cringing at the thought Seven might have overheard. I let out a small sigh when no one's there.

When I turn back, Cyrus is studying me. "We can't really talk in here," he says, his voice so low I have to strain to hear him. "It's killing me having you here, so close, and not being able to touch you or kiss you."

My eyes widen and I lift my gaze to his. The hard Commander mask he's been wearing is gone, he's no longer hiding anything from me. My doubts evaporate like fog under the late morning sun because what's in those amber-colored eyes is pure longing.

"Meet me tonight. Past the vehicle depot where we were the other night."

I nod, not trusting myself to speak. He pushes off the desk, and I stand, our bodies nearly touching, but not quite. My eyes drift shut, and I breathe in his scent. When I open them, he's safely back behind his desk again.

"I'm glad we understand each other, Specialist," he says, loud enough for Seven to hear outside the room.

"Yes, Sir. Thank you, Commander." I turn to leave, but can't resist a quick look back over my shoulder. He's watching me go, specifically my ass. He drops his gaze to his desk and picks up his tablet, but it's too late. I can't fight the smile working its way onto my lips at catching a small glimpse of the boy I fell in love with.

33   The Boy I Love

My eyes fly open to complete darkness, the only sounds coming from my sleeping tentmates. With no concept of time, I rush down the ladder, stuffing my feet into my boots. I tie them quickly before hurrying from the tent. Halfway to where I'm supposed to meet Cyrus, I realize I forgot my jacket, but I don't want to go back for it. I don't know how long I was asleep or how long Cyrus has been waiting for me. Or if he's even still waiting.

Moonlight peeks through the trees, illuminating my way. Cold air skates across my skin, but with any luck, warm arms will be wrapped around me in mere moments. Voices and laughter carry through the night as I approach the vehicle depot. Three soldiers are standing in front of one of the trucks, talking and laughing. Their backs are to me, so I might be able to slip past unnoticed. My other option is to go around the long way, but I'm already so late.

A sudden movement in the middle of them catches my attention. Someone is lying on the hood of the truck, feet thrashing. "Let me go," a female voice screams. Before I totally grasp what I'm witnessing, I push off on my toes, sprinting toward them. The three guys turn in my direction, and the body on the truck pops up. *Liza.* Fat tears roll down her face as she gulps in big breaths of air. Pieces of hair escape her braid and stick out at wild angles. She snatches the bottom of her T-shirt and tugs it down.

Oh god, oh god. The realization of what's happening hits me like an A-Train, and my breath stutters. One of the guys has the number twenty-one printed on his shirt, and my mouth drops open when I recognize the other two as Nine and… "Jefferson?" His eyes drop to the ground. "Liza, get down," I yell to her.

She pushes forward and slides off, but Nine grabs her wrist, holding her in place.

"Let her go," I say, anger pulsing through me. Gang rapes? Really? We're supposed to be on the same team, not…*this.*

"Who's gonna make me?" Nine asks, his mouth lifting into a smirk, his left brow arching, mocking me.

Liza twists in his grasp, and I step forward, applying one of the first lessons we learned in Special Ops. Grabbing Liza's arm above Nine's grip, I rotate it toward his thumb, the weakest connection, and jerk up. She slips free, and I push her back, then nail him between the eyes with my fist. Although I land the punch correctly thanks to this week's training with Three, it stings like freaking hell.

Nine yells a string of obscenities and grabs his face with both hands. Liza scrambles backward, crablike, until she's out of reach, and pushes up, turning to leave. Just as I move to join her, Twenty-

One snags me around my waist, pulling me against his chest. Liza glances back at me, indecision flooding her features.

"Go get Beckett," I yell.

She turns and runs with Jefferson on her heels.

Twenty-One growls, "Wait! Check this chick's pockets for weapons."

Jefferson swings around and closes in on me, my heart pumping adrenaline into my bloodstream at a manic rate, making my body buzz with electricity. I jam my heel on Twenty-One's instep, then swing my leg behind me. He sees it coming and thrusts his hips back in time to avoid getting his junk smashed by my foot. My hand dives into my pocket to retrieve my knife, my thumb sliding across the button.

The blade flicks out as Nine rights himself, grabbing my wrist and twisting until I let go. "You should learn to butt out of things that don't concern you," he growls, wiping the blood dripping from his nose with the back of his hand.

"You're a Leader! What kind of shit is this? You think any one of us is gonna care what happens to your ass in the heat of the battle?"

His only response is to jerk my arm behind my back, pinning me against him.

"You've left us with a problem," Twenty-One says, licking his lips. "We're all dressed up with nowhere to go."

"That's unfortunate," I say, trying for sarcastic, but all that comes out is fear.

"Oh, I don't think so," Twenty-One says, reaching a hand up to my chest and groping me. "Best tits in camp, boys. This is our lucky night."

Anger burns through me. No one touches me without my permission. *No one.* I spin away from Nine, sweeping my leg out, connecting with the back of Twenty-One's knee. He buckles at the same time I drop to the ground like dead weight. Nine loses his grip on my wrist, and I crawl backward, trying to stay out of his reach, my heart pounding against my throat.

Jefferson moves back, seemingly unsure about getting involved. Even if he refuses, I can't take on the other two by myself. My only chance is to outrun them. Nine offers Twenty-One a hand up and they stalk toward me.

I roll to my stomach to push up, but before I can even get to my knees, they're on me, pulling me toward them by my ankles. My fingers claw at the dirt, mud grinding under my nails, my muscles burning with exertion. I flail my legs hard, freeing one leg.

Twenty-One pounces on me, pinning my shoulders to the dirt while Nine unbuckles his belt.

"What do you think Three'll do when he finds out you're messing with a member of his team?" I ask, desperate for anything to get them to back off.

Jefferson's face drains of color, turning a ghostly white in the moonlight. Twenty-One pushes off me and steps back, glancing at Nine, his eyes wide, hands up.

Nine lowers his face to mine, his top lip lifting to reveal crooked teeth. "If you say one word, I'll mess up that pretty boyfriend of yours."

Seriously? He thinks he stands a chance against Cyrus? Then it hits me — he's talking about Colin. Of course. This is how they're getting away with it. They're targeting girls with a weakness. Ones who care about someone else in camp. Bile rises in my throat, and tears gather in my eyes, but I refuse to cry in front of them. Liza will be back with Beckett any minute, I just need to hold them off a little longer.

Twenty-One yanks me to my feet as Jefferson moves behind me, securing both of my arms behind my back and dragging me to the truck. I kick, thrusting my shoulders back and forth as I fight to get loose. Jefferson shoves me up against the hood, pinning me with his shoulder. I lean forward and bite down hard on the fleshy part of his cheek. He screams and lets go, shoving me away from him with both hands. Before I can get past him, Twenty-One moves in and lifts a hand to smack me.

"No!" Nine shouts. "Nothing on the face, man. Seriously."

"She bit me," Jefferson whines.

"You can go second then," Nine says with a smug grin as he saunters over, unbuttoning his pants. My breaths come faster, and I close my eyes trying to calm myself. I focus on my training over the past few days, searching for something that'll help me get out of this. The unmistakable click of a gun being cocked startles me, and my eyes fly open.

It's not Beckett though. Cyrus stands behind Nine, the barrel of his handgun flush with the back of Nine's head. Nine's eyes are wide, his mouth slack. Twenty-One drops his hold on me and backs away with his hands up.

"Hey," Nine says, his voice high-pitched and quivering. "We were just having some fun. Nothing happened."

Cyrus pushes the gun harder against his skull, his gaze traveling back and forth between Jefferson and Twenty-One. I slip out away from the truck and move next to Cyrus. Jefferson closes his eyes and swallows. Cyrus's expression is terrifying. His eyes are hard, his jaw ticking. I almost don't recognize him. He's more pissed than I've ever seen him, and there's something almost wildly irrational about his expression.

"Hands on the back of your head," Cyrus says.

Oh my god. He's going to kill Nine.

Nine lifts his hands, shaking so much he can barely control them, and places them behind his head. Cyrus grabs him by his elbow and spins him around, forcing the gun barrel against his forehead, finger on the trigger.

"Did you touch her?" Cyrus asks, his voice unnaturally, terrifyingly calm.

"No, man," Nine says. "I didn't touch her. He did." His eyes shift to Twenty-One.

Oh, shit.

"Cyrus." I call his name, trying to break the weird trance he seems to be in. Ice water threads through my veins and my chest is tight. Sure, I want Nine punished, and if he experiences intense, ongoing pain, I won't lose any sleep over it. But I don't want Cyrus to kill him because of me. Taking a life changes you. The psychological backlash from revenge killing must be worse than what I'm dealing with after shooting Dantel. "Cyrus," I call again. "They didn't hurt me."

The muscle in his jaw pops, but he doesn't take his eyes off Nine.

I reach up to place my hand on his shoulder, but he's coiled so tightly, I'm afraid if I touch him, he'll fire by reflex. Instead, I whisper, "Cyrus, don't."

He tears his eyes away from Nine and finally looks at me. His gaze travels over my body, and several long, tense moments pass before he seems satisfied I'm unharmed. When he finally pulls the barrel of the gun back a few inches, Nine's body slumps against the truck.

"On your knees, hands behind your head," Cyrus says, then turns to me. "Inside the tent," he nods to the right, "there's a cabinet on the left side. Grab the zip ties and rags in the bottom."

As I pass Nine I connect my foot with satisfying force between his legs. He lets out a guttural screech and falls forward, swearing up a storm. *Damn* that felt good. With a grin, I move into the tent and reach around in the darkness until I find the cabinet and the supplies in the bottom where Cyrus said they'd be.

"You," Cyrus says, waving the gun at Jefferson when I rejoin him. "Secure their hands behind their backs."

I hand Jefferson the zip ties and he scurries over to the other two, kneeling on the ground to bind their wrists.

Cyrus turns to me. "It's time. Get Colin and meet me back here. Hurry."

Twenty-One smirks. "You're banging the Commander? It all makes sense now."

When I turn to head back to the tents, the sickening sound of a fist connecting with flesh echoes through the night air, followed by a loud grunt. "She's the reason you're still alive. Show some respect," Cyrus says.

A brief feeling of satisfaction pushes back some of the anger. Sure, I wish it was me decking him, but Cyrus's punch hurt a hell of a lot more than mine would have. I jog back to the sleeping quarters and duck into the girls' tent first to grab my coat. My eyes drift to Willow's bunk. They'll kill her if she stays, but Cyrus will kill me if I bring her. With a sigh, I turn toward the exit before my feet stop, almost as if they have their own agenda, and take me to Willow.

"Willow," I say, rocking her shoulder.

She doesn't wake, so I shake her harder. Her eyes fly open and she bolts up.

I put my finger to my lips. "Get dressed and meet me out front. I'm getting you out of here," I whisper.

She nods, eyes still wide.

Hurrying to the boys' tent, I realize I don't know which bunk is Colin's. I can't just go in there and start looking in every bed. Before I can figure out a plan, Liza and Beckett come running up.

"Oh my god," Liza says. "Are you okay? They didn't…"

I shake my head. "No."

Liza throws her arms around me. "Thank you so much."

After giving her a quick pat on the back, I twist out of her embrace. I need to get Colin, and seeing Beckett gives me an idea. "Hey, can you do me a favor?"

"Sure, sure, anything," he says.

"Can you grab Colin and tell him to come out here?"

"Yeah." He disappears inside.

I pace the dirt in front of the tent while I wait. Where the hell is Willow? She should be here by now.

Colin stumbles out behind Beckett and glances around, tugging his knit cap on his head. "What's up?"

"I need to talk to you."

"Okay." He looks at me expectantly.

"Not here." My head swivels, looking for Willow. "Hang on." I jog back to the girls' tent, but she's not in her bunk or the tent.

Leaving Cyrus alone with those three guys for this long isn't a good idea. I'm not convinced he won't shoot one or all of them. If Willow doesn't show up soon, we're going to have to leave without her.

Just as I turn to head back to Colin without Willow, a small voice announces, "Ready."

Whirling around, I find Willow standing behind me, her coat hanging on her tiny frame, large eyes framed by long blond hair and the brim of her hat.

"Where were you?"

"Well, I figured it was going to be a long walk, so I went to the latrine."

Laughter escapes my throat, a combination of relief and genuine amusement at her priorities. I grab her hand and tug her along.

Beckett, Liza, and Colin are where I left them, Liza explaining to Colin what happened. Colin's mouth set in a firm line, his fists clenched at his side, he stalks over to me. "Did they hurt you?"

"No. It's a long story. I'll explain later. We need to go."

"Where are you going?" Beckett asks.

"It's better if you don't know." There's no way to know where Beckett's loyalties lie or how devoted he is to the Uprising. He's still got a gun, and last I knew, Jefferson had my knife. *Shit.* What if Jefferson manages to surprise Cyrus, or slips the knife to one of the other guys? Turning, I sprint toward the vehicle depot, hoping Beckett feels he owes me for saving his girlfriend's ass, along with her other private parts, enough that he won't shoot me in the back.

By the time we arrive, Cyrus has all three guys zipped and gagged in the back of the truck. Twenty-One has a wicked shiner developing where Cyrus clocked him. I shudder at the memory of his hands on me, and wish Cyrus had done a little, okay maybe a lot, more damage.

Cyrus glances over his shoulder. "I was getting worried." He spots Willow and his jaw tightens. "Evan…"

"Cyrus, I had to."

His eyes narrow, and I think he's going to say something more, but he only hands me his gun. "Keep it pointed at them. I'll be right back."

He disappears around the corner and comes back a few minutes later with three more handguns. He gives one to each of us, asking Willow, "Do you know how to use this?"

Her eyes widen and she shakes her head.

I'm not sure if she's more terrified of the gun or our Commander, so I lean down to whisper, "He's okay. You can trust him."

"Time to go," Cyrus says, his voice gruff.

Yeah, he's pissed at me now, too. He reaches back and grabs my hand, pulling me along. We sprint from the vehicle depot toward the outskirts of camp where we finally slow, then stop. Cyrus turns his head, listening, before tugging me forward, with Colin and Willow trailing close.

"Where are we going?" Willow whispers.

"Somewhere safe," I say. "Then we'll figure out how to get you back home."

Cyrus drops his gaze to mine and shakes his head. Maybe he doesn't intend to get her home, but I'll find a way. Eventually. It might not be any time soon, but she should be with her family.

With expert stealth, Cyrus guides us through the trees, pointing out twigs to avoid. We're approaching the perimeter and the sentries. A branch snaps behind us, and I whip around, pulling my hand back from Cyrus's and retrieving my gun from my waistband. Two sentries I don't recognize stand ten yards back, weapons trained on us.

The gun sits unnaturally in my hand. It's nothing like the rifles we practiced with, and I wish I had my knife.

"C-Commander, sir, sorry, we didn't realize it was you," one of them says, his voice still somewhere between boy and man, making me wonder if he even shaves yet.

"There's some trouble outside the perimeter," Cyrus says. "You two stay here. I'm taking these three specialists with me to check it out."

"Yes sir!" they both say before turning back.

The breath I was holding rushes out in a whoosh. Cyrus leads the way across a clearing at a brisk rate. A popping sound behind us draws my attention, and I spin around. Out of the corner of my eye, I see Colin and Cyrus dive behind a fallen tree.

Gunfire.

I take three quick steps toward the same tree before I realize Willow is lagging behind. Colin and Cyrus yell for me to get down, but I have to get Willow. Just a few more steps and I'll have her.

She jerks forward, her knees buckling, her mouth forming an O as she falls face down.

"Evan, keep moving," Cyrus yells from somewhere far away.

I drop down next to Willow. A dark stain spreads across the back of her coat and her breath is harsh, angry, as if she has a bad cold. Realization washes over me like an ocean wave coming ashore, slowing everything around me, pulling me under.

No, no, no, oh dear god, no...

What have I done?

When I roll her over, blood seeps through the front of her shirt, too. It's like Lucien all over again, and there's not a damn thing I can do for her. Except make sure she doesn't die alone.

Through great gulfs of guilt and the popping of ongoing gunfire, Cyrus's voice breaks through. "Evan, get out of there now."

"I can't leave her," I yell.

"Evan, get the hell out of there now, or I'm coming to get you." Cyrus says, firing past me. "Colin and I will cover you. When I give the word, run."

I nod and push up, pulling Willow's little body into my lap. Her large eyes stare into mine. "It's going to be okay," I lie.

When Cyrus and Colin begin firing, the gunfire behind stops as the shooters take cover. Scooping Willow up, I start to run. Cyrus yells something at me, but I can't hear him over the pounding in my head and the bombardment of shots being fired around me.

Then something wicked strong knocks me to the ground, forcing the air from my lungs as a sharp, searing pain rips through my shoulder.

34 Searing Pain

gony like I've never known tears through me, savage and unrelenting. Every breath is caustic, spreading from my shoulder to consume all of me like a raging inferno. I lie still for a moment, trying to avoid breathing too deeply, the only sound coming from my heart hammering in my ears. Slowly, the popping of continued gunfire makes its way to my consciousness, forcing me to evaluate my situation. Willow is in front of me, her eyes closed now, but her chest still moves with her rapid, shallow breaths.

I need to get her out of here, but when I lift my head, blinding pain darkens the edges of my vision. Blacking out isn't an option, although that would be a blessed relief. Feet pound the ground toward me, and I want to yell at them to stop making so much noise.

Warm breath fans my face. "Can you get up?" Cyrus asks.

"I don't know…I think I'm…*shot.*" I'm not sure I even realized that's what happened until this moment.

"Where?"

"My shoulder."

"Evan, you need to try."

Nodding, I start to push myself up with my right arm, but it gives way under the excruciating pain radiating from my left shoulder. "I can't," I say on a sob. I glance toward Willow again, but there's no movement in her chest this time. She's gone. Because of me. I can't let anyone else get shot because of me. "Take Colin and go."

"No. I'm not leaving you ever again." He gives me a small smile. "Where you go, I go, remember?"

I nod and will myself to get up. Dirt and leaves fly up terrifyingly close as the ground around us is pelted with gunfire. Cyrus throws his body over mine, his weight presses into me, white hot torture shredding my nerves. Even worse than this pain is knowing Cyrus could be killed trying to save me, and I know I have to get up. He twists and fires off a couple of rounds.

Four deafening bangs from the trees answer, followed by quiet. After the ceaseless barrage of gunfire, this lull is a roar of silence. Cyrus rolls off me.

"I'm going to try, okay?" I say, glancing up at him.

He reaches a hand down and grabs my right arm, pulling me up. A scream tears up my throat and he pauses. Drenched in sweat, my heart racing and shoulder throbbing, I gulp in breaths from a seated position, searching for the strength to stand.

"Wait," I say on a breath, closing my eyes, and attempting to internalize the pain by imagining something wrapping around and containing it.

When I open my eyes my pounding heart skids to a stop. Three is heading toward us, a vicious looking weapon in his hand.

Six-plus-feet of pure muscle, Three closes the distance between us with remarkable speed. His rifle is massive, with a three-foot barrel at least an inch in diameter.

"I'm so sorry," I say to Cyrus. He squats next to me, cupping my cheek, his eyes filled with such devotion, they nearly steal what little breath I have left. There were a dozen opportunities over the summer to tell him how I felt about him, or at the footbridge the day we said goodbye, but I refuse to die without saying it.

"I love you," I say.

The corners of his mouth curve up, and he leans in to kiss me. I close my eyes but the kiss never comes.

"Colin, no!" My eyes fly open to Cyrus, now standing and holding his arms in the air. Beyond him, Colin is pointing his gun at Three. Why doesn't he want Colin to shoot? Hell, why doesn't *he* shoot Three?

Cyrus walks over to Three, and the two do some sort of guy hug arm lock thing. Confusion rolls through me, and I turn to Colin, his expression matching mine. He asked me if we could trust Cyrus, and I told him we could, but now, I'm not sure what's going on.

Colin lowers his weapon and sprints over to me, squatting down. "Where are you shot?"

"My shoulder I think. Or maybe my back."

"Take off her jacket," Three says, standing over me, looking formidable but not particularly menacing.

Colin pushes my coat off my shoulders, and I grit my teeth, trying to force back a scream. It comes out anyway, sounding like an enraged animal. Sweat beads on my forehead as I gasp for air.

Cyrus nudges Colin aside. "I'll do it." He flicks open a knife, *my knife*, and slices up the center of my sleeve until it falls off my arm.

"Take off your shirt," Three says to Cyrus.

Cyrus removes his coat and tugs his T-shirt over his head, handing it to Three.

"How bad does it hurt on a scale of one to ten?" Three asks me.

"I don't know, maybe fifteen?"

Three glances at Cyrus and reaches into his pocket, pulling out a long silver tube resembling a pen. He removes the cap with his teeth, revealing a long syringe. "This'll sting," he says, jabbing the needle into my shoulder.

A groan escapes my lips, but then a warm sensation follows the pinch, radiating out, the pain floating away on feathery wings. With a sigh, I stare up at the sky where the stars are performing a delicate ballet across a velvet stage. Three rips Cyrus's shirt into pieces, making a tearing sound like skates flying across ice. The stars morph into skaters, gliding through the darkness.

A horrific agonizing pain brings me back to full lucidity as Three presses shirt strips into the wound. The stars bounce crazily until the edges turn black and become pinpoints of light. I can't stifle the shriek wrenching through me.

Cyrus squats down, reaching out to me. "Squeeze my hands if you need to."

How is that supposed to help? But when the next wave hits, I do as he suggested, hard, and it helps. A little. When Three's done, he reaches down and grabs my right forearm, pulling me to my feet. My head is thick, as if it's been packed with gauze, and the world tilts before righting itself. The piercing shock dulls to a throbbing ache.

Cyrus takes my hand. "Mateo, this is Evan."

Mateo smiles. "You're everything he said you are and more."

"What?" I turn to Cyrus. "You told him about me?"

Mateo opens his mouth to answer, but when Cyrus shoots him a look, he only says, "He might have mentioned you."

"This is her friend, Colin," Cyrus says.

The warmth spreading through me, chasing away the ache, makes my arms weightless. "What did you give me?"

"A powerful painkiller. It should last about six hours, but it has a wicked rebound effect. When the pain returns, it'll probably be as bad as when you were first shot, maybe worse."

I trip over something and Cyrus reaches out a hand to catch me. I glance down at Willow lying at my feet. "We can't leave her here."

"I'll take care of her," Mateo says. He removes his jacket and hands it to me. "Put this on." Then he bends down to scoop Willow up into his arms. "I'm sorry about all this."

"It's not your fault," Cyrus says.

"I only got about half the ammo replaced."

"Half is better than none."

Mateo glances at me. "Not if it's the wrong half." He turns back to Cyrus. "I shot those clowns with enough tranquilizer to knock them out for an hour, but reinforcements will be here any minute. You need to go. I'll leave a trail in another direction, which should buy you some time."

Cyrus pats him on the shoulder. "Thanks, man."

Mateo turns, and cradling Willow in his arms, takes off, heading south.

"Where are we going?" I ask Cyrus.

He nods north. "Home."

We make our way through a thick wooded area, the frigid air stinging my cheeks. For a while, the only sound is our footsteps and heavy breaths.

Colin finally breaks the silence. "Do you want to explain what that was all about back there?" he asks Cyrus, waving his hand wildly behind us.

"I met Mateo on my first day of Basic. He was my Group Leader. We came from similar backgrounds and we just clicked. One night, things got out of hand between him and another Leader over a girl. Long story short, I saved his life. And now, I guess we're even."

"That seemed like a lot more than repaying a debt," Colin says.

Cyrus reaches up to run a hand through his hair, but when it brushes against his knit cap, he drops his arm back to his side. "Mateo's not loyal to the Uprising. He's a mercenary, hired out to the highest bidder. Right now that's the Uprising. But shooting kids trying to escape never sat right with him. He doesn't think you can win a war if the soldiers aren't fighting for the right reasons. He wanted to level the playing field a little, and decided to replace the ammunition the sentries use with blanks. The rest of the ammo is real, though."

No shit.

"So he's just doing a job?" Colin asks, a measure of disbelief in his voice.

"There's more to it than that, but that's the gist of it."

"Who's financing the operation? We've been trying to figure that out. Evan thinks it's the Northern Territories, which kinda makes sense."

Cyrus blows out a long breath. "That's a really long story."

"I got nothing better to do for the next few hours. What about you, EvTay?"

I stare at Colin's face as he talks. His features move in slow, fluid motion, as if he's under water. "Your lips look funny," I say, reaching out to grab them.

Colin swats my hand away. "Is she gonna be okay?"

Cyrus's response is too low for me to hear, but I feel fine. Better than fine. Little rubber springs are attached to my boots and my arms are filled with helium. I spin around with my arms out to the side.

"That's enough spinning for now," Cyrus says, taking my hand and lacing our fingers together. "How much do you know about the Mexican drug cartels?"

"Not much," Colin says. "Just what we studied in history. About how things got crazy between the cartels in Mexico and the kidnappings and drug wars in the early-to-mid twenty-first century, but they disappeared after the war."

"Not exactly," Cyrus says. "Even people in the Ruins know more than that. The rest I learned from Mateo. During the War, the cartels saw a chance to get a deeper foothold in the U.S. by providing weapons to the Patriots fighting against government regulations. When the war ended and neither side won, the cartels tried to align with the survivors migrating to the coasts. But the Union walled them out, and left the cartels without access to the Ruins or the Territories, back when they were still Canada."

"Caannaaddaa," I say. "That sounds funny."

Cyrus squeezes my hand and goes on. "The cartels spent decades digging tunnels under the Union. They found a market in the Ruins for weapons, food, and clothing, but not much money. Then Canada had their own civil war and broke up into what we now call the Northern Territories. The newly-formed governments had money and a need for what the cartels were selling. So, the cartels infiltrated the Union, using their trains to move goods from Mexico up into the Territories."

"Did they just bypass the Ruins all together?" Colin asks. "I mean, that might explain why everyone in the Ruins is so pissed."

"No. The Ruins still provides plenty of benefit to the cartels. As you rightly guessed over the summer," he says, squeezing my hand, "dairy from the Ruins goes into the Union at an obscene profit."

"Wow, so in a way, the Union is funding their own demise," I say.

He nods. "But the smuggling went on for decades before there ever was an Uprising. About ten years ago, the Union discovered the tunnels. They destroyed them, which didn't sit well with the cartels. The cartel leadership believed there was enough hatred of the Union for a full-blown revolution and began arming the people of the Ruins for war. But they didn't have anywhere near the troop levels they needed. They figured they could recruit Mexicans with a beef against the Union, but couldn't find enough pissed off people willing to go to war against them."

"Seems like an ongoing problem," Colin says.

"Intel says the only place the Union maintains armed troops is along the Mexican border. So the cartels decided to attack from the Ruins, but getting people into the Ruins from Mexico isn't easy. At first, they tried taking them by boat up through the Northern Territories. Although the Territories have no love for the Union, they don't want to be at war with them either. So the cartels stopped looking for volunteers and instead started drafting people from the Ruins, forcing them to serve."

"So the Northern Territories don't want to be involved, but what about the government of Mexico?" Colin asks.

"Mateo says they'd be perfectly happy if the Union walls came down, but they won't be a part of the Uprising. The Union doesn't have much in the way of a defense force, but they have powerful allies. Mexico doesn't want to be on the wrong side of this. They'll let the cartels fight the war and be ready to take advantage of any resulting benefits."

"Do you know their plan?" Colin asks. "I mean, does it have a real chance of success?"

"They stand a pretty good chance. If the information they have is accurate, the Union's limited military is clustered at the Mexican border with short-range aircraft carriers far off the coast. They're going to move the entire Uprising to the walls of the Union, so when the attack starts, any military action directed at the Uprising would result in damage to the Union itself."

35 Rebound Effect

Hours pass, and night gives way to early morning as we continue to make our way north. Stars fade from the sky along with the haze surrounding my brain that had been keeping the pain at bay. It's less of a dam bursting and more like holes slowly boring through the wall, letting pain trickle in, building pressure, until I can no longer ignore it. Soon, every step is excruciating, as if razors are slicing through bone. I grit my teeth, swallowing a scream.

This is the rebound Mateo warned me about, but holy hell, it's exponentially worse. It steals my breath and knocks me to the ground. Kneeling and holding my left arm with my right hand, I count my breaths, attempting to focus on anything except how much this freaking hurts.

Cyrus squats beside me, his brow furrowed. "What can I do?"

"I don't know," I say between pants. "God, it hurts."

"We can't stop. Let me carry you."

"No," I hiss. I can't even stand to have him touch me, much less carry me. Each breath sends pain shooting further into me, igniting nerves I wasn't even aware I had.

"Can't we try to take the bullet out?" Colin asks. "Maybe that'll help."

Cyrus shakes his head, "No. It's a spiral bullet. It has a threaded tip, which splays out when it hits something, making it rotate and burrow deeper, like a screw into wood. That's why she's in so much pain."

"Wait, are you saying she has to live with that thing in her?" Colin asks.

Assuming I live, and at the moment I'm not even sure I want to.

"No. We need to get her up to a hospital in the Northern Territories. They'll be able to get it out."

I wish they'd stop talking. Their words are like someone taking a cheese grater to my nerves. Even though I want to scream at them both to shut up, I can't speak. The pain comes in waves and suddenly my stomach lurches. Bending over, I vomit what little is left of last night's dinner.

"I can't go any farther right now. Just let me rest."

Cyrus pulls the knit cap off his head and runs his hand through his hair. "We can make camp for a little while, I guess. Colin, go gather as many large branches as you can."

Sitting with my good shoulder against the trunk of a tree, I alternate between closing my eyes and watching Cyrus clear away twigs and plants from a patch of earth. When Colin returns with the branches, Cyrus sharpens the ends with his knife and drives them into the ground, making a framework. He and Colin weave leaves, mud, and ferns in between them, creating a shelter.

My shoulder goes from burning agony to almost tolerable and back again. I dig my fingernails into the palm of my right hand to give myself a different pain to focus on.

"Come here, Ev," Cyrus say. "This will help you stay warm." They finished the shelter while my mind drifted on a sea of torture.

I climb inside and lie on my right side. Cyrus and Colin crawl in after me, our breaths mingling in white clouds. Cyrus curls up behind me, resting his hand on my hip, while Colin lies on my other side with his back to me. Before long, the heat from our bodies creates a warm cocoon and I manage to drift off, floating in a world between sleep and wakefulness, surrounded by both physical and emotional torture.

Ever-growing pain invades my dreams until it takes a starring role, before dragging me kicking and screaming into consciousness. The sun is high in the sky, illuminating the ground outside our enclosure.

Blindingly so.

Everything is covered in snow.

Colin's breathing is still heavy and deep in front of me, but my back is cold, meaning Cyrus is no longer there. No doubt he's out patrolling the area. I knee Colin to wake him, and he rolls over, scowling.

His scowl melts into a smile. "Hey, EvTay. You look a ton better." He glances beyond me. "Where's Cyrus?"

"Probably outside."

Colin pushes up and ducks out of the shelter, returning a few minutes later with Cyrus.

"You're not quite so gray," Cyrus says. "How do you feel?"

"Better, I think I can walk some now. But…what about the snow?"

"It's actually helpful. It's coming down hard enough it'll quickly cover our tracks." He clears a spot outside the tent for me to sit while he and Colin tear down the shelter and scatter the pieces to hide our camp. He hoists me up by my good arm and hands me a small silver pouch.

"What's this?"

"Breakfast," he says, opening the packet and pouring some weird jerky square things into my palm. The taste is pungent, gamey, but not as chewy as jerky. I wash it down with a handful of snow.

The pain in my shoulder is too intense to ignore, but not as bad as the rebound effect. Cyrus takes my right hand, lacing our fingers. I let him lead me so I don't need to think too much. The snow is heavy and difficult to walk in, but the large flakes continuing to fall fill in our footsteps, obscuring our path. By midday, melting snow has penetrated the waterproof layer of my leather boots, soaking my socks and numbing my toes.

We hike on through lunch, eating another packet of jerky squares, not stopping until after dark. Cyrus and Colin make another shelter. Then Cyrus gathers more sticks, carving off the wet outer bark to find the dry wood inside to make a fire. When he gets it going, he unlaces my boots, pulls them, off and peels off my soggy, frigid socks.

"Give me your gloves," he says.

Grabbing a finger with my teeth, I pull my hands out and give them to Cyrus. He jams sticks into the dirt near the flames, placing our stuff on them to dry.

"I'll take first watch," Colin says.

Cyrus lies facing me, and for the first time, I notice the dark circles under his eyes. The fact he didn't argue with Colin about taking the first watch is a testament to how exhausted he is. He leans forward, brushing his lips against mine. "Get some sleep," he mumbles, his eyelids sliding shut.

Soon, I drift off as well and dream we're walking through desert sand instead of the snow. It's hot, so hot my body is melting. I wake, shivering, unable to get warm. Cyrus reaches out to tug me closer to him, then pulls back. He props himself up on his elbow, touching his lips to my forehead, and glances up at Colin. "She's burning up."

My skin hurts, like someone's dragging sandpaper across it, and my head roars in protest whenever I move. Not to be outdone by the rest of me, my shoulder throbs deep inside.

"What's wrong with me?" I ask Cyrus.

"You probably developed an infection," he says, and though he tries to hide it, worry laces his words.

I shake uncontrollably, my teeth chattering. "I don't think I can walk."

Colin lies beside me, brushing a piece of hair from my face, and lays his jacket over me.

"We need to cool her off," Cyrus says, removing the jacket. "Go get me some snow." Colin scurries out of the shelter and returns with an armful of snow. "Give me your shirt," Cyrus tells him.

Cyrus wraps the snow in Colin's shirt, making a compress, and applies it to my forehead. The roughness of the cotton T-shirt wrapped around the frigid snow is like a bolt of lightning across my head. I jerk away, but immediately regret the sudden movement. The two of them whisper over my head, but I can't make out what they're saying and close my eyes, trying to sleep.

Vivid images form behind my eyelids, painting ugly portraits of raging infernos, screaming bullets, and barren wastelands littered with the charred remains of children. When I wake, Cyrus is lying on his side next to me, his head propped up on his hand. His forehead crinkles above eyebrows drawn together. It takes me a few seconds to realize he's worried. About me. I want to tell him I'm going to be okay, but I'm afraid I might not be.

"Where's Colin?"

"He'll be back in a minute, I sent him out to search for something. I'm going to carry you on my back. Can you hold on?"

"I think so."

Colin returns with some stringy vine things. "This is all I could find." He gives me a quick smile, but it comes out more like a grimace.

"Those'll work," Cyrus says to Colin, then to me, "Time to go."

He and Colin help me dress. The mere act of moving sends ribbons of pain spiraling through me, making it impossible not to scream. Colin threads his fingers together in a makeshift step to boost me onto Cyrus's back. I wrap my right arm around him, letting my left arm hang, and rest my cheek on his shoulder.

"How's that?" Cyrus asks.

"Good." It's really not, but there are no alternatives. With any luck, I'll pass out again.

Our boots crunch through snow and a soft hiss fills the air as large white flakes settle onto the trees. I close my eyes and listen to the boys talk.

"Why did we change direction?" Colin asks.

"We're going to The Union. It's closer."

"How is it closer? We walked for days before taking a handcar and a horse-drawn buggy."

"How did you get to camp?"

"By truck."

"And the truck took you back toward the Union."

Of course it did. Because why would they locate camps farther away from a target that doesn't even know they exist?

The longer Cyrus walks, the harder it is for me to hang onto him. My arms are like rubber, as if all of my muscles dissolved. With the snow continuing to fall and a blanket of clouds covering the sky, I have no concept of time, but when we stop for lunch, I assume it's early afternoon. Colin clears a spot on the ground next to a tree and helps me down.

Cyrus hands me another foil pouch, but I shake my head. "You should eat something," he says, sitting beside me. I can't stand the idea of food right now. He gives up on the jerky and pushes a handful of snow at me. "At least take this. You need to stay hydrated."

I start to shove the snow away, but the set of his jaw has me reaching for it. As the cold flakes scrunch together in my mouth and melt, I realize how thirsty I am and scoop up another handful while the boys eat. Leaning my head back against the trunk of the tree, I close my eyes. I must've drifted off, because the next thing I'm aware of is a gentle rocking motion and someone calling my name.

Cyrus's face comes into view when I open my eyes, but it's wavy, the way things in the distance look through heat ripples. "Hey, you ready to go?"

I nod and he helps me stand. Colin is pacing in front of us, his hands on top of his head.

"I'll take her," Colin says.

"No, I've got her," Cyrus says.

"I said I'd take her," Colin snaps.

Cyrus whips his head around to glare at Colin, his body tensing. "What the hell is your problem?"

"I don't know what to do, okay? I'm scared shitless of losing my best friend. Just tell me what the fuck to do!"

An unfamiliar sound, like soft crunching of snow, comes from nearby. Cyrus pulls me behind a tree with a sudden jolt, and I let out a groan of pain. The noise gets closer and my feverish mind tries to make sense of what's happening.

"Stay here," Cyrus whispers in my ear, placing my gun in my hand.

A high-pitched whine accompanies the crunches, getting louder, and my brain finally connects the sounds to objects. Tires in the snow. The Uprising found us. I squeeze my eyes shut, waiting for the gunfire to start.

"Rainey?!" Colin's voice is wrapped in confusion.

At least I think that's what he said. But why would Rainey be here? I must be having fever-induced hallucinations, because when I peek around the tree, I see four electric motorbikes and Rainey standing next to one of them. Climbing off another is someone who looks a lot like that kid, Simon, from the cafe in the Eastern Province. And now I know I'm out of it, because the third one looks like my boss, Tony Baxter. And… "Eddie?"

Eddie rushes off his motorbike, knocking it over. He's at my side in seconds, wrapping his arms around me. I whimper at the pain, no longer having the energy to pull away or scream. My father leans in and kisses my forehead and says. "Evan. You're burning up."

"She's been shot," Colin says.

"*What?*" Eddie pulls back from me, his eyes searching my face.

"What're you doing here?" I ask.

He reaches forward and brushes hair out of my eyes with his gloved hand. "I came to get you."

He wouldn't have left Liam and Quinn unless… "Why? What's wrong?"

"Apparently someone shot my daughter."

I open my mouth to ask him how he found me, but Cyrus interrupts. "She needs a hospital."

"Yeah, of course," Eddie says, glancing over his shoulder at the others. There are four motorbikes and seven of us. "Can you ride?" Eddie asks Colin.

Colin nods. I must still be hallucinating. When did Colin learn to ride a motorbike?

"What about you?" Eddie asks Cyrus.

"Yeah."

Eddie starts directing everyone into action. I've never seen him like this — taking control.

"I'll take Evan," Cyrus says. Not waiting for an answer, he swings his leg over one of the bikes and Eddie helps me up behind him. I lean forward, resting my head on Cyrus's back.

"You need to hold on," Colin says.

"Okay." I reach my right arm around Cyrus's waist, resting my left arm on my thighs.

"Use the vines," Cyrus tells Colin.

"Right." Colin dips a hand into the side pocket of his fatigues and pulls out the stringy things he gathered earlier. "I got these in case I had to tie you to Cyrus when we were walking." He wraps them around my torso, securing me to Cyrus.

Cyrus doesn't wait for the others, taking off as soon as I'm tied to him. We bounce along the ground, and I struggle to hang on, wincing in pain with each bump. My body shifts around in the seat and I slide closer to Cyrus, grasping his jacket with my right hand. I close my eyes as we travel, pretending someone isn't twisting blades through my shoulder every time we hit something.

When the bike begins to slow, my eyes pop open. "What's wrong?"

"We're about to run into some old friends," he says quietly. "Stay calm and follow my lead."

36 Old Friends

Cyrus brings the bike to a stop and waits for the others to catch up. Heavy white flakes continue to drift down, but the ground here is only dusted with snow rather than covered like where we were earlier. I peek around Cyrus at a flatbed truck loaded with Uprising recruits. Three soldiers with rifles strapped to their backs flank the sides while two others peer beneath the hood.

Rainey pulls up next to us. "I'll handle this." She removes her handgun from her waistband and checks it. "On my signal, go," she says and rides ahead, stopping beside the truck. The two soldiers in front grab their rifles from their backs and point them at Rainey. Swinging her leg over the bike, she walks up to them and gestures toward us. They glance our way then turn back to Rainey. More words are exchanged, and Rainey puts her hands on her hips, appearing to yell at them. She takes a step closer to one, and I squeeze my eyes shut so I don't have to watch them shoot her.

"Hang on," Cyrus says, and we take off fast. I jerk back and nearly lose my grip. "Hold on tighter, Ev, and lean into the turns with me."

We pitch to the right, curling around the truck. As soon as we fly past, gunfire breaks out behind us. Cyrus zips the bike back and forth, making hanging on close to impossible. In fact, if Colin hadn't tied me on, I'm pretty sure I'd be on the ground by now. I grit my teeth and wait for the next bullet to pierce me.

When it doesn't, I twist around, because they must be shooting at my dad and friends instead. Either I'm hallucinating, or Colin and Rainey have managed to get the rifles, and the soldiers are standing with their hands on their heads. The recruits are pouring off the back of the truck, and Rainey appears to be yelling at them now, too.

I turn around and bury my face in Cyrus's back. The adrenaline that was rushing through my veins begins to wear off as we bounce along, and soon I'm struggling to stay awake. I stop fighting it, and let sleep pull me into darkness.

The slowing of the motorbike and a steady pinging wakes me. "We're about out of juice," Cyrus says. When the bike finally stalls, he unties the vines holding us together, hopping off to help me down. "Can you walk?"

"I think so."

He takes my hand and leads me west. I look behind us for the others, but they're nowhere to be seen. In front of us, a soft glow lights up the sky as the sun sinks behind the massive wall of the Union. We don't get far before Cyrus stops and pulls off a glove, placing his bare hand on my face.

He shakes his head. "You're still burning up. I'm going to carry you again. We'll get there. I just need you to hang on a little while longer."

I nod and he bends down, letting me climb onto his back. Holding my right arm to keep me secure, he carries me. I rest my head on his shoulder and close my eyes.

"Stay awake."

"I can't."

"Tell me what that was all about back there? Who were those people?"

"Rainey…she was a Commander in the Uprising. Do you know her?"

"No, but that explains a lot."

"And my…my dad. And my boss. And the other guy…I think I saw him before."

"Yeah, I actually know him. That's Simon. So, do you want to tell me what the hell you were doing in an Uprising camp to begin with?"

Fuzziness envelopes my brain, but I dig around in the muck, looking for the memory, the moment I made the conscious decision to join up. "I was trying to find out what I could about their plans."

"You went back, you left…to do something in the Union. That was the plan." I hear the tension in his voice even though I can also tell he's working to hide it.

"That *was* the plan, but it didn't work out. Someone knew where I'd been all summer, what I'd seen. We were being watched the whole time. There was no way we could do *anything*."

"What do you mean you were being watched?"

I fill him in on the bugs, Colin's kidnapping, how they threatened us and shot Colin, about Jack finding the memo, and how we split up. Before I can finish, the effort of talking takes its toll. Just the act of remembering is like I'm running up a steep hill after completing a half-marathon. Maybe if I can rest for a few minutes, I can walk slowly up the hill.

"Evan, are you still with me?

"Yes, I'm just tired."

"We're almost there, baby, hang on, okay?"

Baby. He hasn't called me baby in a long time. "Okay." I lay my head on his shoulder and close my eyes for a minute.

"Evan, stay with me."

I want to, but I don't think I can.

Warmth wraps around my body, and a sense of peace flows through me. Am I dead? If this is death, bring it on — I feel good. A shuffling noise to my right destroys my float through the afterlife, and I pry my eyes open. A gray ceiling greets me, or at least I think it's gray. The room is dark, lit by dimmed recessed lights, shadows swallowing most of the space.

The shuffling brings a body into my line of sight. "Hi, I'm Sam. How do you feel?" Sam's massive frame doesn't seem to fit his voice, which is soft and rich, like supple suede.

"Floaty." My voice comes out as a croaky whisper.

He smiles, making his dark eyes crinkle at the corners. "That's the medication. So you're not in pain?"

I shake my head. "Can I have some water?"

He pours a glass of water and inserts a straw before handing it to me. I take a small sip and glance around the room. A chair is pushed up against the wall, a blanket slung over the arm.

"Your friend went to get something to eat," Sam says, following my gaze to the empty chair. "He's been here almost constantly. He'll be glad you're awake."

My friend? Is he talking about Cyrus?

"We don't see many gunshots," he says, his expression questioning. "I've never seen anything like the slug we dug out of your shoulder." He stares at me, as if he's waiting for an answer. When I don't give him one, he says, "The doctor will be by to check on you in the morning."

I watch Sam leave the room, the door closing behind him. Turning to look at the empty chair one more time, I close my eyes again because it's easier than trying to keep them open.

My eyes flutter open to warm yellow walls and sunlight streaming across my bed. A hand squeezes mine, and I turn to see Eddie, heavy bags beneath his eyes and scrubby whiskers dusted with gray. When was the last time he slept? Or shaved?

"Hello, Sleeping Beauty. I was beginning to think you'd never wake up."

"You're here." I can't keep the smile from splitting my face. Seeing him safe fills me with a spiral of relief and joy. "I can't believe you came for me."

His own smile fades, and his eyebrows draw together. "I can't believe you risked your life and Colin's like that. It was a crazy, foolish thing to do."

The words sting, but in a way I know he's right. I try to push myself up, but my left shoulder screams in protest and I only manage to shift my position, angling toward him. "I'm sorry. I didn't see any other way."

He shakes his head, his mouth a tight line. "Any other way for what? Bryce came by, told me what happened with you two. Seeking danger as a way to mask pain isn't the answer."

Bryce told him what happened? Oh god, did he tell my dad we slept together? My face burns and I want to duck under my covers and hide. "It wasn't like that," I mumble.

"No?"

"Okay, maybe part of me was trying to escape into the Ruins. But mostly I wanted to join the Uprising. To get information. Bryce was supposed to go with me, but…"

"And the young man who's been camped out at your bedside night and day?"

I curl in my upper lip, biting it. "That's Cyrus. I met him in the Ruins last summer."

"The one you thought you'd never see again?"

I nod and he waits for me to go on. "Somehow we ended up in the same Uprising camp, but I didn't go there to find him."

Eddie sighs. "He seems rather devoted." He glances toward the door and stands. I turn, curious what he's looking at, but I only see a closed door. "I'll be back later." He leans down to kiss my forehead. "Your mother wants to see you, and for obvious reasons, it would be best if I wasn't here when she arrived."

"Wait, what? Mom is here? Why?"

"You were in really bad shape, and for a few days, we weren't sure if you were going to pull through." A dark expression crosses his face. "I had to call her — she had a right to be here. I would have expected the same from her."

"How…how long have I been here?"

"A little over a week."

"A week? I don't remember anything after…" What is my last memory before waking up here? Cyrus begging me to open my eyes. "Where's Cyrus?" I whisper.

Eddie takes my right hand in both of his. "He's at the hotel. Sleeping. He's been here around the clock since you were brought in. Once we knew you'd woken, I sent him to clean up and get some rest."

I nod. "And Colin?"

"He's fine. At the hotel, too. Everyone's fine. It's a long story, and I promise I'll tell you everything. But it's going to take a while, and your mother will be here any minute."

"How much does she know?" I am not prepared to deal with a ton of questions from my mom and Joe right now.

"She thinks you were injured on the job. She knows about Tony and that you were working on a secret assignment. As far as what happened to you, she only knows you developed a system-wide infection. Your Uncle Dave was able to keep most of the details under wraps."

Movement out of the corner of my eye catches my attention. I draw my gaze away from Eddie to my mother, standing outside the door talking to Joe. She pushes into the room and glances at Eddie, her mouth puckering as if she'd sucked a lemon.

"Hello, Eddie." The disdain drips from her voice, and I roll my eyes.

"Christine. Joe." Eddie stands and reaches out to shake my stepfather's hand.

As Eddie goes to leave, the door opens and a man in a white coat enters. He takes in the group, the tension in the air palpable. "Can you three step out please? I'd like to be alone with my patient."

My family moves into the hall, but as they make their way out, their arguing escalates. "When she lived with us, this sort of thing didn't happen. I'm taking her home," my mom says.

"As I recall, the reason she came out west in the first place was because she landed in the hospital while she was living with you," Eddie says, the door closing behind him muffles the rest of his words.

I hate when my parents argue over me. I drag my gaze away from the door and turn to the doctor, who's studying me. "Hello, Miss Taylor, I'm Dr. Martinez." He thrusts a tan hand in my direction, a pleasant smile revealing blindingly white teeth.

"So, are you the one who saved my life?"

"I lead the team who provided your diagnostic and therapeutic care. I was also the one who had to dig that particularly troublesome bullet from your shoulder." His dark eyes pierce mine, seeking answers.

I glance down at the bed, twisting the blanket between my hands, awkward silence filling the room. "Thank you," I whisper.

He sighs and sits on the edge of the bed. "Look, my team works on special cases. Ones like yours. Your uncle wants what happened to remain quiet. What the Governor wants, he usually gets. You're the youngest patient we've had, and I'm telling you this because I feel I need to. You're lucky to be alive. You might want to rethink your chosen vocation."

I lift my eyes to meet his, wishing it was that simple.

37 Lucky

Mom pulls my blanket up, folding it back on itself before trying to tame my curls with her fingers. "How are you feeling?"

"I'm fine, Mom."

"Eddie said you can't tell me what you were doing, how this happened, but I don't understand. You never expressed any interest in journalism. And embedded reporting? Where did this come from? Is this about a boy?"

Oh my god…seriously? "No, it's not a boy. I told you I needed to figure out what I wanted to do. I like my job. It's interesting, and it turns out I'm good at it."

"Come home," she says, taking my hand in hers. "Work at M Clothing."

"Mom, no."

Joe's been observing our interaction from the corner, arms crossed over his chest. He makes his way to my bedside, kissing the top of my head. He smiles, but it doesn't quite reach his warm brown eyes. "We miss you, honey, but it's your life to live." He turns to my mom, placing a hand on her shoulder. "Christine, you raised her to be the independent young woman she's become. Let her live her own life."

Mom sniffs, wiping a tear with her index finger. "I want her to be safe."

My feelings toward her soften as I realize how hard this must've been on her, being told I might not survive, but the only way to protect them is to find a way to stop the Uprising. "I'll be careful, I promise."

Katie and Rachel spill into my room, filling it with their energy.

"Evs," Katie says, bouncing up to the bed and throwing her arms around me. Wow. She's changed since I last saw her. The unsure twelve-year-old has been replaced by a confident teen, at least two inches taller…and with boobs.

Rachel also sprouted up and out, but she's still sporting the same attitude she's always had. "Hey, sis," she says with a little finger wave.

"How do you feel?" Katie asks.

I'm getting really tired of that question. Luckily, she doesn't wait for my answer and launches into a non-stop barrage of information, covering everything from Joe's new spring line to the latest boy she's crushing on. I get caught up in her enthusiasm, and even Rachel contributes a few interesting tidbits. For a short while, it's fun to pretend the most important things in life are secret crushes and what to wear to school.

"Okay, time for dinner," Mom says with a clap of her hands.

After hugs, kisses, and more tears from Mom, Joe herds everyone out of my room with promises of returning later, leaving me alone for the first time since being awake. I use the solitude to process the events of the past week. There are too many holes in my memory, though, to piece together what happened, and Eddie didn't get a chance to tell me much.

Deep in thought, I startle when someone clears their throat. My head jerks toward the door. "Tony!"

"Can I come in?"

"Of course."

He drags the chair from the wall over to the bed and sits. "How you doing, kiddo?"

"Eh," I say with a little hand motion. "I'm a little fuzzy on the details, but you were out in the Ruins, weren't you?"

He props his elbows on the arms of the chair with his fingertips together beneath his chin. "Yes." I wait for him to elaborate, but he merely stares at me with those dark, penetrating eyes of his.

"Why?"

He pushes up and crosses the room to close the door before resuming his seat. "When you disappeared and I didn't hear from you, I knew something was wrong. After digging around, I realized the signs had been there all along. I can't believe I overlooked them. Guess I'm not as good of an investigative reporter as I thought." He gives me a wan smile.

"What are you talking about?"

"Most girls with your background want to be assigned to fashion or entertainment. I was flattered someone so young showed up at my door wanting to cover crime. I checked into you, found out who your parents are, and assumed you were either rebelling or trying to prove something. But the quick volunteer for undercover, then not reporting back in…I knew there was more to the story."

My cheeks heat under his intense scrutiny, and I fidget with my blanket.

"I studied overseas. In the UK, where they still practice real journalism," he continues. "I was trained to do research, to never stop until I uncovered the truth. There aren't many opportunities for that here, but it comes naturally to me. Once I convinced Eddie he could trust me, he filled in the missing pieces. A quick talk with your friends, and I figured you were in over your head. I couldn't just walk away after what I discovered."

I realize I'm staring at him, my mouth hanging open, and I slam it shut. "But…why? How?" Questions bang around inside my head like a ball in one of those antique pinball games. "Why would you risk your life for someone you barely know?"

"When I found out what you all were up to…" He shrugs. "We all need to take risks when the consequences of doing nothing are too high."

"I…I'm not sure what to say. I can't believe you did that, but thanks." He nods and stares at his hands. "I still don't understand how you found us out there."

He laughs. "It was easier than you'd think. Captain Jackson pinpointed the router your last message was sent from, so we had a good idea where you entered the Ruins. Plus, your friend Jack has some contacts out there who pointed us in the right direction. The town where you stayed up near the border was the logical place to start. Once there, it was easy to find people who'd seen you around. Getting Rainey to trust us was a lot harder. She's…uh…"

I laugh, "Yeah, she's very 'uh'."

"Eddie was able to convince her he was your father and she agreed to help us. There are only two camps in the area. You had to be in one or the other. Rainey was going to sneak in and grab you, but, we ran into you before we got to camp."

"Where did you get the motorbikes?"

"In the Northern Territories."

There are so many more questions, but my nurse, Sam, shows up with his tablet and his needles.

Tony stands and reaches out, cupping my hand between his. "Take care. We'll talk more soon."

Sam checks my vitals and gives me a boost of painkillers, and before long, my eyelids weigh like sixty pounds, and I can't keep them open. Damn him and his magic drugs.

Morning light streams in through my window the next time I wake. The chair where Cyrus had been sleeping is up against the wall, the blanket still folded, untouched since yesterday.

I miss him.

Dr. Martinez pushes into my room, tablet in hand. "Good morning, Miss Taylor. How's the pain this morning?"

"Not bad."

He moves to the bed and pulls a scope from his lab coat, plugging it into his tablet. He presses the end to my chest and watches my heart on the display. Doctors always seem overly invested in my heart and lungs, regardless of the reason I'm seeing them.

"Lean forward, please." He unties the back of my gown, lifting the bandage to peek at my bullet wound. "Keep this up and you can go home tomorrow. You need to get up and moving first. I'll send Amy in to help you."

"Thanks."

"I'll check back in with you in the morning."

Amy enters less than a minute after Dr. Martinez leaves.

"Hi," she says, pushing her tablet into the pocket of her lavender scrubs, her sleek chestnut hair pulled back into a high ponytail that reaches to the middle of her back. "So, Dr. Martinez says you need to get up. Come on, I'll give you a hand."

My first venture out of bed is to the bathroom, and my legs wobble, nearly buckling. Amy's hand slips beneath my elbow to steady me. At least she leaves me alone long enough to do my business. Washing my hands, I take in the horror staring back at me from the mirror. My hair looks like rats took up residence and are planning for a large litter of offspring any day now. Most of the brown has faded, leaving behind a sickly rust color. Dark circles under my eyes make them appear as if they've receded into my skull.

Amy is waiting for me when I open the door. "Can I get cleaned up?" I ask.

She pulls out her tablet and swipes through a few screens. "I don't see why not. Let me get you some towels and a stool to sit on so you can take a shower."

The first hot shower in months feels like a small slice of heaven. The water penetrates my skin, sinking into aching muscles. After three rounds of shampoo, I apply extra conditioner and sit while it works its magic. The added exertion of showering wore me out.

My family is in my room when I emerge from the bathroom clean and dressed in a fresh gown. "Hey, you're up." Joe smiles and gives me a quick hug as I hold the back of my gown together.

"Here, I'll help you with your hair," Mom says, sitting on my bed. She combs through the tangles and applies some product she brought with her. No doubt it was the first purchase she made after seeing me yesterday. Can't have her oldest child looking like she crawled out of a lower-level sewer. When she's done, my curls hang in ringlets the way I wish they did without any effort, rather than the forty minutes it took her.

"So, Dr. Martinez said maybe I'll be released tomorrow." I'm just trying to make conversation, but as soon as the words are out, I regret them.

"Honey, I want you to come home. This journalism thing just isn't a good choice for you."

"I'm not going to run home the first time I hit a setback. Trust me to learn from my mistakes, okay?"

My mom doesn't say anything, but I know she's not done yet. She'll continue to badger me until I agree to go with her, or they finally leave without me. She stands, brushing a few strands of hair from my face.

Loud voices and laughter outside the door draw our attention. Mom bends to kiss my forehead, wiping the lipstick residue off with her thumb, and turns to go. I get a quick hug from Joe and the girls as Colin pushes into my room. Joe pats Colin on the back, but my mom, who's always loved him like the son she never had, merely gives him a tight smile.

Katie and Rachel squeal and throw their arms around Colin, and when Katie bats her eyelashes at him, Rachel rolls her eyes. I lose track of what my family is doing when Cyrus trails in behind Rainey followed by the blond guy from the cafe.

My eyes focus on Cyrus, and I inhale sharply as the rest of the room disappears. He looks good. Rested. Perfect. How does he get sexier every time I see him? My eyes travel over his stubbled face, trailing down the long-sleeve beige T-shirt hugging his torso, to a pair of faded jeans hanging perfectly on his frame. His face blossoms into a smile when my eyes rise back to meet his.

I track his every move as he crosses the room and sits on the edge of my bed. Taking my face in his hands, he presses his mouth to mine. The kiss is long, slow, and deep, as if we're the only two people in the room. I'm pretty sure my heart monitor is going to send a nurse flying into my room any minute, but I don't care.

Someone clears their throat and Cyrus breaks the kiss, pressing his forehead to mine, still holding my face, his eyes locked onto mine. "Hi," is all he says, but that one word sends warmth curling through my body like tender vines.

"Hi."

Colin pushes forward, nudging Cyrus out of the way. Tearing my eyes away from Cyrus, I wrap my right arm around my best friend and bury my face in his shoulder, ruffling his now dark hair, "You look like you again."

He smiles, but it quickly dissolves. "You scared the crap out of me, EvTay. Don't ever do that again."

Rainey shoves Colin aside and stands next to my bed, fidgeting with the hem of her shirt. I grab her hand and squeeze. "Thank you."

She shrugs. "It's not like I had a choice. You're a danger to yourself, but your dad, well, he's a danger to pretty much everyone else around him. I had to save the fate of mankind."

"Don't let her kid you," the blond guy says. "She was already talking about going to get you guys before your dad ever showed up."

I turn my attention to him. "You're the guy from the cafe."

He gives me a grin that crinkles the corners of his eyes. "Small world, eh?"

I shake my head, not sure what he means. "More like weird. I saw you in the Eastern Province, then out in the Ruins. My memory's still a little fuzzy, but you were there, right?"

His grin grows wider. "Yep, I was there helping your friend here get his credentials so he could come find you."

"You were getting Cyrus Union credentials? Did you know who I was?"

"Yep on the credentials, nope on you. Just thought you were pretty and wanted to talk to you. Well, I'm famished. I haven't eaten since yesterday morning. Anyone want to join me?" His gaze swings to Rainey.

"I could eat something," Colin says, heading toward the door.

"I'll be down in a few minutes," Rainey says before turning back to me. "Glad you made it, Uni. I wasn't sure I'd ever see you again."

"Thanks…I think."

She smirks. "I really didn't think you'd make it out alive."

"Speaking of…how'd you disarm those Uprising soldiers?"

"Oh, that. Recruiters tend to be the tough guys. You know, the ones in camp who like to show off and push everyone else around."

I shudder, thinking of Jefferson, Nine, and Twenty-One. "Yeah, I know the type."

"They have more guts than smarts. So, I just acted as if I was their Commander. Gave them a few orders, stunned them long enough for Colin to get into position behind them and grab their guns."

"That was risky. What if it didn't work?"

"I'm a fast shot, plus I was pretty confident they were too stupid for their own good."

"Why'd you help my dad?"

"Simon showed up looking for Cyrus. He was gonna leave the credentials with the family. But then your dad and Tony came barreling into town hell-bent on getting you out, and I couldn't let them go off on their own. Well, I could've, but then you'd all be dead."

"Why do you care?" I'm not trying to be rude, but I'm curious why she'd risk her life for us.

She shrugs. "Like I said, I was paying a debt. Someone helped my sister and told me to pay it forward. And I did, with you, but my sister…well, she didn't make it. I wasn't going to let that happen to you, too, if I could help it. I sort of feel responsible for you now."

"I'll never be able to repay you." I can't bring myself to mention my epically failed attempt at paying it forward. The guilt sits in my stomach like a boulder.

Rainey turns away and inches toward the door. She doesn't want thanks. Got it. "What about Simon? What's his motivation?"

Cyrus smiles. "He's been following Rainey around like a lost puppy for the past week, so I have my theory."

Rainey laughs. "He's…interesting. I like having him around."

"Where'd you find Simon?" I ask Cyrus.

He resumes his spot on the edge of my bed, taking the space Rainey just vacated, and picks up my hand. "I was looking to get my hands on a set of Union credentials, and he came highly recommended. Lots of guys can get forged documents, but Simon has a contact in the government who enters your identity into the Union's database." He smiles, tracing his finger over the back of my hand. "I'm a full-fledged citizen of the Union now. Guess you're stuck with me."

Happiness blossoms inside me like a flower opening to the spring sun. Before it can take deep root and flourish, the gravity of what he said hits me. "Wait, that can't be easy to do. How—"

"No, it wasn't cheap, but it's worth everything I paid."

"What did you have to pay?"

"The only thing I had of any value. My mother's engagement ring. It dates back to before the war. Lucien was going to give it to Draya…"

Holy shit. My mouth drops open. Prewar artifacts are insanely valuable, some are even priceless. He could've traded that ring for everything they'd ever need to survive in the Ruins, but he used it to be with me. Because he wanted something more permanent than fake credentials.

"This little love fest is making me gag," Rainey says. "So…I'm gonna go meet up with the others."

I don't take my eyes off Cyrus as Rainey bows out of the room. What he did is *everything*. How could I have doubted he loved me? "There's something I need to tell you."

"No you don't."

"But—"

He runs his finger across my bottom lip. "I don't know what I would've done, if…" He glances down at the blanket and shakes his head. When he lifts his eyes back to mine, so much is pouring out of them, it steals my breath. "God, I love you, Ev."

The emotion in his voice breaks my heart and warms it at the same time. Maybe he doesn't need to know about Bryce, and maybe I don't need to hear about a girl named Bridget. He leans in, brushing my lips with his, and I wrap my arm around his neck, pulling him closer. The kiss is soft and sweet and full of promise, and I don't want it to end. But we're in my hospital room and yeah, we can't really be making out here.

He pulls back and rests his forehead against mine. "I'm starving, but I'll be back soon. Don't go anywhere."

I watch him walk out of my room and disappear down the hall, admiring the way those perfect jeans fit from the back. With a small sigh and a big smile, I sink back against my pillows. Cyrus is here…and he's not going anywhere. No matter what comes next, we'll face it together.

Thunder rumbles in the distance, drawing my attention. Rain falls from a gray sky, tracing jagged lines down the window. I watch as a drop hits the top of the pane, then zigzags its way down to the bottom, pulling others into its trajectory as it goes. I feel like those raindrops, unable to forge my own path anymore, outside influences dragging me one way then yanking me another.

So deep in my own thoughts, I'm oblivious to someone entering my room until a familiar voice says, "Hey, Evansville."

38 Forging Paths

I guess I always knew I'd see Bryce again someday, but I wasn't prepared for it to be today. With a deep breath, I turn away from the window. Bryce looks beautiful. He always does. The soft gray of his rugby shirt brings out the color of his eyes.

"Hi," I say, my voice barely above a whisper.

Bryce pushes the door closed and leans against it, arms crossed over his chest. He glances past me then turns those slate-colored eyes on me. "You look good."

It's a total lie and we both know it. "Thanks."

"You never answered any of my texts."

My gaze drops from his to my hands twisting in my blankets. "No, I was hurt and angry."

"I should've told you. I wanted to, but—"

"You tried, but I wouldn't let you."

"No, but I should've told you anyway. You had a right to know."

I shake my head. "I didn't want to. That night…I was a wreck waiting for you to come back, terrified something had happened to you. When you walked through the door, nothing else mattered to me at that moment."

"If I *had* told you, would it have made a difference?"

"I don't know. Maybe. Probably."

He's stares at his feet for a few moments, and when he lifts his head, the pain etched across his features tears my heart into a thousand tiny pieces.

"I'm not sorry, though…about what happened between us. I loved you, I still love you, but there's always been someone or something getting in our way. Love shouldn't be this hard. Maybe we were never meant to be."

With a heavy sigh, he pushes off the door and makes his way toward me. "Life doesn't have an undo function, but if I could go back and do everything over, I would. I should've told you that night, even if it meant we never would've…"

"It's not a huge deal, I was just pissed and hurt at having to find out the way I did. I mean, seeing you kissing her like that…right after we…" Heat rises in my cheeks as I remember the moment.

His head jerks up, and his eyes pierce mine while he moves the rest of the way across the room and stands next to the bed. "You didn't respond to my texts, but…did you even read them?"

My gaze drops from his and I'm suddenly fascinated with the pattern on my blanket.

"Evan…"

I blow out a breath, sending a curl fluttering like a kite caught in the wind and peek at him. "No, I was afraid you were going to give me some bullshit explanation and suck me back in."

"What…" He runs a hand over the top of his head and clenches his jaw. "What did you think I was going to tell you that night?"

"About using Alivia."

"Jesus, Evan." His shoulders drop and his hand slides down the back of his head, gripping his neck before dropping to his side. "I went to Benton's apartment to follow up on what I'd found out the night before. After seeing the same three guys enter, I waited outside a few doors down for them to come out. I was going to tail them when they left, but Alivia spotted me. So yeah, I used her, but also I didn't want her ratting me out. I told her I'd missed her, but didn't think she'd want to see me after the way I'd broken things off."

"Okay." I shrug. "And the next morning you had to meet her to keep up appearances. I get it, and I wouldn't let you tell me, but god, I can't think straight when it comes to her. After all the shit she's done to me over the years…"

"No."

"No? You don't think I have a right to have an intense loathing for that bitch?"

"No, that's not what I was going to tell you." His voice is tight, like he's trying hard not to scream at me. "Alivia invited me inside, and after saying I was there for her, it wasn't like I could decline. Plus it was a huge opportunity. Better than I'd hoped for. She went to get us something to drink, and I did some looking around. I overheard a conversation between Benton and someone else. Benton's getting credentials for people in the Ruins. He's got a tech guy who hacks the Union's birth records database. I heard a name, and I knew who the credentials were for. I should have told you as soon as I walked in the door."

So Benton is the guy Simon's working with. Okay, that makes sense. Wait…Simon in the cafe, Bryce needing to tell me something… "Shit…"

"Yeah, I found out Cyrus was coming to the Union. It was a safe assumption he was coming here for you."

Well, double shit. He wanted to tell me the boy I loved was coming for me, even knowing what it meant for him, for our relationship, and I wouldn't let him. I stare at the rain carving rivers that connect and scatter down the window, my thoughts as random as the rain.

"When Colin texted that you guys were heading into the Ruins, I was confused. I was sure you'd wait for Cyrus at Eddie's or at the very least at Colin's up here. When you went into the Ruins, I figured Cyrus found you, and you were all heading out there together."

I turn to meet his piercing gaze. "Yeah, so that didn't happen."

"Your dad filled me in for the most part." He sits on the edge of the bed and picks up my hand. "Everyone was worried about you guys. Lisa…" He shakes his head.

"How is Lisa? And Jack? Are they here?"

"No. They're waiting for us down in the Western Province. Things changed while you were gone. The hit was called off. Max tracked the memo through the system, and although he never found the source, he discovered another memo canceling the hit. Someone saw you and Colin entering the Ruins. They wanted us out of the way so we wouldn't tell anyone in the Union what we knew. They figured we were out of the way for the time being and didn't want to waste their limited resources chasing us through the Ruins."

"But it was only the two of us. I thought they were looking for all five of us."

"Whoever reported back said they saw the kids in question entering the Ruins. It was miscommunication, but this time it worked in our favor."

I chew on my lip and force myself to meet his eyes. "I'm sorry...for everything."

He gives me a small smile and drops my hand. "We've got our work cut out for us. So, focus on healing, okay?" Pushing off the bed, he turns and walks out of my room without a glance back.

"Hey." A deep voice pulls me from that place between dreams and wakefulness. My eyes open to find my favorite face staring at me from beside the bed. "I was afraid you were going to sleep the rest of the day."

I smile and Cyrus presses his lips to the top of my head. I want to kiss him but not before I brush my teeth. "Help me up?"

"Um, are you supposed to do that?"

I roll my eyes. "I wouldn't have asked you otherwise."

He holds out his hand to steady me as I push up with my good arm and twist around, my feet hitting the floor. I'm a little less wobbly each time I get up. Grasping the back of my gown, I back my way into the bathroom as he laughs at me, shaking his head. After taking care of my business and quickly brushing my teeth, I return to my room and Cyrus helps me back into bed.

I pat the spot next to me, wanting him closer. He kicks off a pair of gray athletic shoes and climbs in. He follows my gaze as I take in his Union attire, so different from what I'm used to seeing him wear. "Your dad took me out to get something appropriate to wear. Couldn't let me run around the Union in fatigues and combat boots."

I can't hide my smile at the idea of Eddie taking him shopping. Turning my attention back to the boy next to me, our eyes lock and I suck in a breath. I could get lost in those eyes. When I lean closer, that's all the invitation he needs.

He slips his hand into my hair and pulls my mouth to his, kissing me with soft, lazy kisses that turn me to goo. We spend the afternoon kissing and talking, filling each other in on what we've been up to since we parted ways over the summer. He never brings up a girl named Bridget and I don't mention Bryce is here or what happened between us. Now doesn't feel like the right time for *that* conversation.

Thankfully, we're not lip-locked when my evening nurse comes in with my dinner, but she glares at him all the same. He pushes off the bed and puts his shoes on. "I'm gonna head back to the hotel and get some sleep."

As much as I don't want him to go, he slept in a chair next to my bed for a week, so I don't have the heart to beg him to stay. Grabbing a carrot stick off my tray, he kisses my forehead and walks out of the room. I notice my nurse watching him go as well, her eyes locked onto his ass. The boy can rock a pair of jeans.

Holding the back of my hospital gown to ensure all my assets are covered, I pace my room, waiting for Dr. Martinez to tell me I can get out of here. Bryce's parting words have replayed in my head about a million times. We have so much to do, walking away would be easy; let someone else — the grown-ups — deal with it. But the reason we're in this screwed up mess now is because it was left to the grown-ups the last time.

I open the M Clothing bag my mom brought last night and pull out jeans and a sweater. Since Dr. Martinez is taking his sweet ass time, I might as well get dressed. The jeans fit like a second skin, but the beige sweater is a little large, hitting mid-thigh, and slipping off my shoulder. This must be the latest style, because Christine Taylor would never bring ill-fitting clothes for her daughter to wear. I plop into the chair and pull on a pair of tall, chocolate-colored, calfskin boots.

"You look like you're ready to get out of here," Dr. Martinez says, startling me.

"I am."

He pats the edge of the bed and I sit so he can check my heart and lungs again, as if he expects some sort of change since the nurse checked them twenty minutes ago. He pushes my sweater further down my shoulder and examines my gunshot wound, covering it with a fresh bandage when he's done. "It's healing nicely, but I want to see you back here in two weeks."

"So I'm free?"

He smiles. "Yes, but I'll repeat what I said yesterday. Find a safer line of work or I may not be able to put you back together next time." He reaches out a hand and helps me off the bed. "Is someone coming to get you?"

"I think so. I'm not sure what's keeping them, but I'm going to wait in the lobby." I make a move toward the door then stop and turn back to him. "Thank you, Dr. Martinez."

He nods and I bolt from my room before he changes his mind.

Colin exits the elevator as I approach, carrying two cups of coffee and hands one to me.

"Thanks," I say, taking a sip. "So, where's everyone else?"

He gives me a sidelong glance, and I know I'm not going to like what's coming. "Cyrus and Bryce are having a pissing match in the hotel lobby right now."

A chill rolls through me. "Um, so…how bad is it?"

He shakes his head. "What did you think was going to happen, EvTay?"

I study my feet as the elevator slips back to the main floor. The doors open and Colin waits for me to exit, following me out. "I guess I thought they'd act like adults."

"Maybe if they'd been warned. Cyrus was clearly blindsided."

"Shit. So, he's probably pretty pissed at me?"

We exit into the gloomy morning air, but at least it's dry. I let Colin lead the way to the hotel, sipping my coffee and waiting for him to answer.

He takes several deep breaths before saying, "I don't know if pissed is the right word."

"But he didn't come."

He eyes me again, but doesn't answer. We walk a few more blocks in silence, my thoughts wandering over the past weeks and months, everything we did. Guilt, frustration, fear, all tangle and become inseparable. "Do you ever wonder if what we did was even worth it?" I ask him.

"What do you mean?"

"Going out there. Joining up. Bryce was back east getting leads, Jack and Lisa are probably digging up all kinds of stuff. And Cyrus learned more than we ever had a hope to. Nothing we did mattered. All those things would have happened if we'd never left the Union. But now… Willow is dead because of me, and I could've gotten you killed. I almost got myself killed. These last few months were a dangerous waste of time."

He studies me out of the corner of his eye but he doesn't say anything for a long time. Finally, he turns and places a hand on my arm to stop me. "I'm not gonna say what we did wasn't dangerous, but I won't say it was a waste. Sure, everything you said is true, and I don't know what I would've done if I'd lost you, but we learned so much. I mean, hell, we met Rainey and the others, and I met Ally. And we're soldiers. Maybe not like the kind you read about in history books, but we learned shit out there we never would've learned here. I don't feel like a bystander anymore. I'm not saying if we got a do-over I wouldn't change anything, but whatever it was, it wasn't a total waste."

He drops his hand and we continue on. I let his words sink in, burrow under my skin, settle in and take root. The guilt is likely with me for life, but perhaps the frustration will pale with time. It feels like a million years ago since the night Bryce and I walked on the beach, when he told me stopping the Uprising wasn't my burden alone. Maybe Cyrus is right. Maybe we've all been brought together for a reason. And meeting Rainey and joining the Uprising have a purpose.

We did learn skills, ones I hope we'll never have to use, although I know we probably will. Whatever plan we come up with, I finally feel empowered, ready to take an active role.

I'm still not sure if I believe in fate, but Colin's right about one thing — We're more prepared now than ever.

The end

Dear Reader

Thank you for reading *The Ruins*. As an independent author, gaining exposure relies on readers spreading the word, so if you have the time and are so inclined, please consider leaving a short review on Goodreads, Amazon, or your favorite site for books.

To stay up to date on the latest releases and get access to exclusive content, including the story of *The Union* from Cyrus's point of view, be sure to sign up for my newsletter: http://thhernandez.com/newsletter.

The Union Series

THE UNION (Book 1)

THE RUINS (Book 2)

THE UPRISING (Book 3) – Coming early 2016

Acknowledgements

I drafted this second book in the series a full year before I published The Union. The final version of The Ruins is much different — better — thanks to the help of some really fabulous people.

Once again, a big, huge, thanks to my husband, Ernie, who listens to me ramble as I try to sort out plot holes and makes suggestions for improvements that sometimes I even incorporate.

Thanks to my kids for encouraging me to write, for sharing my books with their friends and teachers, and for creating PowerPoint presentations, trying to further coerce their classmates into reading.

A special thanks to my parents for showing me what a normal, healthy family looks like so I could create a character with a totally screwed up childhood.

Thanks again to my amazing critique partners, Jennifer DiGiovanni, Amanda, Cao Se, Sally White, and Kayla Howarth for helping me make The Ruins the best it could be.

A special thanks goes out to my beta readers Cori Griswold, Elizabeth Parks, Elizabeth Shulok, Emily Kelton, Gen Curry, Inês, Judy Trageser, Kat Wills, Kim Guarnaccia, Lia Trageser, Macy Younkin, Marcie Sheriff, Mattea Hernandez, Natalia Moorehead, Pam Richardson, and Ripal Patel. Your input and suggestions were invaluable.

Thanks to my wonderful editor, Barbara Trageser, for teaching me the difference between blonde and blond, mantle and mantel, and countless other words that never cease to let me forget the English language is HARD.

To my amazing, talented cover artist, Mark Sgarbossa for once again, creating a unique work of art that makes my book look better than I ever could have hoped.

To super talented graphic artist, and one of my BFFs, Suzi Walker, for the wonderful interior graphics.

A special thanks to the many wonderful young adult writers I've met who are so supportive, including Jennifer DiGiovanni, Karole Cozzo, Sally White, Jenny Elliot, Debi Smith, K.J. Farnham, Adam Dreece, Kayla Howarth, and Anya Monroe.

And finally to Jen for keeping me sane, for encouraging me, for the yummy wine, and for just being you because you get me in a way no one else does.

ABOUT THE AUTHOR

When not visiting the imaginary worlds inside my head, I live in San Diego, California, with one husband, three children, two cats, and one dog. In addition to my day job as a writer and editor, I write young adult fiction and read and blog about books. I particularly love the young adult genre with the intensity of teen emotions and the way they're still figuring out life.

When not writing, you can find me with my nose in a book, playing Plants vs. Zombies on my iPad, or binge-watching Doctor Who with my kids. I'm obsessed with pumpkin spice lattes, Comic-Con, microbrewed beers, Bad Lip Reading videos, and my San Diego Chargers.

You can find me online at:

Website: http://thhernandez.com

Newsletter: http://thhernandez.com/newsletter

Twitter: https://twitter.com/TheresaHernandz

Facebook: https://www.facebook.com/thhernandezSD

To stay up to date on the latest releases and get access to exclusive content, including the story of *The Union* from Cyrus's point of view, be sure to sign up for my newsletter: http://thhernandez.com/newsletter.